SAVAGE TRIANGLE

JOHN EMERY

HarperCollinsPublishers

For Ganesha of the Elephant-Head,
who tore out his tusk and with
it wrote down the Epics.

He who lacketh discrimination, whose mind is unsteady and whose heart is impure, never reacheth the goal, but is born again and again. But he who hath discrimination, whose mind is steady and whose heart is pure, reacheth the goal, and having reached it is born no more.

Katha Upanishad.

Tell me a story, tell me a story, tell me a story and then I'll go to bed. Tell me about the birds and bees, and how do you make a chicken sneeze; Tell me a story and then I'll go to bed.

Children's rhyme

HarperCollins *Publishers*

25 Ryde Road, Pymble, Sydney, NSW 2073, Australia
31 View Road, Glenfield, Auckland 10, New Zealand

First published in Australia in 1993

National Library of Australia
Cataloguing-in-Publication data:

Emery, John, 1947-

Savage triangle.

ISBN 0 7322 5034 X

I. Title.

A823.3

Cover design by Head Design
Printed in Australia by McPherson's Printing Group,
Mulgrave, Victoria

9 8 7 6 5 4 3 2 1
96 95 94 93

ACKNOWLEDGMENTS

Extracts from Baynes, Cary F. (trans.) *The I Ching*, or *Book of Changes* — the Richard Wilhelm translation rendered into English. Copyright 1967 by Bollingen Foundation. Reprinted by permission of Princeton University Press.

Extracts from Mullin, G.H. (trans.) *Six Texts Related to the Tara Tantra, by The First Dalai Lama.* Copyright 1980 by G.H.Mullin. Reprinted by permission of Tushita Books.

Extracts from Evans-Wentz, W.Y. (ed.) *The Tibetan Book of the Dead.* Copyright 1960 by W.Y. Evans-Wentz. Reprinted by permission of Oxford University Press.

For his valuable critical guidance through the labyrinths of this book I thank Dr Julian Hafner.

For his encyclopedic knowledge of military history and weapons technology, I thank Dr Peter C. Winwood.

For the supply and installation of my Wordplex word-processing system, on-going training, and late-night service calls, my thanks to Greg Smith of Helicon Technology, Adelaide, South Australia.

For their inspirational guidance, I thank the Venerables Jampa Gendun and Khensur Rinpoche — neither of whom would I have met without the vision and dedication of the people at Buddha House, Adelaide, South Australia.

For her skill in both unfolding for me the mysteries of reincarnation, and healing its wounds, I thank Carla S.

I have, however, chosen to interpret all this good advice after my own fashion. The errors are mine, not my advisors'.

This is a work of fiction. None of the characters in it in any way represent real people, living or dead. The Monastery at Ghenko, and what happened there, similarly, does not exist. However, the courageous stand made by many of Tibet's people against the Chinese invasion is well-documented; as also is the Dalai Lama's different sort of courage in renouncing the way of revenge. May we all learn such compassion for our enemies.

Writing of the final draft of this manuscript was assisted by the South Australian Government through the Department for the Arts and Cultural Heritage.

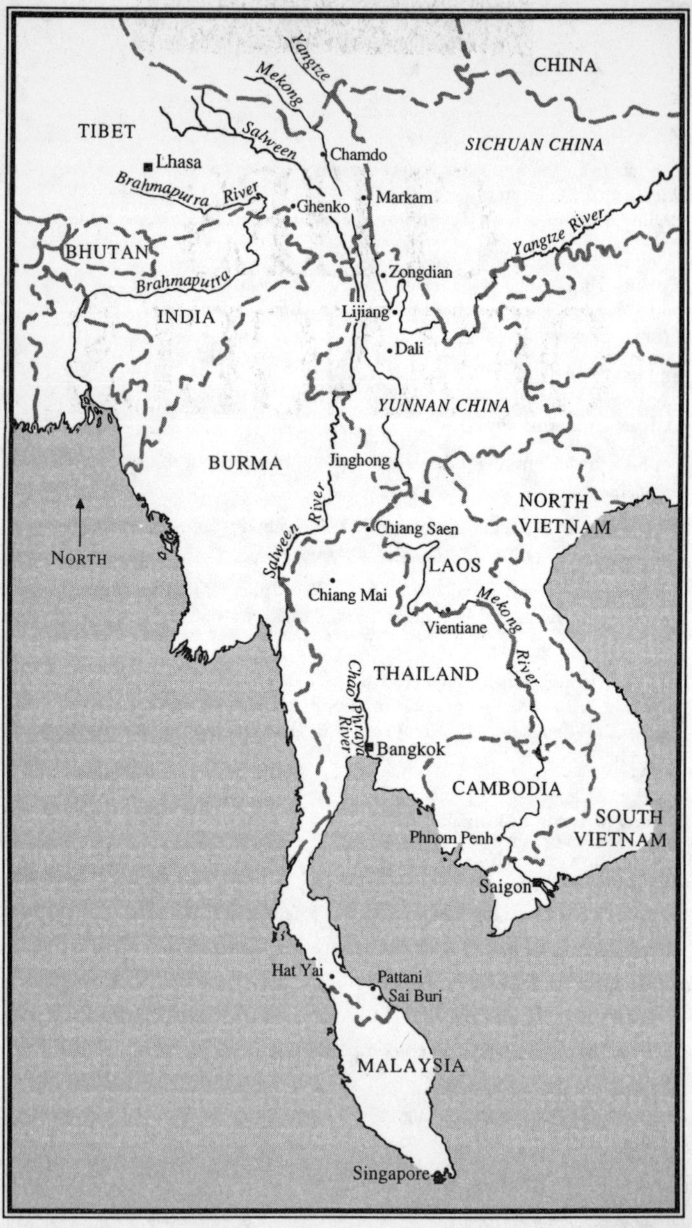

CHINA
Yangtze
Mekong
TIBET
Salween
Chamdo
SICHUAN CHINA
Lhasa
Brahmaputra River
Ghenko
Markam
Yangtze River
BHUTAN
Zongdian
Brahmaputra
INDIA
Lijiang
Dali
YUNNAN CHINA
BURMA
Jinghong
NORTH VIETNAM
Salween River
Chiang Saen
NORTH
LAOS
Chiang Mai
Mekong River
Vientiane
THAILAND
Chao Phraya River
Bangkok
CAMBODIA
SOUTH VIETNAM
Phnom Penh
Saigon
Hat Yai
Pattani
Sai Buri
MALAYSIA
Singapore

BOOK ONE

CITIES OF ANGELS

CHAPTER ONE

He was an old man. Very old. On his back he carried a large straw basket fixed to a frame. He wore an old straw hat against the fierce sun; and he carried a furled, black umbrella in expectation of rain. The black umbrella was grey with road dust. The man's name was Tendzin.

He walked slowly, but with a great certainty of purpose, which enabled him to eat up the miles. His left leg dragged slightly, in memory of an old wound. His right shoulder sagged, worn out with arthritis and age. But when he looked up, his brown eyes were keen, though his vision was haloed by pressure from the glaucoma which the Chinese doctors were eager to operate on.

He had no time for doctors, and less time for the Chinese. But he wanted to halt the deterioration of his vision. So he had agreed to check himself into the People's Clinic in Jinghong, the town on the crossroads and the river. He had agreed to that and let them name a date, and then the Abbot had contacted him.

The Abbot had dreamed about his Master on two consecutive nights. The Abbot had then thrown the yarrow stalks and consulted the *Book of Changes* — the great oracle, the oldest book in the Chinese language. He was given Hexagram Twenty-four. The third, fourth, and fifth lines were moving. The Abbot recognized Tendzin's Master in line three.

There are people of a certain inner instability who feel a constant urge to reverse themselves. There is danger in continually deserting the good because of uncontrolled desires, then turning back to it because of a better resolution. However, since this does not lead to dwelling in evil, a general inclination to overcome the defect is not wholly excluded.

There were tears in the Abbot's eyes when he read that line, for he could see the Master quite clearly.

And the other lines spoke of good fortune. They told him that the Master was ready to face himself again.

When the time for return has come, a man should not take shelter in trivial excuses, but should look within and examine himself. And if he has done something wrong he should make a noblehearted resolve to confess his fault. No one will regret having taken this road.

Consulting the oracle again on the Master's whereabouts he was given Hexagram Twenty-nine, The Abysmal (Water).

Water flows on uninterruptedly and reaches its goal …

The movement of the third line again spelt danger, and counseled caution. But line four was more encouraging.

A jug of wine, a bowl of rice with it;
Earthen vessels
Simply handed in through the window.
There is certainly no blame in this.

Hexagram Twenty-nine went on to describe a river coming out of a ravine. The picture that rose in the Abbot's mind was of the river coming out of the mountains, and out of the place of danger. Because he knew the Master's past, he knew which river it must be. It was the same river as the town of Jinghong was situated on, the Mekong.

The Abbot had pointed to the map, tracing the line of the river over the Chinese border to where it became the border betweeen Burma and Laos, and then following it as it defined the edge of Thailand by the town of Chiang Saen. He had looked up and told Tendzin to take the objects and to go.

Tendzin had spent most of his life crossing borders. When he was young it had been on the cold, windswept plateaus north of Tibet and he had been on horseback. For a while it had been in the company of monks and abbots, in state and in style.

Then it had been on foot, at night, with hunger and terror snapping at his heels. Rumors of the Chinese Army gusting behind him like the wind off the ice fields. Memories of the pit, the bloated corpses of monks. Anguish in his heart, for the Abbot was gone.

The memories tracked across his weather-wrinkled face. He adjusted his load, without losing pace. There was a sound coming from behind and he stepped aside to let the bus pass through, screwing up his eyes in anticipation of the dust.

The bus passed and the dust lifted. Ahead he could see the outline of an old temple crumbling into the road dust and the rotting green vegetation. He heard the bus lose speed as it entered the town of Chiang Saen. He could hear chickens clucking somewhere nearby.

He also heard the throbbing of a diesel motor on the river, to his left. It sounded like a gunboat of the Lao. That was the reason he had abandoned the river above Sop Ruak. He could smell its exhaust in the air, mingling with wood smoke and dust and the last fumes from the bus.

A Thai Army patrol had made him seek shelter in an abandoned, rotting bungalow some time after that. In the bungalow he had found a tarnished bronze statuette, and some compulsion had made him add it to the contents of his basket, as he had also added his own dagger when he realized he would soon be among people unused to men carrying their arms in full view.

He passed the temple without looking at it. He'd seen enough of temples and monasteries in Lhasa and Chamdo. He'd seen them full of gold and ancient images and proud monks and revered lamas. And he'd seen them with artillery-shell holes through walls constructed so long ago it was thought that gods may have built them. But what the gods build, man destroys. And he'd seen the monks cowering naked in the pit, trying not to tread on the corpses of what a few moments before had been their colleagues, while above them the terrified people did their best to obey the soldiers. Did their best to shit and piss all over their former spiritual leaders.

His forehead crinkled. He scowled and spat into the dust. He would never let a soldier touch him, ever again. He sighed and lifted his head and kept walking. No matter what they did, in the end you either died or kept living. Then, in the end, you died, no matter how well you'd survived.

That made him smile, giving his parched lips an ironic twist over his almost toothless mouth. He could see the bus ahead of him, pulled up outside a guest-house. He could smell garlic sizzling and he quickened his pace.

He was right about the garlic. It was frying with red chillies, lemongrass, and dried river fish. The steamed rice was white as Himalayan snow. He was hungry and the food was good and hot and he ate as quickly as he could — which was very slowly, for he had no chewing teeth left and had to chew with his incisors and gums. But that gave him more time to savor the texture and the smell of the food.

It gave him time to be aware of the diners from the bus. The Master was not among them. Mostly they were young Westerners, with backpacks and long-nosed cameras like cannons around their necks. They read guidebooks as they ate and gossiped. Then he realized one of them — a woman with short hair and long earrings — was trying to get him into the barrel of her camera. She was being very cautious about it, hiding the barrel behind her colleague's shoulder.

He swung round and glared at her, waving his hand angrily. She sat back quickly.

'It's all right,' she called, placatingly. 'I just want to take your picture.'

'He probably thinks the camera will steal his soul,' her baby-faced male companion said. 'Offer him some money.'

Angrily, he got up, the rest of the meal ruined for him. The guest-house proprietor stared at him expressionlessly. He picked up his basket and jammed his hat back on his head, remembered his umbrella, and stepped back into the heat.

The guest-house proprietor's Laotian wife was standing by the open door of the bus. She was talking with a man who squatted on the step and who was hungrily scooping rice and fish into his mouth with the fingers of his right hand. The man wore a straw hat and so his face was not visible, but the attitude of his shoulders, the way he picked up his food, made Tendzin stop and look more closely.

Surely it couldn't be?

Then the man looked up and he knew it was the Master. The Master smiled at the woman, thanking her, as he handed back the simple earthen bowl from which he'd eaten. Tendzin stared as she walked past him back into the guest-house.

Feeling the old man's eyes on him, aware of the rigidity of his stance, the Master looked up and smiled at him.

There was no recognition in the Master's eyes. None at all. He wiped his mustache and licked his fingers.

'*Pen yangai, khrap*?' the Master said, pleasantly. But still no recognition.

Tendzin opened his mouth, but found he could not speak.

There was a sound behind him and the old man found the long-earringed tourist was back, holding the camera in one hand, the guide book in the other.

'*Sawat dii, khrap*?' she said.

'No!' her companion interrupted. 'You're a woman, so you say, "*Kha*!" not "*Khrap.*" '

'Shut up, Bob,' the woman snapped. 'I can handle this.'

'Yeah, like you handled the opium seller in Sop Ruak.'

They glared at each other. Tendzin realized the Master had climbed back into the bus. He pushed past the arguing tourists, but now the bus driver was there, barring his way. He didn't have a ticket. He couldn't board the bus. The bus driver was making significant glances down the road to the police station.

The woman tried to engage him in conversation again. Angrily, he thrust her arm away. He saw a moment of shock register on her face, and heard her companion make some kind of warning noise in his throat. Tendzin forced himself not to react. The important thing was to get to the Master, who was now sitting obliviously behind the glass windows of the bus. There was not much time for the driver had turned and was hurrying up the dusty road to the police station.

~

The Abbot had been very concerned that things go smoothly. So concerned he had inquired a third time of the *Book of Changes*; something it was best not to do in one day.

The Marrying Maiden.
Undertakings bring misfortune.

Maybe he'd asked too many times, and maybe it meant nothing.

In despair, Tendzin dropped his basket to the ground and plunged his hand into it and felt around and drew Her out.

'See,' the woman said. 'He wants to sell me something. I told you it'd be OK.'

He knocked against the window of the bus and the Master looked over, into his eyes, then at Her.

And he saw the Master waking up, like a man who has been asleep a long, long time. All the blood drained from his face and he leaned over and attempted to open the window. But the bus was old and the windows were jammed with dirt and rust.

'How much do you want? Shit. I mean ...' She was fumbling with the guide book.

But he had no time for her. He was watching the Master moving through the bus, stepping out into the sun, stepping towards him. No. Stepping towards Her, the image he held up, gleaming green jade, smooth and satin to the touch.

The Master stepped on to the hard earth. He

seemed to sag at the knees, like he was stepping back into something from which he had run a long way to escape. He pushed past the group of backpackers — who could sense something was happening, and were all staring. One raised a camera and the Master had enough presence of mind to reach out and firmly push the lens towards the earth. There was something in his eyes which made the tourist not argue.

Everyone was looking at Her as he held Her aloft. Beautiful Tara — goddess of the earth. She who had entranced the Master way back when he was a tiny child; who had been his plaything and his comfort. He might forget Tendzin. He might forget the river and the sampans. The old man hoped he'd forgotten the pit.

But he would not have forgotten Her.

Tendzin watched him approach, hoping that the third asking of the oracle had been one too many. Hoping that this undertaking would not bring misfortune at the hands of a woman described in the Commentaries on the *Book of Changes* as, 'The Marrying Maiden'.

For a moment he wondered who she might be and when she might appear.

But as he looked into the Master's puzzled eyes, in which fear was now slowly rising to the surface, he felt the horrible certain knowledge that the third asking of the oracle had been right. Someone had made the Master forget everything.

'What a fantastic statuette!' the long-earringed woman said. 'How much do you think it's worth?'

She spoke to the Master, realizing that he was the man to whom it had been shown.

'I don't know,' he replied, like a man waking from sleep. 'A lot.'

'We can afford it,' her companion said. 'The exchange rate's in our favor.'

And Tendzin at last found his voice. He stared angrily from one to the other.

'She is not for sale to you,' he said.

They both gasped, for he spoke in English. But he wasn't interested in their surprise. He looked again at the Master, smiled, and held Her out to him.

'She is his,' he said.

'No!' The Master backed away, alarmed. 'I don't want Her.'

'Take it. Sell it to us,' they chanted behind him.

'Take Her, and give her to your woman,' Tendzin said.

'My woman?'

'The Marrying Maiden.'

'You know her? You know ... my wife?'

Tendzin nodded, and smiled as the Master's hand folded around Her.

'We all know her, just like we know you ... Master.'

They stared at each other. The fear rushed higher in the Master's eyes. Tears began to form.

Tendzin could see the driver returning, the policeman ran beside him, leather holster slapping his thigh as he buttoned his shirt. The old man remembered his doctor's appointment and suddenly wanted to make it. He pushed the basket against the

Master's legs, turned and hurried back into the guest-house.

There were shouts of surprise as he ran through the steaming kitchen. A chicken squawked in alarm as he burst out through the rear door. There was a bicycle leaning against the water tank. He mounted it. He rode. He kept seeing the Master's eyes. He prayed that She would awaken his memory.

CHAPTER TWO

Christmas Eve. Fifteen Years Earlier

In Minnesota, the temperature had been dropping all day. The sky had been overcast, but there'd been no rain. Then, around 3 pm, the snow began to fall and the temperature rose a fraction. There was a light, cutting wind whirling the snowflakes and beginning to pile them against walls and outhouses. But by the time the sun disappeared into the murk over the plains beyond Minneapolis's steel and glass towers, the wind had died. The air was still and the cloud was lifting, and everyone knew they were in for a crackling freeze.

Julia was ten. She didn't want to go to Auntie Esther's and Uncle Ben's, but mom was impatient with her and yelled at her and threatened to slap her good and hard if she didn't do what she was told. Immediately.

'And don't get your new white frock dirty! And don't look at me like that! Just because you played the Virgin Mary in the school play, don't think you can get away with that kind of behavior around here!'

'For Christ sake, go easy on the kid,' her father growled. 'You can see she's got a fever.'

'She's an actress, remember?' mom snapped back. 'She always gets a fever when we visit Esther's. She's putting it on. Oh, God, I feel terrible. Why won't this pain let up?'

'Let's not go to your sister's place if it's that bad,' dad said, too quickly. 'Let's just stay at home and I'll call the doctor.'

Mom just looked at him. Her face was white and pinched with pain. She didn't believe in doctors. And they always went to her sister's, Esther's, every Easter and every Christmas.

So, at 4.30 pm Julia was in the back seat of dad's big '65 Pontiac; his pride and joy. The seats were leather. The heater was warm as toast. They cruised over the Robert Street bridge, over the Mississippi River.

But she felt sick. She felt dizzy. She knew what was going to happen. What had been happening for as many years as she could remember. The thing that happened so often it seemed like it was the core of her life, the event around which everything else revolved. Everything else was the dream. This, towards which she rode, was reality.

She looked down the river, down to where the distant sun glinted on the dark, ice-rafted waters of the Mississippi. She wanted to be somewhere it was hot and the sky clear, and she didn't have to go out there, to that place.

She imagined a city of golden spires, of temples, of swaying dancers and laughing people. She imagined herself to be a princess in that city.

When they got to the farm she couldn't see him at first. Auntie Esther welcomed her sister and brother-in-law with her booming, false voice, and her eyes glittered dangerously as she surveyed Julia in her white frock and her long, blonde hair in an Alice band.

'Doesn't she look like a film star?' she cooed, bending down to poke her painted, carnival face into Julia's. 'I hear she was the belle of the Junior Prom, and she only 10!'

'She'll be a film star all right,' dad said. 'By Christ it's cold. Let's get inside before you-know-what falls off.'

He always said that and Auntie Esther always looked uncomfortable. Julia was sure dad did it to get at her. He didn't like her. He hadn't much time for Uncle Ben, either. He thought Uncle Ben was 'too good to be for real'. Julia knew he was right.

But she couldn't tell anyone, because Uncle Ben was family, and he was an adult, and if she said anything no one would believe her, and Uncle Ben had whispered all sorts of dreadful things that would happen. She would be taken away from her parents. She would go to a home for bad girls. Because she was very bad, to make Uncle Ben want to do things to her. Very, very bad.

And now they were inside and all the family was there except Uncle Ben. She was terrified, wondering where he'd spring from, as everyone called out their false, loud, jolly greetings, and kissed each other. Auntie Esther was watching all the time, with that dangerous, knowing look in her eye.

She suddenly realized that Auntie Esther knew, and would do nothing about it. Julia wondered why.

And then he was beside her. Skinny and tall, with his

lank brown hair and little mustache and his sallow skin, like some kind of mountain bandit. He bent and kissed her — just like he was kissing everyone else, except he stuck his tongue into her mouth. She made herself rigid, made herself not react.

There was all this noise and Uncle Ben was saying he had to go down to the basement and adjust the boiler and Auntie Esther was nodding, but with that look in her eye. Julia tried to catch dad's eyes, but he was having a drink and trying to act like he wasn't there.

She, too, played at not being there as Uncle Ben steered her into the corridor, with no one but Auntie Esther noticing, and shut the door with his foot. He pushed her ahead of him, his thin voice saying, falsely, like a very bad actor:

'Well, now, little Julia, so you want to come down and see how the boiler is fired, eh? Well. Well. Well. If you're a good girl, then I guess I can show you. Mind you watch the hand-rail on the stairs.'

His hand on her bottom, pushing her to the stairs, down the stairs. He locked the door after them. He dragged her in front of the boiler and knocked the door open with a stick.

'You whore. You bitch,' he was hissing. 'I seen you lookin' at my pecker. I seen you thinkin' about it. Here it is, little slut. Here it is. Hey? How d'you like that? Hey? Tell anyone and you're dead. Tell anyone and they'll lock you up and you'll never see your mom again. God, you're beautiful. God Almighty, how'd that stupid broad have one as beautiful as you? Oh, God forgive me. Oh, Jesus, I'm sorry ...'

And Julia was a long way away, looking down from

above at this man with his thing out and his hand inside the girl's dress. He didn't have enough hands to do all he wanted. He was frantic with his clumsiness. Julia watched the girl, who was so rigid, whose eyes were shut tight as his fingers forced her open, forced her to admit him into her body.

Julia turned away and looked into the boiler, into the golden fire. She was a princess, a film star. She lived in a big mansion with a white carpet and she wore a beautiful, silver gown ...

And then they were up in the parlor again and Auntie Esther's dreadful eyes sought her out. Uncle Ben had gone around the back and was making his false entrance through the door, grumbling about having to haul coal while other people made merry. Mom was looking at her oddly, and she knew mom was sorry for yelling, but there was something inside mom that made her go on yelling, and she didn't know how not to yell. And dad, well dad was drunk enough now for nothing to bother him.

Julia moved over close to dad. She could do what he did without needing whiskey. She could wish herself away somewhere else, just like he did. She wondered where he went as he gazed over their heads. Did he have a land in which he was a king and rode around in a jeweled coach?

And afterwards, riding home in the back of the Pontiac, she could feel how rigid she was, how closed off. But she was determined no one would ever notice. She was pleased that, just as they were leaving, mom had smiled and stroked her hair and told her she was good, a good girl, and to always be good and beautiful, and maybe she would be a film star one day.

But she vowed to herself that she would never let anyone do it to her, ever again, no matter how much they wanted to, no matter how beautiful she was. No matter how much she wanted it.

They crossed the big old river again. The night was black and the water was black and she could see the pale ice on it. There were tears in her eyes but she didn't cry.

She always remembered that Christmas because, next day, before she could open her presents, there was an ambulance at the door. They were carrying mom down the corridor on an aluminum stretcher, and mom was sick and moaning, and dad was standing there, not knowing what to do.

Mom died of her cancer six months later, and Julia never had to go back to Auntie Esther's again. Dad sold the house and got a big apartment close to Mid-West Trucking, where he worked. To Julia's surprise, he gave up drinking. It was just the two of them, and although she missed mom dreadfully, in some ways her life got a whole lot better after that Christmas of 1975.

That same Christmas Eve, as the ice choked the Mississippi River and Julia Carr froze inside, the sun set over another river, the Chao Phraya; a river which threaded its way past temples and spires where long-fingered girls danced, just as Julia dreamed of dancing.

A man made his way down that river towards where the sun set over the town of Thonburi, while in the distance Bangkok's traffic smog hung purple over the river.

The old diesel motor of Joe Tobias's sampan idled clumsily as the river's current swept the clumsy craft slowly around the bend that enclosed the great temple called Wat Phra Keo. A powerboat, long and slim, with a rooster's tail of spray shimmering behind it, raced past them. Joe glanced quickly at it, his senses prickling, but it did not slow or alter course. He watched it disappear.

He glanced back at the man at the thick, wooden tiller. He was an old man with an unreadable, mahogany face. They stared at each other and the old man gestured inquiringly at the rusting piece of pipe which served as a throttle lever. Joe shook his head. Neither man smiled, but the old man lifted his chin and pointed across the river, to the temples.

They both listened to the high-pitched, shimmering wind chimes of the Temple of the Emerald Buddha cutting through the sound of the chugging diesel and the distant background muttering of the city's traffic.

Joe sat back inside the thatched cabin of the small sampan, watching his pilot's raised head, following his old eyes as they focused on the distant temple walls.

He knew that the old man would not be thinking about the stories and legends outlined on the temple walls — the stories of the *Ramakien* — but of stories which had never been written down. Stories from the old man's nomadic childhood out on distant plains and steppes. Stories which, long before Hinduism, long before the Buddha, had traveled the great rivers of Asia, adapting themselves to the needs of each small jungle settlement, changing only their outer form while their inner, shimmering dream remained the same.

Joe had no religion of his own. But he was a student of all religions. He liked the fact that the most holy Buddhist temple in Thailand had the Hindu *Ramakien* murals on its walls. He also liked the fact that the most revered image of the Buddha in the land was only thirty-one inches tall. And he liked the fact that the Drug Enforcement Administration was coming to talk with him on Christmas Eve.

Joe always studied the inconsistencies between religious belief and material action.

Liking these things, however, did not make him smile. Nothing made him smile.

His pilot — who had been his pilot, his driver, his servant, for many years now, and yet whose name he never had cause to ask, and so never knew — suddenly looked ahead and then leant his weight against the thick arm of the tiller. Joe leaned from the cabin to see three big steel barges, roped together, drifting ahead of them. As the sampan pulled out to pass them, Joe saw a line of rice-laden sampans being towed by two small, straining motorboats. The motorboats' cabins were festooned with scrollwork and fret-sawn images of mythological beasts. Ferocious, painted eyes stared from the waterline beside their blunt bows.

Both Joe and his pilot looked at the rice sampans. Joe felt no emotion, but he felt his pilot's eyes on him. He tried to avoid them but finally had to look into them. They were full of sorrow and haunted by a deep, yearning question. Joe looked away, into the cabin's dark interior.

Now he felt that uneasy presence again. A presence like a ghost. Compulsively, knowing the old man was watching and had seen him do this before, but unable to stop himself, he stooped into the cabin and prodded at the cushions with his AK-47. He lifted the lids one-handed. He pushed aside the curtain that screened the toilet with the barrel. There was no one aboard except himself and the old man. But he could feel someone watching him. He looked back towards the tiller. His pilot was not watching him. He stepped back into the light.

The river was relatively clear. A few big ferries were tied up along the river bank. Two small commuter ferries were crossing from the Na Phralan Road wharf towards Wat Arun — the Temple of Dawn. The canal, Klong Bangkok Yai, opened to his right, the smaller Klong Lot almost opposite it, and ahead was the Saphan Phut Bridge. The meeting was further downstream of the bridge, by the Krung Thep Bridge, before the river curved in a long arc towards the Klong Toey Harbor. They swept under Saphan Phut, going suddenly from gold to black. Joe tensed. If the Chinese wanted to take him, it could be in this darkness, with all the alleys of Chinatown on his left. But the boat came back out into the gold and nothing had happened.

One of the few emotions Joe had ever experienced was this irrational fear and hatred of the Chinese. It was the force which had driven him to take them on, to beat them at their own business. His meeting with the DEA would finish them, leaving him as the sole contact between the mountain suppliers and the international buyers.

Now the river was wind-ruffled beaten copper, smoothed in places by deep and powerful currents.

Joe could see ahead to the Oriental Hotel. As he passed it he began looking for the DEA's white boat.

He swept the bank with his binoculars, the warehouses and buildings foreshortened into a jumble that ended in spindly jetties, until he discovered the waiting white Toyota four-wheel-drive parked by the water. He could see two men getting into the white boat. He drifted the glasses back to the Toyota and stared thoughtfully at the enigmatic figure inside shrouded by the windshield reflections. He knew it had to be the woman. The DEA had got to her. But had the Chinese, too? Looking at her ghost-like outline, he could tell nothing.

He sensed the razor's edge upon which he walked. He trusted no one. He used everyone. His most fervent belief was that this was the only way to guarantee your personal survival. Yet he still felt a sense of outrage when someone, like the woman, betrayed him — even though the betrayal was nothing personal. They had never seen each other through all their dealings. But she had worked for him, and she had reconstructed enough for the DEA to think they had him. Until he met with them he couldn't be sure of exactly what they had.

The sound of the rooster-tailing powerboat returned. He glanced irritably to his left, seeing it turning in mid-stream, turning back towards the bridge. It was a hire boat from up the other side of the Grand Palace. Probably a hotel boat full of tourists. He studied it with the glasses. He could see their pale faces. A boat-load of fat Hong Kong Chinese. He could see the snouts of their Super-8 movie cameras.

The white fiberglass DEA boat sped across the river, its bow wave almost flat. He focused on the two men aboard it. One he knew — the tall, lanky, blond-headed man. The other — stockier, black, and younger — was new to Thailand. Joe thought he had taken care of the tall one. But the man was made of hard stuff. Here he was back again, dealing just like any dealer; thinking like a crook and acting like a cop.

The long-tailed boat and the DEA boat were on a collision course. The black operative was waving for them to get out of the way. Joe hung the binoculars around his neck and picked up the assault rifle and hunched his way through the cabin to the bows. He sensed something wrong.

He sensed, too, that watching figure. It was like the figure was warning him of something about to happen. For the first time it occurred to him that the figure might be guarding him. It was yelling at him to watch that tourist boat. The boat was wrong. It shouldn't be there. Watch the boat! something was yelling in his head.

Now the racing boat turned and he was looking at its steeply curled wooden bows, and at its knife-like flanks. The water arrowed back from it as it turned to charge his sampan. He swung the AK-47 up, hitting the safety-catch as he did.

The sun was gone. The river's gold was turning black. Joe, watching the boat race towards him, realized that the woman had talked to the Triad. He had only ever recruited women, and yet now he realized that all his life he had never trusted them.

He thought of the river's blackness. He thought of

other rivers; the headwaters of rivers where it all began. He swung the barrel of the assault rifle across the bows of the oncoming boat.

But he was too late. It swung broadside on to him. Bright sparks of light spattered from its side. He heard the thumping of a heavy machine-gun below the chatter of the sub-machine-guns. He felt the sampan shudder as machine-gun rounds splintered the vessel at the waterline.

His own gun kicked in his hands, but it swung harmlessly into the air as his pilot heeled the tiller over, and the rooster-tailing boat fled past them, raking them from stem to stern with rapid fire

Joe fell, windmilling out into the blackness, as the white DEA boat came on, the operatives not quite up with what had happened; staring first at him, then after the disappearing waterspray as the other boat sped back into the deeper blackness under the bridge.

Joe flew out into space, his sight blinded in blood, his face numb, his arm torn and bloodied, a shoulder smashed, pain in his hips. He could see nothing and hear nothing. Then he felt the cold blackness of the river strike him, and he shivered into a thousand pieces.

Dave Watson of the DEA held the spotlight in his hand, beaming it down into the black waters of the Chao Phraya.

'I can't fucking believe it!' he screamed. 'We had him! We had him!'

The water seemed to boil as he scanned it. He saw

something and yelled to Howard Collins, his stocky, black assistant.

'To your left! I got something!'

'We shoulda made the sampan,' Howard said, looking back towards the blackness behind them. 'There was someone else in that cabin. I know it.'

'It was just Joe and his old driver,' Dave said. 'Shit, it's just a log! Where the fuck's he gone?'

'We won't find him, David. You saw what happened! He was hit by maybe four rounds of sub-machine-gun fire. I saw him take one in the face. He's dead, Dave. He's finished.'

'I want that body,' Dave said, quietly. 'I'm not resting until I find that body.'

'What the hell are you going to do with it when you do find it?'

'I'm going to kill him all over again,' Dave said, just as quietly. 'I'm going to chop him up and burn him. I'm going to find a way to make him suffer through ten thousand rebirths.'

Howard could see his pale face in the reflected light of the spot. He could see the pain and the haunting there. He nodded.

He swung the boat out into mid-stream, and throttled it towards the docks.

'Where the fuck's the sampan gone?' he asked.

'It sunk.' Dave's voice was suddenly weary. 'I could hear some heavy weapon firing into the hull. We missed him. We missed Joe Tobias.'

'The current'll take him down to the swamps,' Howard said. 'If he's still alive, the crocs'll finish him.'

'I wanted him,' Dave repeated stubbornly. 'I almost had him.'

'He's dead,' Howard persisted. 'We did our job. We've finished his network.'

Dave turned and stared back at Howard.

'I wanted to kill him myself,' he said. 'With my own hands.'

CHAPTER THREE

On a rainy March night in East Hollywood, seventy-year-old Charles Barnett, ex-bit player and one-time double for Cary Grant, sat watching quietly from a corner chair as one of his tutors led the small actors' master class through its paces in his converted Chapel Theatre. The British spelling of 'theater' was deliberate. Charles considered his pupils had class, and so did the agencies that dropped by regularly, looking for new faces for the relentless machine of production-line television drama.

The theater had begun life as home to a group of Southern Baptists, who had long ago moved on to a large drive-in establishment out in the Valley. Derelict for years, Charles's flair had transformed it into a model soundstage and small proscenium-arch theater.

'Reach,' the tutor, a bony-faced young man with a crew-cut from a week's work on a Vietnam War movie, was saying to the girl with the long, blonde hair. 'Reach right inside and find something of your own. Something you can use. We're dealing with death here.'

Charles realized he was holding his breath as he waited for the girl to move. She had a long-faced, mournful beauty. Hollow-cheeked, with an air of something that drew your eyes to her. Something inside her waiting to get out. It was a quality which had gained her a couple of walk-on moments, and one major/minor role in a low-budget, independent feature. A face the camera liked.

'Think of how it felt when someone you knew died,' the actor said to her. 'Think of how it felt. Have you thought?'

She stared at him. Charles felt her emotions across the room. She nodded. She opened her mouth.

'Don't tell me,' the actor said. 'Feel it.'

She looked down. The whole room was tense, everyone holding their breath. If she could achieve this on the set, if it could translate on to the screen, then she was home safe, with all bases loaded. That early success of hers would translate into a solid career.

Charles frowned. He had seen her latest walk-on moment, on 'City Hospital'. She had looked terrified of the camera. Whatever had got her in front of those independent, Panavision cameras, three years ago, had evaporated.

He shook his head. Oscar Wilde's line came to him.

It takes a brave man to marry, he thought. *And a brave woman not to marry.*

She had not been brave. The chance to marry wealth had come, and she had grabbed it with both long-taloned hands. The truck mechanic's daughter now lived in a Beverly Hills mansion. The American Dream had been vindicated. But where had her talent gone?

Charles clenched his fist with frustration, squeezing his nails into the soft flesh of his palm. He remembered the agony of Cary's marriages.

'Now, give it to me,' the actor said.

She wore a black, V-neck sweater and black slacks. Her hair was in a pony-tail, gleaming against the black wool. She looked up, staring into the actor's eyes.

Charles brought his forearm up, tightening his biceps, biting the nails into the flesh. She lifted one long-nailed hand, like a Thai temple dancer. It froze in the air, halfway between her and the bony-cheeked actor. He stared at her, into her blue eyes. No one in the studio moved.

The two actors stood barefoot on the board floor ... The girl looking up at the boy, her hand frozen, staring with agony into his eyes. The moment drew on. If she was timing it, the timing was perfect, provided she moved ... now.

She didn't move. She hung on a moment too long, and then her hand dropped and she shook her head.

'Sorry,' she mumbled. 'Sorry about that.'

Without the tension of having to try, she delivered the last line like the young Goldie Hawn, whom she resembled.

The actor smiled, lifting his hand in a gesture of understanding.

Charles unclenched his hand and returned his attention to the young actor. He had a good head, and a good body. There was a time when Charles would have acted on that, but he was mellowing with age. Now he could look, without having to touch.

The girl walked back through the silent clutter of haphazardly scattered chairs. None of the other actors looked at her. She sat down next to Charles. He reached over and patted her knee.

'Let it out, Julia,' he said. 'I know it's there. Let it out.'

She stared at him with her deep, blue eyes. She shook her head.

'I can't, Mr Barnett,' she said. 'I can't reach it any more.'

'It'll return,' he said, smiling reassuringly.

She grimaced and stood up and pulled on her jacket.

Leaving so soon?' he asked her.

'I may as well,' she said.

'You have a role?'

She looked at him.

'Not that sort of role,' she said, softly.

She looked away as she tugged out the lapel of the supple, soft leather jacket.

Italian leather, he noted. Bought on a shopping trip to Hong Kong with her reclusive husband. He watched her walk as quietly as she could into the darkness at the edge of the room.

'He could buy her a movie,' Charles thought. 'Why does she bother to come here?'

But he knew the answer. The company of other actors. The reassurance of being around other people whose faces were as blank as your own, until they, too, pulled on the mask of a role.

He sighed and turned his attention back to the pool of light, where the crew-cut actor waited for his next partner to step forward, unconsciously assuming a wrestler's stance as he waited. Charles abstractedly ran a finger over his lips and settled back into the chair. He felt both old and alone, and he knew enough to know that neither condition was curable.

Julia grimaced at the rain as she came down the Chapel steps, and then ran through the puddles to her car. She could feel the water seeping into her thin, low-heeled moccasins. She fumbled with the keys and got herself into the old blue Dodge and sat there a moment, her breath beginning to fog the windshield.

She took off her shoes and dried her toes with a tissue.

Then she pumped the gas pedal and turned the key.

The starter groaned, labored, and groaned again.

'Oh, shit,' she said.

She tried again, listening to the starter drawing the last of the battery's current.

She switched the engine off and folded her arms and sat back, wondering what to do. In her mind she could see her gold Mercedes coupe sitting in the huge barn of a garage. The garage was at the rear of the even huger barn of her house. The Mercedes was his second anniversary present to her. The house had been the wedding gift.

She was unable to explain to him why she liked her old saloon, what it was about big and faded American cars that made her feel safe. When he was home she drove the Mercedes. When he was away, she drove the Dodge.

She knew if she kept cranking she'd simply deaden the battery. She sighed and felt on the rear seat for the old coat that lay there. She jerked the car's hood-release and, covering her hair with the coat, slipped her feet back into the moccasins, and went out into the rain again, to peer under the hood.

The battery terminal was festooned with deposits as big as pigeon droppings on civic hall. Resigning herself to getting soaked she paddled around to the trunk and groped in it for a spray-can that might dry out the shorting electrical system.

The can was nearly empty, but she managed to leak some of the oily fluid on to the battery terminals and the moist cables, all the way back to the distributor. She wrinkled up her nose at the smell of the fluid on her fingers.

She mopped off what water she could see with the coat sleeve. She gave the dirtiest, most-corroded terminal a tug, trying to bed it on to fresh metal, like her father had shown her on his Pontiac.

Then she got back in the car and sat there, methodically cleaning the grime from her long, lacquered nails.

Light spilled out of the Chapel as another student left. She glanced over, seeing a young man hurrying to his Triumph sports car. A yellow cab drew up at the door and the driver honked his horn. The class was finishing.

Satisfied that her fingers were clean, she dropped the coat on to the rear seat and stared at the ignition key. If she turned it on and her cleaning had not been successful, she'd simply kill the battery. Then she'd have to sit here all night. Alternatively, if she didn't turn it, she'd still be sitting here all night.

Faced with that choice, she grimaced and turned the key.

The starter ground and grumbled and the motor wheezed.

She held her breath.

The lights in the Chapel went out and the bony-faced actor came down the steps, with Charles walking close beside him. They both glanced in her direction, hearing the wheezing motor.

'Come on!' she urged it. 'Start!'

The motor caught, coughed, died, and caught again.

Charles opened the door of his two-door Plymouth and the actor got in.

The motor hesitated. She could smell petrol vapor and knew if she wasn't careful she'd flood the carburetor.

Then the motor caught, spluttered, kicked over on six cylinders, and began to rattle the dash.

Julia began to smile.

She patted the old, plastic dash.

'You can do it,' she said. 'Old boy, you can do it.'

The final, errant cylinders cut in and the big old motor began to purr.

Julia switched on the lights and eased the transmission into drive.

The old Dodge lurched against the brake.

Ahead of her the Plymouth wheeled out of the parking lot. She let it go, and then took her foot off the brake. Her old blue car shot ahead, as if eager to make up for its moment of uncertainty.

CHAPTER FOUR

Dave Watson was tired. He'd spent most of the day in Washington with a pair of Democrat Congressmen from the Cabinet Committee on International Narcotics Control, and Fred Tanner, the director of the DEA's Strategic Intelligence Office. Dave no longer worked for the DEA, but for George Vidor, an influential Washington lobbyist. Dave was his narcotics expert, the man they wheeled out whenever the 'war on drugs' heated up; as he was being wheeled out now, flying in to Los Angeles to get the new mayor on side with George Vidor's anti-drug clients.

They'd had a two-hour lunch with the Congressmen and kept arguing on into the afternoon. He'd taken a DEA car to National Airport with Fred Tanner, who'd vented four hours of pent-up spleen on him.

'What the fuck!?' Fred wanted to know. 'What the fuck do these slack-jawed assholes know about conditions out there in the field? They're worse than the fucking generals in 'Nam! Instead of "body count" it's the "kilo count"! Get 'em a kilo of brown sugar and stick 'em on television with it and they're happy as pigs in shit!'

Dave tried to calm him. He knew they could swing the Liberal Democrats round, but it would take time. The President was all in favor of the war on drugs, now that it was getting harder and harder to find commies to declare war on.

Fred had never got beyond major in 'Nam, because of his attitudes, and his mouth. But, then, Dave hadn't even been in the Army. He'd fought his war in Thailand and Burma — the wrong side of the border to pick up any campaign medals or decorations.

The flight had been on time, and that created the next problem. The air over Los Angeles was stacked high with planes waiting for clearance to land: commuters, vacationers, business jets, international flights, all circling like carrion over the kill. The fasten seatbelts sign kept glowing, and the belt was tight across Dave's belly. He was putting on too much weight in this job.

He was forty-five, and felt every day of it. He'd had too much booze, too much food, too much bullshit, and too much sitting on his ass. Too much time sitting in airplane seats circling cities he didn't care for, waiting to land and go to hotels that meant nothing to him, so he could meet with politicians who cared about nothing but votes.

He felt the plane tilt forward and closed his eyes, trying to switch off his entire system until such time as they were safely on the ground.

His last thought was to remember to call Howard Collins, now the DEA's resident LA expert on South-east Asian heroin. He wondered if Howie had also put on weight, and if his tight black curly hair was receding and turning gray.

Diana Walters, manager of Mana: Genuine Arts & Crafts from the Primitive World, was tired, bored, and angry as she waited in the crowded hall of LA International Airport.

She walked back and forth irritably, pausing every now and then to suck at her cigarette. She ignored the glances of the non-smoking public until one fruity-voiced matron glared a little too obviously. Diana told her to screw herself. Shocked, the woman drew back.

The shock was at the incongruously tough voice that emanated from the forty-year-old, suburban-looking woman; a woman dressed in black slacks and a floral blouse, wearing pink-framed spectacles that hid at what first seemed to be timid eyes. But when Diana snapped at her, the fruity-voiced matron found herself staring at eyes full of violent anger. She hastily scrambled away.

Diana forgot about her almost immediately. She went back to the customs desk and tried again.

'We're doing our best, madam,' the pretty black girl there told her, expressionlessly. 'The flight was delayed, and we've had administrative problems.'

If the fruity-voiced matron, now waiting in the nearby Continental queue, was hoping to see an explosion from the angry cigarette-smoker with the pink frames, she was doomed to disappointment.

Anyone in authority — store security men, bus drivers, particularly police and customs officers — had an unnerving effect on Diana. Before them she seemed to grow smaller, to shrink deep into herself, losing her resolve, her aggressive manner — losing, in effect, her ego, to become merely a number. Unconsciously, she crossed her hands at the wrists, rubbing them together compulsively.

'I've been waiting five hours,' she managed to mumble.

The girl reacted to the display of submission with suitable scorn. She shrugged her slender shoulders, pouting her mauve-painted lips. Arching one eyebrow, she watched Diana turn away — just as the computer-printer beside her coughed into life.

She glanced down at the title on the document that was emerging, then called out to Diana.

'Madam? Madam? Miss Walters? Your goods have been cleared!'

For a moment, Diana didn't react. There were such moments when she forgot her new name. Moments when she was still Meredith Grant.

Then, the present caught up with her and she turned back in surprise.

'I'm sorry, madam,' the girl said, still scornfully, but knowing that every now and then Joe Public complained, and the good public servant always, but always, covered her own ass first. 'I'm sorry for the delay, ma'am,' she repeated. 'There appears to have been a computer malfunction. If you take this clearance form over to that counter, you can collect the goods.'

Diana stared at her and the girl suddenly looked

frightened. She saw something glint behind the submissive facade — a darkness and danger, a fascination that stripped away the black girl's make-up, her clothes, even her flesh.

Diana saw the reaction and realized she had let Meredith Grant show again. She grabbed the customs declaration form and hurried away, feeling the startled girl looking after her.

Dave Watson stood yawning at the luggage carousel. He rubbed his eyes. He saw his case emerge through the chute and he waited for it to reach him. He ignored the porters and carried it to the car rental desks, collected his keys, and pushed his way out into the street.

The warm, damp Los Angeles air threw him back many years to the steam-heat of Thailand. He tried to push away the crowding images. But once they were stirred up they swarmed over him like the demons that writhed and swarmed over temple walls.

He opened the car door and ducked to quickly kill the alarm.

He looked up again and his heart stopped.

Then it thudded again. He clutched his chest.

Meredith Grant stepped out of the automatic doors, with a porter behind her. Like him she had aged and put on weight. But she had not lost her impatient walk, and the anger that boiled just below her seemingly placid surface was very evident. She still wore pink-framed spectacles, and now her short-cut hair seemed to him to be almost fashionable.

'Oh, shit,' he whispered.

He watched her and the porter walk to a cab. The porter eased the heavy box into the trunk. She tipped him and got into the rear seat. She didn't look back. She acted like someone eager to be gone.

He started the car and followed the cab.

The rain, which had washed down the streets and filled the air with memories for him, returned. It was a long time since he had tailed a car. He kept losing it and finding it again as they worked their way out from the airport. When he found it he hoped to hell it was the right cab. He thought he'd memorized the number, but he was conscious of tiredness blurring his vision. Maybe it wasn't her at all. But his heart, and his gut, said it was.

They turned on to the San Diego Freeway, heading north. He remembered from years ago that she had studied at UCLA. She was a creature of fixed habits, and he was sure she'd have returned there to pick up the remnants of her life after he had smashed it into a million pieces.

It all came back to him as they picked up speed on the freeway. Tunneling down that road was in a way like following one of the great *klongs*, the canals of Thailand. Like following the Chao Phraya down through Bangkok's glittering spires. Like standing watch on the river's bank as the sampans of rice came to town.

He rubbed his eyes angrily. They were misting up.

Julia parked in a side-street off the Westwood shops and sat there a while, looking at the rain-glistened streets and sidewalks. A few students from UCLA, collars up, dawdled by the bars and bookshops. But the rain had driven most indoors.

She looked across the street to an old Californian Spanish/Art Deco apartment building. She glanced up at the third-floor windows. They were dark. She looked at her watch. It was about 9.30. She wondered if it was too late to disturb Diana.

She bit her lip. She was afraid to go home and face the emptiness of that big, echoing mansion. Since her marriage her few friends had drifted away, leaving only Diana.

She saw a cab turn into the street, slow down, and halt by the apartments. Another car turned in after it and drove past, to pull up further along. As she looked, she recognized Diana's familiar bulk emerge from the cab. Julia got out of the Dodge and hurried across the street to greet her.

Diana looked up at the approaching figure, and Julia had time to see her off-guard, before Diana recognized her. She saw a plump, middle-height woman in her forties. One who had no idea of how to present herself. Who wore whatever her hands first fell to when she got out of bed. Her mousy brown hair was too short to be feminine, and too long to be feminist.

Yet Julia felt a rush of happiness that her friend was there.

'Di?' she called.

'Julia?' Di said, with surprise. Then she remembered where Julia had been. 'You've come from classes? How'd they go? Any agents there?'

Julia grimaced. The cab driver got out wearily and opened the trunk.

'I've been at the goddamned airport for five hours, would you believe,' Di said, 'Trying to get this box through customs. They seem to think it's full of Buddha sticks, or something.'

Julia stared at the large, cardboard box.

'It's stock,' Di explained. 'John faxed me to say it was coming.'

Julia felt a pang that he had not called her. After all, John Chang, owner of Mana, was her husband.

'Oh,' she said.

'It's gonna rain,' the cab driver mumbled. 'You gonna stand all night in it?'

'We've got to get it inside,' Di snapped back at him, her anger only just beneath the surface.

'Put it in my car,' Julia said hastily. 'I can take it to the shop tomorrow.'

Di looked at her, then nodded.

'Can you do that?' she asked the cab driver, indicating the old Dodge across the street.

'Why not?' he said, rhetorically. 'I got nothin' else to do.'

'Come and have a drink?' Di asked her as they followed him across the street.

'Only if I'm not intruding,' she said nervously. 'I just came by on the off-chance you'd be up.'

'I'm up.'

Dave watched them in his rear-view mirror. He saw the box being carried across the street, and he watched the young blonde open the trunk and stand back to let the cab driver ease it in. He stayed focused on her as Meredith Grant went back to pay the fare.

She was the most beautiful woman he had seen in America. She unselfconsciously combed her hair back from her face and looked up the street his way. Her leather jacket was undone and he stared at the shape of her breasts.

'What are you doing with that bitch?' he asked himself. 'She doesn't look your type at all.'

The rain began to fall again and she hurried across the street to follow her friend into the apartment block.

Dave waited a while after the cab had left, then turned his collar up and sauntered down to the Dodge. He knelt by the exhaust. It was many years since he'd done this sort of work. He took the hire car keys and inserted them in the trunk lock and began to jiggle them.

Eventually there was a click, and the lock sprang. He hoisted the lid open and, in the light of the street-lamps, looked down at the box.

It was addressed to Mana Arts & Crafts, Beverly Center, Beverly Boulevard, Beverly Hills, California. He looked at the postmarking and felt his heart thump again. He felt sick and dizzy.

It was postmarked Chiang Mai, Thailand. There was a Customs Declaration sticker and a Thai Government Department of Fine Arts sticker to indicate that these were approved exports of 'artefacts, licenced for sale'. The stickers had been issued in Bangkok, and re-examined in Los Angeles.

Dave had a feeling that US Customs had also gone over the box. He could see where the masking-tape had been not quite properly re-aligned when it had been restuck.

The rain was seeping into his collar. He closed the trunk and stood up. He glanced at the apartment building. There was now a light on in the third floor apartment. He walked back to his hire car and slid in behind the wheel. He opened his case on the rear seat, pulled out a box of tissues and tried to wipe himself dry.

He remembered Chiang Mai, the capital of Northern Thailand. He remembered the night market, between the canal and the river. He had a clear image of himself and his bride wandering hand-in-hand through the throng of Hills people. Mary was enchanted by the piles of bargains: clothes, lacquer-ware, carved elephants, brass opium weights, bargain-priced lengths of rough Thai silk. She was buying for them to set up house in Chiang Saen, way up north on the Thai–Laos border, on the edge of the Golden Triangle. On the edge of the Mekong River. The river that began somewhere in the ice of the Tibetan plateau and discharged through Vietnam's swamps into the South China Sea. The river that began in the heartland of Mahayana Buddhism, the 'Great Vehicle' of Buddhism; that became the supply route for the Golden Triangle's heroin trade; that became the supply route for the Vietnam War; and which finally watered the trawling grounds of the South China Sea's pirates and slavers. A great symbolic river, he thought bitterly.

He could feel the sickening, unnaturally heavy, weight of their dead baby son in his hands as he stood on a sampan in that river, a few miles downstream from their bungalow on its banks at Chiang Saen.

'Fuck it!' he screamed inside the womb of the car. 'Fuck it! Fuck it! Go away! Go away!'

But he knew it wouldn't. He had hoped it was dead and forgotten, but it had re-emerged into his life. He leaned his forehead against the wheel. No tears came to give him relief.

Julia could see that her friend was in a strangely heightened mood, as she restlessly paced her tiny, crowded apartment.

A good fifteen years of Diana's life were crowded into the apartment. The longest internal wall was hidden behind shelves overflowing with paperbacks and old, hardback textbooks. Academic journals piled beside the shelves, relevant articles marked with slips of paper, testified to the dissertation on which she'd been working as long as Julia had known her.

Which was exactly the same length of time she'd known John Chang, her husband. Three years.

Haunting carved masks stared down from the other walls, with slitted, cowrie-shell eyes. A large bark painting from the Australian Dreamtime showed elongated spirit figures moving like wraiths across a hunting track of skeletal animals. A row of black, African fertility statuettes stared from the window-ledge that looked out over the street.

'Five hours!' Diana hissed, staring at her glass of wine, her fingers tightening around it. 'Five god-damned hours!'

'Why did they take so long?'

'They X-rayed the box. Then they opened it and

X-rayed everything in it. They probably X-rayed every goddamned polystyrene bead in the packing!'

'Yes, but why?'

Diana glared at her. She had a wild, distraught air about her. Her hair was disheveled. Julia had an almost overwhelming compulsion to smooth it down. But the glittering eyes held her in check.

'Because they were looking for drugs, sweetie. Why else?'

'Yes, but why us?'

'Because someone must have told them something about someone. Do you know who that could have been?'

Julia felt increasingly nervous. She knew Diana's sexual preferences, but had never let that come between them as friends. Perhaps, in a way, it had deepened their bond, knowing there was that level to her friend's admiring glances and remarks. In some ways, although Julia knew how attractive men found her, she was repulsed by them. She could not let herself go with them.

She shook her head. But Diana persisted.

'Come on,' she said. 'Has someone been spooking around the shop when I'm not there? Some so-called theatrical agent sidling up to you at classes?'

'I don't know what you're talking about, Di! And you're making me nervous!'

Di blinked, and Julia saw the transformation. One moment she was hard, brittle, and tough. Suddenly she was timid. She put down her wine glass and abstractedly rubbed her wrists together as she sat down next to her lovely blonde friend. It was a gesture

Julia had seen many times, always accompanied by a deep hunching of her shoulders.

'I'm sorry, sweetie,' Di said. She took Julia's hand. 'I'm sorry for scaring you. I wouldn't do that, ever. Not knowingly.'

Julia gently extricated her hand.

'It's late,' she said. 'I'd better go. It's my turn to open up the shop tomorrow.'

'I'm sorry, Julia. Please, please don't go. Why did you want to see me?'

Julia stood up. Her friend's eyes were too intense for her. She looked away, to the television set in the corner which reflected back their images in ghostly gray. There was a video cover on top of the set. Julia picked it up.

Di had been watching a Penthouse video. Julia stared at the pouting woman on the cover, her large breasts flopping back. She was naked, except for high heels and a strange, bird-like mask with a curved, cruel beak. She was like one of the goddess figures amongst Di's collection of statuettes. Her nails were absurdly long, longer even than Julia's, like a bird's talons. They touched her painted nipples.

'A girl's gotta watch something.' Di was both defiant and nervous.

Julia put the video cover back on the set. She looked at her friend. The floral blouse was really disturbing. She glanced away, to the open bedroom door. There were more books piled by the single bed.

'I'm sorry,' Julia said. 'I shouldn't have pried.'

'I get so damned lonely,' Di said.

Julia looked at her bent head and nodded, not

trusting herself to speak. Instead, she reached out and smoothed the disheveled hair, suddenly conscious of her own talon-like nails. Her friend kept rigidly still, her head averted.

Julia removed her hand and quickly left the apartment.

CHAPTER FIVE

Dave woke with a start when the Dodge's lights hit his rear-view mirror. The rain had eased to a light drizzle. The old blue car swept past him and he saw her, the lovely blonde, swing it back on to the thruway.

He started the hire car and fell in behind her as she turned on to Wilshire Boulevard.

The rain started again, falling out of the still night sky, reminding him of nights of tropical rain falling into the troubled waters of the Mekong, of the Salween on the Thai-Burmese border, and of the Chao Phraya where it discharged into the Gulf of Thailand.

The old Dodge's wipers beat ineffectually against the rain. Julia had to keep wiping the condensation off the windshield with her hand. There was a car right behind her, with its lights on high beam, and she wished to hell it would either pass or fall back. It made her nervous.

She turned off Wilshire, into Beverly Hills, and was relieved that the car didn't follow her.

Away from the area of clustered apartment buildings,

among the high fences and brick gate posts, she felt the loneliness of the big houses. They mirrored her loneliness. She suddenly wanted her husband's reassuring presence. His calm certainty. His enchanted devotion to the image she had made of herself.

'Why don't you come home, John?' she asked the night.

But the drumming rain erased her question.

'Shit! Fucking shit!' Dave hit the wheel of the hire car. He was sure the blonde beauty would have lived in East Hollywood, and his concentration had lapsed. Suddenly she'd dived into an exit and, before he could react, he was past it. He couldn't get back.

He was booked into a Holiday Inn off Sunset Boulevard and he reluctantly headed there now, aware of his tiredness and his emptiness. But he was also aware that the thing which had driven him for so many years, and that he had thought was at last gone from his mind, had woken up again.

And it was more than one hand reaching out of the grave of the past. There were many, and some had been so close to him that he could hardly bear to look at them as they rose up. Again he was thinking of the swirling demons and people writhing on temple walls. The *Ramakien*, the *Ramayana*, the Hindu pantheon. He had thought he had buried the past. But, in mythology, the past eternally recurs, endlessly, until its karmic lessons are fully learnt. And only then does time renew itself.

~

Julia wound down the window and held the electronic gate-pass out, shielding it from the rain with her right hand as she pointed it with her left. She could never accept that the thing could operate the mechanism through the windshield. The wrought-iron gates swung silently inwards as she dropped the pass back into her bag and took her foot off the brake to let the Dodge creep forward on to the cobbled driveway.

She stopped again to close the gate, and then coasted down past the pool and the white Italianate house. The security lights cast forbidding shadows. The manicured green lawn sloped away, past the few equally stark eucalypt trees, to the stark white fence. John had no time for gardens.

She parked the Dodge over the oil-pan into which its sump would quietly drip. Next to it was the gold Mercedes. John had no cars of his own. He always took cabs when he was home.

She stood a moment, looking down at the closed trunk of the Dodge. She considered opening the box, but she was tired. She turned and walked quietly across the tiled garage floor to the side door and let herself into the house.

There were two security panels in the house. One downstairs, in John's study, and one upstairs, in their bedroom. She checked the downstairs panel, on her way through. The seal had not been broken. Nevertheless, she went around the house and checked every door and window before going upstairs.

Taking off her make-up in the en-suite, she studied her long nose. When she was a teenager she'd fantasised about having it bobbed. But a bobbed nose on a long face would have looked worse than a long nose. For all its faults, at least her face was consistent.

She knew, in an abstract sort of way, that she was beautiful. It was said often enough. But it was something she could not feel. When she studied her photographs, she saw only the imperfections. Similarly, in the mirror, she noticed pimples. Someone who was beautiful, she felt, was that way from the inside out. Her insides felt dead. Whatever it was that people reacted to, it wasn't beauty. It was some kind of mask.

Her face cleansed, she undressed and put on one of her silver nightgowns. She sat down at her dressing-table and brushed out her hair. She would get up early in the morning and wash it.

Finished, she laid the brushes down. She stood up and walked across the white carpet, restlessly turning, glancing back at her image in the ceiling-high mirrors. In the nightgown she was like a twenties heroine. Gloria Swanson, say, in a fantasy palace. Silver and lace and long legs and the crown of blonde hair. But all she could see was a lonely, empty shell.

She slipped into the big, white bed and turned out all but one dim and indirect lamp. She was afraid of the dark. She glanced at the reassuring red blips of light on the security panel. If security was breached, a buzzer would wake her. There was also a direct line to the security company.

She lay there, listening to the house's silence, like the silence of her tomb. She imagined her husband asleep beside her.

She remembered when she had first met him. Three years ago. It was also the day she'd first seen the shop, first met her friend-to-be, Diana. A day when her life was at its lowest ebb.

She was doing a commercial for the Beverly Center. It was being shot on film, with a complete lighting rig. A dozen takes for each lighting set-up. Grips, electricians, make-up girl, all falling over each other, jammed together in the mall. Plenty of time for her to wander the shops while the director and the director of photography argued endlessly over light levels and focal distances.

She was on her way down and could feel it. The only roles she'd been offered called for her to replicate her success in the role of a beautiful young woman menaced, and finally raped and killed, by a nameless Presence in a low-budget, independent film by young graduates from USC: a film that had enough production values to get picked up for video distribution. It was a role she had played very well. Too well. She knew that to keep playing it would trap her.

And, besides, there was her childhood dream. Every scene she did with the monster reminded her of the scenes she was not doing as the princess in the temple garden. For her, even scenes in a semi-professional production of *The King and I* were preferable to more monster movies, no matter how well they paid.

She walked through the corridors of the shopping mall, aware of the posed mannequins in the shops. Her role in the commercial required her to be nothing more than one of them, but with the ability to walk, she thought. In time she would be replaced by a beautiful robot. Or else she would become one.

She stopped at a florist's, and for a while immersed

herself in the sight and scent of flowers. She bought a long-stemmed yellow rose. It came wrapped in cellophane. She unwrapped it and walked on, twirling the flower as she walked.

Walking thus, she came to the window of the shop called: Mana.

It was laid out like a dusty museum display. Half-a-dozen leering masks crowded together, a few beads and artefacts spilled in front of them. A display totally devoid of imagination, and yet it held her transfixed.

The rotting teeth, the lurid hair, the splitting, aged wood, the blank cowrie-shell eyes. She turned and looked across the mall to another window, where the waxed-face models were posed in attitudes resembling those she had to strike, every day. She turned back and stared at the masks.

'Can I help you?' a voice had asked, and she'd glanced up to see an owlish, academic woman with tiny eyes and thin lips staring at her.

'What are these? she'd asked.

'They're aspects of that which is hidden inside all of us, dear. The demons and the gods and goddesses. The spirits of fear and death.'

'They're horrible,' she said.

The woman smiled a thin-lipped smile.

'That's why people buy them,' she said. 'They're horrible. They remind them of the horribleness inside.'

'Why would people want to do that?'

'So they can put on their other mask and go out and pretend to be nice.'

The woman was looking straight at her, and Julia

knew she was talking about her; about her long hair and her careful make-up and her own mask.

'I'm an actress,' she hurriedly explained. 'I'm shooting a commercial here.'

'Why don't you come into the shop?' the woman had said. 'Come and see what else we have.'

Decisively, the woman took her elbow. Before Julia could protest she was being guided into the shop.

And there, with his back to her, standing in the doorway of the stockroom reading from an invoice, was a man. The woman was trying to show her other masks. But Julia's eyes kept going to that still, slightly bent, back. There was a tension in it. She felt a rush of familiarity, as if it was the back of a relative, someone she knew so well that seeing his back she knew his face.

Then he straightened and turned. And the face was what she had known it would be. A man in his forties, thin and of medium height. One eye slightly puckered, graying hair receding. A thin face behind a swooping mustache ... A face that resonated with her dream. A face at home in a temple garden; or on a mountain trail, with a rifle slung across his back. His narrow eyes and high cheeks were Asian, yet his long face and nose seemed European. His skin showed a hint of yellow beneath its tan.

'Hello,' she said, quickly, and felt the woman beside her glare angrily.

The face took a moment to react. He folded the invoice between his long fingers. He glanced inquiringly to the woman.

'She's an actress. Wanted to have a look,' the woman said, sharply.

His eyes, almost black, turned to her. Slowly, they examined her face. They dropped to her hands and the rose she held there. When he looked up again, he was smiling.

'How do you do?' he said in a formal, colonial, English. He extended a browned hand. 'Welcome to our shop.'

She took the hand. Impressions rushed her. The yellow invoice tucked into his jacket pocket. The bandit's mustache ... The unreadable eyes. The silently angry woman beside her, eyes as glitteringly dangerous as her Auntie Esther's. Around them the masks, like mute witnesses, like warning images in a dream.

'I'm John Chang,' he said. 'I'm a shopkeeper. And this is my shop manager, Miss Walters.'

An alarm began to sound in Julia's brain. She gasped and sat upright. The electronic panel across from her all-white bed chirruped for attention. A green light now blinked red.

She swung her feet out of the bed, the images of John and Diana and the shop receding. She pulled on a robe and walked cautiously on to the balcony.

Something moved in the shadows of the eucalypts. She turned on the floodlights.

The cat looked up, its fur bristling.

She felt a wave of relief. She had nothing to throw at it. She waved her hand tentatively, but the cat simply crouched lower and watched her unblinkingly.

She switched the floodlights off, went back to her bedroom and reset the alarm. She would get a technician out to adjust it, so the cats could come and go without disturbing her.

She dropped the robe across her bed and slid back the sheets. Her hand brushed her breast and she let her fingers continue, for a moment, to caress herself.

She stopped.

She could see John's dark eyes as, raised on one elbow, he looked down at her as they lay on the all-white bed.

She could feel his hand, as hers had just done, gently, inquisitively caress. She remembered his face leaning to her, his eyes growing darker. His lips suddenly hard against her mouth.

The feeling of dammed-up, held back power. His hand sliding up to encircle her neck. Tension there, as if he didn't know whether to caress, or whether to close on it and snap the life out of her.

And she, in turn, feeling herself tensing, her own muscles growing rigid, like wire. Wanting to turn to him, to open up to him, but unable to move. Unable to let herself go as her groin drew itself into a knot, a ball of fiber that nothing could penetrate.

And then he would gently kiss her, almost as if they were two actors doing a love scene and now the cameras were no longer rolling they could turn aside, take a breath, and go to sleep.

They would lie there, as close as two spoons in a kitchen drawer, not speaking, not daring to question each other as to why they both stopped at this point.

For her, it was the feeling of impending nausea. Tension screwed so tight that she felt sick. A force rising up inside her that cried out to be released, and the knowledge that releasing that force would destroy her.

He never told her what he thought as he lay there.

She didn't ask him, in case it broke the gentle, hypnotic spell they lived within. Like Gawain, the perfect knight, she had found her way to the magic castle of her dreams. She would not knowingly destroy it by asking the wrong questions.

Or the right ones.

She turned on her side, welcoming the flood of drowsy, jostling images ahead of sleep. She had one final, unsettling thought. It was something her father used to tell her as she watched him working on his cars.

'Whatever you get for free today, you gotta pay for next week.'

She'd got her husband's blind faith, his gentle celibacy, like a gift from the gods. She had never questioned it. How much longer before payment was due?

She slept.

CHAPTER SIX

John Chang wore a light-weight jacket and pants, with leather sandals and a straw hat. He could feel the perspiration under his arms and down his spine as he walked along the side of Silapakorn University. The traffic stink from Na Phralan Road was almost unbearable. Bangkok's early afternoon heat and humidity was always made worse by the fumes, and the noise, of what seemed like every vehicle in Asia trying to jam its way into the Old City.

John bore it, as he bore everything about modern Asia, with sadness — and with the resolute determination that it could be changed. That he could change it.

Other walkers idled, or flowed with gentle Thai grace, accepting the world as it was. Accepting this world of illusion, *samsara*, and making from it *sanuk*: the pursuit of pleasure. Europeans, when they walked, walked in the manner of tourists, as if in a dream. John Chang walked firmly, as if he belonged to this soil, but without a peasant's resignation, without lordly aloofness, without a monk's detachment. He walked like a man determined to change things.

The chatter and laughter of beautiful girls on the university lawns did not distract him, though he did glance at them. His eyes went from them to the gigantic movie poster that loomed in the distance. An idealized Thai beauty leaned forward to show off her Western-sized bosom while, simultaneously, her entrails spilled from her stomach, running in gory detail down the side of the Thai script that extolled the joys of this latest epic-based movie from Thailand's booming film industry.

From there, he took in the towering glass walls of a fully air-conditioned massage parlor, with a sex-tour party of German men waiting impatiently outside. Men so needy that even the looming spectre of the AIDS virus could not curtail them.

John's lips tightened. He did not know how to deal with the lemming-like drive towards extinction which seemed to have transformed man's drive to reproduce.

He looked around quickly, as if suddenly aware that he was being followed. Nervously he licked his lips. He ran his fine-boned hands down his trousers, feeling the sweat there. At last, with clearly a conscious effort, he crossed the road.

Reaching the warehouses by the river, he threaded his way down past open doors where gangs of men stacked rice, laboriously shrugging sack after sack from their deformed backs.

He crossed the riverside roadway and walked on to a rickety dock, where the water taxis fought for the custom of tourists and residents alike. He picked his way past them, settling at last for an old, dilapidated, wooden boat. Originally built for sculling, it had been converted for the tourist trade by the simple expedient of bolting an aging Evinrude outboard motor to its stern.

An old man sat on the stern seat, meditatively picking his nose. He seemed vastly disinterested in attracting business.

'*Sawat dee khrap!*' John called to him. He repeated himself, until the old man glanced his way. They stared at each other. The old man was obviously trying to place him. Not quite European. Not quite Asian. The old man could see a heritage that went way back into the mountains. Under the straw hat he could see a trace of scar tissue puckering the left eye; a thick mustache ... He sensed power. He also sensed a terrible tension.

'*Yaak cha pai Saphan Phut,*' the owner of the power, and the tension, explained patiently.

The old man glanced at the other water taxis, the fast boats, the new boats. They seemed infinitely preferable to his own craft. But, before he could think of a decent reason to refuse the request for transport, John had climbed into his boat.

The old man glanced out into the river's stream, down in the direction this strange, middle-aged passenger wished to travel. Down under the Phut Bridge. A *farang* tourist would have demanded to go upstream, to the glittering temple domes, to the floating market. A *farang* would have tried to ask about a 'water-baby', and the old man would have had to feign ignorance — and listen to the *farang* tell him sex industry fairy stories about beautiful prostitutes in discreetly curtained boats plying their wares upon the waters. The water-babies' granddaughters now all worked from the glass-towered massage parlors. The old man could remember the mothers, and the mothers of the mothers.

An Asian, on the other hand, would not have taken a meaningless ride. If he'd wanted to go down to the docks on business, he would have done so in as fast a boat as possible. Unless, of course, he was on a pilgrimage.

Shaking his head, he tugged the old motor into surprisingly virile life and eased them away from the crowded dock. He had decided his passenger was on some kind of nervous pilgrimage.

They passed under the bridge, and his passenger did not react. The passenger did glance casually towards the Oriental Hotel, but then he glanced up and saw the next bridge, Krung Thep, in the distance. The old man saw his passenger hunch forward, staring ahead, seeking out something in the empty waters ahead of them; searching for something deeply personal in the muddy water of the river, where it mixed with the tidal stream.

John Chang gripped the gunwales with an unconscious strength. He could sense the old man behind him. Since the day on the bus at Chiang Saen all old men seemed to be watching him; all seemed to have a terrible, secret message for him; and a basket-load of objects full of inexplicable beauty and terror. He remembered the texture of green jade, and again felt the tears.

A long-tailed boat roared past, with its rooster's-tail plume. Far in the distance was the thin tinkling of temple bells. John heard nothing. He stared anxiously into the water, down into the colloidal mud. Then, after a while, he sighed with relief, for he had seen nothing. He lifted his hand, unaware of what he was doing — though his driver saw the gesture and recognized it for what it was: a blessing.

John shivered. As if in harmony with him, the water's surface shivered, too. He looked up to see the pattern of wind ruffles swirling across the surface. Soon the kite fighters would be assembling in Sanam Luang. Down one end of the field would be the 'male' *chula* kites, big, awkward, and heavy — handled by excited teams of young men. Down the other the small, light, and maneuverable 'female' *pukpao* kites waiting to be ensnared in the male kites' embraces.

He glanced at his taciturn driver and nodded his head to indicate they could return. Though it was all the same to the driver. He could sit all afternoon out on the river's broad, cooling skin, particularly as his passenger was paying. The old man sighed and leaned on the outboard's handle and the boat turned through the breeze, turning past the bank on which the DEA vehicle had waited with the shrouded woman who had betrayed Joe Tobias — even though she had never seen him.

John remembered packing the objects into the box. What else could he do with them? Leave them for the rapacious tourists? No. In some strange way they were his. They were like his bad dreams made solid. They were a message from himself, to himself. And suddenly he no longer knew who he was.

The shivering of temple bells made him think of Julia, and that was like the sun bursting out of storm clouds. He smiled. He imagined her in one of her long, silver gowns, parading for his benefit across the white carpet of their all-white bedroom. He thought of her hollow cheeks and high cheek-bones, her full lips and her long, lustrous hair. In his mind the gown billowed between her thighs and clung to her firm, full breasts; like the gown on the bronze images of Tara, the Tibetan Buddhist goddess of mercy and love.

Like Tara she had held a long-stemmed flower delicately in her fingers when he had first met her. He remembered the moment. The sound of a musical voice addressing him as he stood in the stockroom of his store.

He had turned and she was there, holding out the flower of hope. Beside him stood the woman who always made him think of the goddess in one of her negative moods. Until that moment he had assumed fate required him to meet Her only in such guise — the guise of Kali the Destroyer — to pay out his karma. But he had turned and there was hope, and a message that he could still save himself. That he could step off his personal wheel of suffering. And so his heart went out to her, binding itself to that image, clinging to it like the drowning fisherman clings to the lifebuoy as the typhoon rages around him.

The boat finished its turn and headed back under the

bridge, among the daily traffic of ferries, water taxis, tourists in fast long-tailed boats, huge grain barges and small sampans strung together like beads behind laboring powerboats.

Like evil prayer beads strung together. Passing them, he thought again of Joe Tobias. What Joe had done on the sampans, so long ago, still locked them together. And, until it was paid out, they would go on through time dancing their interlocking dance, like the patterns of Yin and Yang. Like the blue dragon of heaven fighting the yellow dragon of earth. Like Jesus and his older brother, Satan.

He thought of Joe again that evening as he dined with the Thai government officials he had come to see. They ate French food at the Oriental Hotel's rooftop restaurant. From their table they could see the river curving out around the Old City, a stream of darkness between the shores of lights.

This time John wore a light-weight suit and a silk tie. He knew the value such officials placed on elegance and appearance. And John knew how to play the game of appearances — in Asia as well as in Beverly Hills.

He hoped to win the officials with his easy, unaccented French, and his equally casual command of Thai. As they sat there he could hear the loud voices of Texans and Australians at other tables — sitting there in open-neck shirts, complaining loudly of the heat, while silk-tied officials smiled blandly at them across the tables, and an interpreter kept up a nervous, frowning commentary.

But the world was changing. The Texans and the Australians had already distributed their aid. They were teaching the Meo Hills nomads how to become rice-growing peasants. Out from Chiang Mai they had transformed an area of scrub into the biggest open-cut coal-mine in Asia. Maybe in the world. Now they pressed for contracts to concrete over every last canal in the city. Concrete over the last tourist fantasy of the water-babies.

Eagerly the officials told John of how they were now achieving real growth in reciprocal trade with these countries. The Thai workers at the mines, and soon the ex-nomadic rice-growers, were buying Australian Ford cars to drive on the concreted canals. They washed their Levis in American washing-machines. The power came from the generating plants the open-cut coal was firing. Everyone was winning! The aid givers were selling their surplus goods. The aid receivers were eager to buy. The jungle was being transformed into coal-mines and highways.

This was how Joe had worked. He never personally laid a hand on anyone in violence. He simply offered a choice to someone else. Or simply pointed out that there was a choice.

Plant not maize and rice in this desolate spot, but plant these poppies, that I may refine them in my refineries.

Cast not your nets here, where there are now no longer any fish, but cast them here, where you can fish out packages of powder from my refineries.

Kill not that poor, endangered species of bird. I need someone to kill a man who is doing great wrong to our village-improvement scheme.

You know there is not enough to feed these babies. They are destined to die. Perhaps it is their karma. Perhaps they did great evil in a past existence on the wheel of suffering. Because they must die, let me have their lives, and those of us destined to live will have enough to eat.

'Mr Chang? Mr Chang?'

He returned to the present to see the anxious face of his host across the orchid-bedecked table.

'You have gone white, Mr Chang.'

'Someone walking on my grave,' he joked.

The words were out before he could stop them.

Three polite, but anxious, faces stared at him.

'What were we talking about?' he asked, looking to each in turn.

'Progress,' one replied.

'Modernization,' another said.

'No,' John said. 'I remember. Corruption.'

'You are referring to the heroin trade? If so, I remind you that poppies are also flowers.'

The giddiness, the sense of dread, was receding. John sipped his mineral water and twirled the champagne stem in which it was served.

'Many rare flowers grow in Thailand,' he said. 'Do you wish to destroy all your rare specimens in order to mine coal?'

'We're a nation, not a botanical and anthropological museum, Mr Chang. When you return to Beverly Hills, is there electricity in your house? Is there a car in your garage?'

'I'm already corrupted,' he replied, glancing around nervously, again with that sense of being watched.

'And so is my country. But you have the choice, now, to avoid corruption.'

'There is no avoiding corruption ... unless you give up the Way of action, unless you extinguish all desire. And yet, who supports the non-acting, non-desiring monks in their beautiful temples? The brothel girls and the coal-miners who give them alms, Mr Chang. Without those alms, the monks would starve.'

John looked quickly out to the dark gash of the river between the city's lights. Now he could feel that ghost stirring, a hand rising from the water.

He knew now what the ancient nomad who had tracked him to Chiang Saen was trying to show him in the objects of beauty and terror. Joe Tobias had not died.

CHAPTER SEVEN

At dawn, from her bedroom balcony, Julia watched the light slowly flood the white and red rooftops that nestled among the trees of Beverly Hills. The sky was clear, and every leaf and twig of the spindly eucalyptus trees in her garden glittered from the night's sudden rain-showers.

She sat there, in her silver nightgown, brushing out her damp hair, freeing the tangles with her fingers, the dryer whirring as traffic began to flow into the streets, the sound muted by the distance and the trees. It flowed into the great gray rivers of the freeways like the rain rolling from gutter to gutter, from stream to stream, and then to the ocean.

Once the tangles were free, Julia set herself the task of brushing out the dream images that still clawed at her. Each stroke of the brush was meant to catch one remnant of dream, unsnag it from where it hooked into her memory, sweep it clear into the mainstream, and send it swirling and dissolving out into the rising heat of the day.

As she brushed, the smells of oil and tar began to obtrude over the scent of her fresh-washed hair, obtrude over the scent of the night. The lifting sun brought out the aroma of eucalyptus oil, like an antidote to the smell of distant cars. The rising tide of Los Angeles began to snare away the brittle dream fragments.

She brushed harder, keeping her eyes wide open, hearing the trucks, the roar of the buses, the sound of the day's first ambulance. Above her, in the crystal-like air, the planes dropped down towards LA International.

She shook her hair out, running her fingers through it. It hung loose over her shoulders. Picking up the dryer and the brush she went back inside, shutting the sliding glass doors against the muted traffic noise and the rising smog.

In the quiet peace of her bathroom she put on her face. Staring into the bathroom mirror she remembered the dream she had been trying to cleanse from memory.

She remembered a mirrored door set in brick. Rich, golden light leaked from behind the door into a darkly oppressive room in which she cowered.

Or was it the door of a furnace, leaking golden light and heat into a cold, dark cellar?

She didn't know. In the dream she reached for the doorknob, and as she reached she looked into the mirror on the door.

Staring back at her was a woman wearing a feathered mask; a woman with fingernails grown long and twisted, like the nails of an ancient Chinese dowager. They pointed to huge breasts and their painted aureoles. Then the taloned hand reached up to slide the mask away from the face.

She had woken in a fighting panic, struggling with the covers, dimly aware that, when the mask was ripped aside, the face of that masturbatory goddess would be hers.

She woke, sweating, to the Los Angeles dawn.

By the time she was sitting in the old blue Dodge, at the intersection of Santa Monica and Rodeo Drive, she could no longer see the hills. The rows of tattered palm-trees disappeared into the gritty petrochemical blue that clamped down on all vision of a world beyond LA. So that the city's potential shrank to nothing more than a jumble of factories, apartments, office buildings, and endless freeways that went nowhere.

The lights changed. The Dodge's transmission shuddered in protest as she inched forward. The passenger in the white Lincoln beside her, like the driver a bearded black, gave her the eye. She tried to ignore him, but the two vehicles seemed locked together, like a pair of twigs in the same current.

The two men in the Lincoln had the air-conditioning, and the stereo, turned up high. Their satin shirts were immaculate. The driver wore a cloth cap low on his forehead. He passed a joint to the passenger, who turned and smiled into the Dodge, lifting the cigarette inquiringly to her. She kept her eyes on the road. He shrugged, as if puzzled by her ill will, her lack of manners.

A hole formed in the traffic, and the Lincoln shot into it, as if the driver knew it was about to appear; was reading the traffic in advance, like a surfer on a wave. There was a last, ironic wave of the hand to her, and her companions in the stream were gone. The Dodge plowed along in its lane.

What's gone wrong? she thought. *I always knew what I wanted to be. Always. And even mom came to think I could do it, in the end. So why haven't I achieved it?*

She hadn't consciously thought of her dead mother for months. She thought of her father, still dreamily tinkering with the motors of Mack trucks and rebuilding yet another classic Pontiac. She remembered her mother's wasted face, the pain and the fear, that look of baffled outrage of the dying cancer victim. Outrage against her own body which had turned traitor on her, attacking her at her weakest point.

Her mother had died of cervical cancer. It was something which Julia feared would erupt within herself. It was what nagged behind her thoughts when she stared at her own image in the mirror, or at a photograph of herself, or watched a video of herself in a production.

The painted face. The mask. And, behind it, the rotting corpse.

They had found her weird Auntie Esther three-days dead, her face still painted like a harlequin. She had killed herself a year, to the day, after her sister had died. Uncle Ben, whom Julia could never like, who made her shiver whenever he looked at her, had been 'born again' and now sang the praises of Jesus every night on some local television show. His children had eked out their lives in detention homes and on parole, drunk and drugged, battering and bashing their partners and their own sorry children.

She could remember hideous festivities at their house,

where she removed herself from it all, diving down into her lovely, make-believe world, while the relatives screamed and joked and sang and something else went on, something which she could not recall, except for Auntie Esther's beady, glittering eyes, watching her with what seemed like hate. Hatred of what?

The lights changed and she took her foot off the brake and the old Dodge eased across the intersection, shifting gears with a jolting clunk. She changed lanes for the Beverly Center.

The shopping mall rose, a great gray monolith, above the gray freeway, above the bleached, yellow grass between the streams of traffic and the tattered palms. It stood there, in the middle of the glittering river of automobiles, like a granite peak upon which a mighty torrent was breaking. Julia picked up the exit and eased the Dodge on to the ramp and into the tomb-like interior of the mall's carpark.

She had no trouble getting one of her admirers, one of the center's security men, to find a hand-cart and carry her box for her. The main doors were not yet open for the public, and her heels echoed crisply on the empty floor. She wore a pair of black, pleated, wide-legged pants, cut tight across her buttocks, and a full-sleeved cream-colored blouse. She liked the drape of the fabric against her skin as she walked. She felt the security man's admiring eyes watching where the pants clung tight.

It was moments like this when she did feel powerful, in charge of her life, knowing she was being admired, but from a safe, untouching distance. She gave him a smile.

'You sure look great today,' he told her. 'You can wear them dumb pants better than anyone else.'

'You just like the tight bits,' she said.

'I like your ass, that's for sure. You know, your shop's got the weirdest window in this whole joint. Don't you reckon it scares the customers away?'

To Julia it was the most arresting window in the Center — and yet she had seen other women give it a wide berth as they moved from window to window. Approaching it, they passed a cardshop, its windows jammed with stuffed animals; board games; cute sayings to hang on the wall — 'When the going gets tough, the tough go shopping', 'Where there's a will, there's a relative'. Then a boutique of after-five wear, glittering with sequins and dyed net, lycra skirts and scrubbed leather jackets like the hides of prehistorically sexy creatures. There was a shoe shop with its beautiful, black objects mounted on pedestals, high-arched and heeled, strangely arresting sculptures adorned with satin butterflies.

Then the window of Mana: Genuine Arts & Crafts from the Primitive World.

It was darkly dramatic, containing only two objects. A spotlit mask from Ecuador, with human hair hanging in oily strands across the wooden cheeks, the eyes of broken shell glittering maliciously. Dogs' teeth jammed into the wooden jaws were bared in a ferocious and ironic grin.

Lying beneath it, on a black velvet cushion, was a green obsidian axe from the island of New Britain, its polished stone head having a lustre to it, a depth, that was like looking into still, dark water. Its handle was carved in the long and stylized shape of a crocodile.

She unlocked the door.

'Some,' she said, 'some people look in the window and scurry away. But others keep coming back. I watch them, day after day, staring at the masks.'

'Weird,' he said, lugging the trolley through the door. 'What's the name mean, anyhow?'

'Mana?' She repeated what Di had told her. 'Mana is the power that lives inside something. It's the power of the universe, and it can be concentrated in something and brought out by magic.'

He stacked the box in the storeroom and turned back to her.

'You mean like the way you wear them tight pants around your ass, and how that concentrates my thoughts down into my pecker?'

She felt herself go white. She hated that word. And the situation of the leering man and herself alone in the empty shop induced a feeling of panic in her. She backed hurriedly to the door. He came after her, grinning to show he was only joking. But his eyes weren't joking.

He reached her before she could get through the door. His hand came around and fondled her buttock. She kept still, afraid to move.

She suddenly found herself transported, out of her body. It was like she had stepped aside, leaving a blond stranger there to quiver under his coarse hand. And she was moving along a flower-strewn street in a temple town, listening to the monks chant their prayers. She wore a tightly wrapped, silk dress. She danced rather than walked. On her fingers were long, false fingernails, made of real beaten gold. She writhed her hands in a complicated dance. She was a temple dancer. She was a princess. She was a sacred prostitute, and any act of love with her was an act of love with the goddess.

'Any time you want to spread some of that Mana around, you just call me,' he said, chuckling, sliding his hand quickly up between her legs to feel her sex.

He winked at her and sauntered out of the shop. The keys on his belt jiggled as he swaggered away.

She stumbled back into the shop, into the storeroom, shut the door, and sat on the box he had carried for her. She felt dizzy, sick, and frightened.

Dave Watson had dreamt of Mary, his wife. He dreamt she had been found by monks from some secret, silent order of Buddhists. He had found their monastery in high hills. They were like the hills of Laos when seen across the Mekong, humped and contorted, the hills of Chinese brush paintings. Until he had seen them he'd thought those painted hills were not real.

In the dream it did not surprise him that the monastery's head was Joe Tobias, and that Joe was wearing the saffron robe. And Joe, as usual, was offering a choice. By sign language he indicated that Dave could either stay outside, and keep his peace of mind, or enter the thatched hut where, so Joe indicated in mime, Mary was waiting for him.

He chose the hut.

He woke with a rush, knowing how wrongly he had chosen. She had been dead nearly fifteen years, her drowned corpse dragged from the bottom of Hong Kong harbor, a heavy typewriter tied to her with a silk scarf. He'd bought her the scarf after the birth of their son. She'd lain in the Minnesota soil since then, flown home in an aluminum coffin at the expense of the US government.

And you can't expect to find someone who's been dead that long in good condition, can you? He woke gasping for air, seeing the skull, the brittle, dried hair, the laughing death's head. He thought he could hear the, until then, mirthless Joe Tobias laughing.

That smirking face seemed to say to him, 'You've got your wife back. Want your son, too?'

He woke, trembling, to the boom of LA traffic down Sunset Boulevard.

Now, as he switched off the ignition of the hire car in the shrouded darkness of the Beverly Center carpark, he still felt contaminated by the dream. He got out and checked the locks, then felt his pockets, stalling for time.

He really didn't know what he was doing here, following up what had begun the previous night. He should have been catching some rest in his hotel room, preparing himself for the afternoon's meeting with Los Angeles's new mayor, a fierce anti-drug campaigner with heavy connections in the Republican Party. It was to be a preliminary sortie, a reconnaissance patrol, to see if he could be ensnared into the machinery of lobbying.

Instead, he was walking to the escalators, hands in

pockets to keep them under control. He was heading down to the street-level shops.

Julia felt her panic receding. She stood up and glanced down the long tunnel of the storeroom. A mirror was beveled in wood at the far end, attached to the gray brick wall. In it she saw a frightened young woman looking back, her hair disheveled. She turned and opened the storeroom door and checked the empty shop. Then she found her bag, took out her brush, and combed her hair. Bobbypins between teeth, she fixed it in a high fall.

As always, focusing on her appearance eased her panic. Feeling calmer, she looked down at the box from Thailand. She went and found the shop's scissors.

Kneeling, she slit the tape. She imagined John's patient hands sealing the box. His fingers working methodically, his full lips pursed as he concentrated. Sometimes, in unguarded moments when he was relaxed, he seemed like a monk.

She turned back the lips of the box to find an envelope with the single word, 'Julia', scrawled on it. She smiled and opened it.

In it were three pages from a hotel pad.

Chiang Mai.

I'm at the Chang Phuak Hotel, which has the advantage of some rooms without air-conditioning. I hate the sound of those damned units chugging away all day and night.

It's been a long and frustrating journey. I hardly know

what I'm doing out here any more. Maybe the trail is just about ended. Maybe it's time to come home and do the things you've talked about doing. Invest in some movies. Start a restaurant. Buy a swamp and turn it into a marina. Give up the Asian side of my life and embrace the European.

I suppose you can feel that I've been shaken by something. And you're right. I've never had time for the superstitions that bedevil these lands. But the other night I had a bad dream. Nothing surprising about that, I hear you say. But the dream was set in a horrible little river town called Chiang Saen. One street of mud, dust, chickens, boredom, and misery. And that morning, standing in the lobby of this hotel, fretting about the dream, I saw one of those 'Adventure Package' tour groups being organized on to a bus. Their destination? The town of my dream: Chiang Saen. Not knowing why, but feeling myself in the grip of something far bigger than myself, I tagged along.

We got there at lunchtime, by which time I knew it was all a mistake. I couldn't stand my fellow passengers. I got the bus driver to have a plate of rice sent out to me, and I sat on the bus step and ate.

I became aware I was being watched. Watched by the oldest man I have ever seen. An old nomad with a cunning, survivor's face. God, that face was familiar. I was polite to him, and that was the mistake.

Suddenly, he produced from his ancient haversack a statue ... well, The Statue. The one you will find in this box. The green, jade Tara, priceless beyond belief. He insisted it was for me. My fellow travelers clamored for it, like gulls fighting for scraps. That in itself almost determined me to accept the gift.

But there was part of me that cried out not to touch it. Not to have anything to do with it or with him. I recoiled. He called out to me that it was not for me, but for … 'For The Marrying Maiden'. When he said that I thought immediately of you. I looked at it again, and it was so like you in body and gesture, in the flower it held, in the way the carved fabric molded to the breasts, to the thighs. I began to cry. Why? I don't know. Things were suddenly too much for me. The local policeman puffed on to the scene, intent on arresting somebody.

I managed to stop them pursuing the poor old man — who had vanished, leaving his haversack and all its contents at my feet. He'd disappeared up the road on a bicycle, and despite the shock he'd given me I didn't want them taking him in. I had a feeling he'd seen too much of cops in this life.

So I picked up the straw sack, clutched my Tara, and got back on the bus. I was the object of considerable surreptitious interest now. After all, he had called me 'Master', like I was some Indian guru. I half-expected the backpackers to fall at my feet and plead for pearls of wisdom!

The pearls, though, were in the sack, which I was unwilling to investigate until I returned to the safety of my room.

I know I have seen this Tara before. Just as I have also seen the statue of Kali which you will find here. Vicious, violent. The antithesis of Tara. There's a Malay dagger also mixed up with this, which doesn't belong.

What does belong, though, is the vicious-looking bronze axe head on the relatively new handle. The head

is definitely original! Look at the wear on it. And it has such a … horrible, it's the only word for it, horrible feel to it.

You'll also find a mask and a head-dress! These, too, are really something! Far older than any of the others. Look at the quality of the detailing in them! Whatever you do, don't play with them! I can feel the power there! I'm serious. I know your love of dressing-up. Don't succumb! This stuff, like the statues, has some meaning for me that I can't yet define. I don't want to define. Wait until I'm home and have somehow found out what this stuff means to me.

I would guess that the mask and head-dress are Central Asian, from somewhere out on the high plateau. The ritual objects of some ancient shaman. The drum is his, too. And that bronze could be even older. How come they've been kept together, handed down through time for so many generations, without getting split up? I don't know. I once thought I had answers. Now, all I have is questions.

As I said, the encounter shook me up. I had already decided to give the game away this trip. My meetings with officials have been nothing but frustrating. They don't want the people to be in charge of their own lives. They want the power themselves. And that means allying themselves with the big interests. It's the old colonial system all over again. Except that, instead of the British Crown, it's the American development dollar that buys up the local officials, gives them a cap and a badge, and lets them bleed the peasants dry. Times change, but nothing changes.

I'll sign off now. I'm tired. I'm impatient to see you

again. From here I go back to Bangkok, after I've done the paperwork on these items and shipped them to you and Diana. Then I'll head south to see the fishermen I helped finance. Hopefully, they will still be in control of their own lives. I'll be home within two weeks. Take care my Tara.

All my oceanic love, John.

Julia looked up from the letter. She blinked back the tears. John had never spoken to her like this before. She wondered what had moved him? Was it just the encounter with the old man. Just that and the artefacts towards which he felt what he had written?

There were times when she was afraid to look at the reasons why she had married him. Times when she suspected what this letter told her, that his love for her was far deeper, far more urgent, than hers for him.

Shivering, she stood up and looked out through the shop to where the crowd drifted through the arcade. Water played in a fountain. Totemic poles, part of the water display, peered above the crowd's collective head.

She knelt again beside the box and plunged her hands into the white styrofoam beads that protected the contents. Packed on top was an ornately carved, oval wooden cylinder — a drum with an old, dried and cracked skin held tightly across its top with a black, greasy cord.

The cord was made of long strands of human hair. It made her feel slightly ill to touch them with her fingers, thinking of how long ago they had been collected; how many centuries they had been stretched around the drum head; how many generations of human hands had touched them. The carving was finely detailed and ornate, carved with passion and dedication and with lots of patience.

There was an underworld of skeletons and broken bodies near the drum's open, megaphone-like mouth. There was a heaven, not of celestial angels, but of the sun and the moon and stars. Between them was an upside-down tree, its roots tangled in the stars like hair, and its crown apparently studded with fruit made from human remains.

She turned the drum around. Opposite the image of the world tree was an image of a gaunt, terrified-looking person, rowing a small boat against a powerful stream. Looking closer, she saw that the boat was made from a human rib-cage. The oars were carefully detailed human limbs. The person had an eagle's head.

And the figure was definitely female. For some reason that gave it even more power, more fascination. The idea that, at some time in the distant past, women had such power within their grasp.

She took the projected wooden handle of the drum and tentatively hit the stretched skin.

The sound was surprisingly loud. The boom seemed to fill the small space of the stockroom. She glanced nervously around, then shut the stockroom door. It was just her and the drum, the box at her feet and, down the length of the room, the empty mirror.

She beat the drum again. The skin had a pleasantly

rough and dry feel to it. She put it down and bent over to plunge her hands again into the white beads, like a child with a lucky dip, wondering what treasure would emerge next.

She was looking at a wooden eagle's face. She dropped it with a start. The red beak was hooked and split. She smiled at her fear and bent down and lifted it free of the box. The staring slit eyes were dark. The mask was topped by a cloth head-dress on to which had been sewn a hundred or so bird feathers, sewn so closely that they rippled as she lifted it. The feathers were brown and white, the feathers of some Central Asian bird of prey.

All was silent in the stockroom as she looked at the head-dress, at the narrow, dangerous eyes and the hooked, red beak. She hefted it high above her head. All the weight was in the wood. She held it up with one hand and with the other combed her hair back, and then she dropped it over her face.

There was a cap sewn into the crown and it fitted snugly on to her head. The mask tugged her head forward. She felt oddly dizzy as she leaned with it and looked down the length of the room to the waiting mirror.

A bird-woman-goddess stared back at her. Then it began to walk towards her. It wore her pants and padded-shouldered blouse. It wore her black court shoes. But above the clothes was a cruel beak and slit eyes and a cascading fall of rippling feathers. It lifted an arm to its face and its claws were long and richly orange in color.

It was a face like that from her dream, like that of the

pigeon-breasted model on her friend's video. It was the face of something dark and locked away, hidden in the back rooms of her mind for too many years.

Dave pushed his way through the jogging-suited crowd of Japanese tourists. Among them were flamingo-like, bouffant, Beverly Hills matrons, gaunt-faced and frosted-haired. He scanned the window displays, searching for the curio shop. He saw a bored-looking security guard leaning against a wall, flexing his biceps thoughtfully, and stopped to ask him the way.

The man stared at him over his mustache.

'Mana?' he said. 'What you want with that?'

'That's my business,' Dave said. 'Just tell me where it is.'

The security guard grinned and eased his bulging genitals with a large hand.

'Can't miss the window,' he said. 'It's real weird. And the fox in there ...' He grinned again, and rolled his eyes significantly. 'You go on to where the fountain is and it's off to the left, down the turn there. Third shop after that.'

'Thanks,' Dave said.

'Tell her my offer's still good!' the guard called after him.

Julia stared dizzily into the mirror, into the eyes of the goddess. She reached out her hand, and the goddess's orange-tipped talons reached for her. In the dim light the orange became blood red.

She remembered the moment in Charles's studio, her hand uplifted to the actor, about to throw herself into the emotions of the character on the square of marked-out stage. The actor's eyes staring through her, past Julia Carr, waiting for the moment when the character emerged so he could become the character he was hired to be for the moment. The whole studio waiting for the play to begin.

Dave saw the fountain and steered to its left, down past a card shop and a boutique. Past a shoe store. He saw the darkened window and the spotlight hitting the lopsided grin of the mask. He froze, remembering his dream. Remembering the death's head.

Julia felt the moment about to consume her. The moment she had fought all her life to hold back, the moment of letting go. Her hand trembled. She was afraid. That was why she couldn't act any more. She was afraid. She dropped her hand. The bird-headed mask stared back at her, waiting for her to breathe life into it. 'Human beings made the gods,' she remembered Di lecturing her. 'They made them in every culture, in every tribe, in the specific images of that tribe.'

She lifted the head-dress aside and stared at her own face.

CHAPTER EIGHT

He stared through the open doorway, into the darkened stockroom. He could see her lovely fall of shining, blonde hair, and the garish mask beside it — with its own eagle's plumage. He seemed to be staring into a lost jungle temple, an unknown sect worshiping a goddess in the shape of his own secret dreams.

The mask fell aside and he looked into the woman's eyes.

'Oh, shit!' she said, and dropped the head-dress. It hit the floor with a loud crash, the sound amplified in the narrow room. She stared at the man's astonished face.

He recovered first. He bent down and picked up the mask. Its nose had snapped off.

'I'm afraid I've broken it,' he said.

She shook her head and knelt down beside him.

'No,' she said. 'No. I dropped it. It's all my fault.'

He had the head-dress. She picked up the red-ochred nose. He stood up, holding the mask in both hands.

'I was just passing,' he lied. 'And saw the window.'

'Can we step back into the shop?' she asked him, as she stood.

They bumped against each other. He moved back quickly.

In the brighter light of the shop she felt more composed. He laid the head-dress, broken face up, on the glass counter-top. She placed the beak-like nose beside it, and nervously arranged the feathered cloth.

'I'm really sorry about this,' he said. 'I caused you to break it, didn't I?'

He studied the mask more closely.

'I dropped it,' she insisted. 'It was my fault.'

'If I hadn't scared you, this wouldn't have happened.'

He turned the mask over.

'Where'd you get this, anyway?'

He tried to keep his voice light and casual.

'My husband sent it from Thailand,' she said. 'He's a collector.'

'And you manage the shop?'

'No,' she said. 'I just help out. The manager will be in later if you want to see her.'

'That sounds a good idea,' he said. 'Obviously I'll have to pay for this.'

Or was it a good idea? he thought. *If the manager was Meredith Grant disguised, what was going to happen?*

Grant would make it obvious he had lied to this beauty. Then what would happen?

'Are you all right?' she asked.

He shook his head. It didn't matter what this woman thought. He was back on the path, what Howard, angrily, used to call 'the Quest'.

'Can I see what else he sent from Thailand?' he asked. And tried to smile as he said it.

She looked at him. She liked him. He was tall. His blond hair was receding at the temples. He carried a bit of weight, but not as much as most forty-year-old American males. There were a few lines on his face, but there was also an air of keenness, of searching, about him. He was a man who had been hurt, but had not yet given up.

She could see the admiration on his face, too — but in it was a yearning that went deeper, like John's yearning. A yearning for something which a beautiful woman symbolized. Something beyond her.

And he, too, saw something behind that mask of beauty. He was looking at someone as confused as himself, as lost, as haunted by bad dreams.

They both quickly smiled, trying to cover up that moment of mutual insight.

Standing behind them, in the shop doorway, unseen by either, Diana Walters stood frozen with shock. She could see the girl smiling up at him, and she could see his profile. She knew it and it made her remember everything. She rubbed her wrists together and stepped backwards.

'Let me open the box,' she said.

'If it's not any trouble.'

The phone began to ring.

Julia reached for it, and found herself still holding the

mask's beak, like a red clown's nose. She smiled and put it in the pocket of her pants.

'Good morning,' she said, brightly. 'Mana Arts and Crafts, Julia Carr speaking.'

'Get that bastard out of there!'

'I'm sorry? ...'

Then she recognized Di's voice.

'Di? What ...'

'Don't say another word. I know that man, and he's trouble. Tell him something's come up and you've got to close the store for an hour. Get him out of there at once!'

'I see,' the actress said. 'Of course. I'll come at once. Where did you say?' She paused. 'I know it. I'll close up and come immediately.'

She hung up and smiled at the puzzled-looking man.

'I'm afraid you're going to miss the manager,' she said. 'That was her on the phone. We've got a problem with some stock and I have to close up and go help her.'

God, he thought. *You lie badly.*

He smiled, equally falsely, and held out his hand.

'I'm David Watson,' he said. 'A public servant. And before I go I'll just pay for the damages.'

She took the proffered hand, and then watched him count out two hundred dollars from his billfold.

'Julia Carr ...' he said. 'Is your husband Mr Carr?'

'No,' she said. 'I'm an actress and I still use my maiden name. He's John Chang.'

She rang the money into the register.

'I'm so sorry,' he said, spreading his hands wide.

She smiled, shutting the door after them.

'It's alright,' she said. 'It's not a valuable piece.'

Why did I say that? she thought. *After what John wrote about it? What on earth is the crazy Di up to? How dare she order me about like that!*

'Can I walk with you?'

She looked at him again. She suddenly realized she would dearly like to walk with him, talk with him. He was someone fresh, and she was someone stale. And she did not like being spoken to by Di like that.

She glanced past him, and saw her manager standing across the mall — in the phone booth from which she had rung.

Dave saw her hesitate, her eyes flickering anxiously over his shoulder. He made no move. She looked back at him and smiled sadly. The combination of beauty and sadness went straight to his heart. This time it was she who spread her hands, in apology.

'I've got to go,' she said.

He nodded and stood back, making sure he didn't turn to stare after her.

'I'll see you around,' he said. Meaning it. He moved off into the mall.

This was like the old days, on the job in a crowded street. He took a step, then seemed to notice something in the next window. He peered into it, and scanned the reflections.

She turned back and cut across the mall, past the fountains. He saw her reflection stop at the phone booth, and glance around, then walk quickly towards a shop doorway. Anger trembled in her step. He smiled.

Give it to the bitch, he thought.

Then Meredith Grant appeared in the shop doorway

and he saw the girl stop, one hand on a hip. Grant was rubbing her wrists together and the moment he saw that gesture he remembered the way they handcuffed prisoners in Bangkok's jails. Tight handcuffs, and dragging leg chains. He remembered the humiliation in Grant's eyes as she stumbled awkwardly to the interview bench where he waited.

Tears suddenly blinded him.

'What did you mean by that?' Julia demanded.

'Shut up and walk!'

Shocked, Julia fell in step beside her. They headed for the carpark.

'Who is he? And what was he doing?'

'His name's David Watson, and he was just passing. He ... he broke something and paid me for it. Two hundred dollars.'

'Broke something? What?'

'A mask. In the box John sent. Let go my arm, Di, you're hurting.'

People were glancing uneasily at them as they passed.

'Who is he, Di?'

'He's a creep. He's a ... he's a thief. His photo's in the security file. "Anyone seeing this man is advised to contact ..." '

'Let me go!

'Oh, sorry.'

Di saw a man staring at them. He was smiling, watching the two dykes argue. She glared at him and he hurried away.

Julia rubbed her arm angrily.

'I'm going for a walk,' she said. She pressed the keys into Di's awkward hand. 'You go and open up when you're ready.'

'Julia, please. You don't understand. I was scared for you ...'

'Tell me later.'

Anguished, Diana watched the girl stalk away from her.

Oh God, she thought. *What's happening? Why has it been awakened?*

Desperately, she rubbed her wrists together.

Dave Watson walked past the glitter of the arcade windows, past the splashing fountain with its totem-pole-like columns, without seeing them. He walked until he was outside, in the heat and the exhaust fumes. A different mood of the city assailed him. The stench of buses pulling away from their yellow-flagged stops. The roar of trucks. Then the blast of music from the Hard Rock Cafe, where a line of young girls squabbled with the doorman.

He pushed past them and asked for a table and sat down, still not properly aware of his surroundings, not looking at the legendary, signed guitars above him, not listening to the music that gave the cafe its name.

The cappuccino he ordered came and he took it and stared at the froth on it. He shook his head, not understanding anything. Not connecting anything with anything.

When he had thought it was all over, it had suddenly appeared again. When he had given up the Quest which had driven him for so many years, let life pack him off to its storage area, to its stockroom, where he could put on weight and take off hair, and grow old and die ... it had reached up out of the dark again and grabbed him.

Perhaps in homage to the twin Gibson acoustic guitars above his head, one signed 'Don', and the other 'Phil', the thumping tape changed and he was thrown back into his childhood as those perfectly matched voices began to sing 'Take a Message to Mary'.

The voices intertwined and he leaned forward and put his head in his hands and tried not to cry.

The Everly Brothers. Buddy Holly and The Crickets. Roy Orbison. They all had sung the songs of his youth, of innocence and romance and an inexpressible yearning. Yes, and Mary had been his childhood sweetheart, and he'd said goodbye to her, just like in 'Distant Drums', for he was off to join John Kennedy's Peace Corps.

'Ask not what your country can do for you, but what you can do for your country,' had been the slogan they repeated, in Central America, in the Philippines, in Asia. And, behind the Peace Corps came the CIA to debrief them. Innocence abused.

He came back. He married Mary. But he was now a foreigner to Minnesota. A stranger in a strange land. He had been to Asia, and Asia had taken hold of him, like it took hold of so many others of his generation.

Thousands of young Americans, Britons, French, Australians, Germans, pouring into Asia with their backpacks, and little else, to bum their way from commune to ashram, by ferry and rickety bus. To freak out in Katmandu, have dysentery in Bombay, and be murdered in Indonesia.

It was like some strange, cosmic gate had been opened and Asia had come pouring out. No wonder the older generation ordered a war against it. To them it was some Hydra-headed beast pouring forth from its cavern, assaulting everything they held to be the truth. A beast that threatened to shatter the world. They fought back with the best weapon they had — their children.

David Watson and his bride, though, didn't return to Asia along the hippie trail. And he didn't arrive there in a uniform — wondering if he'd be going home in a zip-up plastic bag. They took the plane, through the embassy. David had shifted from the Peace Corps to the brand new Drug Enforcement Administration. For there was far more than Buddhism — and belief in reincarnation and all the other trash of Eastern religion — pouring out of the hellish gates of Asia. Opium and its derivatives were the weapons that the beast used with most effect.

In 1968 there were three DEA officers in all of Thailand, and he was the most junior. If there was someone who had to get out of the air-conditioning, away from the phone, and up-country, it was him. And that suited him just fine.

The song finished and he lifted his head. He picked up the coffee and took a sip. He recalled the image of Meredith Grant reflected in the window, her hunched shoulders and crossed wrists. Like him she had just grown older and fatter, and nothing else had changed.

She had come to Thailand in her summer vacation, before she went back to do post-graduate studies in anthropology at UCLA. Like all the others — like David, himself — she came to Asia in search of its romance, its dream. Like more than a few she found the underside of that dream: the nightmare which had lain hidden within herself.

He pulled out a pack of cigarettes. He had been almost hounded into giving them up. But he carried them for emergencies. He shook one out and lit it, and drew the smoke down deep, trying to calm his screaming nerves.

Her face burning red, feeling the amused eyes of the onlookers observing their tiff, Julia had hurried from the mall. She infinitely preferred its air-conditioned cool to the stinging air outside. But now she found herself out in it, jammed between the river of metal and fumes and the glaring gray wall of the center, which rose like a granite monolith beside the narrow sidewalk.

There was the usual crowd queuing at the Hard Rock Cafe, standing in the blast of rock music that it spewed out, as other shops spewed out a blast of rejected air-conditioned air. Fighting in line to get into the din and sip a coffee beside someone who just might be the latest, the star of the moment, were the absconding high school students of West Hollywood.

They clustered there, around the door, like a newly discovered tribe, their hair in bright orange ringlets. They wore strips of stretch cloth across their teenage bosoms and another stretch, with a frill, over their thighs. Yards of flawless teenage flesh separated the two cloths. Boys in unzipped leather leaned among them, contriving to look both sinister and gawkish at the same time.

A few of the predatory male eyes flicked over her, drawn by the long, blonde fall of hair. But she was too old to hold their interest for long.

She stood beside them, uncertain, wanting for some inexplicable reason — perhaps to capture a youth of unbridled, satiated desire which she had never had — to join them.

Then she saw him staring at her.

He was seated inside, at a table, a cup of coffee in one hand, leaning back as if he were in a sidewalk cafe on the Seine. He was smoking a cigarette. His sunglasses were clipped into the top pocket of his pale jacket. He was alone.

Seeing her recognize him he smiled and lifted the coffee cup inquiringly.

She pushed past a pair of twelve-year-olds trying to convince the doorman they were eighteen, and found herself, before she could think about it, sitting beside him.

'The return of the goddess,' he said, teasingly.

She felt her cheeks warm. She looked down and felt something pressing against her thigh, from inside her pocket. She pulled it out and mechanically placed it on the table. They both stared at it.

Then they looked at each other and began to laugh.

It was the bright-red, bird-goddess's nose.

~

Diana had the broken head-dress in her hands, and was searching for the missing piece. But her search was vague and erratic. Her mind had almost ceased functioning.

She could feel Meredith Grant moving about inside the persona she had worked so hard to create. Diana Walters, part-time student, suburban shop-manager, single woman interested in the arts. Meredith Grant was gone, shattered by a ruthless drugs cop on a vindictive, personal vendetta. Meredith Grant had got in his way and he had used her and destroyed her, without compunction or pity.

She couldn't find the goddamned missing piece of mask! Angrily she opened the box and tipped its contents sideways on to the floor. There was a flood of white packing beads, and among them the artefacts, like fish thrown up on the shore by a sudden wave.

There was a Kali statuette, the many-armed Goddess of Death dancing on a disemboweled body. There was a wave-bladed dagger, probably Malayan. There was a malevolent-looking axe which gave her a sudden shiver of fear. There was also another statue wrapped in tissue paper.

She unwrapped the paper and held the small, Tibetan Tara in her hands. It reminded her of Julia, with its curvaceous body and its feminine grace. She thought how she'd introduced the damn girl to her employer and how he, in typical male fashion, had fallen head-over-heels in love with her and rushed off to marry her!

And yet the girl was the only friend she had. The only person who returned her own coldness with a gentle warmth.

Angrily, but gently, she put the statuette on the floor and picked up the dagger. She could see where a previous owner had gouged the gemstones from the hilt. She held it firmly in her hand, tensing her muscles.

She looked down at Kali, dancing with glee on the body of yet another victim. Kali seemed to speak to her. Wonderingly, she picked the bronze statuette up. It was like looking at all she loathed within herself.

At that moment, Diana hated herself totally. And what she hated most was her ability to see both sides of things. To see how much she despised Julia and her feminine wiles and graces, and yet how much she loved her. And thinking of Julia made her remember, against her will, the other girls, the girls who had no choice, and whose lives her desires had destroyed.

She could not escape her past. It had come back to her. She closed her eyes in anguish and put the evil statue down.

When she opened her eyes, she was looking at the dagger's blade. It lay in her hand, inanimate, cold. She turned her hand and brought it up against her thigh. She eased it against the cloth of her slacks and felt its tip reach through the cotton, through to touch the edge of her sex.

'I hope I wasn't gone too long,' the girl said, hurrying in through the door.

Diana put the blade down and turned to her. The girl looked at the blade, then at her white face.

'What's going on, Di? Are you all right?'

'I'm fine. Where the hell have you been?'

She saw the girl blink at her forced rudeness.

'I took a stroll.'

The girl spoke like a defiant daughter before her mother.

'A stroll? Where the hell did you go?'

Diana had never known her own mother. She created her now, mean and vindictive, someone who would abandon a baby for her own selfishness. She couldn't stop herself. She needed to push the girl right away.

'Does it matter?' Julia said, calmly, obviously trying to deflect the erratic anger. She put her bag on the counter-top and took out the mask's missing piece and laid it down.

'I put this in my bag by mistake,' she said.

'What do you plan to do with it? Paste it back on?'

'I might just do that.'

Di heard the sharpness and was relieved, and sorry. The girl would not pry any closer to her core.

'Do what you want with it,' she said. 'He paid, didn't he?'

'What's the matter, Diana? He shook you up, didn't he? Why?'

'He did no such thing! I just don't like thieves! Where do you think we should put this stuff? Maybe we could do a new window?'

Julia watched her friend with a strange remoteness. Di was an even worse actress than herself. There was movement in the shop doorway and they both glanced around, relieved to see a pair of Japanese tourists, sleek-haired, bespectacled, dressed in matching His-&-Hers Benneton jogging suits, entering. White Reeboks on their feet. Around his neck a Minolta.

Julia turned back to the stockroom, and Di went to greet them.

She was relieved the conversation had gone no further. If it had she might well have blurted out that she was meeting Dave Watson that evening. She had agreed to have dinner with him.

She stood there, looking down at the objects scattered on the floor. They seemed to produce a strange fascination in her. She knelt down and looked at them, entranced, but afraid to touch. She understood how they had made such an impact upon John, her husband.

She reached out and touched the Tara, stroking its glossy surface. She knew she was about to become involved with Dave Watson. She didn't know why. It was like some kind of fate rushing towards her, summoned by that shivering head-dress and the resonating drum.

CHAPTER NINE

From his fifteenth-floor office window, Howard Collins could watch the afternoon shadows tracking down the steel and glass columns all around him. He could see the sun reflecting back from the river of traffic on Hollywood Freeway. After that the view turned into blue haze and purple fumes.

He sighed and stared at the papers and the computer screen on his desk. The machine was off and he had no inclination to turn it on. Or to open a file. When the phone rang, he picked it up slowly, glancing at the office clock as he did. It was 4.45 and he didn't want to hear about any more work.

'Collins,' he said into the receiver, reluctantly. 'DEA.'

'Howard?'

His hackles rose as he recognized the voice.

'Who's this?' he asked, already knowing.

'Dave Watson.'

Howard wondered if he should just hang up. But he knew Dave was into politics. It wouldn't do. He sighed.

'Hello, Dave,' he said. 'What can I do for you?'

Dave heard the reluctance in the voice as he sat in his brown-on-brown hotel room, the shades pulled down against the rising tide of afternoon traffic out beyond the walls.

'I know you don't want to hear from me,' he said.

'It's not that ...' Howard said quickly. But then his voice tailed off. It was that.

'I ran into Meredith Grant.'

'You still looking, man?'

'I thought I wasn't until I saw her. I thought it was finished.'

'It is, man. All finished. Joe went down with four bullets in him. She got shipped back here, changed her name and tried to become a respectable woman.'

'You know her?'

'We know her, Dave. Diana Walters. Works for some loony philanthropist, name of Chan.'

'Chang.'

'Yeah. Whatever. You seen Mrs Chang? Why he wants to spend all his time trying to get villagers in the Sudan to dig wells and put up windmills, when all they want is a cooler full of Coca-Cola, beats me. He should be home keeping her warm at nights.'

'You've got Meredith Grant?'

Howard grinned. He could hear the disappointment in Dave's voice. Dave loved a scoop.

'We got her. Customs runs a spot check over her business every now and then, just to keep her nervous. They never find anything. She's given it all up. I even think she's given up girls. Like you and me, Dave, she stays home and thinks about the good old days. Did she see you?'

'She saw me. But she kept out of my way.'

'You can't blame her for not wanting to relive those good old days with you.'

'This Chang guy's bringing in artefacts.'

'We check 'em out. He's clean. She's clean. It's boring as can be. Now I'll tell you who *is* bringing the stuff in. The United States Air Force ...'

'What can you tell me about him?' Dave interrupted impatiently.

'British subject originally, but married Miss Foxy Lady, Julia Carr, actress, and thus acquired citizenship. Been in one horror movie.'

'Him?'

'Her. She screams a lot and lets you look at her titties. Which are very nice.'

'I want to know about him.'

'You're too tunnel-visioned Dave. You always were. He's forty-something. Interesting background. Eurasian parents, traders in Indonesia. Killed by the Japanese in the Pacific War. He was just a baby and was brought up by the natives, who hid him at considerable risk to themselves. In fact a bunch of them were massacred when the Japs found out. He's full of guilt and spends all his time trying to reconstruct peasant life as it was before the war. Or wars.'

'What's he do for money?'

'Family fortune. Big investment in Shell Oil when they were in Burma, pre-war. Shell played both sides during that conflict, and came out the winner. You got Shell Oil stock, you got nothing to worry about.'

'I thought it was all over, Howard.'

'It is all over, man! All gone. Finished. You wrapped up the Chiu Chao in Thailand. You were wrapping up Joe Tobias when the Triads got him. We got all his operatives ...'

'We didn't get Joe.'

'Joe's fucking dead, man! We saw him die! Four machine-gun rounds in him. Meredith Grant saw him die, too. Remember?'

'It was a sub-machine-gun and he was on the edge of its range. And it was probably a Peoples' Republic of China sub-machine-gun, made in some backyard shop. And we never retrieved his body.'

'The Thai police did. They identified it and showed it on television, and then buried it. He's fucking dead, Dave!'

'I put half the Thai police force in jail, remember? The Triads owned them. Either them, or the old generals up in the hills.'

Howard was silent, looking at the clock hands jerk around, the distant shadows track down the buildings. When they hit the street so would he. Go home, greet his kids, say a wary hello to his wife, listen to their aggravation. He thought of Dave and all the hotel rooms and all the airplanes and the never-ending quest. He heard himself say, 'What you doing tonight, man? Want a drink?'

'I can't. I'm seeing someone.'

Howard heard the embarrassed edge to his voice and put two and two together.

'Julia Carr?'

'You shit,' Dave said.

'Powers of deduction, Watson. You've got two

weeks before her old man's back in the country.'

'I thought you didn't want to see me?'

'I don't want to get involved. But call me if you want information. That's what we're here for.'

'Thanks, Howard. I'll do that.'

'Take care, Dave. And remember: it's all over.'

Howard hung up.

He thought a moment. He could feel himself getting involved. He got up and came to a decision. He picked up the phone and dialed.

'Honey?' he said. 'How's it going? Look, I'm leaving the office right now. Coming straight home. Let's take the kids and we'll go and eat Chinese and watch a movie.'

He listened to her surprise, and grinned.

'I've been getting too involved in my work,' he said. 'It's time I paid some attention to the family.'

Still smiling, he hung up, then looked at the blank computer screen. The smile faded. He sighed and switched the machine on. He owed Dave something for all the years. A tribute for the Quest. When the machine was ready he typed in, CHANG, GEORGE JOHN.

Julia parked the Dodge beside the Mercedes and wearily let herself into the house. She checked the security panel. Its integrity had not been breached. Unlike hers. She felt as if lights were blinking all over her own panels.

Warning lights. This door has been opened that should have stayed shut. Come quickly, security man.

But the only security man she could think of wore a big mustache and keys that jangled at his belt, and balls that bulged in his trousers.

What about her husband? He was her security, wasn't he?

She stood at the foot of the stairs, on the Italian marble, her hand on one of the white marble polar bears mounted at the banister. She looked up at the gold-embossed plaster above the glass chandelier. The house echoed with its emptiness, and with its phoniness. It was a front for her wandering husband, just as the Mercedes was a front. Just as she, too, was a front.

She walked into his study and trailed her hand around the edge of his big, eighteenth century roll-top desk, bought for him by a dealer. Properly authenticated, built for some famous English explorer and sea captain. The old navigation instruments the dealer had got him were also authenticated. Cook had held this one. Vancouver had peered through that. She walked over and studied the faded parchment on the big globe of the world. It had been crafted for the Royal Society. Yet she knew John wasn't the slightest bit interested in this accumulation of history. He just felt it was the right front for a man such as himself.

She spun the globe, wondering in which Asian country he was now.

Then she began to take off her clothes. She lay her pants carefully across the leather office chair. She almost felt she could sense him watching her. She smiled and lasciviously undid the gold-buttoned blouse and draped it over the pants. She turned, as if expecting to see him standing in the doorway and peeled her bra straps down, squeezing her breasts together with her elbows — just how they liked her to do it in the movie. She slipped her legs out of her panties and let her underwear drift to the floor.

She opened the double doors to the garden and stood there naked, arms upraised, trying to impress her image on to the haunted emptiness of the house and its grounds.

Nothing happened. Naked, she walked down the steps of her white mansion, tucking her hair up as she did. She walked to the edge of the pool and looked at her long-legged reflection. Watching herself, she walked along to the chapel-like cabana at the end of the pool.

Her costume lay on the stone seat, beside the swim goggles and cap. She pulled on her costume. She tucked her hair into the cap and pulled it tight on to her neck. She slipped the goggles over and made them watertight against her eyes. She smiled, feeling like a World War One flyer.

She walked to the end of the pool and launched herself cleanly into the water. She swam with long, strong strokes.

At school she had been known as 'The Ice Maiden'. The fastest girl swimmer in St Paul. The wildest body. And the most unapproachable.

She hit the turn and doubled back, not losing any speed. Swimming was the nearest thing she knew to pure, unthinking pleasure.

~

Dave stepped out of the shower and wiped the condensation away from the mirror. He shaved carefully. His afternoon's meeting had gone well, and best of all, he'd not been subjected to trial by food and booze. Maybe this mayor actually meant business.

He stared at his scraped-clean face. Nowhere on it was there any sign of the turmoil within. He was looking at your average, middle-aged American male.

We are all like this, he thought. *We are all case-hardened shells containing strange gases of incredible volatility. At any moment any one of us can explode. Every now and then, some do, and the rest of us pick up the pieces. And then we all stand around saying, 'How could this have happened? He was such an ordinary guy.'*

He patted a spot of blood on his chin, and wiped the shaving-cream from behind his ear. Mary used to do that for him.

His vision misted over. He closed his eyes and gripped the wash-basin before him.

He opened his eyes and looked again. The face was the same. A little bit moister around the eyes. No matter what turmoil was going on inside, the face would not crack apart. It would hold. He would go on living.

He finished drying and stepped into the room to confront his wardrobe. He only had the one jacket with him. He did have a better pair of pants, plus his good shoes. He considered a tie, but this was Los Angeles, not Washington.

When he put the jacket on and again looked in the mirror, he was forced to consider what he was doing, where he was going, and who he would be with.

Julia Carr. Actress. Married to John Chang. Associate of Meredith Grant. She, too, had an impeccable exterior. At first glance it seemed to be the major concern of her life. No one was that good-looking, that well-groomed, without one hell of an effort.

If he had just passed her in the street he would have turned and watched her walking away from him. If he had staked-out someone like Meredith Grant and Ms Carr had arrived on the scene, he would have enjoyed the look of her, and then considered how she fitted into the set-up. When he made the arrest he would have forgotten her beauty.

But seeing her alone in the shop, playing her mystery game before the mirror, had awakened some deep response in him. He had seen the look of possession in her eyes as she stared at herself in the costume of the bird-god. There were depths to her which she had not yet charted, from which she drew back, and at the same time towards which she was irresistibly drawn.

He and she were on a collision course.

He broke the seal on the bottle of hotel cologne and dashed some on his jaw. It tingled where he had cut himself. He grimaced, and the face grimaced back.

He hadn't done any of this kind of stuff since he'd been married. His wife had consumed all his sexual energy. Then the baby had died, and then she had died. Grief took over. After the grief came the Quest. The lone knight errant battling the wasteland dragons, searching not for the Holy Grail but for retribution, for redress, for an end to the aching void inside the case-hardened shell. And failing.

He stood back and buttoned the jacket. He stared at himself and decided he looked like a minor public servant who thinks he has a hot date with his secretary.

He shook his head and grimaced.

Julia swam twenty-five laps of the twenty-five-yard pool. She clambered out and stood there, breathing hard. She removed the goggles and the cap. She forced the old air from her lungs, bending low, wrapping her fingers around her ankles, feeling the new air make her body tingle.

She stretched, breathing in, her freed hair cascading over her shoulders. Her nipples constricted. There was a tightness in her groin and she pressed her hand against her pubis. She had no idea what was wrong with her.

Thoughtfully, she walked back into the empty house, into her husband's study. She stood beside her husband's study chair, and ran her fingers over the silk blouse, rolling one of the buttons between her fingertips.

She stooped and picked up her panties and bra and dropped them into the seat of the chair. She felt like she was assembling the shell of herself there. All she had to do was slip back into it, and life would resume at some point before she opened the box from Thailand.

She remembered the resonance of the drum in that narrow space. She shivered. John had sent it to her.

She had struck it. And, suddenly, she seemed to have woken, as if from a deep sleep.

She gave the back of the chair a push, setting it rotating, and walked on into the house and up the stairs.

Dave Watson sat on the edge of his hotel bed. He had his feet flat on the floor. He held the fax gently between the fingers of both hands. He wore reading-glasses.

CHANG, GEORGE JOHN. DATE OF BIRTH: UNKNOWN. PLACE OF BIRTH: JAVA, REPUBLIC OF INDONESIA. OCCUPATION: TRADER, PRIVATE AID PROGRAMS. AFFILIATIONS: WORLD COUNCIL OF CHURCHES, EPISCOPAL CHURCH, SMALL IS BEAUTIFUL NETWORK, COMMUNITY AID ABROAD.

NATIONALITY: AMERICAN — NATIONALISED SUBJECT, 1987.

MARITAL STATUS: MARRIED, MS JULIA CARR, ACTRESS, 1987. NO ISSUE.

DEA INVESTIGATIVE STATUS: LOW.

NO CONVICTIONS.

NO ARRESTS.

PERSONAL AND BAGGAGE SEARCHES NEGATIVE.

ASSOCIATES ON DEA FILES: DIANA WALTERS — EX-MEREDITH GRANT — SEE DRUG-RELATED CONVICTIONS FILE: GRANT, MEREDITH, 1949–.

Slowly, Dave folded the page back and looked at the second part of the transmission which the hotel had just sent up to him. It was a photocopy of two news service cables.

CHANG, GEORGE JOHN. ASIAN TRADER AND PHILANTHROPIST GEORGE CHANG IS REPORTED A WEEK OVERDUE ON FLIGHT FROM CHIANG MAI IN NORTHERN THAILAND TO MANDALAY IN BURMA. CHANG'S PRIVATELY OWNED BEECHCRAFT KING AIR WAS REPORTED LEAVING CHIANG MAI AIRPORT, DUE AT MANDALAY WITHIN TWO HOURS. LAST RADIO CONTACT WAS OVER PAI IN NTH THAILAND, BADLY OFF-COURSE. THAI AUTHORITIES HAVE DETAILED A PLANE TO SEARCH NORTHERN BORDER REGION, BUT NO SIGHTINGS REPORTED. NEW CHINA NEWSAGENCY. AUGUST 3, 1976.

CHANG, GEORGE JOHN. BURMESE GOVERNMENT OFFICIALS REPORT FINDING ALIVE MISSING TRADER, GEORGE CHANG, WHOSE FLIGHT WAS REPORTED OVERDUE AND MISSING TWO YEARS AGO. CHANG DESCRIBED AS SUFFERING BADLY FROM EXPOSURE AND MALNUTRITION ON HOME-MADE RAFT ON SALWEEN RIVER IN SHAN DISTRICT. CHANG SAYS COMPASS ERROR TOOK HIS BEECHCRAFT PLANE OFF-COURSE. HE THEN CRASHED IN HEAVY WEATHER IN MOUNTAINS. HE LIVED WITH MOUNTAIN CLAN PEOPLE IN SHAN MOUNTAINS BEFORE FINDING HIS WAY OUT. NEW CHINA NEWSAGENCY. JAN. 25, 1978.

Dave placed the fax on the bedside table. He took the reading-glasses off, walked to the window, opened the shades and looked out at the late-afternoon traffic. He rubbed his eyes.

Two years among the Hills people. A childhood of terror, bereavement, and guilt. A life of shadow and no substance. A character out of a pre-war novel.

The DEA used a Beechcraft to fly photo-reconnaissance over the Golden Triangle, near where Chang had gone down. It was a good plane for mountain work: pressurized, twin-engines, comfortable.

No. The plane was fine. There was nothing wrong with the plane. Aeronautical services being what they were in that part of the world, compass error was all too common. And, the terrain being similar, it was hard to know you were off-course. That didn't worry him.

But the Burmese officials did. Burmese administration was liable to throw you in jail for overstaying a seven-day visa by a day. Burmese administration was absolutely maddening in the dedicated zeal with which it relentlessly pursued paperwork. It could take you three years to get that seven-day visa. It could take your embassy another three to find out you were in jail.

But George John Chang had slipped in, at an unauthorized entry point, spent two years living off the land, and had apparently then been picked up and released. He was not a high-ranking Chinese or Indian official — whom the Burmese might have wanted to treat in a friendly manner. He was one of the Lone Rangers of Asia. Stateless, friendless, living off his wits ... Dave had dealt with them in his previous life. They walked a narrow line along the edge of the law. One slip, and they were never heard of, or seen, again.

George John Chang, though, had some magic charm that kept him safe. And, in Asia, the best magic charm was an important name. A warlord. A Triad leader.

Dave let the name rise up in his mind. He mentally reached out and touched it. 'Joe Tobias.' There was a name to conjure with in that part of the world. 'Joe Tobias.'

A ghostly voice whispered in his ear, the voice of a young DEA officer on his first big case.

'There was someone else in that cabin,' the young Howard Collins had insisted. 'I know it.'

Dave shook his head and sighed. He picked up his room key, slipped it into his pocket and left the room. Waiting for the elevator he realized he felt the kind of nervousness he had felt at high school, waiting at the door of his date's home. He smiled at his nervousness and jangled the key in his pocket.

The elevator doors opened. He stepped inside, pressed the lobby button and descended to meet her.

He saw her step into the bright light at the hotel's entrance. The doorman sprang to open the door for her. Seeing her, Dave felt suddenly clumsy, and badly dressed. He brushed ineffectually at his jacket as she entered the lobby.

She wore a clinging red mini-dress, and her hair was again in that high fall, as if she was trying to remind him of how he had first seen her, in the store-room of the Mana shop. She looked around the lobby, and all the eyes in the lobby followed her. Then she saw Dave and smiled at him. It was a nervous smile. He grinned, just as nervously, and went to meet her.

'You look great,' he said.

She lowered her eyes and self-consciously touched the sleeve of her dress.

'I love wool,' she said. 'I love the way it clings and drapes.'

She looked up at him and smiled again, reaching out to touch the lapel of his old jacket.

'And I love this jacket,' she said. 'It's tailor-made, isn't it?'

'Well, yes,' he said. 'How did you know?'

'My husband had one made when we were in Hong Kong.'

He took her arm, and turned her back to the door.

'Well, that's where this one was made, too,' he said.

He wasn't sure what it meant that she had opened the evening by referring to her husband. She was either letting him know not to try anything. Or else getting the problem out there in the open, so they could both examine it and make up their minds. The doorman was grinning from ear to ear.

'Have a pleasant evening, sir, madam,' he said.

Just for luck, Dave gave him five dollars.

The old blue Dodge was parked around the corner from the hotel. He glanced at her, expecting some explanation for the great distance between her image and that of her vehicle. But she quite unselfconsciously unlocked his door and smiled at him as she slid on to the cracked upholstery.

The battery was running low and the starter groaned before kicking the motor over. She twitched the throttle, frowning momentarily as she cleared the carburetor. The look on her face was the same as on any blue-collar youth's face as he kicked his old car over. She eased the machine on to Sunset Boulevard.

'Where shall we go?' she asked him.

'You live here,' he said. 'You decide.'

'You can have anything you want,' she said. 'From south of the border to the top of the Eiffel Tower. Indian? Chinese? Japanese? Spanish?'

'Spanish,' he said, quickly. 'It means totally nothing to me. I can begin my life anew.'

He meant it as a joke, but it came across awkwardly. She nodded as if she understood him, and eased the Dodge into the right-hand lane looking for an exit.

It was a nondescript, low-rise building in West Hollywood, made of glass and steel, and 'Segovia', the restaurant, was in the basement, down a flight of mass-produced concrete steps bolted to steel runners.

But the door that opened for them was of thick, dark oak; old and gnarled. The restaurant walls were encrusted with plaster, swirled on like daubs of paint from an artist's palette knife. And they walked in to the buzzing rattle of flamenco guitars, their staccato high notes, and the shivering drum beats of a flamenco dancer's heels.

'Tell me about the Dodge,' he said, in an effort to find a peg to hang a conversation on.

She smiled.

'I bought it five years ago in St Paul, for eight hundred dollars,' she said. 'I drove it all the way here to take up my drama scholarship at UCLA. I put in a new motor with part of the check from my first movie role ... I didn't know there'd be no more movies.'

'You know a lot about cars.'

'My dad's an auto mechanic. He works for a big trucking company. I learnt not to be scared about what's under the hood.'

'I'm from Minneapolis,' he said. 'But back before your time, I guess. Else I would have heard about you, for sure.'

She shook her head, deflecting the compliment.

'I wasn't a big deal at school,' she said. 'I was in the swimming team. But I gave that up to act.'

'What did you mean that there aren't any more movies?'

She looked down before answering. The waiter

arrived for their order. When he had taken it and gone she looked up, watching the flamenco dancer — a hooked-nosed, black-haired woman with olive skin. Her fine, red and black cotton dress seemed at first to be cut to conceal, but it subtly highlighted her body in its drapes. Her white petticoats shimmered beneath the hem. Her black shoes hammered the floor, as if her legs were divorced from her hips, beating out their staccato rhythm beneath the aloof face and the twining, mesmerizing hands. Her black-rimmed eyes seemed to dwell on Julia, seemed to look down on her from a great height, as if the emotions she danced cut her off from the rest of humanity. She danced like Julia wished to live, and yet was unable. Julia looked at her escort — the tanned, balding man with the hurt, faraway eyes.

'My face has taken me as far as it will go,' she said. 'Funny thing is, they didn't cast me for my looks, but for my ability to scream. You want to hear me scream?'

'Not now,' he said. 'Maybe later.'

She blushed, and looked down. The dance was building to its thrumming, stamping climax, a climax of tossing skirts and petticoats and flicking fingers and two guitars seeming now to race neck-and-neck for a distant goal. They both turned to watch the dancer's exit.

When the dancer had swept her skirts from the restaurant floor, Julia said, slowly, almost dreamily, like someone waking out of hypnosis, 'I'm a rich-man's wife now. I don't need to act. At least, not on the screen.'

It was out in the open, lying between them. Dave

looked at the table, as if studying what she had mentioned: the husband.

'Tell me about him,' he said, trying to sound indifferent. 'He imports artefacts, I gather.'

'He's an idealist,' she said remotely. 'He was orphaned as a child in Asia, and now his life is dedicated to helping other Asian orphans and villagers.'

'But where does he get the money for that?'

'He ran a lot of businesses in Asia, then he had a bad crash in his plane and was lost for a long time. There was a big insurance payout. He invested it ... I don't know the details. Money is his side of the marriage.'

And what is my side? she asked herself, blushing; afraid to look at her interrogator. Aloud, as if to defend him, she said,

'He's quite different from the usual sort of government "aid worker". He deals direct with the people, the villagers and fishermen and peasants. His cash doesn't end up in bureaucrats' pockets.'

'And he's successful?'

Now she did face her accuser. She studied him thoughtfully. There seemed to be no malice in the question. She shook her head.

'Not very,' she said. 'Not yet. It's a long, hard road for him, alone.'

'But he does have Mere ... what's-her-name, Walters?'

'I didn't realize you knew her,' she said, surprised. 'Yes, he has Di. She's an angel, but a very prickly angel. How did you know about her?'

'I ... ahhh ... it's on the business card. "Diana Walters, Manager".'

She nodded.

'Yes, he has Di, but that's all. He has no one in Asia.'

'How does he operate out there, with no help?'

She began to sense the disquiet beneath the questions. He saw her eyes adjust, suddenly probing him. He smiled, fighting to keep the emotion from his face. Fortunately, she was more occupied with whatever was rising within herself.

He saw her turn inwards, turn to look at what it was he had dislodged.

He suddenly intuited what he needed to say.

'How long have you been married?' he asked her, softly.

'Three years,' she whispered.

The waiter served their paella. She glanced at it, as if puzzled by its arrival.

Watching her, Dave suddenly realized he intended to seduce her, and his object was as much to get information on her husband and his female associate as it was to bring to culmination what had begun in the storeroom of 'Mana'.

'Three good years?' he asked.

'Three years,' she repeated, looking past him. 'I just lived them and didn't know what I was doing.'

He heard the puzzled, self-reflective tone of her voice, and knew that everything was going to work out. And he felt a twinge at the dishonesty of his motives — suddenly realizing that the Quest had corrupted him. Whatever honesty it stood for had to be weighed against the dishonesty necessary to reach those ends.

Then she looked at him, searchingly, plumbing his eyes, and he looked back and saw again that moment in the storeroom, saw again the bird-headed goddess.

He smiled, reached across the table and took her hand. He squeezed it and they sat there, looking at each other. Saying nothing.

But again she thought she heard the thumping resonance of that ancient drum.

CHAPTER TEN

John Chang walked out from the air-conditioned cool of the American Embassy in Bangkok, and the steamy heat hit him like a sledgehammer.

He winced, lifting his hand to shield himself from it. The cab driver who had been waiting in that heat, his white shirt stained with sweat, started up the old Toyota at the sound of John's feet crunching the glaring, white gravel.

John opened the rear door and slid on to the sticky seat. The back windows were wound up. The air-conditioner clattered out ice-cubed air on to the driver's knees. The driver looked inquiringly into the mirror. John found he had no energy for conversation.

'*Yaak cha pai rongrem*,' he said, and sat back, winding down his window.

The driver pulled out on to the road.

John smelt the mixture of Bangkok's scents: flowers and shit. He didn't close them out. He wanted to immerse himself in its reality, to be part of it.

They passed Lumpini Park. Men in loose white shirts and women in halter-tops and mini-skirts were strolling, stopping to buy from trolleys and stalls.

Sanuk, the leisurely pursuit of pleasure, never ceased.

Yet opposite the park John could see a slum. Apathetic children stared at the cab as it passed their alleyway. John looked back at them. The cab kept moving, and the slum disappeared, as if it had been a mistake of the heat and the light.

But, when the cab ground to a halt in the ceaseless traffic of Rama IV Road, as it arrowed towards the city's heart, John wished for more engineering and less *sanuk*. He sat there as motorcycles trailing wreaths of blue fumes behind them wound their way past the stalled cars.

Irritated, John paid his driver and got out. The driver's eyes were expressionless as he took the money and sat back, resigned to a thirty-minute wait in the choking fumes.

John walked as directly as he could for his riverside hotel. But on reaching the river he changed his mind. He hired a water taxi and set off down the Chao Phraya. The cool breeze on the river helped clear his mind. After a while he looked up.

The embassy meeting had disturbed him more than usual. The polite evasiveness of the crew-cut officials — who seemed to ward off the terrors of submersion in Asia by being more American than the YMCA — was harder than normal to handle. If they would only give him something to fight! But all they did was smile, accept the proposals, comment encouragingly on their 'bold originality', and then slip them into the mountain of files and ask him if he'd like lemon in his tea.

If he had come from General Motors, from IT&T; if he could drop the name of some ancient Chinese general eking out his old age in the distant mountains with his army of opium addicts; if he could have pointed to 'reciprocal trade', to teaching peasants how to become dependent on John Deere tractors instead of water buffaloes — they'd have eagerly swept the files aside, leapt up and clapped him on the back, called for a Toyota Landcruiser, and left immediately for those distant opium-growing hills.

The motion of the water taxi eased his mind. Looking up he saw the lovely spires of Wat Arun glittering in the sun. He felt an inexplicable lightening of spirit. Looking back over his shoulder he could see Wat Po. They glided past jumbled warehouses and temples. Temple spires rose above saw-toothed metal roofs. He suddenly wanted to be in the crowded peace of such a holy place.

He turned back to his silent driver and asked him to make for Wat Phra Keo.

The silver zipper in Julia's red woolen dress ran down from the high neck to a point just above, and directly between, the hips. Dave ran it down slowly, uncovering first the base of her long, pale neck, then the two thin, red straps of her slip, and the red lace above the satin.

He lifted the fall of yellow hair and kissed the top of

her neck as his hand kept on traveling, opening up that slash of red satin against the red wool. Then she shrugged her shoulders and he brushed the dress away and she stepped out of it, turning to him with her eyes shy and vulnerable.

'I'm frightened,' she whispered.

They stared gravely at each other.

She stood there, with her dress fallen at her feet, the slip clinging to her hips and breasts, in her all-white room. He could see her back caught in the mirrors, and himself standing in the reflection, looking at her.

She, in turn, stared at the stranger, puzzling at why he seemed so familiar. The way he moved, the phrases he used, his frowns and puzzled smiles. She seemed to know in advance what he would say. At the same time, she felt fear in his presence. Fear at the way she wanted to open herself to him, to reach out to him. Fear at the urgent strength of her need for him. She could see them both reflected in her mirrors. It was like there were at least two couples here, at least two scenarios being played out.

She was outside herself, watching the way the two actors in this script faced each other, and the way the man opened his hands towards her.

He reached up his hand, palm open, to reassure her. She pressed it against her cheek, then turned her face into its warmth, gently kissing the lined palm.

'I'm not here to hurt you,' he said.

'I know,' she murmured, turning away from his hand and looking up at him. She reached up and released her hair and shook her head, so that a blonde wave shivered across her shoulders.

'You're a goddess!' he said, teasingly, yet also in wonder.

She smiled shyly at him.

'Then you must be a god.'

She watched herself watching him; watched the actress slide her long, orange nail under the red strap of the slip. Watched herself tease the slip down over her breast. Watched him stare at the large, pink nipple. Watched herself reach over and slide the other strap down and caress her breast, twisting the nipple between her fingertips like it was a button. She saw herself staring at him, her lips opening.

'Not a god,' he said. 'Just a messenger of the gods.'

The red slip eased over her hips, over the tiny golden triangle of her sex, to the floor. He reached over and drew her to him. She closed her eyes. Her lips were half-open, full with passion. They kissed.

She was no longer watching, she was shaking with passion as her watching self and her acting self became one person at last.

There were many Western tourists in the temple grounds. John strode past them, avoiding their cameras and videos. The porcelain-and-glass-incrusted figures of the pavilions and courtyards glittered in the relentless, energy-sapping heat. He threaded his way through the jumble of buildings, and the jumble of sculpted mythological beasts and heroes, to the cloister that surrounded the temple.

The epic of the *Ramakien* was acted out in swirling

scenes of battles and heroic deeds around the cloister walls. John paused, glancing at the first panel. He looked at Rama and his beautiful wife, Sita. He remembered the words she spoke when she followed him into exile.

I can never be tired walking with you. The reeds, the grass, the thorny bushes on the way will seem to me in your company as soft to the touch as a lawn or the skin of an antelope.

With you it is heaven, away from you hell. So it is. Be certain of it, O Rama, and be perfectly happy with me.

The story of her fidelity always moved him. He thought of his own Sita, at home in his own temple. He thought of himself as Rama, fighting to hold back the powers of darkness as she waited faithfully for him in her all-white bedroom, a glittering goddess in silver.

He smiled and entered the temple.

It was like entering a cattle auction. A hundred or so chanting supplicants were prostrated on the marble floor. Like most Thai temples the building was rectangular, with rows of supporting pillars forming a nave and two aisles. The Emerald Buddha's shrine was on the far wall, a glowing, neon-lit niche in the vividly patterned marble.

The air was thick with burning incense, and with the overwhelming scent of thousands of flowers and hundreds of bodies. John picked his way among the kneeling, chanting worshipers, his eyes always on that tiny, distant, glowing emerald figure.

He knelt among other Thai worshipers. They paid him no heed. He looked up, into the grotto. The Buddha wore his hot-season robes. His green face stared down, its features picked out in white beneath his peppercorn locks, topknot, and the pagoda-like head-dress that was also the leaping flame of Enlightenment.

The throne sat on a pedestal supported by two tiers of figures; the lower tier of humans, the upper of Hindu deities. Buddha himself sat in meditation position, not teaching except by the example of his life.

John bowed his head and closed his eyes. For a moment he saw the river and, rising out of the river, the drifting body of Joe Tobias, blood streaming from it like paper streamers.

He had forgotten that vision for many years. Now it was returning.

Then the body was gone and there was only the river rolling on to the ocean. He let himself be immersed in that ocean. It was black and empty — though he could sense demons crouched on its shores, eager to claim him. He concentrated on the ocean, ignoring their pull.

Without willing it, the Tara Meditation rose in his mind: *Om Tare Tuttare Ture Soha.*

Tara. She who liberates us from unfortunate rebirths and the sufferings of the wheel of fate; from the eight-fold fears that lead us astray; who grants success in all our ventures. May her blessings take root in our hearts.

Some twenty minutes later he came out of meditation. He pushed himself up from the floor, unbending his cramped legs. Around him the other worshipers kept chanting, endlessly and monotonously, to the point where he had forgotten them in his meditation. Now he picked his way between their bodies.

The temple was the noisy, but quiet, center of all things. It was the place where, in his heart, he wanted to reside. But, to get there, he had first to undo everything that Joe Tobias had done. A task almost beyond human comprehension.

But, then, so had been Buddha's task.

He stepped back into the cloister. This time he searched out one of the final panels in the story of Rama. Here his lovely wife, Sita, was about to immolate herself on the funeral pyre because he doubted her fidelity.

The fire, however, knew she was true, and refused to burn her.

As my heart was never taken from Rama, so you, fire, the universal witness, will never take from me your protection, she said.

And, as Rama witnessed the miracle, as the fire lifted her above its flaming heart, so Rama cried:

I knew Sita's virtue, but I wished it to be justified before all the people. Without this test they would have said that Dasarath's son has yielded to desire and despises the traditional laws. But now all will know that she is truly mine, as the rays of the sun belong to their source.

Refreshed, reminded of his own Sita, he smiled and stepped back into the steam-hammer heat, thinking of Julia, and of his return journey down to the south of Thailand, out through Malaysia, Singapore, and then home to lie beside her.

Diana Walters couldn't sleep. She seemed to be back in her Bangkok prison, lying there on the piss-stained straw mattress, listening to the muttered nightmares of the other women; smelling the constant stink of the corner slop-bucket; the fish-like smell of women crowded in on each other. Nights blurring into dark days, into months; the darkness punctuated by the distant rhythm of temple bells. Time's passing revealed only by the regular application of leg-irons and handcuffs to her — and then her presentation before her tormentor.

David Watson, her accuser, lean-faced and sunken-eyed, haunted by something just outside her ken, carrying his load of personal anguish and turning it into a career of revenge.

Always he began each session with the same ritual question.

'Are you ready yet, Meredith? Are you ready to give me Joe Tobias?'

She sat before her interrogator, at first sullenly; then, as the sessions telescoped into one another, with more and more anguish; until she had lapsed again into sullenness, when she'd stopped caring about time.

'I don't know him. I've never seen him.'

'His signature is on checks which you presented at branches of the Bank of Zurich in Amsterdam, in Sydney, in London, but you say you've never met him?'

Or:

'Air tickets in your name were paid for by a company which we know to be his major holding company, but you say you've never met him?'

Or:

'You were photographed carrying a suitcase into a Tokyo brothel. That brothel was bought by Joe Tobias in 1974. It was then a warehouse, not a whorehouse. You did not emerge until 24 hours later, without the suitcase. The suitcase was originally delivered to your hostel room in Bangkok by a woman who has signed a full confession. We know how much heroin it contained, how much money, and that Joe Tobias checked the contents before it was passed on to you. But you still say you've never met him?'

There had come a time when she had realized he believed her. She had never met her employer. But David Watson could not relinquish his hope that she was the key, the final link in the chain, which would deliver him the elusive Tobias.

And then, one steamy day in the exercise yard, she had looked up to see an old, Chinese woman staring at her. Her heart had skipped a beat in fear. It was the first emotion she had felt since she had abandoned time. She knew that ancient, implacable and unreadable face.

The old woman walked beside her a while, saying nothing. Sick thoughts raced through Meredith

Grant's mind. Thoughts, images, memories she had hidden away.

'You will tell the policeman that you can identify Mr Tobias. You will say that you secretly followed his messenger back to a sampan on the river, and there you clearly saw Mr Tobias and his driver. You will say that you clearly identified the messenger, who came to your room with the suitcase, and you heard the messenger call him "Mr Tobias", and that he acknowledged the greeting.'

In the prison exercise yard, the old woman stopped walking and looked at her. Just like all the other times when they had met, there was nothing to read in her eyes.

'I didn't ...' she began.

The old woman shook her head. Was there now a ghost of a smile?

In her apartment bedroom in Westwood, Diana Walters strained to recall that face. Had there been a smile on it?

'What you did or didn't do is not worth a moment's thought. It is what you say to that drug policeman which will determine if you live, or if you die ... and how you die.'

In her apartment bedroom in Westwood, she stared at the ceiling. She had not wanted to die, back then, in the stinking yard of the fouled jail. Despite everything she had done, and the rising tide of guilt which kept threatening to engulf her, she did not want to die.

She was sure she did not want to die now.

So why had she brought the Kali and the ceremonial Malay dagger back to the apartment?

She turned and looked at the dagger lying on her desk, beside the unfinished thesis: 'Women in Thai Buddhist Temple Ritual'.

She once prided herself that no man had dictated the terms of her life. She had never known a father. She had cut herself off from the patriarchy. The old Chinese woman had shown her everything she most secretly desired in the world without men. Through her she had attained her hidden desires. She had taken without pity, and now she was enslaved by two men — by Joe Tobias, whom she had lured to his death, but who would not die. And by David Watson, who all this time wanted most of all to die, but who could not bring himself to do it.

Was Dave Watson coming in search of her, so she could do what he couldn't do for himself? Kill himself. Was he that weak and she that strong? In place of despair, anger surged through her, and she sat up and reached for the dagger and held it in her hand, keeping her head averted from the leering goddess who danced upon her disemboweled victim.

She had been a twenty-year-old virgin on her first trip to Thailand. Asia was something she had read about, dreaming of the day she could experience it directly. She wasn't sure what would happen — but she knew it would clear up the doubts she held about herself. She would throw herself into the deep end of life, and life would reward her by opening up its secrets. As well as Margaret Mead and Malinowski she read Carlos Castenada and Tolkien. She was a secret romantic disguised as a scholarship student, the protege of her Anthropology Professor. In fact the only female protege he had not taken to bed.

She knew nothing about sex. She assumed she was asexual. Campus dykes made her uncomfortable. She thought she could honestly say she had never experienced a sexual feeling before she arrived in Thailand.

The reality of Thailand was dizzying, frightening, and exciting. 'America seems like a poor ghost of reality; like Plato's shadows on the cave wall, when compared to this reality,' the scholarship student said on a postcard to her professor. Here, in this living dream, there was a heightened reality, where nothing was shameful, where everything was permitted. Her dead mother's puritanical credo, the reality which the nuns drummed into the children with the catechism, vanished like a fever dream.

In its place were the beautiful, lissome, slim-hipped, heart-faced, tantalizing girls. Girls who seemed to belong to a different species to her clumsy, androgynous self. She didn't write that on any postcard.

In a bar one night, she met with a group of European airline hostesses. They were all tall, slender, tanned, and as immaculately groomed, as glossily attractive, as the posters advertising their airlines. They made Bangkok a regular stopover on their world-encircling jobs. They were getting drunk and then going on to 'somewhere special'.

They were German, French, and English. They had nothing in common with Meredith Grant, the untidy student from California, with her hacked-off hair, her big, round spectacles, and her rumpled clothes. But, yet, there was a knowledge in their eyes which suggested a bond, one which she had not yet acknowledged. An

English girl bought her drinks and encouraged her to talk about her reactions to the swirling fantasy that was Bangkok. And Meredith found herself talking about the Thai girls and their effect on her.

She remembered they moved on to another bar, where lissome girls cavorted on a garishly lit stage, dressed only in tassles, to the delectation of dozens of drunk men. Yet she found herself staring as avidly as they. And the air-hostesses, too, had ceased joking. They were silent as they watched.

They took two cabs, jamming up in them. The English girl snuggled against her. Meredith's heart was thumping. Her head was spinning. The English girl opened her mouth and Meredith kissed her. Their teeth grated against each other. It was like an electric shock.

They stopped at an old French villa somewhere on the city's edge. They got out of the taxis. The drivers didn't look at them, or at each other, as they took the fares.

She could hear monkeys somewhere nearby, in the grounds of the villa. A peacock screamed. A German *fraulein* tugged her hand and led her up the steps and rapped on the heavy, wooden door.

That was where she first saw the slab-faced, black-eyed Chinese woman. The woman showed no reaction at all. She simply counted the money into her cash-box and nodded for them to continue into the house.

Another door opened, and it opened on to something that had been locked away, tight, hidden within Meredith's being. Something she had never seen before, but when she saw it knew that this was what she desired more than anything else.

Incense smoke clung blue and choking in the dimly lit, warm and fragrant air. Sitting and kneeling about the room on the old Persian carpet, the young, black-haired girls looked up expectantly, starting to smile until they saw their customers. Then their smiles froze, and a dumb passivity came over them.

Diana Walters screamed and dropped the dagger on her bed. She stumbled to her feet and fumbled to the bathroom and dry-retched into the basin. She looked at her haggard face in the mirror. She could not escape it.

John Chang bowed deeply to the round-faced man who sat, cross-legged, on the low platform in one of the monks' cells that lined the outer compound of Wat Phra Keo. The round-faced man was almost bald, and his thick, black-rimmed glasses — redolent of Madison Avenue — sat oddly on his smiling face.

'May we converse in English?' the monk said. 'I must gain practice for my journey to the West.'

'Where are you going?' John asked, struggling to sit comfortably on the floor.

'To England. I must visit some of our people there. What do you wish to speak with me about?'

'All my life,' John began, frowning as he concentrated, 'I have struggled to always do good. Yet I am met on all sides by indifference, by hostility, by the bad actions of others. Ultimately, my own actions cause more bad than good. Why?'

'You desire to do only good?'

'Yes. And also to overcome what is bad.'

'There are two types of desire. One type is bound up with emotions. It seeks to satisfy the ego. It promises that by achieving its short-term goals it will give the ego long-term satisfaction. That is false desire.'

'I'm aware of that, Rinpoche.'

John used the Tibetan form of respect, even though this monk was Thai, a monk not of the Greater but of the Lesser Vehicle.

'Being aware, and knowing, are two different things. We may be aware, but our past karma may be holding us back from knowing. You may believe that your sexual desire for someone will be satiated, will be completed, if you could only possess that person. Yet it never is. Time and again you return to them. Time and again the desire is not extinguished. What begins as love turns, eventually, to hatred of the bond.'

'I truly believe, Rinpoche, that I have mastered that desire.'

'And yet you still have no peace?'

'No, Rinpoche.'

Always, when John thought of monks, the Tibetan term rose in his mind.

'The second type of desire is what you are speaking

of, then. That is when you know what is good, and you desire to see that goodness spread. That is the desire which caused Lord Buddha to refuse the passive peace of Nirvana, and so grasp Enlightenment and return to help us all find the Path.'

'So, if you can see what is good, and know what is good, and have extinguished those other desires, and you still cannot achieve what is good, then you must look at past actions.'

'That's what I'm afraid of, Rinpoche, that in past lives I have, perhaps, done terrible things, and now they hold me back from doing good.'

'We have all done terrible things in past lives. We have all returned, our lives driven by actions committed in those past lives, to struggle on up towards Buddha Consciousness, all bound to the great wheel. You will continue to feel the load of that wheel, until you have paid out your karma.'

'But how much longer will that be?'

'Until you realize that your suffering, here today, in this room, is a product of your mind, and that your mind's suffering is an illusion. What you did in past lives was also an illusion within your mind — for your individual mind, too, is illusory. The wheel of suffering is also an illusion.'

'Are you an illusion?'

The monk smiled at the anger in the man's voice. He had spent a lot of time learning disputation and argument. He was gaining good practice for his trip to England.

He frowned, concentrating, not wishing to treat the man's questions lightly. He looked up at the man and suddenly saw him clearly, very clearly.

'To your perception, I am an illusion. Yes. You do not see me directly, but only through the attitudes of your mind. Those attitudes are created by your past actions — whether in this life or in previous lives.'

'Do you see me directly?'

The earnestness in the man's voice made the monk stare closer, but he did not identify with that suffering. He watched the play of emotions across the tough, bandit-like face. He watched it become like the face of a monk. Then the face of a lover.

'I see a being suffering for what it has done,' he said. 'It sees only the bad it has done. Yet sometimes that bad produced good. Just as the good which it struggles to achieve now produces some bad.'

'You see what I have been?'

The monk stared at him a moment longer, and then nodded. There was a gentle smile on his face.

'You acted out of ignorance,' the monk said. 'When the time is right, you will know why you acted thus, and so be free.'

John Chang began to cry.

The monk stood up, arranged his saffron robe, resettled the heavy spectacles on his blunt little nose, and quietly left him alone in the cell.

Julia turned away from her lover, trying for a last moment to hold on, to not let herself be swept away. But it was too late. Looking up she saw herself in the big mirrors, hair disheveled, lipstick smeared, her nipples seeming huge, her lips heavy. For a moment she saw the painted slut on the video cover, and then realized it was herself. She moaned and took his hands and rubbed them into her breasts.

Lightning seemed to shoot from his grasping fingers; down from her constricting nipples to her squirming thighs; down into her groin. She pressed her legs together. His lips chased hers, pinning her head back against the soft bed. He forced her mouth open.

For a moment there was an image of a roaring furnace, of a young girl. A wave of panic swept up from her depths, threatening to overwhelm her. She stiffened, pulling away from him.

'Easy,' he whispered. 'Easy. Don't rush yourself.'

Anger welled up behind the panic. Who was he to talk to her? What did he know? But his eyes seemed to pin her down, forcing her to respond to him, to look inside him and see the pain behind his desire.

She stared into him. She had a giddy feeling like they had met in some other lifetime, as if some universal law required that they keep meeting again and again through eon after eon. Lovers finding and losing each other, losing and finding.

'You all right?' he asked her.

'A ghost was stirred. It's gone now.'

'We're full of ghosts. We're nothing but the sum of our ghosts.'

'How can we be ourselves, then?'

'I don't know,' he said with male impatience, and kissed her again.

And now she was letting go. She could feel the masks she had worn since childhood falling away. His busy lips moved down, clamping on to her nipple. She felt like the universal mother, suckling her son and lover. A wave of feeling consumed her, both tender and violent at the same time. She wanted to suckle him and consume him. She could feel her hips pushing against him.

Then something possessed her, made her push him aside, and mount his thigh, as if she was mounting a panting, sweating horse. He stared up at her, momentarily at a loss as to how to respond. Her hands shook. She tossed her head, feeling the mane of hair loose around her cheeks. She was alone. She slid along the leg beneath her. Sparks seemed to fly, thicker and faster, like the sparks from the angle-grinder as her dad worked on one of his cars.

She remembered the screaming, high-speed cutter in his hands. She remembered her fear as she watched, and then her delight as the sparks became a cascading wheel of fire bursting from the tool he held in his hands.

She exploded. Her body seemed to disintegrate. She was nothing but a patch of pinwheeling sparks in the blackness of the void.

She exploded again, and this time felt the torn pieces of her body coming back together, renewed. She was crying, tears streaming from her eyes like the moisture streaming from the gaping river mouth between her legs. The river coming down from the mountain upon which she rode — heaving herself up and tossing herself aside, spreading her legs. Gasping. Gaping. The womb of the world opening up.

'Oh, God!' she screamed. 'God! God! Oh, God!'

He was crying out, too. He was calling a woman's name. But then it became just a cry and she felt him explode. A wave seemed to slam through the mountains, bursting, its foam roaring, cascading up through the caves, slamming through her. She felt full. She felt empty. It would go on forever.

It was over.

They rolled against each other, staring in wonder. She traced the lines beside his mouth with her fingertips, feeling the stubble beneath the skin. His eyes smiled back, full of peace. The pain had receded. She smiled at him.

'You are so goddamned beautiful,' he whispered. 'What have I done to deserve you?'

She placed her finger against his lips.

'Shhh,' she whispered.

He sighed and bent his head against her. Although he was a good head taller than her she seemed to be able to enfold him in her arms, to press his cheek against her breasts. They rested there: mother, son, lover, father, daughter, god and goddess.

Dave lay against her back, pressed into her buttocks and calves, feeling how quickly she fell asleep.

He was tired, drained, and empty, but he couldn't sleep. His mind was fired with the return of the Quest. Intuitively, he knew that her husband had to be connected with Joe Tobias.

Again he found himself replaying the moment of Joe's death in the Chao Phraya, Christmas Eve, 1975.

'We shoulda made that sampan ... there was someone

else in the cabin,' Howard chanted in his mind's ear.

He eased himself away from her body's warmth, cautiously, trying not to disturb her. He found himself reaching out to stroke her lovely shoulder, but checked the gesture. He must not wake her. He knew what he had to do.

Since his wife's suicide in Hong Kong Harbor, he had made love twice. Neither time had been particularly memorable. People flung together momentarily, on different roads, with different needs, confusing proximity to one another with destiny. After a while it was like the ache for sex had healed over. There was nothing but the Quest. Then, there was nothing.

But now something had happened. Something which made him feel raw and awkward. He should have felt happy to be the lover of such a woman, but he felt a terrible sadness. It was like all the emotions he had forgotten over the years were now clamoring to be let out, and the bad things wanted out first.

Above all else he felt guilty that he had finally violated his wife's memory. The other two times hadn't mattered. No depths had been plunged. But this time he had challenged her dear memory.

And having done that, he was about to betray the woman who had touched him with such magic. The Quest beckoned. Mary's ghost might well be exorcised, but there was still the horrible weight of the dead baby in his arms. This woman beside him knew nothing about the things he and Mary had seen together. Her body was pure, unmarked by childbirth. In that sense she was virgin.

Dave got up quietly. She did not stir. He dressed, feeling old and tired. He felt like a knight who has a long road to travel and must leave the chapel in the forest because he knows he is not the perfect knight, and that the Grail is not meant for him. Pulling on his clothes seemed to sheathe him in the body of the Quest.

He opened the bedside drawer where he had seen her drop the Dodge's keys. When he saw the three-pointed star on another set he hesitated a moment, and then took them. The Mercedes would be quieter, and it would attract less police attention in Westwood than a battered old Dodge.

He found the electronic gate-pass. He presumed it was coded not to break the security system. He looked back at her, lying asleep, her lovely spine towards him. He covered her and went quickly from the room.

CHAPTER ELEVEN

Diana lay awake. The statuette of the dancing Kali, nimble feet astride her victim's opened belly, leered at her from beside the digital bedside clock. The clock showed 2.23. She was afraid to sleep and face her dreams. She was afraid to lie awake, knowing Dave Watson was coming for her.

She closed her eyes and saw that old, slab-faced Chinese woman, the guardian of the doorway to her dream. The old woman's eyes stared back at her, unflinching. Her loyalties lay with her family, the eyes said, not with Joe Tobias, or with Meredith Grant, or with the girls she bought from starving inland tribes.

Diana opened her eyes. 2.24. Skull-girt Kali still danced. She closed her eyes again and saw herself beside the old woman in the doorway to the incense-lit room of soft, yielding brown flesh, of lips like quivering butterflies and breasts like rose buds. The old woman was silently offering her a choice — to turn and leave behind the room and all it contained; or to enter and accept everything within it.

Diana balled her hand into a fist. How could she have known then what that choice entailed? At the time she had thought its meaning lay only with her own desires. That it went no further than her urge to destroy those desires by trying to destroy the girls. She had wanted to hurt them, like she hurt inside. Her fingers clawed at them. But the girls remained dumb and passive. They would not scream like she wanted them to. Their refusal to scream entered her fingers, worked its way into her body. She stared at that balled fist and knew that their revenge was on its way.

She heard a car pull up somewhere nearby. A powerful, muted motor switched off and the silence redoubled. She opened her eyes and looked at the clock. It was still 2.24.

She remembered the black-eyed madam staring at her on her fourth visit to the brothel, when it was obvious she could no longer afford what she had come to need.

'If you wish to return here,' the woman had said, in soft, lilting English, 'then go first to the Wayfarer Hostel, to Room 34. If you are willing, a man will engage you to carry some items across various borders for him. Do you understand?'

She had looked into the black, gem-hard eyes, and nodded. She understood what was being asked of her. She knew of other students who had been asked the same question. But they had said no.

Faced with the same choice she said yes.

'The money is very good,' the woman had reassured her. 'The risk is very small.'

For the first time there was light in those eyes.

Something stirred in their black depths. 'And you will be able to enjoy my girls again,' she added.

In the still of the night, someone's door buzzer sounded. Whoever had driven up was being let in.

The madam gave her an official-looking, carbon-backed form. It explained that Meredith Grant was to leave her passport, ID, and the completed form, in Room 34 of the hostel. She would be checked over, and notified if she was accepted.

She had often wondered what her fate would have been if she had not been accepted.

But the documents were returned, together with a black and white print of her and a Thai girl of perhaps thirteen. In the print they were both naked, except Meredith Grant still had her spectacles on. It was obvious where her hand lay. The pain on the girl's face was also obvious, as was the violence on Meredith's. Ashamed, she had torn the photo to pieces and burnt it. But she knew she had not destroyed anything.

A week later an envelope waited at her hostel for her. It contained the carbon of the form she had filled in, an air ticket that would take her from Bangkok to Moscow, from Moscow to Amsterdam, and from Amsterdam to New York.

There was also a Bangkok street map with a location circled, and a date and time on it.

At the circled location, at the appointed time, she found a suitcase. She guessed it was false-bottomed. She took it back to her hostel and packed her clothes in it and caught the flight. She was aware she was taking one step at a time, each step insignificant, but their total was transforming her life.

She also realized she was being watched, but she didn't know by whom — and whether they were protecting her or waiting to strike.

Her luggage was not searched going into Moscow. She spent two days there in fear, cold and bored, waiting for her flight to Holland.

The Dutch customs officers, engaged in the war on drugs, read her flight's point of origin: Moscow. They stamped her through, impatient to concentrate their energies on hippies returning from Asia. A young anthropologist who had been to Moscow on a student exchange did not interest them.

In the brothel quarter she left the suitcase in a room, and received the rest of her pay. She also received an invitation to indulge herself. She did, and finally realized she had locked herself into something evil. But something which, all the time, had been waiting inside herself; as if evil was a part of every human being, a part that the lucky did not get to see — and so were known as good.

The clock blinked 2.25. The building was silent. The streets were silent. She got out of bed and went to the bathroom and switched on the light. She ran some water and splashed it on her face. She stared at the face. Meredith Grant's face. She could not escape it.

She went back to the doorway and looked at the Malay dagger lying in the pale light from the street. Lying beside her bed. She imagined it in Kali's dancing hands. Had she taken the statuette because she wanted to invoke the Goddess of Death? The Goddess of Wrath? She who transforms through violence?

She looked up at the black-faced African fertility gods who stared back at her impassively, waiting for her to move, knowing in advance what she would do.

She looked at herself in the mirror. Fat. Mousy. Afraid. Hiding behind her spectacles. She remembered how alive she had been as a student. How she planned to conquer the academic world. How she would be an anthropologist to rival Ruth Benedict and Margaret Mead.

Instead, she sold artefacts in a shopping mall, and watched dirty videos at night.

The handle of her front door moved.

She stared at the brass knob as it twisted back and forth.

She suddenly wanted to hide nothing from him. She dropped her cotton nightdress to the floor. She pressed her spectacles firmly against her nose. She picked up the Malay dagger and unlocked the door.

They stared at each other. He had a lock-pick in his hand. Neither could speak. She stepped back and motioned him in. His eyes went to the dagger, and then to her sagging breasts and belly, to her crotch. She saw him consider running.

But he needed answers before he could ever rest. He stepped into the apartment and closed the door behind him. He watched her eyes.

She retreated, the dagger held towards him. She stepped back to the bathroom door.

'It is Meredith Grant,' he said softly, wonderingly.

She shook her head.

Then she hesitated, knowing that she had to be honest from this moment onwards. She nodded.

'Did you turn Joe over to the Triads?' he asked her. 'Did you tell them about the meeting?'

She licked her lips, saying nothing, but her eyes darted to the bookcase. He realized some answer lay hidden there.

'Or were you still shielding him all the time? Did he fake his own disappearance? Was that someone else we saw die, while Joe stayed hidden in the shadows of his sampan?'

She would not answer him.

'Who is John Chang?' he persisted. 'Just who is he?'

She shook her head again. She hadn't thought she would become mute. She had hoped she could tell him everything, confess it all, make an act of contrition, and die reconciled to the Lord.

Images of her childhood rushed to her. The tolling bells, different to temple bells, solid and irrevocable, spelling out her abandonment, seeming to say, 'Meredith Grant is a bad girl. That's why her mother ran away. Meredith Grant must pay.'

'Answer me!' he hissed, moving closer to her. 'For Christ sake, answer me!'

She stepped back into the bathroom, until her knees pressed against the edge of the old bath. She lifted her right leg and stepped so she straddled the bath.

He halted in the doorway.

Something to his left side caught his eye and he glanced through her bedroom door.

He stared at the dancing, leering figure of Kali.

'What the fuck! ...' he began. He swung back to her.

'Where'd you get that?!'

She stared at him.

'I've got to know,' he said. 'Did John Chang mail it to you from Chiang Mai? Answer me, you bitch!'

She reversed the dagger, holding it against her own belly. She saw his eyes change as he realized what she would do.

'No!' he said. 'Don't do it!'

He moved towards her.

She dropped her hand until she felt the cold steel of the dagger inside her vulva.

Shocked, he stood where he was, staring at the protruding handle. He looked up at her. She smiled at him and jammed her hand as far into herself as she could.

Her mouth opened. A groan issued from it, a moan of shame and guilt. She jerked her hand upwards.

'Jesus forgive me,' she whispered.

The blood burst from between her thighs. The dagger clattered on the porcelain. She fell back against the wall. Blood pulsed from her, jetting against the side of the bath. Her body began to dance and shake. Her eyes flopped open, shut, open. Her tongue danced in her slack mouth.

Dave Watson backed away from the bathroom door. He glanced again to where Kali smirked from beside the bed. Angrily, he lunged across the bedroom and grabbed the figure. To his pounding, confused brain it seemed to wriggle in his grasp.

Clutching the Kali tightly, he opened the apartment door, and suddenly vomited.

The act of being sick cleared his head. His hands were

shaking wildly. He found a piece of paper in his pocket and cleaned his mouth off. He went back to the apartment door.

He could still hear the body thumping in the bath. He locked the door and ran down the stairs. He wadded up the piece of paper and dropped it in a trash-can in the foyer. He let himself out of the building, got in the Mercedes and drove away.

As the powerful engine roared out of earshot, the driver's side window sighed open. Something cut a glittering arc across the street.

With a metallic clatter, the statuette of the dancing Goddess of Death hit the pavement.

The Mercedes was gone.

CHAPTER TWELVE

John Chang took one of the daily flights from Bangkok to Hat Yai, the capital of Southern Thailand. Central and Northern Thailand were too firmly in the grip of the old alliances for him to make any headway there. The attempts to eradicate poppy plantings and replace them with tea and maize had been phenomenally unsuccessful. The drive against the drug warlords had pushed them back into Laos, or into the more inaccessible mountain valleys of Northern Thailand. Their influence still lay heavily across the land.

The south was different. Its allegiances were with the Muslims of Malaysia. The poppy was not extensively cultivated there. The old, colonial rubber plantations hid marijuana plantings and little else. The people were less poor. The land, and the sea, were richer.

John wanted a car and a driver. But when the frizzy-haired drivers clustered in the dust outside the ramshackle terminal heard his destination — fifty miles south of Pattani — their response was unanimous.

'*Mai! Mai!*,' they said, explosively, the clipped tones of their Southern accent chopping their words off short.

No one would go further than Pattani. Beyond that point, they said, there was no law, no safety. They were not interested in risking their lives for anything he cared to offer them.

It was hot, even steamier than Bangkok. They were only seven degrees above the equator. Crowds streamed past them as the drivers gesticulated their fear. The crowds were heading for the monthly, day-long bullfight at Hat Yai Arena. The air was thick with dust, its smell mingling with that of the cattle. In the distance John could hear the frightened lowing of the panicking beasts.

John found a travel agency and haggled a price to rent a car. They demanded exorbitant insurance on it, and he paid. He hated driving, but he had no other option left. He got in and immediately felt the sweat on his spine. He decided first to go to Wat Yai Nai, just off the airport road.

The huge image of the reclining Buddha at the Wat dwarfed the curio shop and mausoleum that was built at its base. The Buddha was still in the process of being restored. Forgotten for centuries, it was now re-emerging from neglect and indifference. Its benign face smiled at John as it rose above the jungle, above the tourists, not indifferent but accepting.

He stood there, entranced by the way it seemed to rise out of the vegetation, as if emerging from the slumber of centuries. But a tourist bus arriving re-awakened memories of another bus, in the north; memories of objects which were charged with dread.

He bought some food from a vendor, and headed on over the river and into the town, past the hawkers, vendors, prostitutes — all selling their wares to eager Malaysians who were on vacation from the strictures of Islam for the day. He headed on towards the mountains and the Malaysian border, driving slowly, unfamiliar with the vehicle in which he had found himself.

He turned off the main road on the edge of the foothills and headed for the coast. John could feel his tension increase as he crossed the railway line. It was the border beyond which pirates flourished.

A large, white Mercedes passed him, with two shirt-sleeved Chinese businessmen in the rear seat. Its windows were up and its air-conditioning blasting.

Pattani was a dirty town, even by Asian standards. Its original character had long disappeared. It was now characterized by cheap concrete buildings with steel shutters for windows. John parked in the shade of a big tree and wandered through the dusty market, looking at the piles of vegetables and fly-covered fish. Many of the vendors squatting in the shade of the awnings wore Muslim head-dresses.

He walked down to the harbor and watched children playing among the Malay-style fishing boats. It was a calm day, the only movement on the water being the wakes of passing boats. And these were few and far between.

His heart felt heavy. He turned away from the water. He found himself looking at the white Mercedes. The Chinese businessmen had also come down to the docks and were talking with a fisherman.

John could see the fisherman handing them a wad of fifty-baht bills.

He thought of his project 50 miles south, and frowned.

In many ways it was the most successful thing he had accomplished. He had set it up with a determined ex-Seventh Day Adventist missionary — who before that incarnation had flown helicopter gunships in Vietnam. He was a young man tortured by memories of fire-raking raids across villages, watching young women and babies splattered by his gunners. All this done in the name of Right at the time; all the villages officially sanctioned as Vietcong sanctuaries. But then, after the war, he had come to the realization that all he had done was to kill people, and nothing in Vietnam, or anywhere else in the world, had changed.

His misery had driven him to preaching, hoping that would atone for his sin. But it didn't. John found him and his Thai wife and their baby at a Seventh Day Adventist guesthouse when he was staying in Bangkok. The wife was from the south. John was keen to find a way in to the south. It seemed they were all made for each other.

'Excuse me,' a polite, English-educated voice said.

He turned. One of the Chinese was smiling at him — smiling with his gold-tipped teeth, his eyes lost behind tinted spectacles.

'You appear lost. Can we help you?'

The spectacles were gold-rimmed. The man was balding and his scalp glistened with sweat. He gestured and John saw his gold rings.

'It is a very hot day,' the man suggested.

'I've got a car parked back in town,' John said, uneasily. 'I'm heading on down the coast about fifty miles.'

'You have business there?'

John nodded.

'I have an interest in a fishing fleet.'

Behind the tinted lenses, the eyes came alive.

'At Sai Buri?'

'Near Sai Buri. There's a little village at the river's mouth.'

'Ahh! I know it. My interests are in the main town! We must have a drink some time, perhaps?'

John glanced at the white Mercedes. The driver sat expressionlessly at the wheel, the door open to get some air circulating. The other Chinese stood in the shade of the tree that also screened the car, hands on his hips, watching their conversation. The only other industry, besides fishing, on that coast was piracy.

'I would be honored,' John said.

The sun was dropping over the inland mountains and darkness was rushing up with tropical speed when John reached Sai Buri. The white Mercedes was there ahead of him. It was parked in the dusty, darkening street beside a ramshackle building in a style somewhere between Chinese and Portuguese — the building was a legacy of two of the powers that had traded this coast, and lost it long ago. He could not see the Chinese businessmen.

A lot of Malay men wandered the street, dazed and drunk. Dull-faced young Vietnamese women watched them from the ramshackle building's verandah.

The young women wore tattered halter-tops that were cut very low, and high-cut tasselled shorts.

John drove slowly past the drunks, and the dazed-looking prostitutes. He realized that the Chinese had to be the owners of the brothel.

A generating plant thumped away somewhere nearby, providing the electricity for the bars and brothels. As well as Malay men out for a good time there were Filipino and Thai fishermen getting drunk in the street. They watched him with narrow, speculative eyes — evaluating the profit in pulling him from the car and taking his belongings. He kept the vehicle moving.

He drove along the river bank, into the darkness. He could see the outlines of the fishing boats. There was something odd with their silhouettes. He stared until it clicked. They no longer carried net booms. And, in the fading light, he could see that their once garishly painted superstructures were now gray. They no longer sported the vivid eyes at their bows — for warding off evil spirits. In the growing darkness, the boats themselves seemed evil.

He drove on, troubled, sensing the evil all around him.

The swampy river chuckled as the tide ran. The sounds of revelry fell away. He began to anticipate his arrival at the village where he and his ex-chopper-pilot agent were attempting to turn the tide of corruption.

It was the village of his agent's wife's people. She had left home to work in Bangkok and, like most other country girls, had found the only work available was in massage parlors and bars. That's where she'd met her husband-to-be. Now they had two children and were back with her people.

John had set up a trust account for the village, and had invested his own capital in renovating their fishing boats. They'd bought new nets and lifting-gear and replaced ancient marine gasoline engines with new marine diesels.

John would have preferred they'd investigated a return to sail, using Jim Brown-design trimarans as some Pacific Islands had done with success. But these people wanted to get their catch back to town as quickly as possible. They'd bought a new truck and it was used to hurry the catch to Pattani. On his last visit to the project, a year ago, John had suggested they invest in buying a freezer unit and market their catch in Hat Yai.

It bothered him that the project had bought into high-tech equipment. In some ways he preferred working with peasants, who were more likely to understand the need to stay with water buffaloes rather than trading up to tractors.

He could see the village lights glittering through the swampy trees. He could hear the muted throbbing of a big marine diesel as a boat left Sai Buri, feeling its way up the channel more by instinct than by pilotage, for there were no navigation marks.

As he entered the village he realized there was another motor pounding away nearby. The village had its own generator, and the lights in the houses were electric. He frowned. His agent had not informed him of the change-over. He wondered if a freezer had also been installed.

He found his agent's house and parked in the dust outside. He climbed onto the wooden verandah and looked through the open doorway.

The wife and two young children were curled up in domestic comfort, watching a video-taped movie. John froze, his hand out to rap on the door. His agent used to preach against the evils of television, once, long ago.

He looked behind him, making out the shape of the family's old Jeep parked beside the house.

He stepped quietly off the verandah, and moved into the shadows down the side of the house, between the wall and the vehicle.

Behind the house was a newly built steel shed. It had a concrete floor. He pushed the door open. It was dark inside. He opened his overnight-bag and found his flashlight.

It showed him a work-bench and power-tools. Like a workshop from any suburb in any Western country. He tracked the flashlight until he found the light switch and switched it on.

There was an inflatable Zodiac boat on a trailer. That also was new. He walked over and looked at it. There was a grappling hook sitting neatly in the middle of a coiled length of rope in the bow. There was a wooden box under the central seat, and he pulled it out and opened it.

Inside was an American Armalite rifle, and a Remington pump-action shotgun. He stared at them a moment, then lifted the shotgun out. It was fully-loaded. Ready for action.

Holding the shotgun, he felt a thumping in his

head. He could see the monk's face, back in Bangkok; the smiling eyes behind the black-rimmed glasses. He could sense a movement, like a great wheel turning on its axis. Instead of being in the vertical plane, though, the wheel turned horizontally. It seemed to turn through mud, its axle buried in mangrove ooze, like that out beyond this shed, where the chuckling tide carried the gray, lightless boats towards the current-snared hulks fleeing Vietnam, across the Gulf. And the boats now coming from mainland China after the smashing of the democracy movement.

Like the ooze at the mouth of the Chao Phraya, where it emptied the body of Joe Tobias into the Gulf of Thailand. The dead body.

But — as that hideous, stone wheel turned, grinding away at the mud, the trees, the shore — John Chang could see Joe dragging himself into the mangroves.

He could see the Shan Mountains, hear the sound of a twin-engined plane, one engine choking to death, the other screaming to lift it higher, lift it higher. John Chang's plane.

He heard a car pulling up outside his agent's house. It was too late to turn the lights off. He had to face what he had created. He heard feet running down the side of the house.

'Who the fuck's in there?!'

He recognised his agent's voice.

'It's me, John Chang!' he called back.

There was silence. John laid the shotgun on the work-bench.

The door opened and his agent stepped in. He carried an automatic pistol in his hand. It, too, was US Military issue.

They looked at each other.

'What's going on?' John asked him.

His agent smiled nervously.

'Nothing's going on. I'm just nervous about intruders.'

'You didn't used to go around armed.'

'Things have changed.'

'Why the boat?' John asked him, nodding towards the Zodiac.

'This is a fishing village, remember? You catch fish from boats.'

'Not from that sort of boat.'

'Well, we're catching a different sort of fish.'

They stared at each other. John tried to smile, and leaned back against the bench so his agent couldn't see the shotgun behind him.

'The Chinamen told me they'd seen a stranger. It sounded like you. So I came back.'

'You deal with the Chinamen?'

'I've got no option, if I want to keep dealing. They sabotaged our truck. We couldn't sell to anyone but them. Then they started lowering the prices.'

'You look like you're making plenty of money.'

Behind his back, John's fingers found the shotgun. He felt clear-headed, realizing he had once again failed to pay out Joe's karma.

'We're getting by.'

'You couldn't buy a boat like that around here. Where'd you get it?'

'You don't really want to know. Surely you can guess?'

'I can guess. But I want to know.'

His agent thought a moment, then slipped the pistol back into the shoulder holster.

'The Chinamen offered us a contract to bring them girls for their brothels. The boats you re-engined were faster than the local craft.'

'Where did you get the girls?'

'Off the refugee boats.'

'What did you do with the rest of the families?'

'It was no different from 'Nam, man! No fucking different! People are born! People die! That's life!'

'And your wife? What does she think of this?'

'Her grandparents had done this before they got religion! That's why the fucking family was so poor! They gave up piracy and tried to make a living catching fish!'

He laughed and sucked air.

'That's why she had to sell her ass in Bangkok, man! My wife, selling her cunt! Why should she?'

'So you killed the families?'

The agent shrugged, and gestured.

'And the Zodiac? That's from a yacht, isn't it?'

The agent nodded.

'Sixty-foot fiberglass ketch, registered in Honolulu. What's a boat like that doing in these waters?'

He was angry now.

'Didn't they know nothing? I don't know how they got this far. They could have been ripped off anywhere between Mindanao and here!'

'How many aboard?'

'Four. Owner and his wife and two young women. I think the old man was balling them all. It had that kind of feel to it. I couldn't bring the girls back to the brothel. There'd have been too many questions.'

'So you killed them all? And took the Zodiac?'

The agent nodded, watching him for his reaction.

John again remembered the monk. Had the monk known where he was going, what he would find when he got there? He felt clear-headed and giddy at the same time. He closed his hand on the shotgun and pulled it out. The agent's eyes went to it. He reached for his pistol. John realized he had committed himself to only one course of action. He had to finish it now, or die.

John pulled the trigger once. The shotgun boomed. The agent flew back against the wall.

The after-shock of the shot seemed to go on and on. It echoed back and forth within the tin shed. There, in that constricted space, two men had just died. One was a preacher turned fisherman turned pirate. The other was John Chang. The man who had vowed never to use violent means to achieve his non-violent ends.

But a man stayed standing, holding a shotgun in his two hands with casual familiarity. He stood there listening. The generator still throbbed. He could hear the distant television. He could hear the boat clearing the mouth of the river, opening its throttle as it boomed into the open sea in search of a target.

Traveling at night like that he realized they must have radar to hunt down their prey.

He stepped over the agent's body and returned to the front of the house, carrying the shotgun at the ready.

The family still sat curled together, watching television. The wife had a contented smile on her face.

Glad she no longer had to sell herself. Glad she had her children. Glad her husband was looking after them.

He got into his car. He started it and headed back into the main town. He wondered what would happen to his agent's family.

The white Mercedes was gone. Drunks roamed the street. The girls in the brothels had taken off their halter-tops. Their faces were dull masks. The same men who now pawed them had thrown their brothers, sisters, babies, and parents into the sea to drown. Now the men drowned in their own fate.

A party of drunks barred his path. Several of the men, who could have been Malay fishermen, carried machetes. He leaned out of the window and showed them the shotgun. They jumped aside and let him through.

He drove into the night, driving hard until he came up behind the rear of the Mercedes just before the road entered Pattani. He wound down the passenger's side window. He drew up next to the vehicle and shot across the seat.

The windows of the Mercedes were bullet-proof. But the driver gasped and wrenched the wheel away as the pellets boomed against his vehicle. The white car left the road and upended itself in the roadside ditch.

He kept going. He hoped the brothel owners were dead. But, if they were, how would the agent's widow support her family?

There were no anwers. Only questions and actions. And then the consequences of actions. And movement. He had to keep going.

CHAPTER THIRTEEN

As always, Julia woke with the dawn. She woke remembering the night and she smiled and turned towards her lover.

She sat up quickly, calling out to him. There was no answer. She hurried through the house, to find herself alone. A hunch took her to the garage and she stared at the empty space beside her blue Dodge.

'You bastard,' she whispered. She drew her hair back from her eyes with one long nail. 'You lousy bastard.'

She heard the security panel demanding her attention, indicating there was a caller at the gate. For a moment she entertained the idea that it was the old tom cat, Dave, dragging himself home. But that fantasy didn't seem right. Angrily, she walked back inside and pressed the intercom button.

'Yes,' she said, shortly.

'Mzz Julia Carr?' an expressionless voice drawled. Not Dave's voice.

'Yes.'

'You own a gold Mercedes coupe.'

It was said flatly, as a statement, not a question.

'Yes,' she said. 'It's been stolen. I just ...'

'Uh huh. You know a Mzz Diana Walters?'

'Yes.' She couldn't see the connection. Then she remembered her lover's obsessive interest in her boss.

'You'd better let me in, Mzz Carr. I'm Detective McNeil, Westwood County Police.'

'Ohhh,' she said. 'Give me time to get dressed, will you?'

She pressed the button, and when the buzzer indicated the gate was opening she hurried upstairs.

The detective was young, short and closed-faced. He wore gray pants and an English-style jacket. When she came down he was looking through John's desk. There was an angry tension behind his every movement.

'Excuse me,' she said, trying to sound acid, but only sounding scared.

He nodded, calmly lifting a notepad off the desk.

'This yours?'

She nodded. 'You can see the shop's letterhead.'

Another cop, this one in uniform, stood in the opened double doors, staring at her. She automatically touched her hair. But the cop didn't react. Both he and the detective were stony-faced, like the world's worst audience, sitting on their hands, watching the actress make a fool of herself. She didn't know which part to play.

'What's happened?' she asked. 'You've found my car?'

The detective didn't respond to the question.

'When was the last time you saw Mzz Walters?'

'At work,' she said. 'Yesterday. Why? What's wrong?'

'You've been here all night?'

She nodded.

'Alone?'

His eyes were stones. She felt herself blushing. She looked down.

'You'd better come with us,' he said. 'And you'd better tell us who he is.'

She sat in the rear seat of the police car as it threaded its way back on to the freeway. The detective radioed his office. He wanted information on Dave Watson, ex-DEA. He described her lover as 'another fucking drug cowboy gone off the fucking rails'.

The radio told him, and her, that Diana Walters used to be called 'Meredith Grant', and that she had a prison record for drug-smuggling in Thailand. The detective thought for a moment and then asked if there was any chance she'd been arrested by a David Watson. The radio replied, 'Affirmative'.

'He's our boy,' the detective said to the uniformed cop, and then to the gray-faced Julia. 'He's ditched the car. I wonder where the fuck he's gone?'

Thai Airlines Flight 24, a 747Sp, was scheduled to leave LAX at 0830, flying direct to Hong Kong. Traveling that route meant they couldn't jerk him off the plane at Honolulu. Assuming they were on to him. And it was always best to assume the worst.

A man may live in the present, but traces of his past

still cling to him. Dave still had a good undercover passport, valid for Thailand, Hong Kong, Indonesia, Malaysia ... all of his old beat. It was in the name of Robertson. David Robertson.

He used his American Airlines Admiral's Club pass to get into their lounge, and plugged in his computer at one of the guest desks. A smiling attendant brought him coffee and a croissant while he worked.

He accessed his old DEA file over the modem and erased the record of his undercover passport issue. He drank the coffee and ate the croissant and then went to the bathroom.

He didn't look too bad. He'd thrown away the vomit-stained jacket after he left the apartment. He'd been too mixed-up to think straight. He shouldn't have left the car there, but he had. He'd taken a cab back to the hotel.

In his room he'd calmed down enough to change and pack. The night clerk was asleep somewhere and the lobby empty. He left a note telling them to forward the bill to Washington.

It was the quietest time of the night, even on Sunset Strip. He knew that if he went walking a patrol car would see him. There was a direct cab-line and he called and waited outside the hotel, in the shadows. No one saw him leave. It was almost dawn when he got off at the airport.

He remembered the warm, alive feeling of the Kali in his hand. He knew that statuette well. He had left it in his house in Chiang Saen a lifetime ago. He had intended throwing the thing in the river, but its power over him had been too great to let him destroy it.

He had left it behind in Thailand, and it had pursued him across the years. This time he had thrown it away, but he could still feel its spell upon him. It should have been burnt and buried with due, magical ceremony, he thought wildly. He should retrieve it.

He shook his head.

There was no going back, not now. He could only go on and find out what force had dragged the statuette out of his past, and find out what had brought the Quest back to life. He could feel, right through his body, that the force, the reawakening of what had been forgotten, was inextricably linked to the mysterious John Chang.

And he knew that he would once again have to stand on the bank of the mighty Mekong River, by the town of Chiang Saen.

Sitting there in the plushly furnished lounge, watching the early-morning passengers trickle wearily in, he wondered how much of a start he had. The abandoned Mercedes would take the police to Julia. Their records would give them him and Meredith Grant, and on that link they could build themselves a murder indictment. Then they might go back to Julia and find out from her about his obsessive interest in her husband and Thailand. Maybe Julia's anger at him would make her his enemy too.

He felt a dreadful pain in his heart as he thought of Julia. It was like the heavens had opened for a moment, and shown him what could be his if he gave up his quest. But he had proven too stubborn to leave it alone. He had used her, like he'd used Meredith Grant, to get at Joe Tobias.

The flight was announced and he again checked the concourse, but it was clear. There was no one loitering behind the ticket counter, or by the security screens. He took a deep breath and committed himself to the only course he had left.

To Chiang Mai and to whoever had consigned the box to John Chang. The mysterious person who could tell him if Joe Tobias had returned to life.

He hurried to the ticket counter and bought a business class seat. The attendant smiled at him.

'You nearly didn't make it, sir,' she said.

'Goddamned head office called me at 4 am,' he said. 'Would you believe it? Trouble with the Bangkok deal. I don't suppose there are any aisle seats left?'

'Here you are,' she said. 'We're only half-booked.'

He took the ticket as she checked the passport. He held his breath, but she gave it back with a smile. He passed his case and computer through and walked away as she ticketed them. As he walked, he heard her phone ring. He forced himself not to look back. He kept walking quickly. There was no turning back now.

For some reason, Julia noticed the video-tape cover was still there, on top of Di's television. The tape was in the VCR. There were people crowding around the apartment. The man in the check jacket pushed his way through and motioned her to follow him into the bathroom.

Di lay face-up in the bath, her eyes vividly wide open. There was blood everywhere.

Julia gasped, fumbled to the basin and threw up. The man in the check jacket watched her coldly.

'Can you identify the body, Mzz Carr?'

She wiped her face and looked at him.

'It's her,' she said. 'It's Di. Who killed her?'

She dared another look. A knife had been thrust between her legs and hacked upwards.

'What was your relationship with the deceased?'

'We worked together.'

'Have you been to this apartment before?'

She nodded, pushing her way out of the bathroom. The walls seemed plastic when she leaned on them. The whole world seemed fluid. Everything was normal, but the relationships between each item within the world had changed irrevocably, and in such a way as no longer made sense to her.

He was close on her heels, remorselessly unemotional in his speech, while his whole body shouted outraged anger.

'During the day or the evening?'

'What? Oh, the evening, after classes.'

'What classes were they?'

'Acting. I'm an actress.' She looked around and sat on the sofa, staring at the television.

'Made any video tapes?' he suggested.

'I've made movies, and commercials. I've done television.'

'Know what tape's in the machine?'

'I can see the cover.'

'Not that sort of movie?'

She stared at him angrily, her cheeks burning like coals.

'What are you after?' she demanded.

He opened a manila envelope and poured a sheaf of old photos beside her.

'Know anything about these?' he asked calmly.

She picked one up, then dropped it. She could recognize a much younger Di, naked, except for her spectacles, with a very young Asian woman, also naked.

'No,' she said. 'Definitely not.'

'Do you have a key to this apartment?'

'No.'

'Know anyone who might?'

'No.'

'Recognize this?'

Like a peculiarly downbeat magician he produced another envelope from inside his jacket and from it slipped a plastic bag. The bag was flat and in it she could see a piece of notepaper.

'No ...' she hesitated. 'Yes. It's the shop's notepaper.'

'Same as this?'

He took the notepad from his other pocket. The one from John's desk. She nodded.

'Did you write on this?' He held out the page which had been crumpled, then flattened. It smelt of vomit. It was stained. On it was hastily scrawled Di's phone number and address.

'Recognize the writing?'

She shook her head. 'I didn't write on it. It's not my writing!'

'What about Mr Watson's?'

'I've never seen his handwriting!'

'He only picked you up last night?'

Again she felt her cheeks burning. She seemed to be falling into a deep tunnel, in which she was losing her identity, the persona she had built up so carefully, so lovingly, the last three years. She could feel the tears in her eyes. Tears of shame.

Someone else put their head in the door and signaled to the detective. She could hear them speaking in the distance beyond her personal tunnel of shame.

'There's a guy out here from the DEA, says they've got a prior claim to this. Calls himself "Howard Collins".'

'I was wondering when the rest of the cowboys would get here. Tell him to fuck off. This is a straightforward homicide. Middle-aged dyke carved up by some mad ex-cop. Happens all the time.'

'Now that's no way to approach matters of joint jurisdiction,' another voice said, quietly and calmly, and authoritatively.

She looked up to see a middle-aged black, presumably the DEA man, looking in the door. He was hastily dressed in jeans and a zip-up parachute-silk tracksuit jacket. He kept his hands jammed into the jacket's pockets.

'One of your clowns fucked up!' the detective said angrily. 'And you're gonna cover for him. No way. If he killed her, then he goes down.'

'The deceased was part of a bigger operation,' the other man said, quiet and patient. 'Her employer is under suspicion of being a major heroin importer.'

Julia stared at him. *That's my husband you're talking about*, she thought.

'What about her?' The detective jerked his head towards Julia. The DEA man glanced at her. His eyes lingered on her body. He sighed and shook his head.

'No,' he said. 'She's clean. He married her as a front, to get citizenship.'

Reality took another lurch. Now she could hear them discussing her marriage. Other men were staring at her, like she was some interesting exhibit at a police lecture: 'How illegal aliens evade the law by marrying silly women'.

The actress who had played the beautiful wife of the mysterious philanthropist was now the actress playing the deceived girl who had played the beautiful wife of the drug baron who was masquerading as the mysterious philanthropist ...

'OK,' the detective said wearily. 'You'd better brief me.'

'What about her?' someone asked, with an angry, proprietorial voice. After all, we found her first, it seemed to say.

'We're holding her for questioning,' the detective said angrily.

'This is a federal matter,' the DEA man said. 'I'm afraid I'm going to have to go over your head.'

'Fuck you, Jack.'

'It's bigger than both of us, buddy. You'll get all the transcript.'

'You cunt!'

'Thank you.'

The ritual change of ownership had been played out. She felt a hand on her elbow. The DEA man smiled tightly at her and guided her past the motionless police, who could only glare their frustration.

He opened the door of his car for her, got in, and smiled at her.

'So,' he said. 'Back to Beverly Hills?'

'You know where I live?'

'Afraid so,' he said. 'Once you start mixing with the wrong people, you get known.'

She tried to reply, but her eyes misted over. He sighed and started the car.

'Traffic'll be hell,' he said. 'Have you got a back way you use between your friend's place and home?'

She nodded and forced herself to guide him back to the high walls and big trees of Beverly Hills.

The young detective in the check jacket had been very deliberately unimpressed by her house's opulence. But the middle-aged black just didn't seem to notice it. He got her a seat in the kitchen, after he'd established there was no help. He bustled about, making coffee for them both and a sandwich for himself.

'They called me at home, about 7.00,' he said. 'Before I could eat breakfast. I haven't stopped since then.'

She nodded. Her own kitchen seemed strange to her. She picked up a white mug with red lettering on it — 'I'm only doing this while I'm waiting for a good role', read the slogan. Di had bought it for her birthday. A joke which, like all Di's jokes, was too sharp to be funny.

'I don't understand anything anymore,' she said, to the mug, to the man eating the sandwich, to the body in Di's bath, with Di's face and Di's build, but not Di's history.

She looked at him for an explanation. She noticed

how he still kept one hand in the jacket pocket. He finished the sandwich and glanced around the gleaming, white-on-white, all-automatic kitchen.

'Why don't you have any help? Town's full of wetbacks looking for work.'

'John didn't like exploiting people.'

God, it sounded hollow when she said it! John. Who was John?

'You gonna have kids?'

Reality tripped her up again.

'What!'

He seemed too normal. He wiped his mouth with his hand and smiled at her.

'I don't know,' she said. 'I guess I tried not to think about it.'

He nodded. 'Plays hell with a girl's career.'

'Please tell me what's going on,' she said, trying to regain control of the situation.

'I'll tell you what I know about your husband,' he said, 'which is less than I told Westwood County. We know he's not a drug-runner, for example.'

'Then why ...?'

'I wanted you gone before they wrung you out and hung you up to dry. You see we've been watching your old man, because of the fact that he hired Miss Walters. Or Miss Grant. Now why would some squeaky clean philanthropist hire a jail-bird like that?'

They stared at each other. He refilled their mugs. His read, 'Don't ask me, I only work here'.

'So, maybe he was a philanthropist, and he deliberately hired a jail-bird as an act of charity. And maybe the jail-bird had repented her previous evil ways ... and as evil goes, she was up there ... well, not with Klaus Barbie, maybe not even with Joe Tobias ... but she was trying for the major league when Dave Watson stopped her. But that's two maybes, two suppositions of good intentions in a world where, I'm afraid, bad intentions tend to be the norm.'

He paused for breath. The coffee pot was empty. He unconsciously rinsed the mug in the white sink. He put it upside down in the draining-rack and looked at her again.

'And then Dave Watson turns up here, literally out of nowhere, and he's stopped being a good boy. He's back on the Quest. And suddenly I'm thinking, shit, Howard — for such is my name — shit, my boy, maybe Dave Watson's been right all these years. Maybe Joe Tobias didn't die fifteen years ago. Maybe he took three in the body, and one in the face, and maybe he crawled on to some mudflat and that old driver of his found him there and dragged him up to the hills ... and maybe he's been quietly running his network ever since.

'Maybe all this. And if maybe, then there are two other people in the world who've got unfinished business with Joe Tobias and they are Meredith Grant and Dave Watson.'

'How can I help you?' she asked him.

The question was reasonable, but to her it sounded strange. Like a line from a play. Maybe the director should get her to do something with her hands when she said it?

'Where's Dave Watson?'

'Why do you care?'

'Because if Joe Tobias is somewhere in this world,

then Dave Watson will be heading there right now. You were the last person he saw. You gave him some information which took him to Grant's ... whatser-name's ... apartment. Information which he was either prepared to kill for, or someone else was prepared to kill for.'

She stared at him. The words formed in her mind and she spoke them.

'Chiang Saen,' she said.

She saw the recognition hit him. She went on.

'I opened a box of things from Chiang Saen yesterday. John had sent it. Dave Watson suddenly appeared, out of the blue, as I was opening it.'

'What was in it?'

She hesitated, and blushed. In her mind was the image of a bird-headed goddess.

'Artefacts,' she said. 'Statuettes ... a mask ... a drum.'

'They at the shop?'

She nodded.

'Let's go take a look.'

'Why does Dave care so much about this man?'

'Dave's wife and infant son died because of him.'

She remembered the pain behind Watson's eyes. But, staring at the image of his face, she saw that of her husband's rise up, superimposed on it. She saw, as usual, the scar on his forehead. She remembered touching it with her fingertips.

'I got that in a previous existence,' he had said.

Howard was holding her kitchen door open for her. She walked, unsteadily, to it. She heard her voice tolling falsely.

'Could a man survive all those bullet wounds?'

'Dave always maintained that Joe was hit by some Chinese peashooter at maximum range. Dave always maintained that, in Thailand, unless you buried the body in a coffin with an open lid yourself, and then covered it with a foot of concrete, you couldn't say with any certainty that it was dead.'

'But surely someone would recognize this man, if he was still alive?'

He laughed, shook his head and clicked the door shut behind them. He escorted her to his car.

'The only person I know who set eyes on him was Dave Watson. I never saw a photo. Joe Tobias was a name, a reputation ... a presence.'

Julia felt a growing nausea, a growing sense that she was no longer functioning normally in the world. Something horrible was pressing up against her, demanding her attention. Something which she had known all along, and tried not to see.

'Mind you,' he added, opening the door for her, 'there is another explanation.'

She stared at him, half in the door.

'Joe Tobias could have been a figment of Dave Watson's imagination. A phantom he conjured up, and couldn't conjure back down.'

He grinned at her and got in behind the wheel.

'But he killed Dave's family, didn't he?'

'He ordered it, which amounts to the same thing — at least in Dave's mind.'

'How did they die?'

'I'll tell you,' he said, soberly. 'But you'd better find a towel before I do, because just thinking about it makes me want to puke.

'I was just twenty when I got to Bangkok,' Howard began, as he eased his car back down through the manicured slopes of Beverly Hills. 'Dave Watson was already a legend in drug-enforcement circles. He'd busted the Chiu Chao Network by hard work, inspired guesses, and finally by sheer guts. He'd rooted out corruption right through the Thai police and military, and finally among the politicians, too.

'I had an image in my mind of how the master drug-cop would look. This was back in the days when Mayor Daley told the Chicago Police Department to crack the head of any guy with shoulder-length hair. Cops and marines had heads like sandpaper! Except for guys like me; we had heads like Brillo pads. And we always wore a tie. But always!

'So, anyhow, I track my new boss down. He's not living in Bangkok, or even in Chiang Mai — the capital of Northern Thailand. He's living in a tumble-down house in a town on the banks of the muddy old Mekong River: Chiang Saen. A one-horse town that's mostly the ruins of ancient temples.

'And what does this drug-enforcement legend look like? Hair down to here,' he looked at Julia, grinning, tapping his shoulder, 'and beard down to here.' He held his cupped hand against his chest. 'Wearing a neck-tie? No, sir! Wearing an old pair of shorts. Skinny. Burnt black by the sun. I tell you ...!'

He laughed at the memory.

'And there with him is this lovely mid-West girl: Mary. His wife. Blonde and cute. Wears skirts and blouses in the heat. She has a little baby. She's totally bemused by her surroundings, and by what her husband's become.

'Her husband wanders around all day studying Hindu and Buddhist scriptures. He stops moving only to stand in front of a statuette he keeps in his study. He talks to it. Hideous-looking thing. Kali the Destroyer. It had half a dozen arms and it squatted on a dead man's chest. The man's stomach was open and his guts hanging out. There were swords in some of the hands, and cobras in others. Around its neck was a necklace of grinning skulls. Its face was ... ugh! It was fucking hideous!'

Julia watched him, entranced by the tale. They moved through the morning traffic, seemingly entombed together, locked into the story, locked into each other's lives.

'Dave told me that the Networks were like Kali. Endless manifestations of Evil. Evil that grew out of what at first glance might seem to be good. Despite having been on US Network News, burning mountains of poppies, and of pure brown heroin, he didn't for one minute believe he'd destroyed the Networks.

'He spoke of the legends of multi-headed, impossible-to-kill dragons that occurred in cultures as varied as the Chinese and the Greek. I thought he was right out of his tree. A total burn-out. I realized head office wanted me to assess the situation, then recommend they ship him out, and me take over.

'Only trouble with that idea was Dave wouldn't budge. Number three and number four heroin was coming down the trails again. We thought we'd closed the Laotian border, but the shit still kept getting through. Dave said it was the wrong time to pull him out. He had a line on the latest warlord to spring up — the newest head on the eternal dragon — out there in the mountains. Some new generation heavy. Not an old Chinese general gone to seed. No sir, this guy was super bad news, according to Dave. Man called Joe Tobias. Where he came from, nobody knew. But everyone could see where he was headed. Right to the top of the industry.

'Dave thought he had a direct line to Mr Tobias. He thought Joe was on some kind of spiritual wavelength that he could tap. He thought there was more to Joe than just dealing shit.

'Dave was reading a lot of stuff. He'd vanish for a week and we'd all think he was out there on surveillance. But no, he was in a cave with some fucking monk, discussing past lives. Dave was big on past lives for a while there. Dave was out of his tree.

'Dave thought that he and Joe Tobias were old enemies from some previous lifetime. Well, I mean, theories are only as good as the results they bring you. Dave's wacky theories had got results up to now. So, who was I to challenge them?

'I mean, whatever the theoretical basis of his actions, in practice Dave belonged to the "fight-fire-with-fire" school. If the Triads cut off the balls of Dave's informer, then Dave would find a way to dump the corpse of a Triad lieutenant on the right doorstep. That's how he got results.'

He looked steadily at Julia. She could not take her eyes away from his.

'I'm not kidding about the surgery,' he said. 'I've

seen a man with his pecker cut off, and it sewn into his mouth. And he was still alive.'

She cried out. He stared remorselessly at her.

'He'd gone mad of course,' he added. 'It would have been better if Joe Tobias had just got someone to shoot him. But Joe wasn't like that. Joe was angry at the whole human race.'

She was dizzy. But it wasn't just the story. It was something else. Some nightmare from which she was reluctantly awakening.

'Everything we heard about Joe Tobias was contradictory. He was white. He was black. He was Asian. Mongolian. Chinese. Russian. He came from the steppes; from the plateau where all those worlds joined up; from where all Asia's big rivers spring.

'Dave found out he'd first appeared in Hong Kong, where he was into waterfront smuggling. No big deal. But he had something that brought him to the attention of the Chinese Triads. They tried to squash him. They cut off the balls of his lieutenant. He had his boys cut off the breasts of the Triad chief's mistress and present them to his wife.'

He chuckled. Julia swayed inside the nightmare, remembering her husband's hand on her breast. She choked and put her hand to her mouth.

'Joe's work had that touch of class. Occam's Razor of Retribution, Dave called it. But Joe's ability to use Asian means to European ends — to secure markets in Amsterdam, San Francisco, and Sydney — impressed the Triad heavies. They stopped fighting him. They offered him honorary membership of the Triad. It wasn't long before Joe was in the Shan Mountains, setting up transportation. It wasn't long after that he was organizing the growers. Some of the old generals tried to move against him — but they'd grown fat and lazy. And Joe, well, Joe had weird connections with the mountain people; and with the Chinese. The way it looked, he had connections all the way to Tibet! And beyond! He ran rings around those old Chiang Kai-shek leftover Nationalist Chinese troops.

'Yes, Mr Joe Tobias was the brand-new head of the dragon, and we were standing around, still admiring the head that Dave had lopped off ... which had ceased kicking by now, in fact was beginning to stink. We were being congratulated by the President of the United States of America — which is, of course, the President of the World.

'Then our people start complaining that heroin's rolling through Amsterdam and San Fran. Exploding into Sydney like never before. Golden Triangle powder. But it wasn't coming across the Laos border. We could swear to that. We didn't know how it was getting past us. All that Dave claimed to know was that Joe Tobias was running it.

'My opinion of Dave began to change as I saw him go into action. He no longer looked weird. He looked possessed, sure. But he was a man with a mission. His family ceased to exist for him. He was like a mongoose watching a cobra. He could see only one thing: Joe Tobias.

'Somehow he got wind of a trucking convoy coming down the National Highway. What a scoop! Five tanker-loads. Half a year's crop! Man, that really hurt old Joe. There was a collective sigh of relief, followed by a collective tightening of breath. What would happen next?'

Julia could now see the great grey monolith of the Beverly Center rising from the river of traffic ahead of them. She pointed it out to Howard, and he began looking for a side lane, searching for an exit, but at no time stopping the flow of words. She had a sudden intimation that he had never told his wife any of this. That it had been locked up inside him a long time.

'Scene shifts back to Dave's domestic arrangements. That crazy house by the river at Chiang Saen. Mary's very uptight. Dave's refusing to budge. Tension's mounting. The little boy's blissfully unaware of anything wrong. Spends most of his time sleeping with a little labrador puppy, his closest companion, as the household drifted closer and closer to all-out war.

'Mary wants Dave to get the hell out. Dave wants Mary to get the hell out. But neither will go without the other. Madness. No one will give in.

'Then, one morning, there's the puppy on the doorstep, disemboweled. Mary starts screaming. After all, it slept in the same room as the baby. They both knew it was a message from Joe.

'What does Dave do? He redoubles his interest in Hindu tales. He re-reads the *Ramakien*, as if the answer's in there. Some story about warring brothers in the time before man.

'Me? I begin to notice how heavy the sampan traffic is on the river. I begin to institute spot-checks. One of them pays off. A boat-load of heroin. I show Dave. He seems to wake out of his dream. He pockets his statuette of Kali and comes down to the river. We find nothing more.

'We search a hundred more sampans. What do we find? Nursing mothers; little brown babies at their breasts. Huge, coal-black eyes telling us nothing. Dave drags the families off their boats and makes them stand there as he torches them!

'Next move is Joe's. And he makes it. The obvious move for a man of Joe's record. The baby disappears. Mary goes into shock. Dave goes mad. He'd been outflanked. Me? I keep stopping sampans at random — but more of them. I figured Joe would contact Dave and strike a bargain. Have your boy back and leave the country.

'But, no. Nothing happens. Except Mary's under sedation in hospital in Chiang Mai. Dave's had a haircut and shave, and is now practicing on an old statue of Buddha in the jungle with a variety of automatic weapons. He's renounced his belief in past lives and karmic retribution in favor of good old-fashioned Western-style revenge. Me, I'm searching sampans, loaded to the gunwales with rice, and all of them with the damned nursing mothers sitting in the rickety, thatched cabins, nursing their babies, staring at me with eyes that were full of some story of untold, appalling misery. And, no heroin.

'But the reports from down river, from Bangkok, are that the heroin's still rolling through. Joe's got us beaten. But how?

'Dave makes a supreme effort and gets himself under control. Comes back, organizes Mary's repatriation to Hong Kong, under sedation. And he joins me on the boats with all those little brown babies with their eyes shut tight and their fingers curled up, all asleep at the breast without a care in the world. The women watching us with those liquid eyes. And the fucking heroin rolling on through! Like we weren't there. How? Where?'

They took the exit. The Beverly Center's tower rose above them like a cliff.

'And then we were looking at a white baby! It was Dave's! This terrified woman holding it to her breast. God knows what Joe had on her to make her do it. Was it only starvation she was escaping? The baby was the same as the others. Asleep. Good complexion. Fingers curled up. Lips nuzzling the tit. Dave's little baby! He cried and grabbed it!'

Now Howard was crying, the tears pouring down his face. He eased the car up the parking-ramp, hardly seeing what he was doing.

'It comes out of her arms, real heavy. Dave almost drops it, but he gets his balance, moaning to himself, and he rips the swaddling clothes off.'

Julia couldn't take her eyes from his anguished face.

'There were rough stitches in the belly. The baby was dead. They were all dead. All of them. Dave dropped the baby and threw up everywhere. I had to get it off the boat. Back in town a policeman cut open the stitches. The body was full of number three heroin. That's how Joe was beating us.

'He was buying babies from starving Hills people. He had his heroin ready to go. He had his couriers standing by in Bangkok — your girlfriend was one of them. His men would kill the baby and gut it and stuff it with heroin. They had about eighteen hours in which the baby would retain its color. They hired other starving women to transport them right under our noses. Somewhere down river his boys would board the boats, unzip the babies, put the heroin in trucks, heave the bodies in the river, and keep on going.'

Julia became aware of a rising, shouting noise in her head. A thunderous roar, like a waterfall. She looked around. It was the vehicles behind them, banked up. Howard's car was stalled on the ramp.

'We're holding up the traffic,' she said.

He stared at her.

'What?'

'The traffic. We're holding up the traffic.'

'Oh.'

He restarted the car and eased it into a parking space. Julia thought she was coping well, but when she tried to open the door she found her hands wouldn't co-ordinate. She had to wait for Howard to come round and let her out. Neither looked at the other as they walked to the elevators.

She let them into the shop and turned on the lights. She could see the upended carton lying in the stockroom doorway. She walked over to it and knelt down.

'So, is it all there?' he asked her.

She touched the head-dress. She looked at the beautiful Tara, but could not bring herself to touch it. He, however, prodded it with his toe.

'You said "statuettes,"' he reminded her.

'One's missing,' she said, hesitantly. 'A statuette ... and a dagger.'

'We saw the dagger,' he said, grimly. 'Is this something like the statuette?'

At last his hand came out of the pocket, and she saw what he had been hiding there, the statuette of Kali, now flattened on one side, but still leering evilly.

She looked at him, and turned the question back on him.

'Is that it?'

'You tell me,' he said, neither of them willing to accept the truth. 'Was this thing in the box?'

After a moment she nodded slowly. She was conscious of the silent tears on her cheeks. He watched the tears, and then sighed, and set the statuette on the ground, beside the beautiful Tara.

'Well, that's it,' he said. 'That's Dave Watson's personal demon.'

She looked at the green jade Tara lying beside the broken, tarnished bronze demon.

'What does it all mean?' she asked him.

'All I can tell you is the easy bit. The statue's back in circulation. The statue which linked Dave Watson to Joe Tobias. The statue came from Chiang Saen. The babies died near Chiang Saen. Therefore Dave Watson will now be heading for Chiang Saen.'

'Why will he do that?'

'Because he'll want to find out if Joe is back there, waiting to resume their game ...' He broke off, and then said, 'You look awful pasty.'

She nodded. 'What will you do?' she asked him.

'Take you downtown, get a statement, call up a few people, then ring the airlines and book a seat for Bangkok.'

'Two seats,' she said.

He stared at her, for a moment not comprehending. She got to her feet slowly, suddenly feeling old. She saw the inquiry on his face.

'Don't forget it was my husband who sent these things. I want to ask him some questions.'

'Isn't he on his way back home?'

She shook her head with certainty.

'I doubt it,' she said, listening to her voice speak from outside herself. 'If what you told me is true, then I doubt very much if he's coming home.'

'What good will going over there do you?'

'I want some answers!' she cried. 'I want to know what's been going on the last three years! I want to know if I'm totally mad, or not!'

He studied her anguish, thinking what it must be like to wake up and suddenly discover that you were living with a different man, in a different world, to the man and the world you'd lived with before you went to sleep.

'OK,' he said. 'I guess we'll have to talk to your husband as well. Maybe he knows if Joe's alive.'

'I think he might,' she said. 'I think he just might.'

CHAPTER FOURTEEN

The canals of Bangkok were being filled with concrete. That was the first thing Dave Watson saw after he checked into his hotel and then emerged into the cooling evening air and set out for the river. The nightmare of traffic was worse than anything America had shown him. Now the cars, buses, taxis, trucks and tuk-tuks competed with earthmoving equipment and large, pink concrete trucks en route to the canals — where they would seal away forever the memories of the city that had been founded in 1782 by King Rama 1. In its place was growing a tropical Los Angeles.

In the original Thai, the old city's shortened name was *Krung Thep*, 'City of Angels'. The original settlement of California's 'City of the Angels' — *El Pueblo de Nuestra Senora de La Reina de Los Angeles de Porciuncula*, Los Angeles, had been made in 1781.

Dave was trying to keep his head clear. But it was filling up with such trivial coincidences as the names and founding dates of the two cities. It was filling with memories of the Mekong River in the flood season. Sampans. Rice. Babies. Memories of a middle-aged Buddhist monk who lived in a cave in what was left of the forest listening to the ravings of the drugs cop with the new crew-cut, and the clean, pale chin. Listening to the story of the bitter duel between him and the man he had never seen, but whose presence filled both his days and his nights: Joe Tobias. The monk who explained to him the universal law of karma. The law of action and reaction. The law which led in the end to the forgiveness of your enemies. And, because of that, a law which Dave had angrily repudiated, for without his quest for vengeance, Dave would have gone completely mad.

He gave a shout and passers-by turned, glanced at him, and nervously stepped aside. He stopped walking and stood there, suddenly struggling to remember where he was. Because he was on the streets of this City of Angels; in that other City of Angels; on a sampan in the Mekong River; on a powerboat in the Chao Phraya ... all these were places engraved into his mind. But now there were other images stacking up, too. Images of mountains and grey stone buildings and ice and a piercing blue sky. It was like David Watson was just a dot surrounded by a field of energy, and that energy occasionally crystallized into realities full of pain and suffering.

Samsara, the wheel of suffering, his monk had called it. The wheel Dave Watson had thought he had relinquished, stepped off by paying with the lives of his son and his wife. And here it was revolving once again, with him struggling to keep up with its turning.

He shook his head. Despite the warm evening, he was cold. The reality of Bangkok was solidifying. He remembered his intention to walk down to the river and take a boat out to where Joe Tobias had slipped away from him. He resumed his walk.

The old man sat meditatively on the stern seat of his wooden boat. He had the metal cover off the top of the Evinrude and was thoughtfully cleaning the spark plugs with a nail file some *farang* woman had dropped in the bottom of his boat. He tapped a plug against the engine block, adjusting the gap by eye. Satisfied, he turned the engine over by hand to clear the cylinders, and began to rethread the plugs into the cylinder head. He was conscious of the fading light, the gathering cool.

He heard a commotion nearby and glanced up to see a middle-aged *farang* arguing with the young driver of a new rooster-tail boat. The tourist wanted to go downstream and the boat's driver was only interested in going upstream. The driver would get a commission from one of the market stalls for delivering them a high-spending tourist. There were no stalls, no markets, down the river — just bridges, warehouses, and eventually the harbor.

The *farang* spoke a halting, but well-modulated, Thai. He was probably an ex-soldier who had spent a lot of time in the city during the war. He had returned in search of old memories — meaning a girl. He would find she, too, had grown middle-aged. His memories, like the canals, were now concrete.

The old man tightened the plugs down with the one spanner in his tool kit, and clipped the plug leads back on. He was not on commission with any stallholder, any prostitute, any black-marketeer.

'*Sawat*!' he called out, and the tourist looked over in surprise.

'You want to go down the river?'

The tourist nodded, smiling politely. He had the dazed look of someone who had just got off a plane and who was about to collapse.

'I'll take you. How far you want to go?'

'Down under Saphan Phut,' the tourist said, climbing gratefully into the boat.

The old man rewound the starting-cord and jerked it hard. Nothing happened. He tried again and the engine spluttered into life. He let go the stern rope and guided them into the stream.

'Down under the Phut Bridge?' he said, thoughtfully, looking at the tourist.

The tourist nodded.

'You got it,' he said.

American. Frightened, wounded eyes. He'd been in the war, all right. He'd seen things it wasn't good to see.

'Why go down the river? Everything happens up the river.'

'Not everything,' his passenger said, shortly.

That's true, the old man thought. *Smuggling, for instance, that's decidedly a down-river activity*. He decided to keep his mouth shut and his eyes to himself. The idea of smuggling made him rethink the memory of his Central Asian pilgrim passenger. He, too, must have been a smuggler. Then, again, maybe this one was a cop. He had something of the air of a cop. The old man debated with himself whether to mention the pilgrim.

They cruised under a bridge, and out into the open again, while he wrestled with the decision. They could see the luxury hotels crowding the bank ahead of them. The tourist passed the hotels without glancing at them. He was staring at the looming bulk of the next bridge: Krung Thep. The tourist raised his hand, staring fixedly into the water, right where the pilgrim had stared.

'Wait,' the tourist said. 'Hold it right here.'

The old man killed the motor. The traffic ground and muttered in the background. Machinery clattered on the distant docks. A rooster-tailed boat came upstream and the tourist started and looked at it in fear. He glanced back and those fear-filled eyes met the old man's and forced him into speech.

'Your friend came here too,' the old man said.

He saw the tourist's face go white. The old man realized he was suddenly into something far deeper than he understood. He was an agent of karma in the lives of two other men. He felt frightened, but he knew that the wheel had to keep turning. There was no other way.

'Your Asian friend,' he touched the skin beside his eye. 'With the scar here. He came to this spot and stared into the water. Just like you.'

'How long ago?'

'A few days. No more.'

The tourist closed his eyes and sighed. The old man saw him give up something he had been carrying, mentally consign it to the river. The tourist sat back in his seat.

'Tell me what else you know about my friend?'

'Nothing else. Like you, he was a pilgrim. He had no business down here. I picked him up at the dock. I returned him to the dock. He paid me and went his way.'

Dave stared at the old man a moment longer, and saw he knew nothing more. He looked down into the river again. His hand clenched the gunwale with excitement.

He could remember the sun setting over Thonburi. The waters of the Chao Phraya shivering gold, while Bangkok's traffic smog hung purple over the river.

Dave was remembering that other evening on this river. Everything was repeating. The wheel was in motion.

He's alive! he thought. *Joe's alive! No one else would come here and do this! All these years I was right! The Quest is not over yet!*

His mind jumped to the other City of Angels, to the woman, the bird-goddess, to the box from Chiang Mai which she had opened; the box which seemed to point north of Chiang Mai to a small and dusty river town.

'Where to now?' his driver asked him.

'Chiang Saen,' he responded absent-mindedly.

'*Mai?*'

Dave glanced up.

'*Pen rai,*' he said. 'Forget it. Just head back to the dock. I'll get a plane.'

The river-boat driver shrugged expressionlessly, rewound the cord, and kicked the outboard over, and swung them back upstream. But his passenger continued to look over his shoulder for a long time. Staring back at that place where several lines of karma had come together some time in a past which was unknown to the boat's pilot.

~

The man half-opened his eyes. He could see a window. He could hear a bird singing somewhere nearby. He thought he might be in the mountains and the bird's song meant he was safe. But then he realized he lay on a bed, and there were no beds in the mountains.

He felt thick-headed from sleeping too long. He opened his eyes fully, feeling wisps of dreams receding. A dream of a boat putting out to sea. A dream of a confrontation between two angry men in a steel shed. A dream of a many-armed statuette with daggers in its hands and snakes about its neck.

He sat up quickly, looking around. He was in a room. There were noises beyond it. High-heeled shoes on wood. The slap of sandals. Murmur of voices. A giggle. The mumble of air-conditioners. He was in a hotel.

He got out of the bed, went to the window and eased it open. The bird sang suddenly, piercingly louder. He looked out over an ancient, waterweed-choked *klong*. The time was just after dawn and he could see old women hunched over even older stoves, thin blue smoke around their seamed faces. He could smell damp heat and leftover food being warmed. He realized he was in Bangkok. He closed the window and looked back at his bed.

Clothes lay on the floor, next to a travel bag. He stepped back to the bed and sat on it and opened the bag. He was looking for something and it wasn't there. What was it?

He remembered a shotgun's weight in his hands as he held it a moment and then dropped it off a humped bridge into a river. He worked backwards from that memory. He relived the boom and the kick of the gun. He saw a white car bucking away from him, careering off a road and into a water-filled ditch. Water erupted silver from among the vividly green weeds.

He went further and saw a man flying backwards, chest caving in as blood erupted. He held that moment and looked at it again. He tried to see it from a different angle, and saw another man holding the shotgun. Was this man himself? He made himself watch the man closely. It wasn't him, but he had come to know the man well.

The man in the Bangkok hotel room moaned and shook his head. He walked across to the white porcelain hand-basin in the far corner and gripped it with both his hands and stared at the oblong of mirror above it. A bandit's face looked back. No. An ascetic monk's face. His face. John Chang's face. But as he stared he saw the same face, but with a different expression, and a different name. The name was Joe Tobias.

John Chang was dying when Joe Tobias first saw him. He lay strapped to his pilot's seat, in the wreckage of his airplane, on the side of a mountain. He lay among the bright, happy, poppy flowers, and their slowly filling pods. The sky was half-blue, half-clouded, and there was rain on the more distant peaks, those rising up towards the headwaters of the river.

Joe Tobias looked back to the track and his silently watchful servant. The old man looked calmly at him, leaning against the cart on which he'd pushed Joe this far. Joe gripped the crutches the old man had made him, and used them to lever himself from the side of the track into the field of flowers. Insects buzzed around him as he labored to the dying pilot.

Joe was pleased that he could now walk so well. He was pleased that he was no longer lying in the darkness of the village hut. The sunlight and the breeze and the sound of insects were all sharp and raw and vivid. The broken metal of the plane glittered among the flower stems. There had been no fire, but some of the metal was still warm.

They had come as soon as they'd heard the impact. Joe had wanted to make sure it was not the DEA and, equally, not the Chinese. The journey had taken them four hours.

Now he watched the pilot die. Terror invaded the dying man's eyes, like the ocean rushing into a rock pool as the tide creeps inexorably higher. And, watching, Joe Tobias felt his own unacknowledged terror rush out to meet it. They clung to each other with their fear-filled eyes. Two men who could have been brothers, their faces so similar. But one of them returning to life while the life suddenly blinked out of the other man's eyes.

Shaking, Joe broke the dead man's grip. He tried to

step backwards, away from the corpse, but then he went down on his knees and opened the dead man's tunic pocket, and removed from it the wallet and the passport. Joe looked at the passport photograph. The photograph made the resemblance between the two men almost identical. Joe read the dead man's name and his description. Suddenly something shimmered in his head and he looked up to his servant and knew he had felt the same message.

The old man frowned. He didn't like what he was feeling. But Joe looked intently, and began to smile.

Joe was seeing himself wearing such a tunic as the dead man wore, holding the same passport in his hand, watching as a customs officer flipped through it. The customs officer smiled at him.

'Thank you, Mr Chang,' the officer said.

Joe gestured at his travel bags. The customs officer shook his head.

'That's all right,' he said. 'You just go through the gate.'

Then the customs officer's interest left Joe and Joe realized he was at the head of a line of people waiting at a terminal gate.

'Next!' The officer called, and Joe passed through, limping slightly.

And Joe realized the airport was that of Los Angeles, USA, and that he was safe.

The vision faded. Joe was leaning against the body, holding the passport, looking at his old, frowning, servant. The old man shook his head.

Joe smiled and pushed himself up and grabbed the crutches. He manipulated them more vigorously now, already thinking ahead to the day when he'd walk, unaided, through that terminal gate.

Joe Tobias moaned again and stared once more into the oblong mirror above the stained wash-stand in the tiny hotel room. Faces like masks seemed to shuttle before his eyes. His face. John Chang's face. Behind them other faces, as if mirrors were reflecting into mirrors, and the faces went on repeating into infinity.

He was remembering too much now. He remembered the old man's name. It was Tendzin. The old man who had nursed him in the mountain hut, and before that had piloted his sampan to the meeting with the DEA men, and who had reappeared in a dusty town by the Mekong with a sack full of memories.

And now Joe realized that it was not just he who had used John Chang. Chang had somehow held on to him. Whatever was in the dying man had grabbed hold of Joe and clung to him like a life-ring in the rising tide of dissolution. They had shared an unspoken pact that he was now breaking, for no longer did the living have a use for the dead. Only the dead needed the living. Joe watched the surging currents of death reclaim the pilot, tear him into a myriad of pieces, and swirl him out of sight.

Joe recognized death's moment of 'fire sinking into air'. The terrifying final dissolution of the last vestiges of duality, when the individual has to accept that he or she is not separate from anything, but is part of one great wholeness. And, without meaning to, or knowing from where the words came, he found himself whispering the last rites of the *Bardo Thodol: The Book of the Art of Dying.*

O this now is the hour of death. By taking advantage of this death, I will so act, for the good of all sentient beings, peopling the illimitable expanse of the heavens, as to obtain the Perfect Buddhahood ...

But he could say no more. He stood up quickly, pressing his hands against his ears. He kicked the travel bag, as if kicking whoever was reciting that text somewhere in his head. He kicked once, and then he kicked again.

It was like he was a small boy in a temper tantrum, kicking and kicking. Not wanting to kick, but once started unable to stop. As if someone was goading him on. It was no longer a bag but a man he was kicking. A man who lay there, refusing to resist as the small boy pummeled him.

And then the man whispered something, but something so familiar the boy had only to see the words forming to know what they were.

Homage to the Female Buddha exquisite with youth.
Radiant as the eternal snows in all their glory,
She sits on a white lotus and a silvery moon
Indicating fully developed compassion and knowledge.

And the small boy within him screamed. Screamed because the things which he had hidden for so long were finally coming out.

Joe heard the sound coming from his throat. He

forced it to stop. He was aware that the sounds outside the room had suddenly ceased, at the instant of the scream. Now they slowly resumed. The high heels tapped out their enticement again. The giggle resounded. He heard throaty European voices raised uneasily. They reminded him of something. He pulled on his pants, grabbed his room key, and hurried into the corridor.

Ahead of him were the high heels, tight, black satin pants, the movement of buttocks, shimmer of long black hair. Two European men and two girls. One of the men glanced quickly at him, fear in his face, knowing Joe was the occupant of the room from where the scream had come. Joe glared back and the man looked away and made his companion and the two prostitutes stand aside to let Joe through.

There was a thread seeming to draw Joe down the creaking stairs of the hotel, down to the bamboo and formica desk behind which a clerk nervously watched his approach.

'I want to make an international call,' Joe said.

The clerk hesitated a moment. Joe drew out a wallet and credit cards in the name of John Chang. For a moment he didn't recognize whose they were. He saw again those repeating images in the mirror. Then he showed a credit card to the clerk.

'You can charge this account,' Joe said, feverish with anxiety.

The clerk took the card, frowned at it and then reached for the phone and began punching in the number as Joe whispered it to him, barely able to control his voice. Joe could hear the signals sorting through the air. The clerk was frowning, then he smiled and pointed to a booth for Joe to pick up the receiver.

'Hello?' a voice asked, puzzled.

With a shock, Joe realized it was a male voice.

'Where is she?' he demanded.

'Where's who? Who's calling?'

'My wife.'

'You John Chang?'

He should have hung up right then, but the need for her was primal. All along he had thought that it had been John Chang who had married her; but now, in anguish and alarm, he knew it was not. It had been that small, terrified, boy.

Homage to the Youthful One with full breasts,
One face and two arms. Sitting in vajra position,
She regally displays both grace and calm
And is filled with great bliss.

'Yes,' he whispered into the greasy mouthpiece. 'Yes. I'm him.'

'Well, if you're calling from where I think you're calling, she's about to land there any moment, with a gentleman named Howard Collins. Mean anything to you?'

'Who are you?'

'I'm the Westwood County Police Department, friend. And I'm afraid your wife has been a very bad girl. And she was a very bad girl with a cowboy name of David Watson. Mean anything to you?'

He put the phone down and stood there, feeling the universe growing smaller around him, shrinking down to be no larger than the size of one man's own karma.

CHAPTER FIFTEEN

From the window of her suite in the Oriental Hotel, Julia could see the river carving a slice through the city. She stood there, staring at its troubled surface, remembering the story Howard had told her about the baby.

She was totally disorientated. The time was now mid-morning — 10.39 the digital clock by the bed told her. But, inside herself, it was early evening — 7.39 Los Angeles time.

She glanced again at the window. In the taxi from the airport to the hotel, after the pampered boredom of their Royal Thai flight, she had felt the sledge-hammer heat, and had smelt the rottenness in the air. She had seen the street-girls and the wrinkled old people. She had felt the whole seething mass of humanity out there living lives of despair.

She didn't want to know about it. She didn't want to know any more about what had become of her husband. He had gone bad; leave it at that. One of life's little lessons.

What she wanted was to wait for as short a time as possible, never leaving the quietly air-conditioned luxury of her suite, until she could slip discreetly away. She'd write Howard an apologetic letter. He didn't need her help to track down the man he sought.

A deep sense of vengeance had got her on to the plane with Howard Collins, a determination to somehow square accounts with John Chang — the man who seemed to have played a sadistic game with her life, who had used her weaknesses to create a woman who didn't exist as partner to a man who wasn't himself. But the squabbling touts at the airport, offering more forms of sexual deviance than she had ever envisaged, and then the garish, glittering hell of Bangkok's morning streets, had got rid of that — forcing upon her a realization that this was a different world to hers. Totally, impenetrably different. Whatever fantasies she'd once indulged, about temple dancers, about water lilies drifting on ponds and lacquered boats poling above the sacred golden carp shimmering in the depths, had vanished in the smell of fumes, in the thumping heat, in the blankness of the prostitutes' eyes. She was not of this world and had no wish to enter it. The man who had married her, and then come here, had obviously died, and this was the hell of his imagination.

Julia recognized she was suffering the symptoms of shock. All that she had been through since she had woken to find her short-term lover gone was crowding in upon her, pressing her to accept it as reality, or else accept that she was mad. Julia knew one good way to keep her sanity, to reassert herself against a world that threatened to destroy her.

She would take a shower and change. The hotel advised its female guests that a long skirt and high-necked blouse would be suitable garb; anything that hid flesh, which sold so cheaply out there on the streets beyond the self-opening doors of the lobby. She would put her hair up. She would spend an hour on her nails. When Howard returned from his investigations, she would be gone. This hell belonged to him, to Dave Watson, to her husband, but not to her.

The old city was different, but the old city was the same, Howard thought, smelling the benzine in the air, hearing the traffic's roar. More concrete. More vehicles. But the same heat. By Jesus, he'd forgotten the heat! Even by the river it was more than he could bear.

He envied Julia, waiting in her suite, wondering which button on the phone to press to summon room service. He didn't like that spoiled-child aspect of her. But her looks made him put his dislike to one side. That was one lady he would dearly like to get to know better ... in more ways than one. She obviously liked dangerous characters, and Howard Collins had a bit of a reputation in that area. He preened himself as he paid off his taxi and crossed through the warehouses and sheds, down to the roadway beside the river's edge.

He stood there, looking across the river, and back towards the bridge. Out there was where it had all come together — where Dave had thought he had finally nailed Joe, and Joe had pulled his final disappearing act.

That was if you assumed Joe actually existed. What he had said to Julia in jest, back in her Beverly Hills driveway, returned to him. Maybe it was true. Maybe there was no Joe. There was just Dave fighting phantoms of his own devising, and he, Howard Collins, had been sucked into the vortex of Dave's obsession.

But that didn't account for the babies, did it?

He shivered. There was a small, flat-bottomed workboat tied to a piling and drawn up in the mud. He scrambled down to it and then searched around amongst the rusting steel, the old drums and discarded black rubber conveyor belts that lined the banks, until he found where its crew had stashed their oars — hiding them from just such a would-be boat thief as Howard.

Grinning to himself — picturing Julia's reaction to this minor act of daring — he slid the boat into the river and set off, pulling himself out into mid-stream, out towards the bridge, out to the spot where Joe had gone down.

On the far bank, two people in the curtained barge saw the dinghy pull away from the shore. They waited. Several other boats had left the docks in the hour since they had stationed themselves here, knowing that whoever was on the Quest would be unable to resist coming back to this spot. They held the heavy, silk curtains apart and watched the rower labor out to the center of the river, and then ship the oars and let the current twist the boat about, as the rower stared into the water.

One watcher eased back through the rearward curtains, to the rowing bench. Slipping one bare leg over the single oar the watcher began to scull the ancient, gold-leaf-encrusted barge out towards the drifting dinghy.

'Well, he's not here,' Howard said to himself.

He looked up and smiled at his own incredulity. At some level he had still thought Joe floated there. As if time had ceased to operate at this place, and all his life since then had flowed out from this center — as Dave's had.

He looked up and saw the antique, blunt-nosed barge, heavily-curtained, gold-plated wood worked in the shapes of dragons and demons and full-breasted maidens, coming towards him.

'Water-baby?' he asked himself.

The barge glided on, a boat out of a distant, almost mythological Bangkok past, when prostitution had been a matter of choice and not of necessity, and royal courtesans plied the water trade in such craft. He found himself smiling as the vessel moved silently, eerily, towards him, circling upstream so that it could drift down to him.

He found himself entertaining the possibility that Julia had dived into his secret heart, discovered his desires, and had come to fulfill them. That it was her, bare-breasted, face painted, fingers tipped in gold-leaf, waiting inside the silk curtains.

The barge bumped against his boat, and he stumbled against its side.

He grabbed its gunwale and tried to see into the

curtained interior. But he could see nothing. He let go the gunwale and pulled himself on to the barge, sensing his dinghy spring away behind him and float clear.

He collected himself, hoping he didn't smell too stale. He pushed aside the curtains and crawled into the barge. The interior was dark, but there was a shrouded figure waiting in the stern. Disappointed, he realized it was male.

The figure was familiar. He assumed it had to be his old boss.

'Dave?' he asked. 'Is that you? What the fuck's going on?'

'I'd like you to tell me that,' a harsh voice whispered.

Howard could see a gaunt face. A thick mustache. He realized. He turned to grab for his dinghy, and saw it floating downstream, still powered by the kick he had given it when he came aboard the barge. He grabbed the barge's gunwale, about to throw himself into the river, but then his head exploded into stars, and then into blackness.

Joe watched the unconscious cop for a moment. He had lost that feeling of disassociation, of being himself and not himself. He felt the man's pulse and grunted with satisfaction. He pulled the body in behind the curtains, carefully redraped them, then slipped back to the stern and took up the pilot's position. He lifted the ancient, long-handled oar and slipped the blade into the water. He wrapped his leg around the handle and eased it against the wooden chock on the transom. He splayed his bare toes for grip.

Then, in the way boatmen of Thailand have done for a thousand years, he stroked the barge up the river, powering it with his leg, guiding the restored antique back to the inlet where he had found it under restoration.

There was an empty shed there, with a large ceremonial barge half-restored in it. There were a number of sharp chisels and gouges, boat-carvers' tools, lying on a bench beside the hull. He had noted them before he'd removed the barge and begun his patient wait for the black man's inevitable pilgrimage.

He thought of the gouges. He could feel growing in him a real combination of sexual pleasure and intense power. A feeling he had discovered many years earlier.

The *Bardo-Thodol* said that one could, *obtain the Perfect Buddhahood, by resolving on love and compassion.*

So, if one wanted, above all else, to avoid such personal obliteration, such monkish mumbo jumbo, such pain and terror, as sticking to the Path inevitably brought, then one had to avoid love and compassion, had to replace them with their polar opposites.

The small boy would keep on kicking until that whispering mouth ceased to recite the Praise of White Tara.

But even as he docked the barge and his cargo, and eagerly went to grasp the gouges and find himself a roll of tie-wire, the words were whispering away.

Homage to the one whose face unites
The beauty of a million autumn moons,
Whose wide eyes gaze with compassionate warmth
And whose joyous mouth smiles equally on all.

Angrily, he jabbed the gouge into his own palm and was suddenly startled at the red pulse of blood, and then the pain. He sucked at his hand as he walked back to the barge and looked down into the confused eyes of the cop as he struggled to sit up.

Joe grinned and kicked him in the groin with his heel and was gratified by the explosion of pain in the man's eyes.

The eye specialist who served the hospital at Jinghong, the capital of Xishuangbanna prefecture, hard up against the Thai border, was a prim young woman. She came regularly from Kunming, two hundred and fifty miles away, across both the Da and the Hong, two rivers gouging their way down deep gorges through jungle and rock before their tranquil spill and juncture on the plains of Hanoi.

She believed that anything was possible — provided it was done with technology and the apparatus of the Party that served the People. She believed that when an old man's eyes went bad it was because of some little technical thing, a blocked duct, too much pressure, or a few cells growing awry. She didn't believe it was because he'd seen too much and that the things he'd not wanted to see, a long time ago, now kept returning to his eyes.

'You must not leave this bed!' she said to the old man firmly, thin lips snapping off the syllables like they were pieces of cloth and her mouth scissors. 'You must not put pressure on the eyeball until it is fully healed. If you do not help yourself, then we cannot help you!'

By 'we', of course, Tendzin knew she meant 'The People', that mystical power created by pure materialism — which denied all mystical power. The People who had 'liberated' himself, the Abbot, the Master, even the Dalai Lama, many years ago.

If he'd had true courage he would not have even checked in to the People's Clinic in Jinghong. He would have let blindness overcome him and let himself go on to the next stage in the story that was the life of a man. A story with many chapters and with only one guiding rule: you cannot stop it happening, so submit!

But he had only the kind of courage which permitted you to face swords, rifles and mountain guns; to keep on walking down a road when ahead of you your comrade had disintegrated when his foot came down upon the trigger of a mine laid by the hands of those emissaries of The People. Walking with that feeling going all the way from your toes to your testicles. Which step will be my last?

He drew his lips back over his few teeth in a death's-head grin. That was the test of earthly courage.

The grin faded. Now he needed unearthly courage. The courage possessed by the Abbot.

This reminded him of the Master — who possessed neither kind of courage. He shook his head in anger and sorrow. The Master had not been given the chance to grow into his courage.

If only things had happened differently, then he could have served the Master with pride rather than with sorrow.

Long ago, in the golden light of dusk, when he had seen the long-tailed boat turn and begin its run at their sampan, he had immediately known what was coming. But there was no escape. There was only the possibility of limiting the damage. The long-tailed boat turned side-on, showing them its rooster's plumage of spray. The Master had his AK-47 in his hands. Tendzin could see everything that was about to happen. He cut the motor, grabbed the foam-rubber cushions from the seat, and threw himself over the side as fire spattered from the attacking boat. Machine-gun rounds thumped methodically into the sampan at its waterline, bursting the teak, shooting water steaming on to the ancient twin-cylinder diesel.

He could hear the screaming outboard motor of the DEA boat approaching. The sun had died and the river was purple and black. The Master would have gone over the bows. Holding the cushions, the old man sculled and dragged himself along the settling gunwales of the sampan, keeping it between him and the white American boat.

The sampan was settling stern-first, the dead weight of the engine dragging it backwards into the black water. As the bow rose above him he saw something floating and grabbed it. It was the Master.

The white stab of a spotlight lanced past him, and struck against the hull as it slid into oblivion. He shoved the cushions under the Master's arms, not knowing if he was dead, alive, or somewhere in-between. He could smell the blood and thought about crocodiles, sharks, sea-snakes — it was like thinking about land-mines. They either got you or they didn't.

The tide was flowing, combining with the river's current to drag them downstream. The spotlight returned, one more time, and lanced him in the eyes. But it moved on over him, dismissing him as debris as an excited voice called,

'To your left! I got something!'

'Shit, it's just a log ...'

'We shoulda made the sampan ...'

The voices were receding. Tendzin guided his precious burden, aware of its labored breathing, thankful for that sound, knowing they trailed a veil of blood all around them. The tide and the current were holding them in mid-stream when they needed to reach the bank. Tendzin began to fight his way across the flow.

'It's good to see you took her advice and rested that eye.'

Tendzin smiled, recognizing the voice. With his eyes closed he said, 'I found him. I gave him the objects. But he ran.'

'His destiny is with us,' the Abbot said. 'He'll return.'

'And if he does return, what then?'

'My friend, the scholar Pin Li, wants me to return to Ghenko,' the Abbot said. 'I'll take the Master with me.'

'Back to Ghenko?'

Tendzin opened his eyes in surprise, opening them on the white ceiling of the People's Clinic and the beaming, round and brown face of the Abbot. The

Abbot's right hand was wrapped around a staff. The old man blinked and realized the staff was a broom handle.

Tears filled Tendzin's eyes, remembering a time when the Abbot had only to look at one of the servants and the nervous young man would grab a broom, a shovel, a pitchfork, whatever was at hand, and bend his back, anxious to please.

'Tears are good,' the Abbot said. 'They lubricate the eye. Sweeping is good. If done vigorously enough it exercises the cardio-vascular system — like bowing before an altar and reciting the sutras at the same time. Neither of which you ever did with much enthusiasm, I might add.

'Sweeping and walking among the beds of the dying would be a good exercise to give a novice,' the Abbot continued thoughtfully. 'It would concentrate his mind wonderfully. I really do understand what we did wrong, all those years ago.'

Tendzin said nothing, watching the round, brown, almost wrinkle-free face, the smiling eyes behind the clinic's wire-framed spectacles.

'We separated the spiritual from the earthly. I had two sets of rosters, you see. One set for monks to meditate by. One set for our servants to cook and clean and wait upon us. I should never have split the two like that. I had not known what valuable spiritual practice the act of sweeping can be.'

'It was the custom of the order,' Tendzin said, prickling defensively.

'It took the Chinese to teach me this lesson,' the Abbot said, his brow creasing thoughtfully.

Tendzin realized he was not speaking ironically.

'They taught us a few others,' the old man growled, '... in Ghenko.'

'They are already paying,' the Abbot said, lightly. 'You must address your compassion to the painful lessons they are now learning.'

'And what they did to the Master? Is that worthy of our compassion?'

The Abbot stared at him.

'To turn someone aside from a thousand lifetimes approaching the moment of Buddhahood? To have that on your conscience?' He shook his head. 'Think how they will have to pay for that.'

'I'm thinking,' he growled. 'I'm thinking about having them dig a pit and take their clothes off and get in it and ...'

The Abbot held up his hand to silence him. The hand moved on and touched his dry, wrinkled forehead.

'What did Buddha come to know during his moment of realization beneath the Bo Tree?'

'You tell me.'

'No. You tell me.'

Tendzin sighed and felt the anger draining from him as he spoke.

'He realized that as long as there is one person on earth who has not experienced realization, then no one is free from the wheel of fate. As long as one person denies it, then we are all trapped.

'The Master's spent a lot of energy denying it,' he added.

'He will return. The more he denies it, the closer he comes to it,' his smiling Abbot told him.

'And what does the scholar want from the ruins of Ghenko?'

'She wants what I want,' the Abbot said. 'Information that will answer certain questions.'

The black man's red blood ran in a small rivulet into the open drain at the barge shed's center. The drain connected with the inlet. The inlet connected with the river. The river with the sea. Both Joe and the dying man looked at the way the blood dissipated in the water. The dying man closed his eyes. Joe considered jerking them open again. But there was no point. There was no more information to be extracted. There was nothing else that torture would achieve.

Joe unwound the wire that had held Howard Collins tight against the post. The wire had cut deep into his flesh as he'd heaved against it. Joe unbound the cloth from his mouth and pulled out the small block of wood that had prevented him screaming. In the end the black man had screamed with his eyes. He looked up the river, to the spires of Wat Po. He could not see as far as the Oriental Hotel, but he thought of the woman waiting there for Howard Collins to return. He felt hollow in that space inside him where she had resided, remembering the dead man's tale of her infidelity.

He was very tired; as drained as if it was his own blood streaming away. In the end he had stopped enjoying what he was doing. But he'd had to continue to keep the other stuff at bay.

The other stuff was the dreadful memories of a little boy. A little boy kicking hard, desperately, kicking and crying, but still hearing a voice whispering the Praise of White Tara.

Homage to the Majestic One whose sparkling ornaments
Of crown, earrings, necklaces, arm-bands, bracelets,
anklets and belt,
So elegantly arranged,
Surpass any worn by men and gods.

Homage to the goddess before whose lotus feet
Vishnu, Indra, Shiva, Brahma, anti-gods and spirits,
Men, apparitions and all the world
Submit themselves in complete devotion.

Angrily, Joe Tobias threw the bloodied gouges into the water. Their wooden handles bobbed and drifted past the ornately beautiful barge that had borne Howard Collins, Head of the United States Drug Enforcement Agency's South-east Asian Bureau on the American West Coast, to his place of death. Joe glanced back at the slumped body. The blood was beginning to congeal. Glistening black and gold flies were settling on the wounds.

The buzzing of the flies grew louder in the silence of the deserted boat-yard. They buzzed like monks reciting their mantras. Joe began to think he could hear them intoning, *Om. Om. Om. Om.*

The sacred syllable, the sound which was born with the birth of the universe. *Om*. That which is now and ever shall be. The eternally created moment.

Om. The sound which, intoned correctly, leads to the heart of Enlightenment.

It was being recited by a thousand black and gold flies as they milled in the cuts that striped the black man's body. Black and gold flies on black and red flesh.

Joe whispered the syllable himself.

Om.

He closed his eyes and spoke again. The syllable seemed to shiver right through his body.

Om.

He began to shake. Visions flashed before his closed eyes with every recitation as the busy monk flies kept up their chant. Now they were reciting the other syllables which would bring Her to life within the utterer's mind.

Against his will, and yet with a deep, despairing need to evoke Her, he picked up the chant.

Om Tare Tuttare …

Joe could feel Her growing within him. And yet he still resisted Her. For, with every shiver of the whispered syllables, other visions rose up unbidden. The visions of a little boy, crying with anger, pouring his rage down into his foot, slamming his foot into a face, as if it were a football. And yet the face continued to whisper.

May all sentient beings after death take rebirth.
Before Amitayus in Sukavati, Land of Pure Joy,
May they live in the ways of the great Bodhisattvas,
And equal Avalokiteshvara, Lord of Compassion.

May I realize the oceans of sutras and tantras,
To be able to pass them on to others...

And then the voice was silent and the struggling boy stopped heaving against the coarse cotton tunic of the soldier who held him and everyone stared at the broken face of the monastery's young Abbot.

And, at that moment, the first shell from the resistance fighters' captured mountain gun smashed into the high walls of the monastery. The soldiers let go of the boy. The soldiers ran for the gate, in a melee of shouting, of plunging horses. The boy ran like the wind, ran until he was grabbed by familiar arms.

'Keep low,' a familiar voice — that of his servant — growled. 'Wait till they're all in the courtyard.'

His servant pressed him against the stone wall. He stared back across the courtyard to see the Abbot's broken face and his now peacefully closed eyes and the blood weeping from his open mouth, and then his own tears drowned his eyes.

'Mummy,' he whispered. 'Mummy.'

'Shhh.'

The servant's hand gently stroked his neck.

'I want my mummy.'

'Let's go.'

He knew he could not have her, but he was thinking about the lovely Tara, his bedtime companion, the glossy green jade polished by his blankets. He wanted to find her and take her with him. But there was no time. The Chinese were firing back at the white puff high on the cliffs across the valley. His servant pulled him towards bushes growing by the monastery wall.

'We're going to beat these dog-turds yet,' the servant whispered in his fierce, growling voice; a voice which the boy had never heard be gentle, and yet now could feel a strange gentleness beneath it, and feeling that gentleness realized he could trust his servant with his life.

They ran, not knowing that the Abbot's eyelids fluttered weakly, and the lips picked up where they had broken off:

And may I strive until samsara is emptied,
To uphold the victory banner of practicing exactly as taught.

CHAPTER SIXTEEN

The second coat of polish had dried and now Julia was applying the hardener with small, precise movements of her left hand across her right nails. Her left elbow was supported on the antique desk. She was thinking about nothing but the meticulous job before her; working at keeping the brush strokes out of the sticky fluid, so that each surface of lacquer was blank and featureless, and each coat added depth and lustre as she watched.

Glancing up she saw herself in one of the suite's many mirrors. For a moment a shop-window dummy's perfect, blank face stared back. She suddenly wanted to shatter the mirror, shatter the image. She raised her hand, then remembered her drying nails. She turned so she could not see herself.

The beautifully decorated barge moved slowly down the river under the flattening white light of midday.

There was no breeze. Everything waited, hanging in suspense. The ships crowding the wharves were motionless. No tourist boats moved. Only the one, anachronistic barge drifted slowly downstream, towards the shadows under Krung Thep Bridge.

Joe dug the oar into the water at the barge's side and it began to rotate about a spot in mid-river. The spot. The place from which it had all begun. He kept his mind clear of the memories of the white police boat, of the black snouts of Super-8 cameras which became the black snouts of sub-machine-guns. He pushed them to the side and concentrated on slipping Howard Collins's body over the side.

Freed of the weight, the barge rebounded slightly. The sound of the oar scraping over the stern rattled across the still water. The weighted body disappeared quickly from sight into the featureless, muddy depths of the estuary.

Om Tare Tuttare Ture Soha, a voice whispered in his mind.

Angrily, he shook his head. He had sought the reality of Tara, not some ghost which moves within the mind. He had sought Her reality in a woman. A blonde and silver goddess all his own. To love and to honor. To be faithful all her life.

He was crying, his throat tight, veins stretched like the paintings of souls enduring torments in one of the ten thousand hells.

With each sob he jerked the barge back up river. He wanted to be free of her hold over him now. Forever free. As long as she lived, he would not be free.

Looking up he could see the white towers of the

luxury hotels clustered by the river. Convulsively he jerked his leg, driving the barge towards them.

She stared at the drying lacquer as she moved her hands back and forth before the upended hair-dryer on the desk, nestled there in a little cradle so that its blast of hot air was directed straight at her.

She tried not to see the mannequin in the mirror moving in time with her own movements. She tried not to think about the world outside the floridly over-furnished room.

But she could feel it threatening to break through, to shatter the image and reveal the darkness she could sense at her own core. She screwed her eyes tight, feeling the tears threatening to seep out.

The door-buzzer rang and she froze. The hair-dryer's whine became a roar.

'Just a moment, Howard!' she called.

She looked around desperately for a way to prevent time catching up with her. She took a quick glance at the mannequin in the mirror. It stared back at her with haunted, sunken eyes.

The buzzer sounded again. She switched the dryer off.

'My nails aren't dry!' she yelled.

But they were, and the buzzer sounded a third time. Staring at the door, she slowly stood.

The model in the pink slip, in the mirror, also stood. Her heart thumping, Julia opened the door.

Her husband stared at her.

She willed her hand to close the door, but nothing happened. His face was lined and gray with exhaustion.

There was blood on his shirt. There were tears behind his eyes. He was carrying a kitchen knife.

'John?' she said.

He looked at her, and she could see he was trying to speak, but didn't know what to say.

'Come in,' she said, stepping back to let him through.

He reacted to the sound of her voice. The tears broke through. His eyes glistened. He gave a choked-off sob. She could see his hands shaking.

She looked at the knife and, without thinking, reached down and took it from his faltering grasp.

She closed the door.

He made to reach for the knife, but then let his hand drop. And with that movement he gave a sigh and something seemed to leave his body, so that all his strength evaporated. She realized he didn't have the strength to stand much longer.

She sat on the bed and looked at him.

If she tried she could hear Howard's voice recounting the horrors which the man standing before her had caused. She ignored the memory. What she could see was a lonely, confused man at the end of his tether. His reality far outweighed Howard's tale. Here was the man who had caused something to open up within her, who had protected her from her own demons for three years. All Howard and Dave Watson had were words. This man had given her his love. Now he needed something from her.

And with a moan of surrender she realized that there was a way of shattering that false image, that painted dummy which she had made to hide her terror behind.

All she had to do was touch him. And, as she watched, he reached out a hand to her. She could see a crescent-shaped cut in the palm. The blood had dried.

She could see a crescent-shaped cut in the palm. The blood had dried.

Then he moaned and rolled on to the bed, his head falling on her lap. She dropped the knife on the carpet. Howard's tale was whispering in the back of her mind. But her hand reached out and stroked the shivering head that lay in her lap. Like a mother she half-sung a reassurance.

'It's all right, you're safe now. No one can harm you here.'

He looked up at her. She had never before seen such haunted eyes as his. Looking into them she felt a dreadful realization that she and this man were locked together at a level far deeper than she had yet suspected.

He glanced away from her, to the knife lying on the floor. He had only to pick it up, plunge it into her, and life would return to normal, wouldn't it? But if he did that, he knew the monk flies would come for her. Buzzing monk flies with their endless, murmuring mantras. And once they started, he would pick up the refrain.

Om Tare Tuttare ...

'John?' a voice whispered to him. 'John? What's wrong?'

He blinked and focused on her.

'I came to kill you,' he whispered back. 'That's why I'm here.'

They both looked at the knife.

'And are you going to?' she asked him.

He shook his head.

She could see that the blood on his shirt was not his own. It was splattered there as if someone had been flicking it at him. She slipped his head from her lap and stood up. Alarm showed in his eyes.

'Give me your shirt,' she said.

He looked at it, and saw the blood. He shuddered.

'Come on,' she said. 'It's finished now. Let me clean you up.'

'The black man,' he said.

She flinched.

'Howard?' she asked him. 'You killed Howard?'

He nodded, his face like that of a guilty child awaiting mother's punishment.

The shock must have shown on her face for he looked alarmed.

'I'm sorry,' he said. 'I didn't mean ...' He gestured, unable to explain.

'Give me your shirt,' she said, holding out her hand.

He stripped off.

'He told me about you,' Joe said, as she took the shirt and poked it in the hotel laundry bag. 'He told me about you and Mr Watson.'

'He told me about you and Mr Watson, too', she replied, dryly. 'And Mrs Watson. And their baby.'

He lay back down on the bed, shivering.

'You're a monster,' she said, wonderingly. 'A human monster.'

'It wasn't me,' he tried to explain. 'You don't understand what it was like then.' He cupped his hands over his face, then took them away and looked into her eyes.

'Whatever I asked people to do, they did it. Can you understand that? Anything at all. I just spoke words, and other people made those words into deeds.'

'What can you do with a monster?' she asked herself, because the monster lying on her bed was now a frightened, disorientated person.

She sat down beside him and touched the shivering flesh along his side. She touched an old, round scar. He flinched.

'That's why we never made love, isn't it?' she said. 'Because you were really a monster pretending to be a man.'

But she knew that was only half the story. She had encouraged their celibacy for her own ends. If he had been a monster-in-hiding, it had suited her only too well.

She felt the old, familiar tension in her body. The refusal to surrender herself to anything — especially the touch of a man.

'God damn you!' she hissed. 'Why did you have to come back? I could have coped real well without you!'

But that wasn't true, either.

She was crying now. She brushed at the tears. She ached for someone to comfort her. She stretched herself out beside him on the bed; her breasts and her thighs against his back and his legs. She burrowed one arm under him and slid the other around his chest. They lay together like an old married couple. She had seen her parents lying like this many years ago.

She remembered her mother's secret pain.

That made her think of something else. Something which tightened her up inside, so that she unconsciously squeezed against her husband. She shook her head, trying to stop the tension.

'No,' she whispered. 'Go away! Go away!'

Joe forgot his own pain and turned to look at her.

'What's wrong?' he asked.

'I don't know. Something scared me. Not you. Something inside me.'

Now it was her turn to hide her face in her hands. She felt his hand, gentle on her hip-bone.

'You were always so tense when we lay down together,' he said.

He took her hands away from her face and stared at her. His eyes were now those of her husband.

'Who are you?' she asked him. 'Where did you come from? Why have you become what you are? Who was John Chang? Did you kill him, too?'

Questions saved up over three years burst from her. Questions she should have asked back then.

He sighed and lay down beside her.

'Chang died in a plane crash,' he said. 'I took his passport. I tried to take over his life, too.'

He stared at the ornate light-fittings above them, in the off-white ceiling with a hint of pink to it.

'I thought I could make it work,' he said. 'I thought I could really become him and that I could make up for what it was Joe Tobias did.'

'Who was Joe Tobias?'

Haltingly, he said, 'I think it was me.'

'Was you? Does that mean you are not him any

more? Does that mean you weren't born with that name? Come on! You owe me an explanation, buster!'

She was angry now, raising herself on her elbow. He flinched from her anger.

'I don't know of any born names,' he said. 'But I do know that once when I was young I was standing in the shadow of a big ship on some docks. Maybe Hong Kong. Maybe Singapore. I remember the sound of engines. A Chinese man called out to me, 'Hey, Joe, come here.' He pointed to another ship in the harbor. A thin rope hung from its rudder, he said, and there was a waterproofed package on the end of the rope. If I brought it back then the man would feed me. As I was very hungry, I did so, and he called me Joe.

'Some years later I needed a passport, and that was the name on it: Joseph Tobias. So I became Joe Tobias.'

'But you weren't born under that name?'

'I don't know who I was born!' he cried, angrily. 'So don't ask me! I don't know my father! I don't know my ... my mother.'

His voice cracked on the last word.

'I'm sorry,' she whispered. She reached for his hand and took it in hers.

'I know this!' he said. 'I hate Chinese. I hate Buddhists. I hate all religious people, but Buddhists especially. But now I find myself saying Buddhist things. I keep seeing Buddhist things in my mind.'

'You sent me a parcel of artefacts, remember?'

'You got them? Is She safe?'

His face was a child's again, full of fear, and also hope.

'Is who safe? Your manager certainly is beyond that ...'

'The green Tara. Is She safe?'

'Yes,' she said. 'The green Tara is safe.'

'An old man showed her to me and I started to cry and I felt terror, and since then everything has gone wrong.'

'And the other things the old man showed you? How did they make you feel?'

'They made me frightened, too. But only she made me feel both fear and something else. Something I can't describe. Something I felt when I first saw you.'

He stared at her.

'That I still feel when I see you,' he added.

They looked at each other. After a while he reached out and touched her cheek. She put her hand on his.

She found herself leaning towards him, and then she found herself kissing his forehead. Her kisses continued until her mouth was on his, and her hand had shifted his hand to circle her breast.

She slipped the shoulder strap of her slip down her arm, and his fingers were now warm against her breast. One shivered across the nipple, making little sparks in her closed eyes.

She felt his lips brush the breast, and then hesitantly touch the nipple. She opened her eyes, smiling, holding his head gently.

She held him there, suckling him, feeling the tenderness growing inside her, and then the tenderness turned to something else.

It was the familiar tension. She tried to will it away. She felt as if a furnace were burning her cheeks. The feeling grew hotter and harder and she wanted to cry out. With the feelings came wild images of heat and burning light and a leering face. She could feel herself beginning to panic.

She pulled away from him. They stared at each other.

'You always pulled away?' he said, with a questioning inflection.

No, she thought. *It was you. You pulled away. I'm sure it was you.*

'We'd lie there and I could feel how tense you were,' he said. 'I wanted to touch you. I wanted to ... to worship you ... but I couldn't. There was too much hidden inside me, and something hidden inside you. So we lay there and did nothing.'

'Have you ever made love to anyone?'

'No,' he said.

'Is that what's made you what you are?'

He shook his head, his eyes puzzled.

'I don't know,' he said. 'I don't know what it was has made me ... hate!'

His voice cracked upwards. His sorrowing face suddenly snarled.

The overwhelming maternal feeling returned to her and she cradled his head again. This time, when the feeling came, she was relaxed. This time what started as a cry of fear became a simple moan of surrender.

But she could only surrender to him if he were ready. He hunched against her, nuzzling like a baby. To him it was like lying in blackness and cold, with only the thought of the nipple sustaining him. That was warmth. That was life. But the more he drew from it, the more he seemed to change. Its energy flowed into him. Its erection became his erection. As he grew harder and fiercer so she seemed to let go, to fall, until she was lying down and he was on top of her. Now she was open and accepting and he was passing the energy back into her, the energy he had taken from her.

He was afraid she had fainted, she was so limp. But her eyes moved and a cat-like smile showed on her lips, and when he tried to draw away suddenly she was strong, clinging to him with her fingers.

He felt the energy building inside him, and he grew afraid. It was so fierce, so ferocious. It was the energy he had met many times, and each time before he had directed it another way. He had directed it out into the world, instead of in here, into a woman. And, each other time, someone had died.

He shook his head, tears streaming down his face, thinking of the waste of it. The waste of other peoples' lives. The waste of his life. When all he had needed to do was this. But then panic seized him again because it was so ferocious, and he was afraid of hurting her. He yelled out. Then he seemed to explode. His body seemed to disappear.

He remembered the swirling field of force that had been John Chang. He remembered the energy that sucked that wraith away, flinging it into emptiness, like a dye in water, like Howard Collins's blood in the river. Then he was the water, the emptiness. Then it was all over.

She let him roll off her. His eyes opened, then closed. He fell instantly asleep, leaving her shivering with need. She turned on her side and moved her thighs against each other, watching his sleeping face as she did. She came quickly, and cried out, but he didn't hear. He was sound asleep, his face smiling and peaceful. She came a second time, crying a second time, and then she kissed the sleeping face and turned on her side.

She wondered why she had never been able to make love with John Chang. But within an hour of meeting Joseph Tobias — Monster of the Mekong — with the blood of a man he had just killed on his shirt, she now lay beside him, clutching his seed between her thighs.

What if he had impregnated her? Would she mother another monster? It didn't matter to her right then. She had broken loose from whatever had chained her down. She was adrift on a river of uncertainty. She smiled and stretched and let it swirl her out into mid-stream, let it take her and use her for ends which were not hers any more. She closed her eyes and slept.

~

There was an evening wind sweeping across Northern Thailand. It cooled the burning land and swept away the blue smoke from the forest fires and the diesel fumes in Chiang Mai, four hundred miles north of Bangkok.

The breeze set the bare light bulbs dancing on their wires above the marketplace, so that their light flickered and wavered, making it seem that the market was taking place underwater.

Dave Watson felt like he was lost in the depths of an ocean, feeling the pressure grinding down remorselessly on him as he stood on the concrete, surrounded by bustling tourists, artefact buyers arguing with stall-holders, drunks, *bhang* smokers, old men lost in opium dreams, and whole families urging their wares upon the wandering crowd.

He was on a fool's errand, not a Quest, he thought — brought here by the label on a box. Who had labeled it? How could he tell which of these cunning old men had helped Joe Tobias parcel up that particular time-bomb?

He remembered the woman. Julia. He remembered that shimmering first enchanting sight of her. He remembered the night with her, when what had first seemed like a mirage became real. He remembered the grotesque death he had witnessed in a crowded Los Angeles apartment.

Three memories. Three points in time when he was offered a choice. The choice was to give up the Quest, or plunge deeper into it.

He had chosen the latter, and here he was, waiting for Joe Tobias to appear. And then what?

His fists were clenched. He sweated. There was only one thing to do now, one act to heal the jagged scar within him.

He shook his head to clear it and focused again on the traders, the tourists, the silently watchful cops and soldiers. When they glanced at him, their eyes moved on without recognition. He was just another tourist.

But when he felt their eyes upon him he felt a new tension inside. When the eyes left, he felt a surge of relief. He realized that, somewhere along the Quest, he had changed sides. He was no longer a cop, no longer a good guy.

Feeling one cop's eyes come back to him, puzzled at why he stood rooted to the spot, he pantomimed being a tourist looking in his travel guide. With the cop still watching, he walked on, opening out the hotel brochure. The cop looked away. Feeling the sense of relief, Dave walked to one of the wooden poles that held up the shivering lights.

He inspected the market traders again. This time he was using his old cop knowledge. Somewhere here there would be a man who could sell him a gun.

BOOK TWO

THE ASCENT INTO HEAVEN

CHAPTER SEVENTEEN

The same evening that Dave stood in the markets of Chiang Mai, the Abbot watched the sun drop behind the Longlanshan mountains. He had finished his cleaning duties for the day and had returned his brooms and mop to the central store.

For a few minutes he felt the peace of mind which had often been his many years earlier, when he could watch the sun set over the ice field behind the monastery at Ghenko, in the years before he became Abbot of that monastery.

Now he watched as the far — north-eastern — bank of the Mekong River still showed patches of light. The banners above the army camp there still fluttered in the sun. But the bank on which he walked — the south-western — was in shadow.

Naturally enough, the Abbot's mind fell to speculating on the alternation of light and darkness upon the river banks. The northern bank was the bank in light. The Yang bank. The southern bank was the bank of darkness. The Yin bank. At noon both were bright. At night both were dark. Here were the fundamental precepts of Chinese philosophy.

The word 'Yin' originally meant 'cloudy', 'overcast'. 'Yang' had meant 'banners waving in the sun'. Banners were human inventions. They invariably meant war, for they stood for pride. And pride, when challenged, meant war for most men. The cloudy and the overcast were nature. Nature was what suffered during war. But nature, in the end, asserted itself. It flowed.

It flowed like the river. And the Chinese sage, Confucius, writing centuries after the great *Book of Changes* had turned the doctrine of Yin and Yang into the most exquisite philosophy, had remarked:

Everything flows on and on like this river, without pause, day and night.

He was not speaking about the Mekong River, but of the Yangtze. But that river, and all China's great rivers, as well as the Brahmaputra and the Salween, all flowed out of Tibet's ice fields. Just as those ice fields fed the Ganges and the Indus — the rivers which witnessed the great pilgrimages, and the transfer of great wisdom.

The Chinese sage's words made him think of other words.

Plato, the Greek philosopher, had drawn from his predecessor, Heraclitus, when he remarked,

You cannot step twice into the same river; for fresh waters are ever flowing in upon you.

He smiled. Plato had been bent on refuting Heraclitus. Plato hungered after the unchanging form behind the ever-changing effects that form created. Yet even through Plato's enmity shone Heraclitus' vision.

Nothing ever is, everything is becoming.

Man hungered desperately after form, yet was condemned to know only flux.

The Abbot reflected that if you were to follow this surging stream through all the valleys and canyons of China, you would come finally to cold and half-frozen grasslands and swamps with high ice-capped mountains looking down on them. You might find a spring, and you might claim that the spring was the source of the mighty river. But the spring was fed from somewhere else. The ice of the glaciers was only water in a form which moved more slowly.

Of course, on your journey up the valley, you would discover huge land-slides choking its course as deforested hills shed their soil after every rain. You would find silted-up lakes. You would hear no animals or birds, but only chain-saws and engines. And you would pass the ruins of many monasteries.

Angrily he brushed the tears aside, shook his head and looked up. Emotions rose unbidden and he fought them. Everything flowed. What had happened to his monks was part of the flux. After all, they had created the conditions which led to their end. Just as he had created the conditions which led him to suffer even more, to remain alive and feel the guilt and the anguish.

He began to intone a hymn to Tara, to calm himself, letting Her lovely image rise up before him.

He walked to the lodgings where he rented a room along with other street-sweepers and laborers.

In the evening, after his meal, he returned to walk along the banks of the river as was his usual practice. He was sure he had not been followed. His landlady was one who kept a careful eye on his movements, and sometimes she released a grandson to follow him.

But he had finally convinced everyone, through his actions, that he had recanted, that he had learnt the errors of his previous ways, and that he was happy to serve now in the role required of him.

He came to the footbridge, stopped and looked beside the empty drum positioned by the foot-track. Someone had dropped an old newspaper beside the drum, not in it. Frowning at such a thoughtless action, and with a meticulousness you might expect from a man who had been sweeping corridors for fifteen years he bent down, refolded the newspaper and dropped it in the bin.

He walked on, head bowed, obviously lost in reverie.

But his heart was thumping and his adrenalin was up, and after a while he put his hands into the pockets of his cotton jacket, and felt the forged identity papers — which the newspaper had hidden — with his fingertips.

And when he was safely in his room, with his jacket draped casually across the landlady's spyhole, he took out the two sets of papers and stared at the photographs of himself and Tendzin.

His eyes blurred, and he cried silently.

To take the final step in this life both he and Tendzin had to surrender their identities, and become two old men with two totally different life-stories, outlined in the emotionless anonymity of Chinese bureaucratic shorthand. The nomad warrior and the proud Abbot were dead. In their places rose up a pair of antiquated peasants, citizens of Yunnan Province. One of them, he who had been a warrior, was identified as a 'Long Marcher', a soldier who had fought for the establishment of the modern Chinese state. His companion, obviously a man with a head for figures, had become a book-keeper for his work unit. And now the pair of them were identified as involved together in yet another project designed to bring rewards to the people of China. They had permission to run a trucking business.

The tears were not for their past happiness. No, what surprised the Abbot, and made him angry at his own grief, was that he cried because now the Re-education Camps would be buried forever. He remembered the cruelty and savagery that he had fought with the only weapon a monk has: his mind. He was ashamed at the pride which still lived within him — pride which had survived manacles, chains, starvation, lice and disease, and the deliberate attempts of his jailers to drive him, and all his compatriots, insane.

He remembered what it was like to wake in the morning and count the number of newly dead. And he remembered the earnestness which hid the sadism of their guards — the earnestness which required each prisoner to believe that the cruelty, the madness of it, was actually a higher order of goodness, and that the prisoners were the mad ones for not seeing this.

Angrily, he brushed the tears away. Emotion was still not dead in him. How many more lifetimes must he endure until he could burn it all away and escape into bliss?

He sighed, slipped the papers between two pieces of cardboard and hid them under his mattress. He lifted his jacket from the spyhole. It must have been more than five years ago that he'd discovered the spyhole. He had no idea if it was still used. But the habit of caution had become ingrained.

He lay on his bed and, as so often happened, imagined a life where the Master had been enthroned and he had stepped down to resume his simpler duties as Master of Studies. He thought of the library as he had last seen it, embedded in the deep silence of the centuries, all its wonders and its texts there to be explored. He saw the young Master standing in it, saying goodbye to the life to which so many incarnations of his had led.

Then the boy turned and looked at him with his burning man's eyes, and he knew why that life could never have been.

Instead of becoming a bridge across the river of knowledge, the monastery had become a dam holding the waters back. And he, the Abbot, had known where the key to unlock what was wrong lay. He knew, and he refused to look. And so error flourished unchecked. The monastery had become self-sufficient and self-serving. In the end it was all Yang and no Yin.

The other meaning which had accrued to the word

'Yin', the meaning which he had forgotten as he walked by the river, was 'the female'.

His mind jumped back to the question he had asked after he had recently dreamt of the Master. The question, and the *Book of Changes*' reply.

Hexagram 54. The Marrying Maiden.

Thunder over the lake:
The image of the Marrying Maiden.
Thus the superior man
Understands the transitory
In the light of the eternity of the end.

And the commentary?

Every relationship between individuals bears within it the danger that wrong turns may be taken, leading to endless misunderstandings and disagreements. Therefore it is necessary constantly to remain mindful of the end. If we permit ourselves to drift along, we come together and are parted again as the day may determine. If on the other hand a man fixes his mind on an end that endures, he will succeed in avoiding the reefs that confront the closer relationship of people.

A curious hexagram, with its suggestion that knowledge rested upon human relationships — particularly for a celibate monk, raised all his life with men.

Perhaps the one thing which had turned the monastery from a bridge into a dam had been its turning away from the feminine? Instead of sexual intercourse with real women they had turned to cerebral intercourse with the Tara.

He smiled and rolled over. Sleep was coming. It surprised him to feel his old, forgotten sexuality stirring. That *Chakra* — that focal point of the great snake Kundalini as it rose from his feet to explode out of the crown of his head and reveal to him the world beyond this world — had been passed a long time ago. He let his mind linger on the image of the young, beautiful Tara in Her many-colored silk robes, with Her globular breasts. He felt a rising sense of anticipation, and he fell asleep wondering what the morning would bring.

CHAPTER EIGHTEEN

'This is where it began,' Joe said uncertainly.

Julia looked at his wondering face. Something had opened him up and plunged him into his inner darkness. His movements had become slow and uncertain, as if he had aged. And yet he also had the raw fear of a child about him. She took his hand, but he did not respond. She looked at the broad river, jungle against the far bank, and strangely shaped hills in the far distance.

They stood on the side of the road at Chiang Saen, with a guest-house and kind of diner behind them. The road was dusty and empty. Chickens squawked in the hot, empty midday silence.

She suddenly remembered the moment in her storeroom. The moment when she dropped the head-dress over her face and was transported into some other world. She imagined she could hear the rhythmic thumping of the drum.

'The old man came out of the restaurant and saw me, walked up and handed me the ... the objects,' he said, as if recounting a dream.

'And you didn't know him?'

'I think I did know him. But I think his face had altered. It was screwed up around his left eye. He was squinting. He had aged. I think I knew him.'

'Who was he?'

'My servant.' He hesitated, then said the man's name. 'Tendzin.'

'Joe Tobias's servant?'

He nodded, feeling the resonance of the name bring up memories.

'It's horribly hot,' she said. 'Can't we go in?'

He nodded again and turned to the guest-house. She followed his slumped shoulders up the steps.

Dave Watson put down the binoculars and rubbed a bead of sweat from the bridge of his nose. He turned his back on the view of the road and the guest-house, leaned against the wall and let all his breath out in a long sigh.

It was him, all right. Joe Tobias.

And it was her with him.

He smiled. If Joe had got out of the car by himself, Dave might not have picked up the glasses. He'd have just assumed it was some government official poking his nose in where it wasn't wanted. But the shapely blonde and her honeyed bare legs had reawakened Dave's prurient interest as he sat musing in his old house by the river.

Those legs. That chest. The silken hair. His lust became confused with the rage that the man with her engendered. He stroked the butt of the pistol he'd bought. Maybe he could satisfy both desires yet.

He remembered the sickening weight of a dead baby. He slid to the floor and began shaking. He put his head in his hands, but no tears came.

There was marginal relief from the heat inside the restaurant. Their rented car wasn't air-conditioned, and they had made the journey with all the windows down, preferring dust and smoke to stifling heat. She drove. They'd taken an old Toyota with vinyl seats, a column shift and a plastic steering-wheel which was soon slippery with her sweat. It changed ratios with a thump that spoke of major problems fast approaching in its transmission.

She thought how she had met John Chang and, with hardly a thought about it, surrendered her own life to unite herself with that closed enigma of a man. Now he had suddenly split apart to reveal something dark and primitive at his core. And with that split they had changed roles. He now relied on her to answer all the needs of his life. The hesitant terror he now displayed was like her own anxiety back in Los Angeles. And her calm competence was what had once been his. She felt uneasy at the rising strength within herself now that she no longer lived in his shadow, but he instead lived within hers.

'Are you hungry?' she asked him.

He looked at her uncertainly.

'You're going to have to order,' she said, firmly. 'I don't know the language.'

He blinked, and she watched some shred of the old

John Chang struggle up from the depths as a woman, her black hair in a lustrous bun, came smiling and nodding to them.

She glanced past him, through the open side screen of the building, to the verandah.

She found herself staring at Dave Watson. His ashen face stared back. And then, as she watched, his two hands came up together. There was a pistol held rock-solid in them and it was aimed at her.

For a moment, she froze. Then the barrel wavered fractionally and was pointing at her husband.

A voice was screaming. Hers. She threw herself across the table, slamming her arm against Joe.

They crashed to the floor, and she could hear the waitress taking up her scream.

'Run!' Julia yelled into her husband's dazed face. 'Come on! Run!'

From the corner of her eyes she caught the glimpse of movement as Dave crashed over the screen and into the restaurant. He fired two more shots quickly, and the waitress's scream cut off with a dreadful grunt.

The restaurant's owner was frozen in the kitchen doorway, watching his wife die. He had a cleaver in his hand. Julia dragged her husband past him, into the heat of the kitchen, where an untended wok was hissing and spitting over the flames of an ancient wood stove.

She pushed Joe to the door and followed him outside.

Where to go? And how to get there? The car was clearly the fastest, but Watson could get to it quicker than she.

But Watson and the restaurant owner were shouting at each other inside the building. She grabbed Joe's hand and dragged him past frightened chickens and a cat that arched its back and fled.

As she started the car Dave came stumbling down the steps, the pistol still locked in his hands. She found herself at the center of a violent explosion as the rear window blew out and the air was full of glass. She slammed her foot to the floor and the car spun dust and stones back into Watson's face, throwing him sideways, as the vehicle slid, then fishtailed as she corrected it, spinning the plastic steering wheel wildly.

The transmission thumped into drive and they lurched down the road in the direction they had come.

'I know him,' her husband said, with mild astonishment.

'You surprise me,' she said.

The dirt road was rutted and potholed and the steering had plenty of play in it. The wheel slipped back and forth between her hands, but the car kept on pointing down the road. They passed a bungalow overlooking the river and she suddenly remembered Howard's tale. She jerked her head at Joe.

'Do you know that place?'

He stared back after it. He turned around and put his head in his hands, and shook his head. But she knew he meant yes.

'It was Dave Watson's?' she asked him.

After a moment, he nodded.

Then suddenly the road ended and she was heading straight for the river.

'Shit!' she said, and hit the brakes. They slewed to a halt.

Out on the river a Laotian patrol boat thumped past, a hatchet-faced soldier staring at them from behind the machine-gun mounted on deck.

She tried to throw the transmission into reverse, but it jammed.

'What's the matter?' he asked her.

'Linkages are jammed,' she said.

She sat there, not knowing what to do, her mind refusing to focus on the reality of the situation. Instead, she thought about how sweaty her hair was, and how the heat made her fingers puff up.

Angrily, she realized she'd split a nail on the manic steering wheel. She stared at it, not knowing whether to cry or to curse. Instead she sighed, reached on to the back seat and found her cosmetic bag, and in it scissors and an emery board.

She trimmed the broken nail back and buffed it smooth. The patrol boat thumped on past, around a bend in the river, leaving them alone with the silence.

She studied her face in the mirror. She'd put on a little eye shadow and mascara before they'd left, and touched up her lipstick when they'd arrived. Her cheeks were beaded with sweat, and her color was high.

She turned the mirror and studied her husband's dazed face. She then shifted it so she could see back through the jagged hole in the rear window to the waiting, passive jungle.

She was calmer now, and her mind was beginning to work again. She realized that if it was Watson's house they'd passed, then he'd know the countryside very well. She wondered how long they had before he found them.

Fixing the car was probably just a matter of attacking the linkages with a blunt instrument. She smiled. Her husband's head, for example.

But she didn't want to have her head under the hood when Watson arrived. And even if she did sort the problem out, the only way back along this road would return them to him.

She remembered Watson's gentleness when they'd first met. Was there a vestige of it left, or had his vendetta totally consumed him? Should she abandon Joe to his richly deserved fate, and strike some bargain with Watson?

This time she turned and studied Joe openly. He looked over. They stared at each other. His face was haunted, frightened. She found herself smiling softly and patting his hand. She frowned. Where did this strange softness inside her come from?

'You went with him?' Joe asked her. 'You went to bed with him?'

She stared back, feeling the tears in her eyes. She nodded.

She saw the raw pain on his face. He closed his eyes and leant back in the seat.

'It was my fault, wasn't it?' he asked, softly.

'It was both of us,' she said. 'We were both dishonest. And now ... here we are.'

'I thought I could save myself through you. I thought that by having you I had somehow found ... Her.'

'Found who? What's wrong with me?'

He didn't hear the sharp second sentence. He only replied to the first.

'Found whoever it is inside that won't let me rest.'

'How long has this person been inside you?'

'There's been an aching emptiness there as long as I can remember. And an image of ... someone ... someone who can rid me of it.'

It was on the tip of her tongue to say 'You mean your mother', but she bit the words back. Californian psychology only went so far. It no longer explained her best friend's death, or the behavior of the man beside her. Or that of the man out there looking for them.

She hastily looked in the mirror again. Then she touched Joe firmly.

'Come on,' she said. 'He's out there looking for us while we sit here agonizing over things.'

'You went with him,' he repeated.

She opened the door, got out and looked back at him.

'I went with him because you weren't available. Now come on!'

He fumbled his way out as she removed their overnight bags from the rear seat.

The road they had followed had to have a purpose. It ended at the edge of the river, so its purpose had to do with the river. She walked to the bank and looked along it.

There was a small, rickety landing platform just up from them, with three blunt-prowed boats tied to it.

'Come on!' she called to him, pointing up the river.

Two of the boats had outboard-motor mounting

brackets on them, but the owners had wisely taken the motors home with them. The third, and oldest, had an old motor bolted inside underneath a loose sheet of iron protecting it from the weather. She pulled the iron off, laid it on the landing-stage, and climbed aboard. She opened the fuel tank and sniffed its contents. It was a gasoline engine. The tank was maybe half-full.

There was an empty jerry-can lying in the bows, and a length of hose. She smiled, wondering if the owner acquired his fuel in the same way as she was about to.

She brushed past Joe as he sat on the landing-stage.

'Put our stuff aboard,' she said, testily.

She siphoned the car's gas-tank and filled the boat's, then refilled the jerry-can with the remaining gas from the car, and fastened it in the bows with some of the loose rope that lay about.

Joe had seated himself in the stern. She glanced at him, saw he was OK, then studied the engine again. It was a four-cylinder Isuzu. A car engine that had been clumsily marinized.

She made herself think clearly and logically, using all the knowledge she could remember from her dad's workshop and applying it here, on the edge of the jungle river. There was no radiator, but the inlet and outlet hoses indicated it drew cooling water from the river. She wondered how the filters were. She rocked the flywheel back and forth, feeling the compression. It was OK. The sheet of iron had done its job and there was no obvious water damage.

There was a puddle of water lying in the bottom of

the boat. She found a bailer and thrust it into Joe's hands.

'Bail,' she said to him.

He looked at her uncomprehendingly.

'The water! Get rid of it!'

So this is what it's like to have a small child, she thought, turning back to the motor.

She suddenly realized that it had no battery.

'Fuck it!' she said, and sensed Joe glance up quickly.

She smiled reassuringly at him and went to get the battery out of the car.

The Toyota had a small tool kit tucked in next to the spare. She took it, and took the jack and wheel-brace, too, trying to think ahead, to anticipate trouble and be there with a solution before it occurred. Or maybe she was just trying to avoid thinking about Dave Watson and what he wanted to do.

She broke a second nail getting the battery out of the Toyota. She got dirt under the others. She was hot and sweaty and exhausted by the time she was finished.

She made herself stay patient. She checked the carburetor for fuel-flow, and only then did she press the big, black starter button.

Nothing happened. Not a thing.

'Shit!' she screamed into the silence.

Then she heard the distant sound of a vehicle on the track.

She looked at the inert motor.

Think! she told herself. *Think! Nothing happened. Not a whisper. So there's no current getting through anywhere. There's a short or a break in the line.*

'You idiot,' she muttered aloud.

She reached behind the plywood panel on which the ignition switch, starter button, and choke had been screwed, along with an oil-pressure and temperature gauge.

She found the ignition wires and twisted them together.

The electric shock made her gasp and let go. But she knew she had current now. Her thumb and forefinger were blistered and she dipped them in the river to relieve the pain. Then she pulled the choke half out and pressed the starter.

The motor coughed and wheezed. She imagined she could hear a vehicle very close.

'Come on!' she said. 'Come on, you bitch!'

She could see the agony on her father's face as he tried to coax life out of dead metal.

The motor caught. A great puff of blue smoke ejected beside Joe. She eased the choke in, and the motor settled into a lumpy rumble.

She cast off the bow line, reached past Joe and untied the stern rope. The boat drifted out into the river, the current dragging it back down towards Watson's house.

She revved the motor, but nothing happened.

'Idiot!' she said, for the second time.

She grabbed the steel rod that stuck out from the back of the engine and pulled it towards her.

There was a clunk, and she felt the propeller bite. They stopped drifting and began to move upstream.

The sun flashed on a windshield and she glanced back in time to see Dave Watson getting out of a car.

She opened the throttle and stuck the tiller under Joe's arm. He grasped it uncertainly, then began to comprehend what was going on.

She looked back at Watson on the landing-platform, both hands outstretched, the weapon held rigid. She nudged the tiller so they headed for the farther bank. Watson lowered the gun and looked at the two boats tied to the shore.

She adjusted the tiller so they headed upstream, into the current. She smiled at the perplexed-looking man in the boat with her.

'Just keep us heading upstream,' she said. 'Because that's where we're going.'

As Dave Watson watched the boat disappear around a bend in the river, his vision began to clear. He was suddenly aware how blurred it had been, and how much he trembled. The images of the guest-house replayed in his mind. He tried to brush them away, but he kept seeing the look of surprise on the Laotian woman's face as she folded up around the bullet, like a boxer caught unawares. He kept seeing her crashing to the floor: dead.

He wiped his brow and shook his head. The police would be after him soon. He walked back to the car and dropped the gun on the seat. He shouldn't have bought it, he thought. He should have used a knife, or his bare hands. He had descended to Joe's level now, and there was no going back from it, not until Joe was dead. Joe was obviously running for his old killing fields in the Golden Triangle. He must still have agents up there over whom he had some control. Dave figured he had to get Joe before he left the river. Before the Burmese border. Where could he get an outboard in a hurry?

CHAPTER NINETEEN

Now the sun was dropping over the west bank of the river and the long shadows were coming out to meet the boat as it headed towards the night. Joe liked the welcome vibrations of the motor in front of him, and the feel of the tiller's bite along his arm.

He felt warm and glad that Julia was with him, even though he knew of her infidelity. She was tarnished, but still a goddess, maybe more human now. And she had lain with him and in so doing had transformed his whole life.

But what was that life? Joe wondered. It seemed as insubstantial as the play of dying light on the river's surface. A pattern of mirages and myths, memories and reflections; dreams that he woke from screaming, to then wonder if maybe they had been reality and this that he had woken into was the real dream.

The movement of the boat had a reality about it which suggested he had been in such a boat before, on this river, or one like it.

Julia glanced up from watching the motor's gauges,

and looked directly at him and smiled. The smile was so genuine, so full of love, that tears sprang to his eyes as he smiled back. Then he blinked and looked away.

He couldn't have been evil if he could love like this, or could engender such love. Love prevented you from doing whatever it was that Joe Tobias had done.

He glanced at his arm. The entity's arm. The vehicle for his consciousness. But the consciousness was now different, and wanted nothing to do with whatever consciousness had inhabited it before.

He suddenly saw a sampan on the river and cried out and pointed.

She glanced where he pointed then stared back at him. To her the river was empty.

But it couldn't be. It swarmed with rainy season sampans, laden with rice. He cried out and pointed again, and saw a warning look on her face. He retreated into himself, watching the boats bearing down on them, afraid now to draw attention to the ghost fleet that they were sailing among.

She watched him and frowned, seeing how he shivered and drew back, his anxious eyes obviously focusing on things all around him that she could not see. His lips moved, whispering words she could not hear. She remembered an old, alcoholic actor she had known, and his fits of delirium. This was the world the man she had married now inhabited.

She looked ahead, sensing a change in the current. It was bucking against their side and she could see a change in the water's color. A different stream, from an as yet unseen tributary, was discoloring the river, and confusing the current.

For the first time she thought about borders, border guards, police. They would have to stop soon. They could not go on. But stopping meant exposing themselves to Watson. And there was always the risk of a patrol boat.

She leant against the tiller and guided them towards the far, Laotian bank. At least they could reduce the risk factor by eliminating the chance of Watson finding them.

The last of the sunlight caught Joe's face as they bucked across the current towards the eastern bank. He cried out and shut his eyes. But the sampans kept coming, surrounded now by golden light. And each sampan had a woman in its prow, standing there bare-breasted, with a baby clutched at the breast.

Then, together, all staring at him with their huge, wounded eyes, they released the naked babies.

Joe cried out again, gripping the gunwale and knocking the tiller sideways, so that the boat slewed across the chop, and Julia had to grab the tiller and knock them back on course.

All the babies except one fell into the river and the river consumed them, swallowed them whole, without a trace showing on the mottled gold and copper surface. The one remaining child flew upwards and all the women looked up after it as their rice-heavy sampans glided on. As it rose it caught the sunlight and glowed, released from its earthly bonds.

Joe fell on to his knees, lurching the boat again. Julia cut the throttle back, so they had just enough motion for headway. Tears streamed down her husband's face as he stared blindly into the heavens, his eyes wide open.

'I'm sorry,' he whispered. 'Forgive me. Please, forgive me. I didn't know what I was doing. Oh, forgive me, please!'

Julia had to concentrate on the bank looming towards them. Trees grew down to the waterline, their heavy branches arching out like fleshy arms over the gentler flow away from the tumult in the river's center. She threw the motor out of gear, scrambled forward and grabbed a branch, and the boat slewed around. With one hand she snatched up the bow line and wrapped it around the branch. They came to a halt, then began to swing back until they lay alongside the bank, with the water chuckling past them.

She tied a laborious knot and then made her way aft. She knelt down beside her husband and looked into his eyes.

At first they were vacant and far away, with pain in them. But then consciousness began to return and his eyes came to focus slowly upon her.

'Joe?' she whispered. 'Joe? You all right?'

He blinked and nodded vacantly.

'I've tied up against the Laotian bank, to keep away from Watson. But a border patrol could come by any time now. Do you know where to go from here?'

The light was fading and he was rapidly becoming just a dim shape in the stern of the boat. She saw him turn his head, looking out at the river. When he spoke, his voice was a haunted whisper.

'Go back,' he said. 'Don't go on. Too dangerous.'

'More dangerous than Watson and his gun?'

'More dangerous,' came the whispered reply from the shrouded shape.

She was unused to the way tropical night came down so suddenly, with no twilight, no preamble. The river was now black. The branch to which they were tied was losing its shape. Joe was just a voice.

Then she heard, from down river, the unmistakable sound of an outboard motor revving loudly as it was pulled into life.

She reached up and felt for their mooring line.

Joe realized what she was doing, and cried out.

'No!' he said. 'Don't. Not up there, please!'

'Sorry, Joe,' she said, uncoiling the line.

The current flicked the bow out of the overhanging branches. She pressed the starter button and the motor kicked over. She listened and heard the outboard heading up river.

Their own motor revved more slowly. She hoped its sound would not travel to Watson.

Joe moaned as she pressed the tiller against him, feeling her way out into mid-stream, back into the bucking current.

Dave heard the distant throb of the inboard, and smiled. He knew these waters as well as Tobias did. Hell, hadn't they met up along these banks to discuss their proposed deal?

He remembered the dark, unreadable eyes in the ascetic face. There had been a shiver of recognition in him when they met, as if they knew each other at some deep and terrible level, a level hidden from daily consciousness. Was it a precognition of how their lives would lock together? How the image of Joe Tobias would come to dominate his every thought for so many years to come?

The inboard was keeping to the Laotian bank. Dave figured Joe wanted to keep away from the Burmese, who were steamed up against the Karen people, and who would probably shoot at anything that moved in the night. Or the day, for that matter.

Dave was worried that the inboard would carry better than his short-shaft outboard through the chop of the current. He opened the throttle out full, but the boat's speed didn't seem to change. He mentally cursed the unwieldy hull, and slacked the motor back to save fuel. He had no idea how long this would take.

She heard the motor in the blackness behind them surge louder and then cut back and she guessed the reason. Watson had made some ground, but obviously felt that he wasn't going to catch them. She relaxed enough to stop worrying about him and peer ahead, trying to somehow guess what might lie ahead of them.

But the river was pitch black. There was no distinguishing water from air, or from land. There was no moon. No stars. No lights on the bank. Just the buffeting of the chop indicated the river beneath the boat. Without that she might have slipped into madness, with no reference point at all for reality. The slap of the waves seemed to shiver right through her, setting up a second rhythm above that of the motor's vibrations.

For a moment she thought she was in her dad's big Pontiac when it was running rough. She could almost hear him muttering to himself. 'Change the plugs, change the plugs.' She could almost hear her mother's seemingly ceaseless whine. 'Why don't we get a new car, Ray? Why do you carry on with these old heaps?' 'This ain't no old heap, this is a classic. Just needs a new set of plugs. Why we have to put up with your god-awful sister, I don't know.' 'There's nothing wrong with her! What have you got against my family? At least they weren't grease monkeys.' 'Jesus, Sylvia. Lay off, will you. Hey, Julia, you OK, honey? You're mighty quiet back there.'

Julia shivered. *Why am I crying? What's the matter? What's the secret? What's the secret?*

'She's allowed to be quiet, you big log.' 'I tell you, that brother-in-law of yours gives me the creeps, and that's a fact.' 'You got something against him, Ray, you say it. You got something against him?' 'I got nothing against him. He's a great guy. Except he drives a Volkswagen. What kind of man drives a Volkswagen?'

Why am I shivering? Why am I crying. What's the big secret? What's the big secret?

Dave guided his boat across the chop, even though it was taking him away from the sound of the other boat. He wanted to get into clear water. He was thinking that if they both made enough noise then the Burmese, or maybe a Laotian patrol boat, would hear them coming and turn on their searchlights. The lights would pick out the first boat, and then some trigger-happy trooper would let fly with his M-16, and that would be the end of the Quest.

Or would it? Could he live without personally sending Joe to the beyond? Could he live after Joe had already cheated death? If it were to happen, he would have to scour the river until he found the corpse.

He found himself thinking strange thoughts. He found himself thinking that the best thing for the good of everyone would be the death of the Master. Now why did he think that? He seemed to hear murmured voices — they must have been in the water's movements — voices muttering in corners, suddenly ceasing as he walked by, or as the Master walked by.

What Master? What the fuck was happening?

He shook his head. His heart had given a strange lurch, as if discovering that it had suddenly stopped beating, and now resumed at double speed.

What fucking Master?

Joe was glad that the baby had gone up into the sky. For a Christian that meant heaven. For a Buddhist it meant, what? The Buddhists believed in many worlds all intersecting this one. Just like this world was made of a million different moments, and each moment was a tiny world in itself.

It was a terrible thing that the entity which had previously inhabited this body had done. That entity could not have been him. Could it?

He remembered the bespectacled face of a monk in Bangkok. A man who seemed to look through the face of John Chang, into the face of Joe Tobias. Had he seen through that face into the next one down? It was like an onion, this face. Layer after layer peeling on down and down towards some unknowable core.

He stared into the layers, to see the face of a small boy, a boy whom he now recognized as himself, years ago, living a life of which Joe Tobias had relentlessly tried to destroy every trace of memory. A small boy growing up alone, lonely, frightened, in a huge, cold, stone building peopled with Buddhist monks who treated him with an uneasy deference, as if he contained something special — but something which frightened them, too.

A small boy whose only comfort was a jade statuette of a goddess.

CHAPTER TWENTY

1959. Ghenko Monastery, Tibet

The sound of engines jerked the nine-year-old boy out of a frightening dream. A dream pounding with the roar of powerful engines. Instinctively he clutched for Her, found Her, and stroked Her smooth, jade flesh. She had been in the dream, too. His penis was hard.

'Tara,' he whispered. 'Tara. Tara.'

Being a statuette, She said nothing, but he could feel Her lovely presence; the feminine aspect of Enlightenment.

He thought to call out for his servant, but lately Tendzin had not answered his cries in the night. Either his servant was sleeping heavily, or had decided that it was time the boy gave up the ways of childhood. Perhaps the servant thought that by not coming the boy would learn virtue and right behavior.

This time, though, aware of light beginning to fill the ornately curtained corners of the room, he began to wonder if, perhaps, the reason the servant did not reply was because the servant was not there. Lately he had noted a certain tension between Tendzin and the Abbot. Tendzin had a very cryptic way of muttering asides when the Abbot spoke about the necessity of not resisting the Chinese.

The boy's face was cold, and he snuggled back down into the covers. But he didn't close his eyes. His dreams were too frightening. His penis was too hard. He didn't know what to do with it. And the rising sound of trucks intrigued him.

Tendzin had given him a toy truck and he kept it under his pillow. He found it now and, keeping one hand on the Tara, he fondled the truck with the other. From the highest tower of the monastery — next to his sleeping-room — he could see the forest road and the logging trucks going by. They excited him, even though he knew they filled the Abbot with sadness, and Tendzin with anger.

Then there was a sudden crash! A rending sound of tearing metal. He sat bolt upright, clutching both the Tara and the truck to his chest. The sound changed, but continued. A sound now of something crashing and bumping down the side of a ravine. Squealing metal. Another crash. And then he heard the distinct popping of rifle-fire.

Down in the courtyard he heard the Chinese garrison coming to life as the guards shouted urgently. He heard their high-pitched, excited voices. He could hear horses snorting as troops tried to rouse them. The whole monastery was waking up.

The shooting had died down. There were occasional, sporadic shots. He strained his ears and wondered if he could hear voices. He heard the squeal of the centuries-old gates swinging open, and the clatter of horses' hooves heading for the bridge that would take them across the river and on to the logging road. Then, with a devastating boom that punched him in the ears with its shock-waves, something exploded. He cried out in fear, and with relief discovered that someone had come to his aid.

It was the Abbot.

'Where's Tendzin?' the Abbot asked, glancing around.

'I called, but he didn't come. Is he all right? What's happening, Rinpoche?' He was relieved to find his penis had subsided.

'I'm sure he's all right,' the Abbot said. 'He'll be here in a moment, with a good excuse.'

'But what was that bang?'

'Somebody blew up the bridge,' the Abbot said, 'and so prevented the garrison riding to aid whatever trucks have been attacked in the mountains'.

'Who would have done that?'

'Somebody who thought long and hard about what he was doing. But didn't think at all about the consequences.'

Before the boy could follow up that remark there were other people in the room, carrying torches. They were other monastery officials. The Bursar was there. The Chief of the Monastic Guard was there. And there were Chinese, too — the captain of the garrison, with his uniform hastily buttoned and disorientation in his eyes. His pistol holster was unfastened, and the polished wooden butt could be seen. The boy stared at it.

'What's happening?' the Abbot asked.

'I thought you could tell me that,' the captain said. 'You are in charge, aren't you?'

'In charge of the monastery, yes. Not in charge of the mountains and the river.'

'You're in charge of the hearts and minds of the peasants. You can incite them to violence.'

'I speak only of non-violence, and you know that. It is my passionate belief.'

'Are all your monks accounted for?'

The boy felt a sudden tightening of the Abbot's grip. He was a man who, by his position, was committed to always speaking the truth. He hesitated a moment.

'I believe I can account for all the monks, yes,' he said.

But Tendzin is not a monk, the boy thought.

This was how an honest man lied. Indirectly. By omission.

'It is on your head if there are any missing.'

'I will call them all together, if you like.'

'Thank you. I will await you in the courtyard.'

The captain was almost at the door. He glanced back.

'Oh, and account for all your cooks, servants, and hangers-on, too,' he said, and went out.

The Bursar looked at the Abbot.

'What shall we do?' he asked, in fear.

'You heard me. Get everyone into the courtyard.'

'But what if someone is missing?'

'Why would that be so? Are we not all sworn to non-violence?'

The Bursar, an old, fat man, stared at the young and slender Abbot.

'Non-violence is the only way of avoiding bad consequences,' the Abbot said. 'Isn't it? It alone will not provoke men into violence which they do not understand. Men need very little provocation to discover those bad things inside them. And a monk must ensure that the discovery is not made. He must lead by example.'

The Bursar was looking guiltily at the floor.

'So. No one will be missing,' the Abbot said. 'Because I have given my word on it. And so, if the impossible were to happen, and someone were unable to be found — perhaps they had gone to the outhouse and got lost on their way back — then I, and only I, will receive the punishment. Is that clear?'

The Bursar looked up and, frightened, nodded.

'Make sure everyone knows that. There is always unpaid karma in our lives. It may be that I have the chance to redeem some of it. But I want no one else to respond. No one. Understand?'

'Yes, Rinpoche.'

'Tendzin is the sort of man who gets lost going to the outhouse. Find him before the Chinese are properly awake.'

'Yes, Rinpoche.'

The Abbot released the boy gently.

'Come,' he said. 'Dress yourself. We must help the Chinese in their head-count.'

He went to the window and looked out in the direction from which the sounds had come. The rising sun struck him in the face, shafting gold all around him. To the boy it was as if he was being blessed. He smiled back at the boy.

'We must help them, but we must help them slowly, very slowly.'

The Abbot helped the boy dress, not in his everyday clothes but in the red and gold ceremonial robe. The boy was surprised and looked to the Abbot for an explanation, but the Abbot's face was set and far away.

'I had a bad dream,' the boy said, to call attention to himself.

The Abbot glanced at him.

'I dreamed I was in a strange place where there was ...' he hesitated. 'It was like a lake, but a lake that went on forever. I was standing on the side of the lake, on a sort of bridge, but it wasn't a bridge. There was a building floating on the water, but it was made out of iron. Then I was in the water. I dived down and I went deeper and deeper, and as I went deeper there were all sorts of monsters. Then I held something in my hands. It was a parcel, but I wasn't allowed to open it. I knew it was full of bad things, but I wanted to open it. I wanted so much to open it!'

He had the Abbot's full attention now.

'And then?'

He hesitated. Tara's hands still caressed him, disturbingly. He edited Her out of the dream.

'I woke up and I heard the trucks, and it was like the sound of their engines had been in my dream, too. Like I was in a place where there were many engines.'

'It's called the future,' the Abbot said, gently, settling the tall cap on the boy's head. 'It will be full of engines.'

He stepped back to study the young monk, the reincarnation of the Master who had established this monastery, and whose tenth reincarnation had died fifteen years earlier. For seven years the monastery had remained leaderless. The Dalai Lama had directed that he, Gyalwa Mukpo, Master of Studies at the monastery, should assume the role of Regent Abbot until such time as the Supreme Abbot's reincarnation was discovered.

The monastery continued without a head until one night the Bursar had dreamt of a circle of tents on an arid, icy plateau. A baby lay at the center of the circle, laughing and playing with its toes, even though snow fell all about. The baby looked at the Bursar and the Bursar looked at the baby, and they knew each other.

Now the baby stood before him, a boy, and locked within him was all the wisdom of those succeeding incarnations.

The Abbot sighed and removed the head-dress. The boy looked puzzled.

'What is it, Rinchope?'

'Take off the robe.'

Puzzled, the boy hesitated, but the look on the Abbot's face made him obey.

'Give it to me and put on the clothes the Chinese gave you.'

'Why?'

'Do it!'

He had never seen the Abbot angry like this. He hurriedly obeyed, watching the Abbot carefully return the robe and the head-dress to the inlaid box in which they resided.

The Abbot's reverie was interrupted by a pair of Chinese soldiers pushing open the door.

'Come,' one of them said, in halting Tibetan. 'You are wanted now.'

They were only young, and they spoke roughly to hide their uncertainty.

The Abbot looked at them and nodded. He reached out, took the boy by the shoulder and, escorted by the soldiers, they left the room.

'The servant?' the soldier asked. 'Where is he?'

'Coming,' the Abbot said. 'He had to visit the outhouse.'

The boy had been told that he had known this monastery for many lifetimes. Until now he had not properly felt it. But the dream had plunged him into dreadful feelings of being lost and adrift through space and time, and it seemed highly possible that the person walking down the dark and cold stone corridor could have done so many times before.

They walked down the slate steps, and he suddenly felt how the feet which had worn them away over the centuries were his own feet. He shivered and the Abbot felt the tremor pass through him.

'It will happen as it must,' the Abbot said.

The Abbot was very careful to keep his voice neutral. Last night he had consulted the oracle and it had told him:

If you are sincere,
You have light and success.
Perseverance brings good fortune.
It furthers one to cross the great water.

But it added:

Waiting in blood.
Get out of the pit.

The image of the pit, and of blood, was very vivid. He feared it.

The boy stopped at the bottom of the stairs, beside two dark, wooden doors carved with dragons. He looked inquiringly to the Abbot.

'You want to visit the library?' his Abbot asked.

The boy nodded.

The Abbot glanced at the two soldiers.

'A moment,' he said. 'The boy needs something from the library.'

The soldiers glanced at each other uncertainly. The Abbot seized the initiative, and threw open the doors.

Butter lamps always burned in the library, and its tall, slit windows caught as much daylight as possible. The four of them stood, looking in at the cubicles and the pigeon-holes of stacked, rectangular manuscripts, the gold-leafed *tangka*, and the gold-leafed statues whose gilt surfaces had turned black from centuries of candles and incense sticks wafting smoke across them. They gazed at the slat-like ancient wooden books and the modern books in German and English.

The boy walked two steps into the room and looked about. The Abbot knew he was saying goodbye.

The boy's eyes swept the room, fastening at last on the tapestries that depicted his previous incarnations in meditation pose.

'Come on,' a soldier grunted. 'It's us in the shit if we're any later.'

The Abbot sighed.

'Come on,' he said. 'Time to dream later.'

The boy turned and looked at him and the Abbot felt a sudden, dreadful chill.

The boy's eyes were blank and dark and totally unreadable.

'I'm coming,' he said in a deep, dark, adult voice.

The boy and the Abbot emerged together in the monastery courtyard. The boy had grown accustomed to the Chinese garrison which had arrived, one day, and simply taken up residence. His eyes quickly found the captain in charge of the garrison. He often had given the boy favors, had talked with him and indulged in occasional play — though always, the boy had noted, with some underlying, unexpressed, meaning to whatever he did. As if the captain were conscious of the necessity to teach the boy something about why the garrison was there. But the boy had welcomed the attention as a diversion from the harshness of monastic life.

But when he found the captain's face this time, he felt his heart grow chill. The captain was very angry, and there was a deep coldness to his eyes. And why were the poor villagers assembled between the garrison soldiers and the bewildered, frightened monks? These people, dressed in rags, had no idea of what was happening — of explosions and troops and the airplanes which appeared from nowhere and disappeared into nowhere. They were peasants who were now finding that their fields, woods, and forests had been invaded by smiling Chinese soldiers with trucks and axes. Smiling that same cold smile as the captain smiled.

'We're here, captain,' said the Abbot.

The captain said nothing. He studied the boy's face. The boy kept his face set. Looking at it made the captain grow thoughtful.

The captain's political officers had done as much as anyone could to dismiss the superstitions of the people, to turn exotic legends around so that the monks became the enemy in the people's minds. Reincarnation was the corner-stone of their theory of the world. It was the rock upon which the whole edifice of Tibetan Buddhism, and its repugnantly feudal system of lifetime serfdom, rested.

Until now he had simply sneered it off. There was no scientific basis for such a belief. But politically you could see how it benefited the priests — and how they strove to maintain the belief in it, and so maintain their power.

He'd at first felt sorry for the boy, caught up in a battle that was patently not of his making. He knew the boy's background probably better than the boy did himself. There were things he planned to tell the boy which would surely change forever the way he thought about the Abbot and the other monks. Captors pretending to be benefactors.

But now, looking into those darkly anguished eyes, eyes like those of a man who has suffered much and seen more, he lost his certitude. A boy should not have such eyes.

Bad dreams began to re-awaken in the captain. The sense which he'd had right from the start, that this was a place of real evil, began to return.

He looked up from the courtyard to the slit windows high above him. The blank walls of the monastery were as featureless as the walls of a concrete dam. They were a tribute to slave labor. Until they were smashed the memory of the old system would not be eradicated.

He looked down at the ancient cobblestones upon which they stood. Symbolically it would have been best to commence the punishment here, in the heart of the monastery. But logistics dictated against it. Just outside the walls was a cellar, hand-hewn into the rock and covered with cedar beams. It was the obvious place to do what was necessary.

He glanced back, his eyes again resting on the old, fat Bursar. Then he looked again at the Abbot, and smiled. He would begin the symbolic action here.

'Have your people remove all their clothes,' he said.

The Abbot stared at him.

'I beg your pardon?'

'I am searching for saboteurs, for hidden weapons and explosives. Have everyone — except yourself and the boy, of course — remove their clothes.'

All eyes were on him. He spoke fluent Tibetan. They all had heard what he said. The old Bursar had turned quite pale.

'I can't allow that,' the Abbot said.

The captain lifted his pistol from its holster, and all eyes followed the movement. He walked over to the Bursar, who was shivering with terror. He placed the pistol's barrel against the shaking head.

He screwed up his nose, smelling the ejecting urine. He pulled the trigger.

As he re-holstered the pistol, they were stripping off.

He jerked his head to two of the soldiers, and they came and secured the Abbot and the boy. The boy the monks called 'the Master'.

Once the monks were naked he ordered his troops to herd them out through the monastery gates, into the stone-walled cellar. Then he had the villagers follow them out. He kept the Abbot and the boy back until he judged the time was right.

The boy kept staring at the lifeless body of the Bursar, one of his friends in the hierarchy of the monastery. The Bursar lay motionless. The boy watched the blood trickling from his head.

He looked upwards, aware now of the murmur of sound outside the gates. There were the high-pitched shouts of the Chinese and the uneasy muttering of the villagers. There was also a dreadful, muffled wailing.

The captain gestured to the soldier holding him, and the boy squirmed, trying to break free, but he couldn't. He and the Abbot were dragged to the gate and pulled towards the old cellar.

The villagers were crouching on the cedar beams across the cellar. The troops were shouting at them, gesturing with fixed bayonets, prodding men, women and children alike into loosening their robes.

The prodded bayonets began to have their effect. The boy saw a yellow jet of piss arc out in the morning sun. A woman groaned, unable to hold herself any longer, and evacuated her bowels down into the cellar.

The wailing rose higher, and the boy realized where the monks were.

Expressionlessly, the captain stepped to the edge of the pit.

He turned back to the Abbot and gestured for him to be brought forward.

The boy watched the struggle on the Abbot's face as the captain indicated for him to step up. The captain pointed significantly to the Abbot's groin. The Abbot shook his head.

The captain's face did not change. He turned and pointed at the boy. Again the boy saw how lifeless the captain's eyes had become. The captain glanced back inquiringly at the Abbot.

The Abbot lifted his robes and jetted down through the cedar grating, down on to the huddled backs of his naked, moaning monks.

The soldiers were beginning to relax now, to smile a little. One of them moved to open his trousers. The captain roared at him and he drew back in fear.

The boy understood. The humiliation must not come from the Chinese.

Four soldiers now led a horse to the edge of the pit. They turned it and patiently backed it up, stroking its flanks to soothe it.

The captain smiled and turned to the boy. The boy again tried to break away, but the captain put his arm on the boy's shoulder, and turned him away from what was happening, all the while taiking earnestly to him.

The boy listened to the voice beside him, speaking at almost a whisper. His mind was whirling. He could not understand why he felt such a fascination with what was happening all around him. The soldiers. The shock of the pistol and the Bursar's face erupting.

It was as if he was seeing through it, seeing himself in the role of the Bursar, and in the role of the captain. He felt he could understand the captain, and so he found himself listening closely to what he was saying.

'Do you remember the horses out on the plains?' the voice was saying. 'Horses running like the wind. And riding those horses people who were wild and free like the wind. People riding all day without seeing a single tree, or a hill. Grass rippling before them, like they were riding in a huge lake. Oh, the feeling of it! Do you remember?'

The boy gave a tentative nod. Something had stirred, the ghost of a memory. And the ghost of a dream, of Tara, Her beautiful hair and Her globular breasts. He was hard again.

'Do you remember the beautiful young woman who rode with them? And tied across her breast, her infant son. Tied so his flesh was warm against her flesh. His mouth had only to pucker and her nipple was in his mouth. Do you remember?'

The boy did not nod. The captain glanced at him, saw the tears, and kept talking.

'And nights under the blazing stars, with the sound of the wind in the grass, and the horses shifting uneasily about the tents, and the fire blazing up at the stars. And the mother stroking her son's head as she laid him to rest, leaning forward to sing him a lullaby. Leaning forward to give him the breast he desired so much.

'And then they came. Remember? The foreigners? The monks?'

The boy's head jerked as if he had been hit. He stared at the captain's face, seeming to see it clearly for the first time since he had begun talking.

The captain stared back at him, his own truth, his own beliefs in his eyes.

I am doing this for all your people, those eyes said. *It hurts, but it must be done. They must be freed from the errors into which they have been led.*

'The monks. One had dreamed of a child in the snow, on the plains. There were other omens. A mare gave birth to a two-headed foal. Someone else dreamed of the plains. Dreams. Superstitions. They packed their bags and set out.

'They found the boy with his lovely mother, out in the open plains, out where the air was free and pure. They told her lies, so many lies. They promised her so many things. They stole him from her.

'They brought him here!'

He gestured up at the bleak walls of the monastery. Each slit window like a prison cell.

The captain let the boy drink in the bleak image. Let him see it as the captain had first seen it. A grim facade dominating the river valley, forcing down its terrifying bleakness on the lives of the villagers huddled at its base.

The captain turned him back to face the Abbot.

'This man ordered that the boy be captured and brought here. This man ordered that his mother be secretly killed.'

The boy gasped and looked at the captain, and then at the Abbot, who was too far away to have heard what was said.

'Yes. He sent out his Bursar and his troops, with orders to slay her, so they would not have to pay the compensation they had agreed on.'

He gestured to the two soldiers standing guard over the Abbot. One lifted his rifle and clubbed the Abbot in the spine. The Abbot gasped and fell forward. The captain led the boy up to stand looking down at the Abbot's gasping mouth.

'He did it. Now he must pay for it.'

The Abbot was whispering something. The boy could not understand it clearly.

The captain made a face, and kicked the Abbot's mouth. The boy stared up in astonishment. The captain smiled at him.

'Your turn,' he said. 'He had her killed to save his money.'

The boy shook his head, tears streaming down his face. There were half a dozen horses standing around the cellar now. The smell of horse dung was pungent in the morning air. Why was his penis so hard? Why was he shaking?

'If you don't kick him, she will not rest easy. Her ghost will remember you.'

The boy shut his eyes and gave a gentle kick. It was like kicking the football Tendzin had given him.

He kicked again, a little harder.

'Kick him hard!' the voice whispered.

He gritted his teeth, eyes closed, and swung with all his might.

Something snapped within him. He cried out. He kicked again. He lifted his foot and stamped it down.

But the kicks seemed to give the Abbot strength. He

half-lifted his head and now the boy could hear what he was saying, very clearly.

Homage to the Female Buddha exquisite with youth.
Radiant as the eternal snows in all their glory,
She sits on a white lotus and a silvery moon
Indicating fully developed compassion and knowledge.

'Kick!' screamed the captain.

He kicked, and the Abbot's face collapsed on to the ground, into his own blood. The boy cried out and kicked again.

And then there was a smashing sound above them and they all looked up. Something exploded against the monastery wall. Away across the river, on the logging road, there was a puff of smoke hanging in the air. A moment later there was the concussion of the shot.

'The gun!' the captain shouted.

His troops were already running.

The boy stepped backwards, realizing he had been forgotten. Then he saw, crouched against the edge of the monastery wall, the familiar figure of his servant. Tendzin. He cried out and ran for the outstretched arms.

'We're going to destroy those dogs turds yet,' the servant whispered in his fierce, growling voice — a voice which the boy had never heard be gentle, and yet now he could feel a strange gentleness beneath it, and feeling that gentleness realized he could trust his servant with his life.

But he did draw back when Tendzin thrust him into the bushes and he was suddenly confronted with a black hole in the foundations of the monastery. He looked back at his servant fearfully.

'Come on! We haven't time!'

He took a deep, shuddering breath, and stepped into the blackness.

CHAPTER TWENTY-ONE

The night was warm and Julia could feel that the motor was now running hot. Some debris must be jamming the cooling-water inlet pipe. There were no lights on the plywood dash. She stretched out her hand over the manifold, trying to tell how hot it was, how much longer she could keep going before she would have to pull into the bank and somehow grope around to find the inlet and free it.

It was hot, but not too hot. She held her hand there a moment longer.

'You whore. You bitch,' he was hissing. 'I seen you lookin' at my pecker. I seen you thinkin' about it. Here it is, little slut. Here it is. Hey? How'd you like that? Hey? Tell anyone and you're dead. Tell anyone and they'll lock you up and you'll never see your mom again. God, you're beautiful. God Almighty, how'd that stupid broad have one as beautiful as you? Oh, God forgive me. Oh, Jesus, I'm sorry ...'

She gasped, withdrew her hand and looked

around quickly. Where had that voice come from? Why was she shivering?

Then a light appeared suddenly out of the darkness to her left. It stabbed out, a giant's finger flicking across the sullen black surface of the river. A metallic loud-hailer voice rasped a message in a language she didn't understand.

She lunged at the tiller and pointed them towards the black bank somewhere ahead in the darkness. At the same time she cut the throttle back, not wanting to ram the bank at full speed.

'Fuck!' Dave Watson swore, seeing the light. He quickly used it to map his position, checking the banks. There was no sight, nor sound, of Joe's boat.

There wasn't much they could do. They had to either go on, or go back. The Burmese would have them if they went on. And he'd have them if they came back. He grinned, and eased his throttle back, more to cut the noise than to lose speed. He heard the loud-hailer give a burst of rapid-fire orders, presumably in Burmese. The orders were repeated in Laotian. Then in Thai.

Dave reflected that they could spend all night repeating the same order through every possible language and dialect you could encounter here where so many nations, tribes, and histories came together.

'Identify yourselves,' the loud-hailer said. 'Be prepared to show your papers and be searched.'

As Julia probed towards the distant river bank, the harsh orders echoing back from the unseen bank, she heard another boat engine start. She glanced back and saw a light beneath the stabbing arc of the searchlight.

The light was a torch in the hands of a soldier. Then the boat's own spotlight flicked on as the motor revved, and she realized a fast launch was cutting away from the garrisoned bank, and arcing around, under the searchlight's beam, to hunt her down.

She could feel the heat pouring off the Isuzu's manifold. She leaned down to look. The rising heat, and the first faint suggestion of a dull red glow from the tortured metal, suddenly snapped her mind back to the ugly image she kept trying to ignore — had, perhaps, spent all her life trying to ignore.

'You whore! You bitch!' he was hissing. 'I seen you lookin' at my pecker. I seen you thinkin' about it. Here it is, little slut. Here it is. Hey? How'd you like that? Hey? Tell anyone and you're dead. Tell anyone and they'll lock you up and you'll never see your mom again. God, you're beautiful. God Almighty, how'd that stupid broad have one as beautiful as you? Oh, God forgive me. Oh, Jesus, I'm sorry ...'

She jerked back in surprise from the glowing motor. The searchlight was now lighting the far bank, turning the black jungle a ghostly white. She spun around, for a moment thinking there was another person in the boat with them. But there was only the semi-comatose Joe hunched over the tiller, staring vacantly at nothing at all. But, then, just as her consciousness was opening up a huge hole in time, stripping away veils of illusion she had treasured over the years, so, she thought, Joe's mind might also be revealing equally confusing images from a past he had attempted to forget.

She gripped the plywood dash and tried to clear

her head. But the voice had been so real, so insistent, and it hit her with a dreadful sense of truth. Had she really been fleeing that voice all her life? That voice, and now the memory of her uncle's fingers, and the way she had cut herself off from all her emotions, the way she had became just an actress imitating the actions of others, these were the limits, the edges, to the life she had built herself.

'Go away!' she whispered. 'Please, go away! Go away!'

The fingers of light kept probing, searching, winkling. They made her think of other fingers probing.

I don't want this, she thought. *I didn't ask for it. I don't want it!*

Then she thought that it didn't matter because when the searchlight found her, she was going to die anyway.

'Fuck you all!' she screamed. She swung the tiller around. As the old boat pointed towards the oncoming launch, she opened the throttle right up, and dropped down on to the oily ribs of the boat.

The soldiers' light picked up the lumbering shape of the boat, but too late for them to react. She heard a startled shout as the light pinpointed them, and then the old boat slammed against the side of the launch as the helmsman tried to swing out of the way.

She heard two shouts of surprise, and two splashes, as the crew was knocked into the water. The old boat scraped along the side of the launch. She picked up the Toyota's wheel-brace, and leapt aboard.

The helmsman had been thrown across the cockpit by the shock of impact and was struggling to his feet.

She hit him across the face with the steel wheel-brace with all her force. He grunted and fell forward, blood pouring from his head.

She grabbed the wheel and swung it so the two boats still nuzzled each other, tracking together as they idled, the current beginning to twist them downstream. She went forward, on the launch's deck, found its mooring line and threw it to the hunched, staring shape of her husband, as he sat up in the stern of the old boat.

'Get aboard!' she yelled at him.

He took the mooring line and examined it thoughtfully.

'Joe! Get out of the boat!'

He looked at her questioningly. She grabbed the line and pulled it, jerking him towards her.

The action got through to him. Slowly, a man dreaming, he climbed aboard, and stood on the bows, looking at her.

'There's a man in the cockpit!' she snapped at him. 'Get him over the side. Come on! Move it!'

Dave heard the collision and a confusion of shouting. Obviously the troops had found the other boat. He was disappointed. Now he would not have them. But, then, as he motored slowly towards the blundering finger of the searchlight, he suddenly heard the launch rev up, and accelerate away, up river. The searchlight chased after it, as if surprised.

Dave kept heading towards where he'd heard the collision. He bumped against something in the water, put out his hand and found he was touching a man's head.

His first thought was that it had to be Joe. Then he felt the shirt-pockets and knew they belonged to an army uniform. And he realized that Joe had escaped him once again.

'Son of a bitch,' he said. He shook his head. The bastard was incredible. It was almost like he was super-human. As he had thought in the past he began to think now that Joe Tobias was some force from outside of time, a force sent down to mock him, to torment him for some crime that he had no recollection of ever committing.

Passing the guard-house on the far bank, he opened the throttle a little more. No one paid him any attention. He could hear a couple of vehicles heading up a riverside road, in search of the vanished motor-launch. He mentally wished them luck. This territory had been Joe's long before it was theirs.

But the only territory Joe now inhabited was the country bordered by the edges of his mind. He sat on a bunk in the cruiser's cabin, staring at his hands without seeing them, his mind lost completely to the blackness and the water outside the thin fiberglass hull.

He seemed to exist both within time and outside it. It was as if there was a thin shell that was Joe Tobias, in the reality of a boat on a river, but that thin shell contained echoes, or ghosts, or memories — traces of things which Joe Tobias could remember from other times, centuries before the time of sitting inside the boat.

He kept coming back to an image of a black tunnel, a cave, of hewn stone steps, and with it a feeling of great fear, a feeling which — all of this present life — had worked to keep him from looking into that tunnel.

But there was no longer any avoiding it. It was as if he was being pushed towards it. Eventually, come what may in the world outside, Joe Tobias would have to enter that tunnel.

He shivered and momentarily roused, looking up to orientate himself, hearing the motor's roar, and the sound of the hull slicing through the water. He could see a doorway, and out through that doorway the outline of the boat's cockpit. He remembered heaving a body over the side, hearing it splash into the water while all the time a searchlight carved into the blackness around them.

That's right! he told himself. *She's here with me. She's at the helm.*

He smiled and swung his legs on to the bunk and stretched out.

Then he found himself staring into the tunnel's mouth, and he knew he had to enter it.

He, who had been the murderous Joe Tobias, the saintly John Chang, and once a small boy trying to make sense of a terrifying world, could see that he had also been other people, at other times.

And yet all these people were one, all living out one destiny throughout time. He suddenly understood, right throughout his body and his mind, what the Buddhists meant by reincarnation, and by the wheel.

The tunnel delved into time, and into something solid and real. The boy monk took a step inside and felt the immense weight of the ancient monastery pressing down all around him. But the weight was also like the weight of all history banked up about him, all incarnation and reincarnation. He could hear water trickling nearby and the smooth rock at his fingertips was clammy and coated with furry moss.

Then he could hear a moaning sound. It reminded him of the moaning in the pit and he started with terror. That's when he remembered his guide, his servant, behind him.

'What is it?' he whispered.

'There's been a rock fall,' his guide said, his voice choked in the pressing blackness. 'The passage is constricted and the wind moans through it.'

As he advanced into that rising moan he began to feel a breeze plucking at his face, bristling the fuzz on his shaved head. There was an inkling of light in the far distance and his eyes gratefully fixed on it.

He gashed his knee on a rock and winced. He bit his lip, determined not to cry. He found himself clambering over the rubble, into the face of a howling banshee-like wind built up where fallen rock half-blocked the tunnel. The howling seemed to consume him. It took him back to the pit, to the contact of his foot with the Abbot's face, and then into something else.

He had been in this tunnel before. He had been in it as a man, in some other time, and as he advanced, so that reality, that memory, grew more solid, more real, until he could feel himself pushing back his robe from his shoulder, hitching up its skirts, knowing he was on his way to meet someone. He knew that the meeting must be kept secret, which was why it was down here, in the ancient tunnels beneath the monastery.

Then, in the blackness, a light. This other incarnation of his moved towards the light, until he could make out a face in front of him.

There was such happiness, such joy, on that face. Her eyes were bright and moist, her lips half-parted in a welcoming smile. He stumbled in his eagerness to be with her. He went down on his knees and embraced her in the dampness of the cave.

Then time seemed to telescope itself together, and suddenly there was a third person with them, and everything had changed. She was terror-stricken, and he was yelling with both anger and fear. She was somehow pinned to the floor, unable to move, and the third person loomed over them, plying something in his hands, something like an axe.

He flung himself at the third person, and then whatever it was that he swung came slamming down into the side of his head.

He fell into the blackness once again, dissolved out of that lifetime and into another, fell with rage and fear inside himself, and a sense of betrayal and loss. He raged against her, for he felt she had lured him into a trap, and then not come to his aid. He raged against the third person, someone he knew but could not recognize, a friend perhaps. He raged, and fell, and then he was a small boy once again. Once again in the tunnel with his servant, again terrified of whatever secrets the tunnel contained, as the servant urged him on to once again stand upon the spot where, in that previous lifetime, he had met his death.

The boy stood there, swaying, in the grip of a fear he could not understand, until he lost consciousness.

'Master? Master?'

His eyes opened slowly. He was lying in the shade of a spreading juniper, on the banks of a stream. A face looked down at him with concern. His servant's face. Seeing the movement of the eyes, the face registered relief, and then joy. Such a simple reaction that the boy — or the man within him — smiled, and took the servant's hand reassuringly.

'You fainted in there,' the servant said. 'I carried you through. There are many branching paths under that old building. If it wasn't so damp and cold and dark we could have stayed there.'

'What are we going to do?'

'There has been much shooting. We still have the mountain gun, and you and I will attempt to rejoin our troops when it gets dark. I want you to lie here and rest. I can get to the wrecked truck. I might be able to salvage a machine-gun.'

'Rinpoche? Is he ...?'

Tendzin's eyes started with tears. He brought his hands together, touching his forehead and his chin.

The boy cried out and tossed his head to deny it.

'No!' he said. 'No! It didn't happen! No!'

But he knew it had happened. He knew the world had suddenly got much bigger and much darker. So big and so dark he did not think he could live in it any more.

'Shhh. Be still. I must try and get back to my

troops. I want you to stay here and be still and sleep.'

'No! Tendzin, no! I don't want to sleep!'

'Well, stay here and keep awake, but I'll be gone some time and you must not show yourself.'

'I'll be quiet as a mouse, truly.'

Tendzin smiled and caressed the boy's forehead, then stood up, dusted down his clothes, and hurried away.

The boy did not want to sleep, but he was tired and exhausted, and although he fought against his closing eyes, they got the better of him and took him down into restless, ugly dreams.

It was with a sense of relief that he was pulled out of the dreams by the sound of droning engines. He opened his eyes quickly and sat up. The day was pleasantly cool, with a breeze blowing up the valley, keeping at bay the chill of the distant glacier-topped mountains to the west. He looked up, realizing that the droning engines were above him.

Planes were a special delight to him when they made their rare appearances overhead, flying to the Chinese airstrip at Jyekundo, or from there en route to Chamdo. He got to his feet and stepped out from the cover of the juniper to watch the three silver craft, their twin engines making diamond-like circles before their wings. Excitedly, he waved.

As if responding to his wave, one of them broke the formation they flew in — the same formation as geese. It peeled away from the others and began to pick up speed, arrowing straight towards the mountain road.

It swept over him with a roar that seemed to make

the whole valley shudder. For a moment he was engulfed in the roar. He looked up and saw the doors hanging open beneath the plane. He thought he could see someone up there. Then something dropped from the doors and began to whistle earthwards. The plane's momentum carried it past him, towards the road and where the mountain gun had been firing.

He realized that the other two planes had turned and were on a similar run, heading directly for the monastery.

Then the ground began exploding, throwing him on to his stomach. He looked back to see huge blasts erupting inside the monastery.

'No!' he shouted. 'No! Stop it!'

He had thought at first they had come to delight him. He had waved to them, and they had responded like this. Was he responsible for what they were doing?

Forgetting Tendzin, thinking only of the Abbot, he scrambled down to the stream and plunged across it, and began to claw his way up the hillside.

Behind him came the sharp, staccato shouting of a machine-gun as the first plane returned, with fire stammering from it, like a dragon out of the sky. A Chinese dragon.

The ancient, elemental beast, the creator and guardian of the earth. It had turned against humanity. Was he responsible? He had waved. He had seen that horrible vision. He had done those ... things ... to the Abbot. He was responsible. He was guilty. He must somehow find a way to stop time, to turn it back, to reverse things so that whatever had started this chain of events could be erased and life could return to normal.

He remembered how he woke with an erection. Was that it? What had Tara done to him in the night? These were things which the Abbot only spoke of guardedly. Why were they so secret? Why were there no women in the monastery?

He reached the top of the bank to find the earth still exploding. He could hear terrified horses somewhere nearby. Dust and smoke billowed all around him. He could hear his name being called. Was a demon coming to punish him?

He ran, but his foot caught in a juniper root and he fell full-length on the ground. Whatever was chasing him was closer. He screamed and tried to stand up, but fell again, and the thing was on him.

'No! No! No!' he screamed.

It was Tendzin. The man wrapped him in his arms, and they lay together as the earth shook and shivered all around them.

When it was all finished, when the dragons had departed, and the earth had ceased crying, they returned to the monastery, and they walked to where the pit had been.

They could see only one half of the pit. The other half had become a ragged crater. The bodies of all the monks had been torn to shreds. Pieces lay tossed together, their blood and gore mingled into one giant, shredded corpse. There was no sign of the Abbot. They found the spot where he had lain, and they saw the darkened earth. But the Abbot had gone.

'He's still alive,' the boy said, eagerly, hopefully.

Tendzin touched the top of his head gently.

'We've got to get out of here,' his servant said. 'The Chinese will come back.'

'Where can we go?'

Tendzin glanced up the rocky mountainside, out of which the monastery buildings grew.

'We'll start by going up there,' he said.

They began the long climb, pausing occasionally for breath as they labored past the different levels of the monastery. All was silent after the bombing, but great clouds of dust hung in the air, billowing from jagged holes in the ancient walls. Newly broken stone gleamed where it had been fractured. The boy could look in on rooms which previously had been sheltered by their roofs, by their walls. He looked in on furnishings suddenly made naked — on pots and pans, beds and cushions. He and Tendzin paused to watch a section of wall lean slowly forward and crash down past them, down past the other levels of the monastery to thunder into the ravine and finally come to a dusty rest in the stream. They looked at each other, said nothing, and resumed their climb.

At last they crested the mountain and could look past the broken and disordered top-most rooms of the ancient building and on to the vast, white expanse of glacier. Tendzin looked further north, towards the distant ice fields. Up there was Lhasa, the heart of Tibet. It was where they belonged. In particular, it was where the boy should go for his enthronement. But up there were more Chinese. More guns and bombs.

Tendzin was very weary. Through the shock he was beginning to comprehend just how wrong his actions had been. He was beginning to see what he had unwittingly unleashed through his arrogance and pride.

The Abbot had been right all along. But not right in a prissy, monkish way. He had been right in the way a general is right. He could see beyond the valley, beyond the skirmish, to the whole war, and he knew this was one battle which should not have been attempted.

Now the boy waited for guidance, Tendzin thought. But his guide was gone, leaving only a stupid ex-bandit to care for him. A man with no more brains than a fieldmouse. He looked to the boy.

'What do you think?' he asked uncertainly. 'Where do you think we should go?'

The boy looked down on the room where, only a few hours earlier, he had been woken from his bad dreams by the first sounds of gunfire. His bed was broken, tipped at a crazy angle across the floor. The bedclothes were shredded like the ribbons carried on carnival days. He shivered and turned and looked down the valley.

'Away from here,' he said, firmly. 'Down the river.'

'And leave Tibet?'

'I never want to return,' the boy said.

As he spoke, the boy felt his mind locking away the world that had existed before the bombers came. All memory of his lonely childhood. All memory of those dream-like, time-shrouded monks in the tunnel. All memory of that lovely woman. All memory of the task set for him in this lifetime. And yet, with that locking away came a dreadful sense of loss, and a dreadful compulsion to keep coming back. Back to the edge of the pit. Back to the face of the whispering, bloodied Abbot.

'Never ever return,' he repeated.

His servant, seeing and hearing only what was on the surface of his young Master's words, nodded understandingly.

'I think you're right,' Tendzin said. 'So, let's begin walking.'

CHAPTER TWENTY-TWO

Julia drove the boat on into the night as fast as she dared. The sky was not completely black, for the stars were vividly bright above the tendrils of river cloud, and their light outlined the jungle on either side of them.

Even after Joe had dumped the soldier's body over the side he had shown no signs of comprehending the world about him. She had no idea what was happening within him. She had got him into the cabin, and laid him on one of the twin bunks, only to have him grow agitated and insist on sitting up. She had left him there, sitting on the bunk, staring at his hands.

Then clouds rolled in and the blackness became total, and so she headed the boat towards the bank.

She felt far enough away from the border post to turn the spotlight back on. She gasped as it showed her a primeval, dream-like landscape of whitened branches and hanging vines. Throttling back the engine, she ran the launch slowly along the jungle's edge, aware now of her tiredness, of a feeling of nausea. Her mind replayed the moment of contact between the wheel-brace and the soldier's face. Her hand still tingled with the shock of it.

Then the solid line of dream landscape beside her parted and she could see the spotlight glittering on water. For a moment she thought she was imagining it. Her tired mind, her gritty eyes, playing tricks on her. She kept staring at the reflected light bouncing back at her, and slowly realised that there was a lake just the other side of what she could now see was a jungle-clad sandbar. She shook her head and rubbed her eyes and forced herself to concentrate. Soon she saw a break in the sandbar, where the black river met the black waters of the lake, where the sandbar jungle petered out. She swung the boat into the gap.

The black foliage loomed over them and suddenly the night sky was cut off. She sensed the trees all around, and felt their greater humidity. She ran the boat further into the blackness, and then cut the engine. There was a sudden, almost shocking, silence.

She could hear the boat's engine ticking as it cooled. Foliage dripped into the water around them. Something splashed, and she jumped. But she made herself go forward and find the mooring line.

The spotlight shone into the water, shining through to a clear, sandy bottom. She stepped over the side and waded ashore. She slung the rope around a strong tree trunk, then pulled on it, and eased the boat in under the overhanging foliage. She tied the rope off and returned to the boat, dousing the light. She sat listening to the inexplicable sounds of the jungle all around her.

Slowly, and faintly, the sound of an outboard motor

emerged from the delicate symphony of water noises, rustlings, gruntings, and the shimmer of insect sounds. She tensed, sitting atop the cabin, staring back down the river.

The sound grew clearer and she imagined Watson sitting at the tiller. She remembered him as she had first seen him — staring in at her private moment in the storeroom. She remembered the look of the lost man in his face. She heard the motor drawing abreast of her, and she stopped breathing.

The motor's pitch changed as it buzzed on past, nosing into the river's current. Her breath returned as the sound descended through the scale, and once more became like another insect on the river.

She groped her way into the cabin, to find Joe curled on his side on the bunk where she had left him. She closed the door to the cockpit and then felt her way to the opposite bunk, to find it stacked high with the belongings of the soldiers. Her hand recoiled, remembering the wheel-brace, the shock of impact.

She retreated to Joe's bunk and sat there beside him. She reached out, seeking comfort, and took his hand.

He murmured something and drew her towards him. At first she hesitated, but then she let herself go; let herself stretch out beside her husband.

The hull muffled the river's relentless growl, and hid the sounds of the jungle. The air was humid and warm. She closed her eyes, then opened them, unable to differentiate between the two states.

Joe stirred again, and this time she heard him whisper, 'Tara? Tara?'

The question was filled with uncertainty and loneliness.

'Shhh,' she whispered. 'I'm here.'

'Tara?' Now eager hope replaced the uncertainty.

'Yes,' she said, firmly as any mother lies to a frightened child. 'Yes, it's me. Now sleep.'

Julia dreamt. She dreamt she was back in the shop in the mall. She smiled in her sleep, because of the reassurance and the safety of that place. She was there in her high-necked blouse and her tight pants and high-heel shoes. The crowd passed by outside, murmuring, growling, sounding like a river. In the far distance was a sound like car horns blasting in unison, as if there was a traffic pile-up on the entrance ramp to the carparks. She came out from behind the glass-topped counter and walked to the door to see what was happening.

She found herself looking at a procession. It was a procession of Buddhist monks in orange robes, with strange hats on their heads. Bringing up the rear were four huge musical instruments — long, curving horns, each being blown by one monk, and with another monk supporting the curved bells at the ends of the horns. The sound they made was hideous.

Suddenly the dream wasn't fun any more. The procession was halting outside the shop. The monks were gathering around, and the horns were blasting and drums pounding and great brass cymbals shivered. There was now a woman at the center of the group of monks, holding up a human skull. The woman also carried a stone-headed axe.

She shrank back from the shop entrance — only it was now the entrance to a cave. A flight of stairs had been cut through the living rock and she stumbled down them.

Dave Watson and her husband were waiting for her at the bottom of the stairs. She was suddenly very pleased to see them. They stood together, their relaxed poses indicating they were old friends who trusted each other intimately. They both reached out to her, smiling, eager to embrace her.

Now there was a new tension in the dream.

Now she was sitting on a bed like the bed in the Bangkok hotel where she had opened herself up to her husband. She wore a beautiful silk robe. She felt its delicate roughness between her fingers. Then she looked up and her husband was there and she smiled at him and lay down, lifting the delicate robe from her thighs. Again, he lay with her, and again she opened herself up to him. But Dave Watson was standing beside the bed. And he was frowning. He had something in his hands. Was it an axe?

She tried to look at it, but her eyes wouldn't rest on it. Her eyes kept darting away, like the way a child won't look at the doctor's needle as it approaches her arm. The woman in the dream was crying.

She struggled, trying to push her eager lover away. She could see Dave's face transforming — from the smile when he had first seen her, to the frown when he discovered her with Joe, to a vicious snarl.

She was on her knees, in the storeroom of the shop, screaming at him. She was chained to the floor, unable to move, as a monk, who was also Dave Watson, lifted his hand as if to bless her — or was it a violent curse? Joe was now yelling, too.

Joe threw himself at the monk, knocking him backwards. But the monk recovered his balance and, before her eyes, as she struggled against the chains, he turned on Joe, snarling, punching Joe in the side of the head. And then he threw himself on the chained and helpless woman, his hands ripping the delicate silk from her breasts.

Julia woke, gasping, and found herself in pitch blackness, with an inert body against her. She screamed and flung herself away from it, crashing on to the slippery floor of the boat.

She lay there, bewildered and confused, suddenly unable to move, as if she was still shackled to the floor, her wrists pinioned together.

Then there was a voice in the blackness, and she recognized it as her husband's.

'John?' she called, then remembered. 'Joe? Is that you, Joe?'

'Julia? Where are you?'

She felt for the edge of the bunk, pulled herself back on to it and found herself burying her head against his side.

'What's happening?' she asked him. 'I don't understand any of it.'

'Where are we?' he replied. 'What can't you understand?'

'I dreamt Dave Watson, and some monk, were killing you, and I ... I was there and couldn't stop it.'

She felt him grow tense.

'Where did it happen?' he asked carefully.

'Back in Los Angeles, but it was also a cave ...'

She felt him sit up.

'Where are we now?' he asked her.

'Further up the river, hiding in some kind of a lake. Dave went past in another boat, I don't know how long ago.'

He climbed over her, fumbled to the door and pushed it aside, and suddenly they could see each other in the half-light. He stared at her, then smiled — but the smile didn't get past his mouth; his eyes were deeply troubled. He turned away from her and stepped into the cockpit of the launch.

He saw that they were tied to a big, overhanging tree which arched out from the dense jungle crowding the lake's edge. The sandbars beside them supported enough vegetation to screen them from the river. In the opposite direction from the river, to the east, light was spreading — revealing ranges of steep hills.

The day was already sticky. Low cloud hung on the hills.

Joe was light-headed. The daylight was evaporating the memory of dreams that had been far more than dreams. Dreams which were beginning to make sense of the lives he had led — lives lived like dreams. Now dreams had returned him to a life in far keener focus than any life he could remember. The world he looked at seemed vastly different to the world he used to know. It was more profound, and his own, insignificant place in it more certain. Even the sense of insignificance was liberating — as if he could start out all over again, and this time get it right.

He stepped to the side of the boat and looked down into the clear, green water. Tiny fish darted in and out of the weed. Suddenly aware of his need, he steadied his knees against the boat's side, and urinated into the lake.

That simple act threw him into painful memories. Anguished, he saw the tiny fish flee from his polluting stream. He realised how complex things were. There was some remorseless morality at work, and he was part of it. He was not free until he had absolved himself of all he had done.

When he looked back, she was standing in the doorway, watching him.

'There's canned food on board,' she said. 'Are you hungry?'

He nodded, and then realized there were tears in his eyes. He suddenly found himself embracing her — and he could feel, at the same time, that he was a monk, his arms around another woman in a cave.

'Joe?' she said, puzzled at his fervor.

'Tell me your dream again,' he whispered.

'The dream?'

'You and me and Watson ... and the monks.'

'Why?'

'Because I've had such dreams myself.'

She pulled back and stared up at him, feeling her flesh crawling, feeling cold despite the growing heat around them.

'You've had the dream?'

'Just tell me what you saw.'

'You and me ...' she hesitated. 'You and me making love and then Dave Watson was between us, and then a monk ...' It sounded silly when she said it.

They stared at each other.

'This is crazy stuff,' she said. 'I've been through

some horrible things last night. This is all some kind of psychological reaction.'

'What were you wearing?' he asked, ignoring her desperate rationalizations.

'Look! What does it matter? ... Silk, I think ... I was ... if you must know, I felt like I was, I don't know, chained up and stuff. I don't know where I got the idea. Do we have to talk about it?'

He nodded.

'I think it might be why we're here,' he said uncertainly. 'It might be why all this is happening. Maybe it's so we can discover each other again ...'

'If you're talking about reincarnation, I just don't believe in it Joe. I'm sorry. I think it's just cheap California junk! The kind of stuff I had to put up with at college!'

He stared into her eyes.

'But what else is there to believe?' he asked her. 'That all this we have lived through has no meaning? That ... that our love is something ...' he spread his hands uncertainly, '... something just chemicals and hormones.'

'And all the things you did?' she asked him. 'How do you feel about them?'

A terrible shadow crossed his face. She was suddenly ashamed of having reminded him. She took his hand in hers, but he pulled away from her.

'I don't know what I can do,' he said. 'But I know I have to do something. I have to stop that wheel going around and around, generating its misery. And the only way to do that is to face everything I have done and accept it ... and I don't know if I have the strength for that.'

He turned back to her. This time it was she who embraced him, and lifted his hand and kissed it.

'What you did, you did out of ignorance,' she said. 'And whatever your explanation is doesn't matter. It's the fact that you're sorry which is important.'

'Can you accept what I did? Can you know that and ... and love me?'

She looked up at him. She remembered what Howard Collins had told her, in the mall carpark. She remembered her husband standing in the Bangkok hotel doorway, blood on his clothes. Howard's blood.

She looked at him and saw it all there; all the violence, and the fear behind the violence. She stared at him gravely, and nodded. Then she touched her lips against his.

She pulled back and shook her head.

'I just can't help it,' she said. 'I don't know what it is, but I just can't help it.'

They stared at each other a moment longer, and then she took his hand and led him back into the boat's cabin.

They lay down together on the bunk.

She was right. She didn't understand any of it. And the only explanation she had was what he called 'hormones and chemicals'. She just needed him, and she needed him right up against her, and then she needed him inside her. She sensed that he was somewhere else, in his head, somewhere disturbingly mystical and nonsensically beyond time. But that was him. If you loved someone, you loved all of them.

CHAPTER TWENTY-THREE

The Abbot woke with the dawn. He lay in his bed a while before getting up to make his devotions. He lay there thinking about all the years he had waited in this place, doing penance for his errors: for failing to lead the monastery correctly; for not anticipating that Tendzin would act as his nature dictated, and antagonize the Chinese; that the Chinese would act as their nature dictated, and seize the opportunity to terrorize his people. He did special penance for not having anticipated what would happen to the Master.

The Chinese had arrived in 1954, and an astute man could have easily predicted what would happen. There had been five good years in which to educate the Master properly. It would have been difficult, for he was only a little boy at the time. But less difficult than the task which confronted them now.

Alternatively, he could have got the Master away before the massacre, so that his eyes would not see it and his confused mind not grasp hold of it and cling to it as it had done over all these years.

All these years in which the Dalai Lama thought him, the Abbot, dead with the other monks, and the Master dead, and the whole line of the monastery destroyed. The only people who thought him alive were the Chinese. And Tendzin.

He smiled in spite himself. Tendzin, the old warrior. He was close to the end of the road now. Next time around he would probably confront life as a helpless woman, and learn different lessons in the almost eternal march towards Enlightenment.

He sat up. He must see Tendzin today. The more he thought about it, the more certain he was that the Master would return the way he had left. By the river. He would return to the place where Tendzin had handed him the objects. The river was right next to it. Yes, he would come up the river as far as he could, until the rapids prevented further progress. He and Tendzin must evolve a plan for getting to him before the Chinese found him.

The Book of Changes indicated the Master would not be traveling alone. The Marrying Maiden accompanied him. As yet, the Abbot did not know her part in the scheme of things. But he was certain she must have a part, or else she would not be on the journey. This was not a journey of chance, but one of fate. This was a coming together of forces which had been moving towards each other for centuries. Forces which would never have had the chance to meet if the Chinese had not done what they had done.

He got out of bed and bowed to the image of the Buddha and the photograph of the smiling Dalai Lama. The Dalai Lama kept reminding his people that the Chinese were their best friends, not their worst enemies, for the Chinese had issued them with their greatest challenge. He sat back and let his heart contemplate this. It was the hardest lesson he had ever experienced.

The Laotian Army major poked at Dave's open wallet on the desk before him. He looked across the desk to where Dave sat in the other metal chair.

'DEA?' he asked.

Dave nodded. His eyes were gritty with exhaustion.

'That why you so far up the river?'

He nodded again.

The major sat at a metal desk in a cabin of a Laotian patrol boat. There had been no way of avoiding the boat when Dave rounded a bend as the sun burst on to the river. He was aware that he had overshot Joe, and was just thinking about turning around and heading back. A shout from the patrol boat's bow and he had immediately raised his hands in the air, staring at the wavering barrel of the forward machine-gun.

'You got permission, Mr Watson?'

He shook his head.

'A freelance operation, eh?'

The major chuckled. It was a hopeful sign.

'That's right. They got away from us in Chiang Saen and I had no chance to get clearance, not if I wanted to catch them.'

'But you lost them anyway?'

Dave nodded.

'You want to use the radio? Call your people?'

Dave licked his lips.

'Err ... not yet,' he said. 'Not until I know where they are.'

'That might be never, Mr Watson. There's a lot of bends in this river, a lot of tributaries, lakes, hide-aways. This man, he knows the country?'

Dave nodded again. He could see the futility of the Quest being laid out before him.

'He also took on a Burmese border patrol. Killed at least one of them,' Dave added.

'That don't surprise me. Those Burmese are good at killing villagers; not good at killing smart people. This man seems pretty smart to me.'

Dave nodded again.

'So, what you want to do, Mr Watson?'

'I want to find him,' Dave said, simply.

The major got up and took a fragile chart from the top of a metal cabinet.

Dave stood up, and his head hit the roof. The major laughed.

'This is not a boat for Westerners,' he said. 'Even though the French built it.'

The major spread the chart on the desk and Dave looked down at it. It was a series of photocopies of a hand-drawn chart of the river — all taped together.

'Our chart,' the major said. 'The original is kept in a vault in Vientiane.'

Dave couldn't tell if he was joking or not.

The major stabbed at their position with his dividers.

'We are here. We have come from ... here. As you can see, we could not have missed them. But down here, see this big bend.'

Dave followed the dividers downstream.

'The river breaks its banks during the rainy season. It makes lagoons. There are also tributaries coming down this big valley. If I was them, that's where I'd go.'

'Can this boat get in there?'

'No. But we can position ourselves outside and send a force in. Are they armed?'

'I don't know.'

'Let's assume they are. Why get an unpleasant surprise, eh? I can send a squad around here, on the land, and send another squad in with the dinghy you so kindly provided. We wait here with the rest of our force.'

'Is it possible to take them alive?'

'It's possible. If they don't shoot at us. If they don't run. And if my men don't get over-enthusiastic. They haven't shot at a live target for a while. I might not be able to restrain them.'

Dave stared at his smiling face questioningly.

'And maybe I'm not too interested in restraining them,' the major added. 'Who knows? We hold our fire. They shoot. I lose a man. We capture them. I then got to hand them over to Thailand. Maybe their government's changed again. We got to hang around for extraditions. There's a court case. You know what happens if they've got friends in high places in Thailand? They walk away. Right?'

Dave reluctantly nodded. The major studied his face a moment longer, then smiled sympathetically.

'I know what you want. You want them on television. Major drug bust. Much better footage than a couple of coffins. But you've been around. You know how the system works. You know it's simpler if we just shoot them. Yes?'

'Yes,' Dave said.

Joe had made a methodical inventory of the equipment on the boat. They had one AK-47 assault rifle. Holding it was like a reunion with family. One with whom you are totally familiar, and yet don't necessarily want to know. There were two full banana-clip magazines, and a box of rounds. There were also four hand-grenades.

The main fuel tank was less than half-full. The reserve tank was OK. There was enough canned food to get them wherever they were going. Where that would be, he didn't know as yet. The water tank was three-quarters full, but he was dubious about the quality of its contents. There was no stove on the boat. But an opened tin of instant coffee and three dirty mugs suggested there had to be a gas-ring somewhere.

He found the gas-ring and bottle in an old box up in the bow. There were six matches in a box. There were also some crumpled-up shirts and army-issue trousers. He found a roll of tobacco and papers, and a full box of matches with them.

'There was a patrol boat going up river just before you took that boat,' Joe said. 'It hasn't come down, so it's still up there. Watson has to meet it. If they don't shoot him then he'll tell them about us. They'll know where to look.'

She stared at him.

'So, what do we do? Can we go further up this stream?'

'Not for very far. These hills are held by old Nationalist Chinese troops who went missing years ago. If they find us, they'll take us and have some fun with us before we die. They don't get much entertainment, other than smoking opium. They like hurting people.

'The patrol boat could send out a search party. They'll stay close to the river, though. They don't want to end up on the same entertainment program as us.

'The Burmese are waiting for us to return. Joe's influence with them is out of date.'

She noted how he used the third person when he spoke of his former self.

'We have to go up river. The question is whether we start before the patrol boat reaches us, or wait for them.

'If we wait for them, we may be able to hide. But if they find us, we're out-numbered, out-gunned, out-provisioned. We're stationary, and a moving target is harder to hit.'

'So we have to go up the river?'

He nodded.

'We have to see them first, and shoot them first, and get past them while they're recovering from the shock. If we can do that, then by the time they've turned around we'll have a clear start.

'We might even get lucky with the rain. If it really comes down they might not see us, and we can slip past them.'

'Then what? They'll get us eventually.'

'The river gets too shallow for them. Eventually

it'll get too shallow for us. Too shallow. Too fast. Too many rocks and rapids. But by then we're in China.'

'Then what do we do?'

'I don't know,' he said.

They stared at each other. She now wore a baggy green army shirt and trousers, with her hair tucked up under a fatigue cap. But when he looked at her he still saw her as she had been when they'd grasped each other in the cabin.

And she. When she looked at him, she could see his face, and behind it her uncle's face, and way behind that, dimly through a mist, a young woman struggling desperately in a cave.

Again she tried to explain away that woman's presence using the language of psychology. But words would not dissolve her. They stared at each other as if they were looking across the centuries.

She shook her head. She spoke, both to him and to the image in her mind.

'I don't think I can do it,' she said.

'There's not much choice,' he replied. 'You pilot the boat. And I get ready to shoot.'

She nodded, and he handed her two grenades.

'What do I do with these?'

'When I start shooting, you remove this pin here. But you keep holding this lever down. Make sure you hold it down. When I shout, "Throw!" you hurl it towards the patrol boat.'

'I'm not very good at throwing.'

'You've got no choice,' he reminded her. 'If things get tough, throw the second one.'

He saw the doubt in her eyes.

'You have no choice,' he repeated. 'If we meet a patrol boat on this river there is only one way of surviving the meeting ... shooting first.'

'And how does killing these people fit with your reincarnation theories?' she snapped.

'If it is neccesary to kill,' he said, ignoring the sharpness, 'then it should be done with regret.'

They stared at each other, and again she felt the weight of time, of centuries gone by. She dropped the grenades into each of her shirt pockets. She felt their heaviness against her breasts.

He nodded, cast off the line and pushed the bow back towards the trees and the river. He left the mooring rope trailing in the water as he hurried to one side to fend them off another huge, sweeping tree limb.

'Start her up!' he yelled.

She grimaced and twisted the key.

'So where are we now?' Dave asked.

He and the major stood side by side in front of the cabin. Above them the helmsman, standing on the roof, kept a nervous eye on the jungle as he guided them downstream. The bow machine-gunner swiveled uneasily back and forth, keeping his twin barrels pointed low so that the lightly armored shield in front of him covered as much of his body as possible.

The weather was closing in and they moved towards the end of a rainbow that seemed to hang in the river.

The other troops were spread along the decks and across the stern, carbines at the ready. They wore flak vests and helmets. They chewed gum nervously.

The major pointed at the chart. 'We're here. This is where they'll probably be hiding. We'll cut our motor this side of the bend, drift over to the bank, and put a party ashore ... there.'

Dave nodded. He felt his pistol in his pocket. The major had not invited him to join the hunt. The major was probably thinking of the paperwork involved if something went wrong. But Dave wanted to get a shot at Joe very badly.

He felt a stab of guilt, thinking of Julia. She was in the firing line now. He found himself remembering the image of her in the mirror; like staring into a jungle pool and seeing a mythological beast. He remembered their love-making. Then he remembered how he had abused her trust, and he remembered how her friend had died.

He shook his head wearily and stepped around the side of the cabin to stare at the river.

Julia held the boat in mid-stream, and at less than half-throttle. The bow was trying to climb up the forward wave and get the hull up on the plane, but she had no intention of going any faster, even though this way they were using too much fuel. Joe was stationed forward of the cabin, sitting there with legs outstretched. He was an easy target, but he could think of no way to make it safe for himself while at the same time having the freedom of rapid movement and unrestricted fire.

The jungle grew thickly against the bank, and cliffs

rose right behind the line of trees. They were wedged into the river, with no way out except ahead. Julia saw the bank and the jungle sliding towards her and realized they were into a steep bend. She turned the wheel and the open river appeared before them. There was nothing in it. Her heart surged with relief, and then the fear crept back. If they met the patrol boat on a straight stretch of river, they were gone.

Abstractedly, she glanced at her hands. She'd cut her nails right back, with a file from the boat's tool kit. She couldn't remember when she hadn't had long nails. Or worn make-up on an important day. Or not thought about her appearance. She felt a sudden sense of liberation, and lifted her head and smiled. She felt like all the things which had clung to her over the years, and which had begun their life by her uncle's basement furnace, were breaking away, like ice in the half-frozen Mississippi River, and swirling downstream behind her.

Dave gripped the rail and looked past the bow to the point where the river cut off as it swept around a bend. They had a good five miles to go before they reached the spot the major had designated. He tried to think himself into Joe's position. He couldn't imagine Joe hiding himself away in the jungle. Joe was an extraordinarily good strategist. He had to be one jump ahead of the major.

Dave looked around and saw the major now standing beside his bow machine-gunner, pointedly putting himself outside the flimsy safety of the gun's armor.

Dave looked at the bend ahead of them and knew that this would be the one.

'Major!' he called.

The major glanced back at him.

Joe heard the throb of the big diesel ahead of them. He twisted his head and screamed at Julia.

'Full throttle!'

She stared at him.

'Full throttle! Now!'

His eyes forced her to obey.

The boat leapt on to its bow wave.

She was crying with fear, the tears blurring her vision. She put her hand in the shirt pocket and took out the grenade.

She eased the wheel over, feeling the boat respond.

'Major!' Dave shouted again.

The major was looking at him, frowning. Then Dave saw the white spray ahead of them, the bow wave, and then the bow of the boat.

They rocketed towards the patrol boat. Joe fired a low burst from the AK-47, spraying it under the machine-gun's armor. He saw the gunner fall, and the man standing beside him, outside the armor's protection, go windmilling backwards. Joe kept firing. He had the second magazine taped piggy-back to the first, so that as soon as it was empty he could simply switch them around.

Fire flared from the patrol boat as the troops responded, shooting by reflex, not aiming, spraying the water with bullets, as the boat hurtled towards them.

'Throw!' he screamed.

She couldn't get the pin out. She had to let go the wheel and tug it with both hands.

She heard Joe cry out, and knew he had been hit.

'Bastards!' she yelled, and hurled the grenade with all her might.

Dave saw her standing in the cockpit, screened by the cabin. His heart leapt. He lifted his hand up as if to greet her, even as the troops fired at the boat as it skittered towards them. He saw Joe in the bow firing back, then hunching up as he took a hit.

Then Dave saw her let go the wheel, struggle with something, and then throw it.

He saw the grenade go high in the air. He gasped and threw himself over the side, into the river, as the grenade exploded above them.

The explosion threw her backwards. The boat slammed sideways and took off for the far bank, out of control. She forced herself upright, grabbed for the wheel, missed it, and hit the throttle forward.

The boat came down off its bow wave, dropping almost to a standstill. She grabbed the wheel, reefed it around, and they headed again for the patrol boat, but the firing had stopped.

She swung the wheel again, and then the boat snagged on something, and lurched sideways. She grabbed the throttle, pulled it towards her, and the boat took off, just as a soldier got his wits back and started firing again.

Whatever they had snagged was still there. She swung the wheel to shake it free, but it hung on.

Then she saw the man clinging to the mooring line. He gave another desperate heave, and pulled himself aboard. It was Dave Watson.

She flung the wheel over, hoping to throw him off. He grabbed the edge of the cabin and clung there. Instead of dislodging Dave, she saw the wounded Joe slide sideways, and fetch up against the stainless-steel railing around the anchor.

Dave grabbed another hold and dragged himself to the cabin.

She glanced back. The patrol boat had come to a halt in mid-stream, its bow half-turned towards them, but already it was beginning to drift. Its stern was swinging, and she knew that if the crew didn't get their act together quickly, they'd be into the trees.

She steadied herself, easing the throttle back so she could have time to react to any snags. She looked again at Dave Watson.

He was grinning, holding a pistol in one hand and pointing it to where Joe was doubled-up on the foredeck.

'No!' she shouted. 'Dave! No!'

Her words momentarily roused Joe, as Watson swung the pistol around to level it at her. Joe's reaction was instinctive. He rolled the carbine across his outstretched leg, blood now oozing from his thigh, and fired.

'No!' she screamed.

But she was too late. Watson grunted, as a bullet punched him towards her.

'Joe! No more!'

She had his attention.

'Let it all stop,' she said. 'Right here and now.'

Her words registered with him and his face suddenly relaxed and he sagged back against the railing.

And now the clouds opened up and rain thundered on the deck, sluicing the blood over the side, drenching Julia, and forming puddles in the cockpit. She grabbed the cabin door and closed it to keep the water out.

The rain was warm and it cut visibility almost completely. She throttled right back, nosing slowly forwards, aware of the two wounded men lying in the bows.

She tried to work out what to do. The two men needed urgent help. But if the patrol boat came after them they were all dead. Should she sacrifice these two men — without whom she would not have come here and put herself in this situation — or should she try and save them?

She could sense a strange pattern emerging. A triangle of forces. As if the three of them had been dependent upon each other once before.

She couldn't work out why she had stopped Joe killing Watson. On the one hand she completely rejected Joe's reincarnation nonsense, and yet she accepted that forgiveness was the thing; that retribution, revenge, the blood vendetta between these two men, had to end. And she, somehow, was the agent who could end it.

The river nudged and buffeted the boat as it crawled through the pounding rain. Darkness loomed to her right and she realized it was the river bank. Suddenly a great arm reached out for her. Its fingers dripped tendrils of flesh. She spun the wheel, and the overhanging branch, laden with trailing creeper, slid along the side of the boat. The creeper touched her shoulder, wet and clammy, and she screamed.

I've got to keep it together! she told herself, angrily.

She swung the wheel again and headed back for the bank, remembering what Joe had said. The patrol boat couldn't see them in these conditions.

Keeping the engine ticking over she hurried to the bow, climbing over the sprawled men, and retrieved the mooring line, and flung it at the branch, which had re-emerged through the gloom as the current took them slowly backwards.

The boat jerked up tight as the line held. She hastily secured it and turned back to the cockpit.

Dave stared at her. There was blood all down his right side. For a moment she thought he was dead. But then he blinked, and again she felt that dreadful giddiness, a lurching nausea, as if she was staring down through a tunnel in time.

She could avoid it no longer. She had to stare at that other woman, and to taste that woman's reality as if it were her own. It was like looking at the repeating ghost images on a faulty television.

All at once, with her whole body, she felt a shock of absolute terror. She felt that woman's moment in her dream, the moment of approaching death.

She felt it with a conviction that overpowered the last

desperate attempts of her mind to rationalize it.

Julia found herself in the cockpit of the boat, vomiting. She was shivering. She pulled herself to the side seat and looked into the water.

The rain had stopped and now the sun broke through and sparkled on the freshly cleaned leaves and glittered on the wavelets on the river. The motor was still idling and she switched it off.

The pattern was all around her. A pattern of action and reaction. It was as clear and sparkling as the jungle leaves and the glittering water, and just as impersonal.

She was at the center of it. Only she could bring it to a close.

She took off her cap and wiped her face with it. Then she went to find the medical kit to see if she could stem the bleeding of her two lovers.

For Joe it was as if he hung suspended over the rushing river of time. The river on which a young boy had set sail, many years before, fleeing a castle, a monastery, that was shattering down all around him. Joe could see that boy and his servant picking their way through the juniper bushes, over the rocks, climbing towards the peak, leaving behind the horror in the pit.

And yet the boy was glad to be leaving. He didn't look back. There had been something dark and unwholesome in the depths of that ancient, cold and shadowed monastery. A memory of water trickling over stone, fallen masonry; a secret hidden deeper than the foundations. Perhaps a secret that was the foundations. Perhaps the bombs had brought the monastery crashing into the river's ravine because of that hidden, dark secret which had undermined the builders' intentions over the centuries.

But the river rushed on, and the only reason Joe could find for why he no longer rushed with it was the image of Tara now before him, kneeling over him. Her gentle, lotus-bearing hands reached out to touch his forehead, to loosen his shirt and feel for his wounds.

The boy's deepest regret had been losing his jade Tara when he fled the monastery. He had snatched her from a box hidden deep, deep, in a cave within the monastery's bowels. There had been other things he had seen in that box, things which he had firmly driven from his mind.

It was all returning to Joe, now. He lay immobile, unable to stop the flood of images as the river seemed to rise up, break its banks, and pour its contents back over him. Contents which he had held at bay for so long.

'Keep still,' a faraway voice whispered. *Her* voice. 'Keep still while I fix this.'

But it wasn't the present agitating him. He was reliving the moment when the boy stood there, lifting the black, wooden lid, and stared in at two hideously grinning skeletons that stared back at him; one of them dressed, as if for a ceremony, in a feathered head-dress and an eagle's mask.

Clutched in the bones of one hand, an ancient ceremonial axe.

The other form's twig-like fingers encircled the jade Tara.

Even in his terror, the boy managed to grab the gleaming, green statue, and slam the lid down tight on the other things.

The boy's scream seemed to echo through Joe's head as he writhed on the deck of the boat. Anguish lanced right through his belly.

The boy was running down dark corridors, stumbling up ancient, stone stairways, fighting through cobwebs and dust.

'Nearly there,' she whispered. 'Nearly there.'

The boy threw himself into the Abbot's lap, trembling, crying.

'Got it!'

He jerked into consciousness, into the moment when Joe Tobias lay on the foredeck of a small, fiberglass cruiser, tied to a tree on a rushing, glittering river, with mountains high above. His wife was sitting back, smiling at him, her lovely blonde hair tossed back from her face. She was holding something in a pair of forceps.

'Got it!' she said again. 'The bullet.'

She tossed it over the side. He watched it arc out and disappear into the hungry water.

'I didn't think I could do it,' she said.

She gently sponged his side, and then wrapped the crepe bandage around him.

He cried out as the bandage tightened. But also because the way she knelt over him reminded him of something, and he didn't know what. Some terrifying memory that seemed to belong with the image of the small boy in the dusty room, the ancient bones, and the things which the old man had thrust into his hands further along this river; the things which had set in motion that which was now happening to him.

'It's all right,' she reassured him. 'You're safe now.'

'No you're not!' said another voice, weak, but full of excitement. 'No fucking way you're not!'

She'd forgotten Dave Watson. He had dragged the AK-47 to his side and now held it across his body, aimed directly at Joe. His eyes glittered fiercely with hatred.

'Dave,' she said. 'Don't. Please don't.'

'This is the only reason I'm here,' he said. 'The only reason.'

'We've got to help each other,' she said.

'Like he helped my family?'

'You can't live like this. Your hatred will kill you.'

'So? I'm dying. He's coming with me. And you, too, if you don't get out the way.'

She stood up slowly, still holding the roll of bandage and the scissors and forceps in her hands. He jerked his head to indicate she should move out of his line of fire.

'Please, Dave, don't,' she said. 'I'll give you whatever you want.'

'It's too late. Anyhow, I've had you. All I want is him.'

She moved around level with his shoulder. She looked at his neck. It was as if she was watching that other woman's neck, exposed like this, back in the dreams which seemed to make a mockery out of time.

'Fuck you, Joe!' he said.

His neck was stretched taut like the neck of a sacrificial victim. Her hand was tight on the half-opened scissors. He lifted the gun waveringly, and she saw his body tense.

She couldn't do it. She dropped the scissors and Dave half-glanced at her. She could no longer live in the world of action and reaction. Dave saw her moment of weakness and laughed. His lips were set in a sneer.

She kicked with all her might, smashing his hand against the gun. He shouted with surprise and pain, and ripped a reflex burst of fire across the river.

She saw her chance, grabbed the carbine and wrestled it out of his tenuous grasp and swung it around, pointing it straight at him. They glared at each other.

'You bitch,' he whispered. 'I'll have you.'

There was no understanding, no remorse, in his eyes. He was a lost man, lost in bitterness, in anger, in the inability to forgive.

She stared at him, wondering what to do. When the solution came, she smiled. It was bizarre. It was a coincidence. Or, it was the pattern repeating.

Holding the weapon pointed at him, watching his eyes now beginning to cloud over as the adrenalin receded and the pain returned, she stepped past him, picked a long crepe bandage from the medical kit, and bound it around his hands and feet.

His eyes opened. He began to struggle, but he had no strength left. She looked into his eyes and smiled — but he could not comprehend the meaning behind her smile. He could not feel, as she could, the bonds on her own limbs, placed there so long ago by him.

She returned to the cockpit, rubbing her wrists and ankles, and restarted the motor and guided them back into the stream.

CHAPTER TWENTY-FOUR

The Abbot and the servant walked in the grounds of the hospital, along the gravel path under the shading trees. Rhododendrons bloomed beside them. They walked slowly, like two harmless old men, their minds dwelling on times long ago.

'I think she will be with him,' the Abbot said.

'Who?'

'The Marrying Maiden of whom the Book spoke.'

'It's a Chinese book.'

'It's a good book. The Chinese are good people. But in some things they have a very narrow view.'

Tendzin restrained his anger. He knew his own narrow view had not helped them in the past.

'Why do you think that?'

'Because there is a woman somewhere in the whole pattern of things.'

'I didn't think monks and women went together.'

The Abbot stopped and took his old friend's arm and stared at him very earnestly.

'What has happened to us can only have happened

because of our faults, my friend,' he said. 'Whatever we did in the past contained faults, otherwise karma would not resolve itself as it has. So, if there were no women in our past, then I expect them in our future. It is the way things work.'

'They were very difficult times when he was a boy,' the old servant said. 'I remember how badly he slept. He'd cry out and I'd go in to him and his eyes would be wide with fear.'

The Abbot nodded and resumed his gentle, measured pace.

'They were difficult times,' he agreed, nodding thoughtfully. 'There were years when we were adrift, with no Master. The oracles would not speak. He did not reincarnate when we expected. Then there were false oracles. I myself had dreams which I knew were false omens. Images of cities far away from where Buddha had traveled, where no Enlightened One could reincarnate. Yet the dreams were so insistent. So clear. It cost me much to deny them.'

They reached a fork in the path. Ahead they could see the banks of the river, studded with vegetable gardens. But as they walked down the riverside fork they could see how the increasing floods had cut great scars through the cultivated ground, truncating the gardens. And now men and women worked together, sandbagging where the river had broken its banks and chewed away their livelihood.

'The river has grown far more vicious,' the Abbot said. 'It was never like this before.'

'It's the Chinese,' Tendzin growled. 'They strip away all the trees up in our land, and the water has nowhere to go but straight down here. Soon all of Tibet will have washed down the rivers and out into the ocean. And that's what the Chinese want. An end to Tibet.'

'I'm sure you are wrong,' the Abbot said gently, but unconvincingly.

'So what do we do now we think there are two of them, and they are coming up the river?'

The Abbot glanced at him. Was there an edge of sarcasm to his voice?

'We go and meet them,' he said. 'What else?'

His old friend stopped and stared at him.

'We do what?!'

They looked at each other. The Abbot smiled. Tendzin ground what was left of his teeth.

'You live with your head in the clouds!' he said. 'The river is unnavigable from here! What do we do? Walk? And where do we find them?'

'As to the last question,' the Abbot replied, 'we'll find them where they run out of river. As to the first ...'

He kept walking. Irritated, but intrigued, Tendzin kept pace with him.

They came to a fence that ran around a compound. The Abbot looked over it, then looked at Tendzin, and smiled.

'Oh, no we don't,' Tendzin said.

But the Abbot kept smiling.

'What about my eyes?' the servant asked. 'I can hardly see my hand in front of me!'

'I can see. You can drive. It's simple co-operation. The heart of communism. Who could find fault with that?'

Tendzin glared at his beaming face, then stared through the fence at the hospital vehicle compound.

He glared at his old friend, who was still beaming. Irritated, the servant found himself smiling.

'No one would stop an ambulance,' he said.

The Abbot laughed and clapped him on the back.

It rained on and off all day as the boat moved slowly up the river. She was glad of the cover the thunderous showers gave them, even though she was wet and soon shivering with cold. She was not strong enough to shift Joe from the foredeck, but she rigged a shelter for him with a tarpaulin. She knew he was still alive, seeing his eyelids flutter, and occasionally open, and a look of sudden comprehension show on his face. Comprehension and fear.

She kept remembering the dreams, the feelings. The feeling of nausea — the disorientation and fear — would not go away. Only the thought of the patrol boat searching behind them kept her at the wheel. She longed to tie the boat to a tree and curl up and sleep.

They passed no sign of human life as they motored northeastwards. There was only the rippling stream they floated on, the crowding, silent jungle, and the clouds overhead. When the clouds did part it was to show high mountains on either side. The river's current grew stronger as the river itself narrowed between the mountains, and she needed more throttle to keep them moving against it. She was now conscious of their dwindling fuel supply.

When a fierce tributary joined them, from the left, its

current was so strong it pushed them towards the other bank, and she needed a full turn of the wheel to keep them on course. The engine labored, and they struck the bottom.

For a moment she thought they were finished. She opened the throttle full, twisting the wheel desperately, and they kicked through the gravelly bar.

Looking back she realized that if they were in danger of grounding, then no patrol boat could follow them. She realized it was time to think about whatever dangers lay ahead.

The river was now in the shadows of the mountains on her left side. When the clouds broke there was no sign of the sun. A long twilight descended upon them. She saw a small tributary rushing in from the right, and she forced the unwilling boat into it. They brushed through overhanging branches, but she was immune now to their clammy feel and the shower of dislodged water. She kept the boat going until finally it ran solidly aground on gravel and sand.

She revved it hard, and blue fumes rose up all around them. But the boat remained fast. She tried reverse, and it dug itself in deeper. They had come as far as they could. She switched off the motor.

She waded over the gravel bed, dragging the mooring line, and made them fast to a tree on the tributary's bank.

Returning to the boat she gazed at her two wounded lovers on the foredeck. Watson's eyes were half-open, watching her with baffled rage. The wound, superficial, raking a long tear across his ribs, had stopped bleeding.

'Come on,' she said to him. 'Let's get you inside.'

She dragged him across the slippery deck, tumbling him into the cockpit, and then pushing him into the cabin, not particularly worried that he began to bleed again.

Returning for Joe she discovered how exhausted she was, and she was afraid of tearing his wound open. But as she bent over him, his arm came up to embrace her.

'Push, Joe!' she commanded. 'Help me, Joe!'

They fell together against the cabin and she managed to drag him to the edge of the cockpit. She was weak with exhaustion, her whole body trembling. She collapsed into the cockpit and stared at him as he lay against the roof.

'Please, Joe,' she said. 'Please make an effort!'

He responded to the tone of her voice. She saw his legs draw up. He kicked out. Encouraged, she took his weight under his shoulders.

He fell on top of her into the cockpit, bruising her back and her ribs. He kicked and got himself up and somehow rolled into the cabin.

She crawled after him, jamming the door tight behind her.

It was important not to give up, a dull part of her mind told her. It made her light the gas-ring, made her grateful for its heat as she clumsily stripped off her sodden clothes, moving awkwardly in the confined space of the cabin.

The hand-grenade in her pocket surprised her. She took it out carefully, suddenly remembering its twin and the moment of explosion. All that had happened to someone else, in a land far away.

She boiled water and made coffee and got him to sip a little. She opened the last tin of tuna and spooned some into his mouth. His eyes opened and stared at her. She stared back at him. She was too exhausted to smile, and all the memories kept jumbling in her mind, confusing her reactions.

Then she turned to Watson with a spoonful of tuna. Angrily, he shut his mouth and turned away. She sighed and ate the fish herself.

But guilt made her ignore his hate, and bandage his wound, even as her eyes tried to close.

Sleep. All she wanted was sleep. With the last of her strength, she turned the gas off. Rain fell again, thundering on the plastic roof and deck. She could hear it pouring into the cockpit. She thought that at least they couldn't sink, being aground. Her mind grappled with what would happen if Watson freed himself. But before she could resolve the problem, she was asleep.

'Slow down,' the Abbot said.

'Why?'

Tendzin peered myopically at him and the ambulance veered off the road. The Abbot hastily pushed the wheel back, centering it.

'Because there's a soldier ahead and he wants us to stop.'

'Just what we need,' the servant said.

'That's it. Stop right here, and let me do the talking.'

'Old age has really sent me soft.'

'Good evening, soldier. What can I do for you?'

Tendzin kept his hands on the wheel, one foot near the throttle, and the other foot pushing the ancient clutch in. Any trouble and he'd let go the clutch, floor the throttle, and race away.

'Me? I'm Doctor Lin Yutang,' he heard the Abbot say. 'Yes, from Jinghong. I'm an epidemiologist.'

A what? he thought. *Where does he get these words? Does he make them up, or what?*

'No. I wouldn't advise searching the vehicle. You see we've had quarantine cases aboard, and it has yet to be fumigated. I beg your pardon? Smallpox. I understand your dilemma, and I'll happily sign any documentation you have. I'll gladly take responsibility for you not searching the vehicle. That's all right. I know how it is. You have your orders, but they don't think what it means to get smallpox germs under your fingernails in the course of duty. They don't get any germs under their fingers, do they? Just ink.'

Tendzin worked hard to keep himself from laughing.

'Thank you. No, don't phone ahead. We'll sleep at an inn along the way. I've no idea how long this old jalopy will go before a wheel falls off. Good night.'

'Driver! Snap to! We've got a job on our hands!'

He let out the clutch and the old vehicle shuddered away.

They drove in silence for a while.

'What's an epi-what you call it?' he asked eventually.

'A doctor who specializes in the study of the origins of diseases.'

'Where do you get these words?'

'I worked in a hospital. I read the journals.'

The old servant sighed and shook his head.

'That's something I regret,' he said. 'Never having been able to do that. Read, I mean. Now I see small children doing it. Children you pass in the street. I used to think only monks were meant to read.'

The Abbot sighed heavily, glancing at his myopic old friend, his screwed-up face, his lizard-like hands on the wheel. The wheel seemed to have a life of its own, twisting back and forth in the old hands, while not seeming to have any effect on the way the vehicle pointed. The Abbot knew enough about motor vehicles for this to cause him some concern.

'They say the Chinese make people learn to read now,' the servant said. 'Force them to do it.'

'It's good,' the Abbot said. 'Out of much pain has come some good.'

'I'll never understand you as long as I live.'

'I know. You're the hardest case I've ever dealt with. You'd have made Lord Buddha tear out his hair in frustration. If I'd have caught up with you after you stole that mountain gun I'd have kicked your bum all the way to Lhasa.'

There was a guilty silence. Just the roar of the motor and the rumble of ancient wheel-bearings and a differential grinding itself slowly to dust.

'I'm sorry,' Tendzin said after a while.

'That's all right. You didn't know.'

'There's not a week goes by I don't remember that.'

'You weren't to know that they were waiting for an excuse to do what they did.'

'Yes, but it was me that gave them that excuse. It's my

responsibility. My karma. I started that. Then I lost the Master in Hong Kong.'

'Who knows,' the Abbot says. 'It was all our karma. You were just the Judas.'

'What's that?'

'The Christians believe that the Lord Jesus was betrayed by a man called Judas who gave him to their enemies — the Romans; like our beloved Chinese. The Romans then killed Jesus. For centuries every good Christian loathed Judas and told stories about the torments he suffered in their hell. But more recently some scholars have argued that Jesus had to be betrayed in order to meet his karma. Someone had to do it. Judas was the chosen one. He was as essential as Jesus.'

'And you're saying what I did was essential?'

'That's right. Jesus and Judas are now together, united and forgiven. They both know that what they both suffered was inevitable.'

'I'm glad I brought you on this trip. I can see I'll catch up on all the sermons I've missed over the years.'

'That would be impossible. Would you like me to be quiet?'

'No, you old goat. Keep talking. You make me angry and that keeps me awake. Tell me more about the Master. Where does he fit into all this? And why are we thumping through the night on this wild goose chase?'

'There was something wrong with the Master before the Chinese arrived. You mentioned his nightmares. Nightmares speak of bad karma, of the fear of some previous incarnation. What could a reincarnating Master fear from his previous lifetimes? We'd had our troubles. We'd been raided and abused over the centuries. And we'd fought back once or twice. Only a *Bodhisattva* is perfect. But there should have been nothing which made the little Master so fearful.

'I remember one day when I was presiding over a civil court, hearing a case against a peasant guilty of theft. He was a hopeless case, always causing trouble by stealing. He was on his knees, wailing and blubbering. But the law speaks, and we ignore the law at our peril. Suddenly the rear door to the chamber burst open. My own private door. I glanced around in surprise. The little Master came rushing in, like all the demons of hell were after him.'

He was silent a moment, watching the road in the yellow beam of the headlights.

'I thought I saw a fox,' he said, after a while. 'Where was I? Yes. He came tearing in, crying his eyes out, and leapt on to my lap. The guards dragged the peasant out and I turned my attention to the Master.

'He couldn't tell me what had frightened him. I calmed him down and carried him back to his chambers. I sent for you. Much to my surprise, you came. I found the green jade Tara hidden under his pillows. It was obviously a great comfort to him, so I let him keep it.'

'I remember,' Tendzin growled. 'I would have liked him to have had a puppy.'

'No attachments, remember? A monk has nothing between himself and infinity. Nothing but his robe and his begging bowl.'

'Some of those fat old birds had a bit more than that.'

'The system wasn't perfect. No system is perfect, not even communism.'

'There were horses I have owned who had more compassion than people like the Bursar.'

'He paid, remember? Where was I? You keep interrupting.'

'You were sentencing a hopeless peasant, and then you had to turn your attention to the Master.'

'Yes. I went for a walk in the monastery. The dust that was on the boy's hands, and on his head, was very old. I went walking and found some doors open which I knew were rarely opened.'

For some reason Tendzin felt the hairs on his arm prickle.

'I went down to the lowest level, to where the cellars had been carved into the living rock by our ancestors. I took an electric torch with me, courtesy of the Chinese.

'What had brought him down to this level, if he was so terrified? He could hardly sleep at night for fear of the dark. Yet he dragged himself down old, dark steps, looking for something. I'm sure he found the Tara down there somewhere. I could see dropped fat from his lamp in places where he'd stood, terrified, trying to build up the courage to keep on going.

'There were no more doors, just crude archways, and piled-stone walls which had now become part of the earth itself. These were the very foundations of the monastery — of our order. I came at last to a point where I could go no further. Piles of stone gave way to the bare, hand-chiselled rock. But I saw a deeper darkness behind the rocks. And I found where he had wriggled through, into a tunnel. I followed in his footsteps, shining my torch. I could see I was in another chamber, and against the far wall was a huge, black, wooden chest.'

Now all the flesh of Tendzin's arms, his thighs, up and down his spine, was shivering. He glanced in the mirror, feeling as if a devil stood behind him. He felt as if it could reach out and encircle his throat with its hands.

'Looking at it, I felt a rush of some strange fear. This is what had scared the boy so badly. And yet I suspected this is what he had come looking for. I opened the lid and looked into the box.

'I was looking at ancient, human bones; at the still-surviving grin on not just one, but a pair of skulls. Two old skeletons lay there, on top of brittle scrolls and palm-leaf manuscripts.

'One of those skulls wore an ancient shaman's costume — a mask and a head-dress. It lay among other relics of its trade.

'I was filled with a dreadful fascination. I reached in and picked up the ancient axe. The handle was so brittle that pieces fell from it. I took out the drum and looked at the images wrought on its side. They spoke of the shaman's journey to the land of the dead. I lifted the head-dress from the skull, as if I was lifting a crown. I stared down at the manuscripts lying beneath the bones. I knew they must contain the real story of the origins of our monastery. But I could not bring myself to touch them. I closed the lid, and I hurried away, taking with me the shaman's relics.

'I kept those things in my room and they seemed to challenge everything I did. They confronted everything I knew about our order. We had our history, of which we were vastly proud. Too proud, of course. The first incarnation of the Master had crossed the ice fields from India, back in the eighth century. He came to what was then the fertile valley of Ghenko, and established a center of teaching. So what was the meaning of this hidden, ancient, shamanistic material? Way out on the steppes there are still relics of the crude beginnings of religion; the shaman's hat and drum are still used. But the Hindu texts demonstrated how all this was just a manifestation of *Maya*, just part of the ongoing web of illusion that humans spin, which keeps them on the wheel of fate.'

Fear still held Tendzin tight, and he had to force himself to concentrate on driving into the night, along the narrow mountain road.

'I did a lot of thinking, a lot of reading,' the Abbot continued. 'And yet I could not bring myself to go back down there and face whatever those brittle manuscripts contained. Someone had placed those skeletons together, atop those manuscripts. And at what point had the green jade Tara joined them? For I was sure she had to have been there in the box with them. A jade Tara which came from China, but was heavily influenced by our own culture.

'Thinking about that Tara led me to reread our history, and I read about the young wife of the warlord who once controlled the valley — a beautiful Chinese princess, sent as a conciliatory gift from the people of

China's northern province to our own warlord. One day she had simply disappeared.

'And listed among the gifts at the wedding? A green Tara, made of the finest jade, and given by the monks of our monastery, through the personal request of the Master himself. The Master who, one day, like the beautiful bride, simply disappeared — never to be seen again.'

He fell silent and watched the road, listening to the rumbling of the vehicle. He resumed speaking, more to himself than to his driver.

'The Master had disappeared. There was great confusion. One of the monks, young, strong, hotheaded, took over. There were years of confusion before the new incarnation of the Master was recognized. Years when the monastery lost focus, when its implacable stand against the Feminine became ingrained to the point of instinct. That monk hated women with a passion. He tried to breathe his hatred into the incarnate Master.'

The lights suddenly veered out into nothingness. He grabbed the wheel and wrenched them back on course. Tendzin woke up with a start.

'I think we'd better stop soon,' the Abbot said gently. 'This vehicle is not equipped with wings and there is a lot of air out your window.'

'I was awake,' Tendzin said defensively. 'I just got something in my eye.'

'It must have been a dream. Slow right down and when you get a chance, pull over. There are two comfortable bunks behind us, continue your dream in one of them.'

'I was awake. Let me ask you something. How did those relics survive the Chinese, and all those years you spent gaining a Chinese education?'

'They survived through my cowardice. I couldn't stand the challenge they made. I parceled them up and sent them away. I sent them to a monastery in Yunnan Province of China, where a student of mine had recently become Abbot. He kept them for me. Now, let's sleep so we can be fresh for tomorrow's search.'

'How do we continue the search tomorrow?'

'Searching on land, we use a truck. Tomorrow, we must search on water.'

'So?'

'So tomorrow we need someone to cancel a karmic debt by lending us a boat.'

'I'm glad I've got a monk along, to explain the morality of theft.'

CHAPTER TWENTY-FIVE

Julia woke. The air was stuffy, and there was an unpleasant smell. She lay beside the sleeping Joe. Dave Watson, still bound tight, slept on the other bunk. She sat up and discovered her aches and bruises.

She had slept in her panties. She took them off to rinse them and opened the door. Water lay over the cockpit floor. Her motion made the boat tilt and she realised they were no longer aground. She looked around quickly, but the mooring rope still held. The previous day's rains had swollen the river and lifted them off the bar.

The day was cloudy and she didn't know the time. She leaned over the side and rinsed her panties. It was all so normal, except she was naked and hiding in the jungle with a pair of wounded men, and a bunch of outrageous ideas about why they were all so cozily together.

She had no dry clothes. She couldn't even brush her matted, itchy hair. To be perfectly truthful about herself: she stank. And the swollen river made her nervous. She couldn't imagine slipping over the side to wash.

Then she heard voices and for a moment thought she really was mad. Except she'd read somewhere that a mad person thinks they're normal, and the rest of the world has the problems. She didn't think that.

By now she was standing naked in the bow of the boat, straining to work out where the voices came from. She froze, not knowing if she should try and cover herself. Would movement alert them? She remembered the hand-grenade, but it was in the cabin with Joe's gun.

The voices got louder. She realized she could see glimpses of the larger river through the foliage. It, too, was swollen. Then she saw the two men.

They were on a barge made out of logs, poling downstream, arguing between themselves. Two old fishermen.

One of the fishermen glanced up, and was suddenly staring straight at her.

She kept perfectly still, her lips half-open, her arms bent at the elbow, hands spread.

The other old man, who wore spectacles and had an oddly scholarly air about him, glanced up, sensing his companion's distraction. He, too, stared at her. They were two old men struck by a vision of bare-breasted loveliness.

The scholarly one reached out and touched his companion's arm.

But the men forgot their navigational tasks, and the river slowly took the clumsily shaped craft, and gently spun its stern out towards the river's center. And that movement precipitated the blunt bow into the bank.

The old men stumbled, flailing about, one of them

dropping his pole in the river. The scholar windmilled on the edge of the boat, about to follow the pole into the water, but his friend grabbed him and they tumbled together on to the flat, wooden deck.

Julia couldn't help it. She laughed. Then she saw the elder of the two, who seemed to possess the greater presence of mind, grab a branch to hold the barge against the bank, and urge the scholar to clamber ashore.

'Hell!' she said aloud, aware of her nakedness. She scrambled back to the cockpit and dived into the cabin.

She shook Joe awake.

'Joe!' she said. 'Joe! Wake up!'

He stared at her blankly.

He was a long time coming round. She could see him trying to rise out of the depths of his mind. Had he been seeing what she had seen?

Then she realized she wasn't the only one who stank. But the smell coming from Joe was not of stale sweat. It was a smell of rottenness.

'Oh, God!' she cried. Her nakedness was suddenly unimportant.

'What did you say?' he whispered.

'It doesn't matter.' And it didn't either. There was nothing she could do about the fishermen. 'Let me change this dressing.'

She got the bandage off him and released the rest of the smell. It made her choke, but she forced herself to go on.

What do I do? she thought. *Clean it out. I've got to keep it open, don't I? Oh, God, look at this muck! I really can't handle this! I'm not a nurse.*

There was a handbook with the medical kit, but it

was in some alien tongue. She almost screamed with frustration. There were pictures of broken limbs, sores, dressings, wounds. A diagram of mouth-to-mouth resuscitation. All useless.

She remembered how her mother had hoarded her own illness, like a precious secret, not letting anyone in on it. She had a sudden memory of that Christmas day, long ago, waking to a different pattern of sounds, of whispered urgencies, and then a knocking at the door. A strange, male voice.

'You called the ambulance, mister?'

She was out of bed, and lunging for the door. There was dad in the hall, his shoulders sagged. Two ambulance men. There was the doctor whom mom visited only occasionally. There was a lot of congestion in the hall. Where was mom?

'Mom?' she'd called. 'Mom? Where are you?'

The four men looked at her and she froze. Then the tears welled into her father's eyes and he knelt down and put his arms around her.

Mom was between the two ambulance men, lying pinched and gray on a collapsible, aluminum stretcher, covered with a white hospital blanket. There was a dull, faraway look in her eyes as she gently whimpered. There was blood and vomit on her parents' big bed, and a horrible smell, different from vomit. Then the doctor took Julia's arm and shepherded her back down the hallway.

Tendzin let go the branch and lunged for the shore. He mistimed his leap and floundered in the water. The

Abbot grabbed his arm and for a moment they teetered there together, before the last of his momentum, and the last of the Abbot's strength, brought them back on to the bank.

'Did you hear her laugh?' Tendzin asked.

The Abbott nodded, standing up and trying to get some dignity back to his bearing.

'Who could she be? A water spirit? Did you see her breasts?'

'Of course I saw her breasts! Come on, stand up.'

'The barge! How will we return?'

The barge spun slowly into mid-stream, setting a course for the gorges of the border country.

'We'll ask the water spirit for help.'

'Are you serious, monk?'

The Abbot nodded, helping Tendzin up.

'Trust me,' he said. 'I've dealt with the spirit world before.'

'Yes, but were those spirits as beautiful as this one?'

They pushed through the undergrowth and then stopped on the edge of the tributary, staring at the white, fiberglass boat which the jungle had hidden from them.

'She travels in style,' Tendzin said. 'I last saw a boat like that on Hong Kong Harbor.'

'Come on. Wade the stream.'

But Tendzin hung back, suddenly nervous. The Abbot studied the fear on his face, and smiled.

'Come on. If she's supernatural, I can handle her. If she's real, I'm sure you can rise to the occasion.'

His manhood suddenly on the line, Tendzin had no option but to ease himself into the swiftly flowing, shallow water, and follow the Abbot to the boat.

'Hold it steady while I climb aboard,' the Abbot said.

He grunted as he dragged himself over the white gunwales. Sliding on to the cockpit floor he suddenly smelt the putrefaction, and a gust of fear swept him.

It was the smell of approaching death. Perhaps she was a demon en route to the land of the dead with her cargo.

'Oh, Tara,' he prayed. 'Protect me from the presence of demons.'

He crept to the cabin door and glanced in.

The beautiful, naked demon was crouched over the body of a man. For a moment the Abbot thought she was engaged in torture. Then he realized she was cleaning a putrefying wound, and suddenly his vision of her transformed.

'Tara?!' he said, with wonder.

The goddess looked up at him.

And it was Her, the Feminine principle of the Buddha. She stared at him, her expression one of care and concern. Instead of a lotus blossom, she held a wad of cotton-wool in her hand. It was stained with pus.

'Tara,' he whispered, and knelt in the cockpit, bowing his head until it touched the teak at the bottom of the doorway.

'What is this?' said Tendzin, coming up behind him.

He too saw the vision, and checked himself. But he could also see the face of the man she was tending.

'Master?' he exclaimed in wonder. 'Master!'

The Abbot looked up, focusing on the man.

Tendzin was right. The oracle had led them to the Master, and to the Marrying Maiden. But the Master was ill, and the Maiden had transformed herself into the Tara. And who was the third person? The wounded, bound man with the burning angry eyes?

CHAPTER TWENTY-SIX

'What are we going to do with you?' she asked Dave.

'Get these fucking chains off me and I'll show you what I'll do!' he yelled back, kicking out against the heavy, rusty, cast-iron chain which she had found to secure him with among the rubble of this decaying temple in the mountain jungle, a few hours ambulance drive from the river. He glared at her ferociously from the mildewed corner of two ancient stone walls, his eyes full of hatred.

'Get rid of him,' Joe said from his place across from the corner, his wounded right leg stretched before him on a box. 'Do it quick and clean, and with remorse.'

She glared at Joe, and the new etchings of pain on his lean face.

'I'll get you, you bastard!' Watson growled.

The two men stared at each other, and she watched them both.

Doubt had replaced the initial shock of the visions. Doubt and confusion. The sense of a repeating pattern, too, was gone. The world had shrunk back down to its normal size.

Her period had not come. Perhaps inside her was growing the child of one of them. Or perhaps what she had been through had simply confused her cycle. But she had a feeling that it was not the latter. The feeling grew out of the moment when she thought she was inside the body, and the mind, of the woman in the tunnel. She had been certain that the woman was pregnant by one of the men. Now, a week after the event, the images had receded, had lost their reality. The image could have been her imagination, an hallucination. It could be fake, but her body wasn't faking.

'You'll never learn, will you?' Joe whispered to Watson, his eyes dark and burning in his pallid face. 'You'll just keep coming back again and again to this point, and never let go.'

'I'll never let you go, that's for sure! You've got one hell of a lot to answer for, buster!'

Joe nodded, closed his eyes and put his hand over his face. Watson's angry eyes swung to Julia.

'So, what's it gonna be, sweetheart? You haven't got the nerve to do me in, have you? You won't let your boyfriend do it. That leaves those two old birds, and whoever else is spooking around this goddamned rat's nest!'

He held his eyes on her.

'I thought you were something,' he said. 'I really did. I thought I was going to free you from yourself!'

He laughed bitterly. She looked away.

'This bastard here has killed ... how many people? He tortured them, for Christ sake! He's a fucking monster! And you ... you accept that?'

She looked back at him, and nodded.

'Christ!' he said. 'Christ, no wonder the world's a fuck up! Women! Jesus!'

'You know nothing,' Joe said, so quietly they both had to strain towards him to hear his exhausted voice. 'What I did I must pay for. I know that. But what you did, you must pay for.'

'I've done fucking nothing! Except try and bring ass-holes like you to justice! My conscience is clean! Now, if you bastards kill me, that's your lookout!'

Julia shook her head. She didn't know what to do. She did not have Joe's certitude about what he had seen — what she had seen. The old men were on Joe's side, treating him like some long-lost saviour. They were busy organizing fake travel documents for Joe and herself. As far as those three were concerned, the journey had entered its final phase — an all-out assault on some far-off monastery, and the enacting of some mystical rite that would ... would, what? Would redeem them all?

And if she was pregnant? What then? Did she have any right to endanger the child? Did she own her body, like she'd always believed? Believed until waking that morning and counting the days and knowing what was wrong — and suddenly being transfixed by a feeling that seemed even older than the vision of the woman in the cave.

Some instinct had surged up in her, an instinct that made her feel that her own life was suddenly meaningless. Biology had taken over. She was in the grip of a power greater than herself. The power of life.

'We can't kill him,' she said to Joe. 'Regardless of whether what you experienced back on the river was real, or not.'

'What the fuck are you talking about the fucking river for?!' Dave yelled.

'It was real,' Joe said quietly. 'It was real, and for that reason he must not prevent us reaching Ghenko and the monastery.'

'I'll do a deal with you,' Dave said.

She heard the desperation in his voice. She looked at him.

'Get me out of this country, and I won't report you to the authorities. You go and do whatever fucking mumbo jumbo it is that the old fart out there wants, at his fucking monastery, at fucking Ghenko, and I'll get back to Hong Kong, and I'll wait until you're finished ...'

His voice died off. She glanced at Joe, raising her eyebrow inquiringly.

Joe hesitated, thinking a while. Then he shook his head.

'No,' he said. 'He wouldn't keep his word. No.'

'Can we keep him here?' she asked.

They looked at each other.

'OK,' Dave said. 'I'll accept that. I won't try and escape.'

Joe laughed weakly, and waved his hand dismissively.

'It doesn't matter what you promise,' Joe said. 'Your anger will decide how you act.'

He looked at Julia again.

'OK,' he said. 'He stays here, but he stays in chains, and he stays in a nice, safe cellar.'

'You cunt!' Watson said.

'Well, on that note,' she said, 'excuse me.'

'Bitch!' he snarled after her.

Outside, in the cloudy mountain air, she discovered herself trembling. She took a deep breath to calm herself, and then realized the old, gap-mouthed man was grinning lecherously at her. She let out her breath and smiled at him.

'Where's the Abbot?' she asked him.

He indicated the valley that appeared through the surrounding jungle. The valley was ringed by distant mountains, rising in tiers ahead of her.

'He'll be back soon,' he said.

She nodded, looking around at the ruins of the ancient temple to which the old men had transported her and her two lovers. It was not just age which had brought it down. China's recent past showed in the systematic shattering of the Buddhas, and the defacing of frescoes showing what looked like ten thousand different versions of hell.

Yet sometime recently someone had begun rebuilding the place; laboriously collecting up scattered tiles; piling up pieces of broken Buddhas prior to reconstructing the images; fixing a roof to keep out some of the incessant rain of these mountains.

Feeling the old man's enjoyment in watching her, she smiled at him, blushing as she did so. Despite the bulky peasant clothes the Abbot had found for her, she was conscious of her body, and of the old man's appreciation of her.

She walked past him, to the truck and stood there, examining it.

When she had first seen the truck, half-hidden in the undergrowth beside the river, it had been quite clearly an ambulance. It had taken them a day to pole the barge back to the spot from which the old men had set out on their river journey. And part of that day had been spent by her swimming down the river after the runaway barge to retrieve it.

The elder of the two men was the driver, and the one most fluent in English. He had the border-dweller's gift for languages. His scholarly friend's speech was more pedantic, more the product of learning than experiencing. With their help she had got her two lovers into the ambulance, and trusted the old man's driving to deliver them to this spot — where they had now been a week. In that time she had stripped all trace of ambulance from the truck. Now it looked like an early 1950s Chevrolet delivery truck — although its origins quite clearly lay in a Polish factory. The communists had done General Motors the honor of imitation.

'All fixed now,' the old man said brightly, hobbling over to stand close to her.

'All fixed,' she said. 'Though I don't know how long the differential will hold together.'

'You'll fix that too?'

She smiled at his faith in her mechanical ability, and shook her head.

'If we meet another truck on the road,' she said, 'we'll do a swap. OK?'

He laughed with evident pleasure at the prospect of larceny. She smiled and took his arm.

She felt so good! Standing there in the steamy heat, under a hazy sky, with this old man. She felt like she had been here all her life. She felt clean and clear and with absolutely no worries, no neurotic fears. The struggling actress living out her masquerade was long gone. It was as if Julia was dead and this new woman had been born from out of her husk.

The old man squinted, and pointed through the trees to the distant road that wandered down the valley beside the glistening ribbon of the big river, and plunged eventually into the mountains. His long distance vision was remarkably good.

'Here he comes,' he said.

'How's he traveling?'

'He found a bicycle.'

'Found it?'

'Well, perhaps he's convinced some sinner to lend it to him in return for a few prayers.'

She shook her head and laughed.

The Abbot, though, wasn't laughing. It was a long, hard push on the old bicycle. And where he had come from had not helped him generate a mood of eagerness and strength. Even though the scholar's hand was as unerring as ever, she was not well. And now her employer had let her know that her services were no longer required.

Inside Pin Li's mind was an encyclopedia of ancient poetry. Her skill with calligraphy had been a legend. She had supervised the production of many a beautiful book — before beauty and the truth it contained had been banished from the world. Her inability to stop producing beauty and circulating truth had led her as unerringly to the Re-education Camps as had the Abbot's arrival in China with no papers, no ready explanations, no money, and no patrons.

Now that the convolutions of history had spat them both out — old jail-birds washed up in the same town — they had reverted to their past errors. They argued philosophy and religion when they could. The Abbot wanted her to recite works which vindicated his view that the Chinese were a people every bit as cultured as the Tibetans. And she wanted to hear what the Buddha, and before him the Hindu sages, had to say about the nature of Mind.

The scholar created beautiful documents. She created them quietly, and only for cash customers who were also members of that huge, underground society teeming beneath the dying skin of communism. The society of fellow re-educated, ex-convicts. The men and women who had looked madness in the face and lived through it.

But the Abbot could see how the effort of denying other people's madness had caught up with Pin Li. That, and living the lie which she had found herself caught up within. She had taken help, once, from people outside her world's borders, and now she was their agent.

He, too, had taken that help, and he, too, was trapped. But at least, he told himself, at least I recognize the moral dilemma of it all.

The Abbot pictured the young Pin Li, during that first flush of freedom, when women's feet were unbound, and the rest of the world hammered at China's door. He saw her toiling with her pen and ink-block, mastering the exquisite beauty of the script — her young mind eagerly playing with the storehouse of wisdom that was her inheritance. And then he contrasted that image with the old woman, hiding in a cheap room, by day proof-reading the people's newspaper, and by night toiling over not poetry or essays, but travel documents, and identity papers.

One day a month they both went into the mountains, to the old Buddhist temple, to carry on the renovations which they would never finish. She would leave him there, picking up broken tiles, and go on to the river, where she conducted some secret ritual of her own.

Now the newspaper no longer wanted her, and so the beautifully wrought American passports and the new visas and travel documents that the Abbot carried were the last examples of the scholar's art. For without access to the newspaper's dilapidated linotype machine, the even older letterpress machine, its photographic equipment and darkroom, the Leica camera which ought to have been in a museum of technology, and supplies of paper, the business of document reproduction — or forgery, as a pedant might put it — had to cease.

The editor's eagerness to receive a percentage of the scholar's income from this source had obviously diminished in proportion to the sudden hardening of the official line. Whatever events had occurred in Beijing, in Tiananmen Square — and no one would ever know for sure what they were — the effect had been the creation of a feeling of fear throughout the land.

The only good news was a sudden loosening of travel restrictions into Tibet. For reasons the Abbot could not fathom, the party suddenly wanted to act like a friend of religion.

The Abbot got off his bicycle and resigned himself to pushing it the last mile as the broken-down road climbed into the trees, heading on to crest the mountains and plunge down to the river. Along the way it wandered past the almost-forgotten entrance to the temple. A temple begun, as he had once assumed Ghenko had begun, by wandering Buddhist scholars seeking to spread the word. He knew, now, that there was a deeper level to Ghenko, just as there was a deeper level to his relationship with the scholar.

'Nothing is as it seems,' he reminded himself. '*Maya* is everywhere.'

Although Dave Watson raged and swore his hardest, kicked, screamed, and lunged at them, they took him down into the temple's half-cleared cellar.

Julia — with a giddy feeling of a dreadful unreality, as if she were stepping into the dream, the nightmares of revelation — had fashioned a pair of shackles to fit the chain, and padlocked Watson to a ring-bolt in the cellar's floor. A bolt probably installed for just that purpose, but whether this century, or in the distant past, no one could say.

They left him a drinking trough, and what blankets they could spare, and some food. They left him a promise that someone would come to look after him until they returned from their pilgrimage.

Not until they pulled two old doors over the cellar entrance and cut out all light except those bright stars which could winkle through rot holes in the wood, did he really believe they would do it.

'This is the fucking twentieth century!' he screamed after them. 'I'm an American citizen, for Christ sake!' And then, more quietly, 'You can't do this to me.'

Then, straining his ears, he heard the old truck start up. He heard the gears grate as one of the old men took the wheel.

'Why?!' he screamed. 'Why?!'

But there was no answer. He had been abandoned. Except he had a strange feeling that he was not alone. A feeling that, if he looked quickly to one side, he would catch a glimpse of companions in his nightmare.

He looked. For a moment, he thought he saw a man and a woman. The woman was kneeling. Then he shut his eyes and yelled again, and they disappeared.

'Get out of here!' he screamed.

'I don't like it at all,' she said, as they labored down into the valley.

'I have a very reliable friend,' the Abbot said. 'She will come and check on your companion in a few days.'

'A few days? He'll go mad by then.'

'No,' said the Abbot. 'It takes longer than that. A month will do it. I have seen men driven mad by a month of solitary. If he has any faith at all, he will last.'

'Or his anger will sustain him,' Joe said, quietly.

'But he's all alone!' she protested.

They ignored her. What she really wanted to say was, *But he might be the father of what I can feel within me, groping towards form. He lay with me and I thought we shared something. I can't let him go!*

Instead, she said, 'But what if we don't come back? What if something happens to us?'

The Abbot looked over his shoulder to her as she crouched on the bench in back of the truck. He smiled gently, and touched her hand with his.

'My friend has the keys,' he said. 'She will release him within the week, and show him how to get back to the river. He came up the river, and he can return by it.'

'Once he's released,' Joe said quietly, 'he won't rest until he's found us. We should have killed him.'

The Abbot turned to face the divided windshield again, trying to ignore the chill that Joe's quiet words caused in the air. It was the chill of truth.

'He doesn't know where we're going,' Julia said.

'Yes he does,' Joe said. 'He knows exactly where.'

She stared at him.

'How?'

'Because I told him.'

'Why did you do that?'

'I was talking to you, and I let the words slip out because I was sure we wouldn't be mad enough to let him live.' He shrugged. 'So it's on me if anything happens.'

'We aren't mad to let him live. Madness is killing people,' the Abbot said. 'There is only one way off the wheel, and that is the way of non-violence.'

'Where did you get the American passports?' Joe said, suddenly changing tack.

Julia saw the Abbot's confusion. She saw his lie.

'My friend made them up.'

'Your friend had a remarkably good source of paper,' Joe said. 'That's genuine State Department stationery, if ever I saw it.'

'How can you be so sure?' Julia demanded hotly.

'Because I've traveled under false documents in the past.' He held up his new passport. 'This is the real thing. There's only one organization that could make this available to a group of renegades way out in the backblocks of China — out near the border, where there's a lot of international tension ... the CIA.'

She stared at the back of the Abbot's head. The old man refused to look at them.

'Is that true?' she asked him.

'My friend ...' he began. 'My friend had access to a source. I did not question it.'

'But you knew,' Joe said, gently. 'Of course you knew. How many other travelers have you helped along the road to Lhasa? How many hitch-hikers with tiny little cameras have you suggested take a few photos of People's Liberation Army convoys?'

The Abbot's shoulders had hunched.

'How much does it cost to bribe enough people to enable you to make these documents? Where's your source of funds?'

There was a long silence.

'It's OK,' Joe said, eventually. 'You take help from where you can get it.'

The Abbot let out a long sigh. He shook his head.

'No,' he said. 'The greatest evil grows out of the smallest seed. I was very sure my friend was in contact with the people you mentioned. And you are not the first Westerners to have stayed at the old temple. Yes, we took help from where we could get it. The more help we took, of course, the more that was demanded in return. And we tried to pretend that the fruits of those actions would be peace.'

'But they will be,' Julia said, earnestly. 'Won't they?'

The Abbot turned and looked at her. He shook his head.

'The fruits of violence are always violence,' he said. 'And I have seen too much of it to think that will ever change. It would have been better if we had lain down and died than accepted help from those people.'

'What nonsense!' she said. 'The most important thing is staying alive.'

She realised that biology was speaking through her — that a voice was echoing inside her, 'Stay alive so you can bring me into the world.'

'It's a question I have often asked myself,' the Abbot said, 'when I remember what it was like waking up in the morning to see men frozen to death beside me — men who had died because they could no longer bear what living entailed. The question was this: perhaps they made the right choice? Perhaps I was the coward for staying alive, for sanctioning what my captors did to me? Because, always, those of us who survived did so because we committed some small evil. We stole someone's scraps. We informed on some petty misdemeanor. We smiled at the journalist's camera — pretending our bellies were full — so the guards would reward us later. We wrote out confessions of idiotic crimes we had never committed, so they would stop torturing us.

'The Christian church was founded upon the man who denied he was a disciple, remember? Isn't that odd? The very foundations built upon the denial of faith. I have often thought about that since I was released ... since I denied the Buddha that I might find some rest. Nothing I do now can make up for that cowardice. Nothing.'

They were silent, listening to the differential howling as the truck rumbled down into the valley. Eventually Julia leant forward and wrapped her arms around the Abbot's still shoulders and pressed her cheek against his.

CHAPTER TWENTY-SEVEN

Julia was glad that the only view of their travels she had from the back of the truck was over the shoulders of the Abbot and his driver, through the ancient windshield. Even though it meant that the inside of the truck was soon hot and sticky. For even looking straight ahead she kept seeing the precipices as they corkscrewed now up, now down, the mountains. It took all her effort to retain her seat over the bone-jarring thudding of the rear suspension, bouncing about among the bedding, the food, and what spares and tools she had been able to gather together for the truck.

They wound down to a river valley, bypassing the town of Jinghong, and then made their way westward, climbing beside a river which fed back into the Mekong behind them.

She had taken the precaution of strapping Joe to his bench. He was still weak, and his wound still wept from the upper thigh. He cried out a number of times as they crashed down the road, which was no more than a track scoured out by rain. His face gleamed with sweat.

Eventually, she gave up trying to peer out at their journey. She jammed herself against the hot metal side of the vehicle and, wedged there with blankets, fell into a dull reverie, while the old driver crouched over the wheel, trying to second-guess the rain-cut washaways that scarred the surface of the road.

'CIA?' Tendzin said softly.

The Abbot glanced quickly at him, but Tendzin kept peering ahead at the forest, the pot holes and washaways.

'So that's why we're enduring all this?' he continued. 'You, a spy.'

'I am not!' the Abbot said indignantly. Then he glanced at his old friend, sighed and nodded.

'I'm nothing that exalted,' he explained. 'The scholar is the real spy. I am merely her assistant.'

'You collected information from the hospital?'

'A lot of military officials came through that hospital. All I did was empty their wastepaper bins. In return, Pin Li photographed journals for me; or copied books.'

'So your love of learning was your undoing?'

'Love of anything is our undoing. I should have cultivated ignorance.'

'If you had, we would not now be returning the Master to our home.'

'Don't expect too much from our old place of residence.'

Tendzin wrenched his eyes from the road. The Abbot had a look of fore-knowledge on his face.

'Watch the road!' he snapped.

'What do you know about the old place?'

'I know nothing — except that the scholar's contacts keep wanting her to get photographs of "the installation at Ghenko".'

'What installation?'

'Exactly. When we left, you'll recall the Chinese were in the act of knocking it to pieces. I remember a hospital patient, a colonel in the Construction Brigade. He had come down from Tibet with a broken leg. Ghenko was a word which occurred in his conversations.'

'What does the scholar want you to do?'

The Abbot was silent a while, looking ahead at the climbing road and the crashing river beside them. Eventually, he dug into his robes and pulled something out. Tendzin glanced at it.

'What on earth is it?'

'It's an automatic Pentax camera, supplied by the scholar's friends. Look, watch this!'

To Tendzin's surprise and delight, the Abbot held it up and pressed a button and what looked like a stubby, glass-eyed penis erected itself from the middle of the apparatus.

'Abbot! What is it doing?'

'Not what you think. That is an automatic zoom lens. Even an idiot like myself can take perfect pictures with it.'

'And if an army patrol stops us and finds it?'

'All the tourists have them. I'd be more worried about the army patrol's reaction to our pasengers and their luggage.'

'I thought it was all right to carry passengers?'

'Yes. Their papers are in order for travel by road.

But I could not dissuade the Master from bringing his weapons.'

'A man's entitled to carry a rifle.'

'And a woman's entitled to carry a hand-grenade?'

'Ahhh, but what a woman! She can make me act like your automatic zoom lens!'

'Cultivate detachment, you rascal.'

'Your sermons are losing their effect as I learn more and more about you.'

'Look out ahead, you fool!'

Tendzin looked up, and slammed his foot on the brake.

Julia crashed against the back of the Abbot's seat. Jerked out of her half-sleep, she stared through the windshield at what had brought them to a jarring halt.

They were caught behind a huge timber-jinker, on which one enormous forest giant was precariously fastened.

'Where are we?' she asked.

'Still a long way from our destination,' the Abbot said. 'How's your patient?'

She glanced at Joe who, like her, had been rudely awakened by the sudden halt. She smiled at him and he gave her the ghost of a smile in return, and reached out for her hand. She could feel the fever in him.

'It would have been better to have left him behind,' she said.

'If we'd left him with your other companion, only one of them would have survived. What is the cause of their enmity?'

'I don't know,' she said. 'Something that happened a long time ago, I guess.'

The Abbot nodded.

'Yes,' he said. 'It has a karmic feel to it.'

She gritted her teeth. She didn't want to hear about that. She tried to concentrate on her belly. Growing within there was all the reincarnation she needed. In the end, that's what all the theories meant: life goes on.

'Trouble,' Tendzin said warningly.

The timber-jinker had come to a complete halt. They soon saw why. A small group of soldiers appeared from around its side.

'Hide!' the Abbot said to her. 'And cover him up, too.'

'What are we going to do?' Tendzin whispered.

'Get our papers out, what else? Tell them we took a wrong turning.'

The leader of the army patrol was young, hatchet-faced, and with an air of brutal efficiency. He would have been an infant at the time of the Cultural Revolution. A child brought up to respect no authority but that of the party. A child who had taken part in all the mad brutality which had been visited upon the Abbot.

The old man shivered, but made himself nod politely to the young officer.

'What are you doing on this road?' the officer demanded.

'My idiot driver took a wrong turn.'

'Papers?' grunted the officer.

The Abbot handed them over and sat, trying not to show his internal agitation. The officer read at first with boredom, then with a sudden interest which made the Abbot's heart sink. The officer looked up sharply.

'Which of you is the Long Marcher?'

'My driver,' the Abbot said, 'has that honor.'

'Then calling him an idiot is not a patriotic act, is it?'

'I spoke ... it was a joke.'

'What does he want?' Tendzin asked.

The officer's sharp eyes flicked to Tendzin. But his attitude became mildly deferential.

'Which brigade were you with, honorable sir?'

'I ...' Tendzin glanced to the Abbot.

'He was with the 25th Army Corps,' the Abbot said. 'His home was near Dali, and that is where we are now going.'

The officer's eyes came back to the Abbot.

'And you are the book-keeper?'

The Abbot nodded, his throat suddenly too dry for him to speak.

'We do not joke about veterans, do we, book-keeper?'

'No, sir. No, we don't.'

All the Abbot's memories crowded back around him. Those glittering, humorless eyes, and the mind refined to torture point, all in the pursuit of some future heaven on earth. This man would kill for the good of the party.

And I, I am killing for the good of Buddhism, the Abbot thought. *I am encouraging the Americans in their war with these people. I lie and cheat and steal, always with the excuse that my long-term goal is honorable.*

The officer turned away from him and walked around the truck.

What error of doctrine had the officer committed to wind up patrolling this distant border, the Abbot wondered. What error of doctrine had he himself committed to continue to suffer rebirth? From the corner of his eye, the Abbot saw the officer outside Tendzin's window. Tendzin turned and stared at the officer.

The officer straightened his back and saluted. Then he nodded to indicate they could continue.

Tendzin crawled the truck past the parked timber-jinker. The driver and his offsider were engaged in a loud argument with the troops. The truck's crew were brightly, colorfully, dressed in some minority group's clothing; some mountain tribe which, like the Tibetans, had been swallowed by the Chinese dragon.

They edged past the old road-tractor, its bonnet festooned with animistic symbols and its cowled headlights painted like eyes. Neither Tendzin nor the Abbot spoke for a long time.

They camped that night on a logging track. Although Julia was weary to her bones, the nearby rumble and coughing of a tiger on the prowl kept her awake.

In that insomnious weariness, her mind freewheeled, until she was suddenly facing her childhood memory, her favorite fantasy. A young princess in a garden of ponds and ornately carved temples. *The King and I* had been an early favorite movie. How she had loved that film whenever she caught it on late-night television, or at a revival cinema. And then there had been the production of the musical.

She had used every trick she could to get into the chorus and wear the silk gowns and the long, false gold nails.

She had forgotten it entirely on this trip until now, lying awake in the forest near the Burmese border. Now she could feel the texture of fine silk between her fingers. Both rough and smooth. She stretched her fingers out in the dark, remembering how she used to wear her nails.

It couldn't be, could it?

Life couldn't reach past death. Even if there was something more to reincarnation than she was willing to admit, surely things as simple and ordinary as the clothes you wore could not penetrate that supposedly impenetrable barrier.

She shut her eyes and found herself staring at that mysterious woman's approaching killer. His eyes were wild. His hands grabbed the folds of her robe and wrestled with it, and then ripped it apart. The woman fought back, trying to claw him with her manacled hands and her long, golden nails.

'Julia? Julia?'

She opened her eyes to his worried voice. Joe had dragged himself beside her as she mumbled and twisted on the bench. She reached up and grabbed hold of him and pulled him against her.

'Don't leave me,' she whispered. 'Please. Not this time. Not any more.'

He chuckled.

'It took a long time to find you again,' he said. 'I won't let you go in a hurry.'

And she found herself wanting it to be true, all of it, every unbelievable image and feeling.

~

Suddenly, there was a shaft of light. Dave Watson stared at it. He had lost track of time. He sat indifferently in his own filth. He looked at the shaft of light falling from above, as he heard the sound of the door being dragged away from the cellar entrance.

'Hello?' inquired a nervous and high-pitched old voice.

Dave's hackles rose. He said nothing. He shuffled himself quietly upright.

'I've brought you some food,' the voice continued.

Dave had no weapon. He looked down at his spread hands. They had only chained his feet. His hands would have to do.

A wooden ladder came into his view and it slid down to connect the floor to the light.

A figure in some kind of robe descended the ladder.

'I told him that leaving you here was not good. But he said you were a wild man. Is that true?'

Dave caught a glimpse of a mild-mannered, but lined face. A shrewd face. The hands carried a satchel, with a ring of keys looped over a finger. Dave's eyes went to the keys, then back to the old face.

'He told me to wait a week.' The person paused just out of Dave's reach. 'But that didn't seem right. After all, both he and I have been imprisoned.'

Dave moaned softly, and the old person looked at him sharply.

'It's only been two days,' the person said.

Dave moaned again.

Worried, the person stepped closer.

Dave grabbed the old throat, and jammed his thumbs into the wind-pipe.

'No!' the voice croaked. 'No. I let ... you go.'

'I'll let myself go!' Dave grunted back.

He saw the panic in the old eyes. Then he saw terror. And then he realized it was an old woman.

He started, and released the pressure, and she collapsed, choking, to the floor.

Dave grabbed the keys and fumbled with the leg irons.

'You mustn't ...' the old woman's voice was badly strained. 'You must stay here. Please! Trouble will come to me!

'Tough shit!' Dave said, recovered now from the surprise. He stumbled away from the filth-soaked earth, and grabbed the satchel.

'No! Give it back! It's not yours.'

Dave shook his head, jerking it out of her reach.

He grabbed the ladder and hauled himself towards the light. Feeling hands behind him, he kicked out. There was a cry and he heard her thump back on the ground.

Dave dragged the ladder up next to him.

There was a battered old bicycle propped against a tree. Dave looked at it. He could hear the old woman crying beneath him. He ignored the cries.

He opened the satchel and he wolfed down the bread, tearing it between his teeth. There was a piece of acrid-smelling goat's cheese, and he tore at that, too.

Hunger sated, he looked further into the satchel. He pulled out a 9 mm pistol. He stared at it with surprise. It did not compute with the old woman. What else did the satchel contain?

There was an old Leica camera, and there was also a topographic map.

Puzzled, he examined the map closely. He could see the Mekong, and he found the point at which the borders of Laos, Burma and China converged on the Golden Triangle. He followed the river up and then, checking the topography around him, pinpointed his position, and the nearby town of Jinghong.

Intrigued, he went right through the satchel, and found another map, and a postcard. The card was written in Chinese characters, and showed a view of Beijing. One set of characters occurred twice, and was underlined both times.

He could make no sense of it and opened out the other map, recognizing it as a bilingual, Chinese/English, map of Southern Tibet.

And he suddenly recognized the Chinese characters from the postcard again, on the map, with the English name printed beside them. Ghenko.

He looked back at the cellar in surprise. Then he dug into his back pocket and pulled out his wallet. His out-of-date DEA badge was still readable. He took the ladder and walked back to the cellar and looked down.

She stared up at him anxiously. He smiled, holding the ID up in one hand, while he slid the ladder down to her. She stared at him questioningly.

'You and me are on the same side, sister,' he said. 'I think we oughta sit down together and have a long talk about things.'

CHAPTER TWENTY-EIGHT

Julia woke to the sound of rain. She lay a while, listening to it pouring on the metal roof of the truck, for a moment forgetting where she was. Remembering, she sat up quickly. Joe was asleep. The Abbot was curled up on the front seat. Through the fogged-up windshield all she could see was the wall of forest, and the rain.

As she looked out into the rain, something appeared at the forest's edge, staring towards the truck. With a sudden thrill she realized that it was the great cat's face of a tiger. It peered unblinkingly, inquiringly, towards them, then suddenly turned, as if making up its mind about something, and was gone.

Julia eased the back door open and peered out. The rain showed no sign of easing. As she squatted in the doorway she heard a sound under the truck. Something scraped and slithered. She edged back, putting out her hand for Joe's gun.

She pulled the AK-47 as quietly to herself as she could, eased the safety catch off and lined the gun up through the doorway as something slid up from under the truck.

Tendzin's bright eyes and gap-toothed grin appeared. He took in the girl and the gun and the grin grew even wider.

'Where have you been?' she demanded.

He pulled himself into the truck.

'Slept underneath,' he said, pointing down.

She felt suddenly guilty.

'I saw a tiger,' she said. 'Over in the jungle.'

'Tigers are OK,' he said. 'We should really worry about bandits.'

'Oh?'

He nodded.

'Lots of bandits,' he said, seemingly happily.

'Relations of yours?' she suggested.

He looked at her with his grin, and raised an eyebrow.

But they saw no bandits that day. The track they traversed gave up all pretext of being a road. It was merely a series of linked pot holes. Julia took over driving to relieve Tendzin — there was obvious tiredness in his eyes. They spent most of the day in second gear, with an occasional burst into third. They never reached top.

They seemed to have disappeared into a green world. When the rain eased they found themselves in fog. She could only trust that the Abbot had some notion of where they were going. They carried a drum of fuel wedged into the back, along with their belongings, and she knew they'd be making use of it before they hit any kind of real road again.

Once she thought she saw some other jungle beast

through the gloom. Several times they passed ruined temples. With no sign of the sun, no horizon or shadows, directions became meaningless. The only thing she could do was keep on driving.

Eventually, the grey light of day merged with the blackness of night and they came to a halt in the middle of the track.

The good news was that Joe had improved. His wound had stopped weeping and his face was losing its striated, strained look. To celebrate, Julia doused some semi-rotted wood with gasoline and made a fire. They had hot tea, with butter — Tibetan-style — and dried fish.

She also topped-up the fuel tank from their gas drum, and checked the engine over with the aid of the Abbot's Eveready torch. Holding it she remembered what Joe had discovered about the Abbot and his contacts with the more sinister elements of her country. She had come to inhabit a world where nothing could be taken at face value. Nothing at all.

This time she made space for Tendzin to sleep inside the truck, and they bedded down and lay in the blackness again, listening to the sounds of forest animals roaming nearby.

I'm free, she thought. *Free to pursue any of my fantasies. Free to give up the things which never worked out in my life — like my acting.*

But I'm not free,' she reflected. *I'm pregnant, and that is the ultimate way of being 'unfree', isn't it? And I'm stuck with these bandits until such time as we either run into a bigger group of bandits, or into an army patrol that is not fooled by the venerable 'Long Marcher'. Or, if the impossible does happen and we reach wherever we're going, what then?*

Does the Abbot take his photos, and do whatever it is he wants Joe to do, and then we turn around like any other bunch of tourists, and drive home? What do I mean: I'm free? she wondered. *I'm mad! That's what I am. So, why do I feel so good?*

She slept a dreamless, deep and refreshing sleep.

Next day, some time in the afternoon, they floundered out of the forest on to a real road. By the standards she had come to accept, it was a highway, a freeway even. No concrete. No blacktop. But the pot holes were reduced to the size of oranges, and spaced a yard apart in solidly packed earth.

She felt like getting out and kissing the hard-packed earth as she surveyed the road carving its way around the mountainsides.

'You like the road?' the Abbot inquired.

She looked at him and nodded.

'It's the finest road in the world,' she said.

'I helped rebuild it,' he said. 'It's what they call the "Burma Road".'

She looked at him again. He smiled back at her and lifted his hands.

'They bled for the first two weeks,' he said. 'I carried rocks from out of the way of surveyors, and dumped them down the ravines. I worked on this road I don't know how long. By day I carried rock. In the evening I learnt about the mistakes in my philosophy. And when I finally understood all my mistakes, I was carrying rocks up above the snowline. All my compatriots had died. I was repatriated to Jinghong.'

He sighed and looked at the road again.

'And now I return,' he said.

'Now we all return,' she said. 'Where to next?'

He pointed ahead with his chin.

'There is a town this way. It is called Dali. We will drive straight through it. And, out through the town, we will find a road which goes all the way to Tibet.'

She heard the emotion in his voice. His eyes had a faraway look in them, and a slight glaze of moisture. Then he became businesslike again.

'But I think Tendzin had better return to the wheel. There are many different sorts of non-Chinese people in this area, but none of them have yellow hair like you.'

She pulled over and surrendered the wheel to the old man, while the Abbot sat there, not sure whether to smile or weep at the prospect of returning to his native land.

The Public Security Official examined the backpacker's papers one more time. It wasn't that the papers were out of order. It was just that in the past five years the official had grown used to backpackers, and he knew what to expect. They were often filthily dirty. They could be male or female. They came from all over Europe, from America and Canada, from Australia and New Zealand. They came seeking the 'mystic Orient', hoping to find it above the snow-line, in Xizang Autonomous Region, as it was now called. Tibet, as it once was. But they were all young.

This man was forty-five years old, pot-bellied and balding. He was American. He had that slightly crazy look to the eyes of a religious seeker, so perhaps he was some guru chaser. Someone for whom the world had become too much and now he was on what they used to call the 'Hippie Trail'.

The passport photograph matched him exactly, even down to the shirt he was wearing. It was so good it could almost have been taken yesterday. It did not have that 'frozen in time' look of most passport photos.

Something was wrong, but the official could not pinpoint it. And, in the absence of any reality to anchor his intuition upon, he smiled at the tall American, and handed him back his papers.

'Thank you, Mr Wilson,' he said. 'You will find the bus station just down the street. The bus will return you to Kunming, where you can re-book for Lhasa.'

The official looked through the door and pointed to the dusty main street of Jinghong.

The tall, middle-aged backpacker thanked him and picked up his pack — which the official noted was very old, and which looked as if it had indeed covered millions of miles — and walked back out into the street. The official came to the doorway and made sure he did walk down to the bus station.

Jinghong was the last town before the Golden Triangle border. The People's Republic of China had no interest in what went on down there, but it did pay to keep an eye on strange characters traveling alone.

Dave Watson bought his ticket from another official, this one younger, more bored-looking, who reluctantly examined his papers and seemed disappointed that they were in order. Dave was conscious, all the time, of being under scrutiny. First by the security official who had vetted his papers, and then by a pair of young female European backpackers who sat on their gear in one corner of the concrete bus station. He made sure not to let them catch his eye. He wanted to be alone.

Jinghong was once a sleepy, hot and dusty tropical town. Almost like Chiang Saen, he thought. But now there were army trucks parked in the street, and a sense of purpose in the dozens of people hand-mixing concrete and shoveling it into the rising, bamboo-reinforced walls of some new building. The Chinese dragon, if not fully awake way out on its borders, was at least twitching.

Fellow travelers came drifting into the bus station, to stand and stare in open-mouthed fascination at the dirty, long-nosed girls, and the tired, angry-looking long-nosed man. There were whole families of peasants: rangy-looking mountain nomads with craggy faces and erect, defiant bearings; and ancient and wizened old women whose life-force no political turmoil could ever crush.

He made sure he got seated next to a foul-smelling peasant, composed his mind and prepared to sleep his way on up out of the tropics to the snow. The girls had smiled at him, and now probably assumed, from his lack of reaction, that he was either gay or simply a cranky old misogynist. It didn't bother him. Nothing bothered him but the end of the Quest, now that it was in sight.

CHAPTER TWENTY-NINE

As Dave Watson slept, the old truck bypassed the town of Dali, bouncing and scraping its way through many a creek-crossing, and rattling over bridges older than many civilizations, as it jolted along the edge of Erhai Lake, on the road to Lijiang.

This was China, Julia realized, peering from behind the Abbot. Here were elegant pagodas and Buddhist temples, and green, green fields that had been cultivated for thousands of years. Something within her responded to the sight of the lake through the trees, of the snow-capped peaks ahead of them, and of the work-weary peasants who didn't bother to look up at the truck coating them with dust as they toiled homewards — their backs misshapen by a lifetime of servitude to the earth itself.

Again she felt the sickness. The nausea. She groaned, clinging to the rattling side of the truck. It was the baby, wasn't it? It was morning sickness?

But she felt dislocated in time. She could feel the presence of that other woman again. It was as if her rough tunic had become fine silk. She stared at her hands, finding it hard to believe that the nails weren't long and thickly lacquered.

And the fear that surged up with the image was overwhelming. A fear of ... what? Of the end of everything? Of the end of life? Of approaching, and violent, death?

The Abbot heard her cry out and glanced back at her white face.

'Pull over,' he said, quickly.

Outside, on the hard-packed road, it was little better. She was sick, and that cleared her head for a moment. But the world felt rubbery. Everything felt like it was about to collapse in on itself. Like the world, time, her life, was a card table being folded up.

She climbed back aboard, trying to avoid their anxious, concerned faces. She smiled bravely. The Abbot was puzzled. But the driver's shrewd eyes went to her belly and she realized he knew at least part of the conundrum.

And perhaps, she thought, *he knows more of it than I want to know.*

The road wound into the town of Lijiang around huge, snow-capped mountains. In the truck, they were hot and sweaty, but looking up through the windshield Julia could see that far-off tantalizing vision of icy coldness.

Then the twentieth century intruded into the ancient landscape ahead of them, and Julia felt a rush of aesthetic outrage.

The town lay in a small river valley studded with sudden, absurd, small steep-sided hills. Atop one of the hills the huge steel lattice of a radio mast looked down on a street of ugly, grey concrete buildings.

On the wall of one building a vividly colored poster depicted some famous battle, with a group of brightly pink peasants lifting the Red Flag against darkly menacing warlords with Genghis Khan mustaches. She realized it was a movie poster, and that this was the local cinema.

The bus station lay ahead of them. A crowd of people gathered there with their cane baskets. She saw tall women in bright-blue clothes, their backs loaded down with wicker baskets, as the truck rattled past. It drew the eye of some local Mao-suited official standing in the doorway of the Public Security Bureau.

'Keep driving,' the Abbot whispered.

Tendzin just grunted.

They passed a statue of Mao Tse-tung mouldering in an unkempt garden, and then they were through the town. They passed another hill, atop which sat a well-kept building in the old Chinese style half-hidden among bushy trees. They passed another group of people, the women again outfitted in bright blue.

Tendzin laughed.

'Good people,' he said. 'Hate the Chinese.'

'Who are they?' Julia asked.

'Naxi,' he said. 'Came from Tibet a long time ago. The women are in charge and the men are just ...' he waved his hand dismissively. 'If the women like you ...' He grinned.

'Be quiet and take the next turn left,' the Abbot suddenly said.

Tendzin glanced at him in surprise, and then did as he was asked.

'If you like the Naxi so much,' the Abbot said, 'we'll stop in their village — which is just up ahead of us — and you can keep all those immodest women at bay while I climb up to the monastery that sits above their village.'

'How about we leave the prayers till we get to Ghenko?' Tendzin suggested.

The Abbot turned angrily to him.

'I'm not going to this monastery to pray, you idiot! First, there is someone I must thank for risking his life for me. Second, I need information about roads that will take us on to Ghenko that will avoid the Public Service Bureaus! Now, when we reach the village, you stay with the truck and make sure the local children don't run off with the wheels!'

Tendzin kept his eyes fixed straight ahead as he took the turn.

And again Julia felt the sickness and the nausea.

Alone, leaning up the steep climb into the clouds, the Abbot let his breath out with a sigh. He needed to get away for a while. Being cooped up with Tendzin was bad enough, but the presence of the woman made it far worse. Something about her troubled him.

Pausing for breath he looked back and saw the truck parked at the beginning of the monastery path. The village children had formed a half-circle around it, kept at a distance by the menacing figure of Tendzin, who was armed with a long stick. The Abbot laughed and released his anger and turned back to the path. Now he had time to notice the vividly green vegetation and the sudden, outrageously bold orchid blooms that sprang up from old, fallen logs rotting in the undergrowth.

Smiling, the Abbot leant into the final steep part of the ascent, into the clouds, until he arrived in the monastery grounds.

All was silent as he entered the flower-choked walls, picking his way between more vivid orchids and huge clumps of hydrangeas. And there, among the flowers, lay the shattered statue of Sakyamuni Buddha, smashed by the Red Guard in one of their rampages.

He stopped and bowed to the broken statue.

'All display is mere illusion,' a voice said behind him, in Tibetan. 'Although the image is broken, the example lives on.'

He lifted his head and looked into the face of a monk. They stared at each other a moment, then tears filled both their eyes and they embraced.

'My Abbot!' the monk exclaimed.

'And keeper of my secrets. I'm glad you have survived.'

'Every day they threatened me. And every night I took refuge in the *Dharma*. Did the package you requested arrive in good order?'

'Yes. And I can never thank you enough for keeping it so well all these years.'

'And I can never thank you enough for your teachings, O Abbot. But, what brings you here? I did not think people like you could get travel documents.'

'As to the documents, all things are possible. As to our destination ...' He took a breath, suddenly discovering it was difficult to say. 'As to our destination. We're returning to Ghenko!'

The monk's eyes opened in surprise.

'Ghenko is to be re-opened?'

'Ghenko is finished, my friend. I saw its destruction.'

'You were always ahead of me in your thoughts, my Abbot. I had better make us some tea while you instruct me once again.'

'I bet that old goat is drinking tea and swapping tales with his counterpart up the hill,' Tendzin said. 'By the time he gets back, these brats will have made off with half the truck.'

'Let me out and I'll deal with them,' Joe growled from behind the seat.

'Not likely!' Tendzin said. 'If they see any more strangers we'll never get rid of them.' His voice suddenly changed, as he switched to Tibetan.

'Hello, my dear! Say, while I'm waiting for my venerable Abbot to pay his respects up the hill, you wouldn't have something to eat, I suppose?'

'What's going on?' Julia asked Joe, in a whisper.

'He's chatting up some local woman,' Joe said.

'We need to get moving, don't we? It's dangerous to hang around.'

'We're moving as fast as we can through this country.'

When the Abbot returned it was to find Tendzin and Julia in the front seat of the truck, eating cheese and tomatoes while Tendzin translated between the yellow-haired woman and a tall, hawk-faced woman dressed in bright blue.

Behind them, Joe was sitting up, the color returning to his face as he bit into a serving of plate-like bread.

And, surrounding the vehicle, was that constant circle of grave children's faces silently absorbing everything.

The Abbot found the track his ex-pupil had described to him — a cart-track that wound around the mountainsides, climbing slowly with each turn. Eventually the mountain slopes became vertical ravines dropping to a river that crashed and roared far below them, as the track grew narrower, seemingly clawed out of the mountainside.

'If that monk was wrong, and we run out of road, we can't go back,' Tendzin growled.

'He knows the road,' the Abbot said. 'Have faith.'

'If we get one wheel over the edge,' Tendzin continued gloomily, 'we'll go straight down there into the Yangtze River, and come out in Shanghai Harbor'.

But the monk wasn't wrong. The road pressed against the river, then took a leap over a ridge-top pass. The air was now chillingly cold, and so thin that Julia could only breathe by gasping. She shivered, wrapping first Joe and then herself in the blankets they had brought.

'Don't move about too much,' he advised her. 'Try and let your lungs get used to taking in lots of air.'

'How high are we?'

'A mile or so, I'd say. We'll drop down again on to the main road. I don't think there's any way of avoiding it, no matter how hard the Abbot tries.'

Joe was right. Their cart track twisted and turned, and then, seemingly reluctantly, descended from the mountainsides on to a road wide enough for two vehicles to pass.

The road swept across the Yangtze River on a huge stone-sided, but steel-spanned bridge.

And, in the town of Zhongdian, their luck ran out.

Perhaps lulled into relaxation by being on a street where the people wore the red turbans and sheepskin jackets of his nomadic ancestors, Tendzin grew forgetful, took his eyes off the road, and they all heard the thump as the truck struck something.

'Pull over!' the Abbot said, anxiously.

'What was it?' Tendzin asked, craning out of the side of the truck to look back. He saw a dazed goat stumble about before collapsing on to its knees, as its angry turbaned owner came striding towards them, followed by a Public Security official.

'Oh, Tara!' Tendzin exclaimed. 'Get your weapons out of sight. We're going to be searched.'

Then he began a torrent of conciliatory Tibetan to the angry nomad who loomed up at his window.

'Papers, please!' the official said, pushing the goat's owner aside. 'And open up your vehicle for me.'

Julia stared back at the surprised Chinese official as he looked into the rear of the vehicle. A large crowd assembled behind him, consisting mostly of red-turbaned men, women with weather-beaten faces and black hair in many tight plaits, and delighted children pushing and shoving as close as they could get.

The official found his voice at last, staring at the Abbot beside him.

'This area is forbidden to foreigners,' he said.

'We took a wrong turn,' the Abbot said. 'You must forgive us. Their papers are clearly in order. They can go to Lhasa.'

The nomads heard the name of the Tibetan capital, and a buzz of comment grew behind the official. It clearly made him nervous. He shut the door on the foreigners, and glared at both the Abbot and Tendzin.

'They are not to leave until I say so! You two come with me!'

The official yelled at the nomads, ordering them to keep clear of the vehicle. With relief he saw a pair of soldiers hurrying to his asssistance.

'We could be in for trouble,' Tendzin mouthed to the Abbot.

The Abbot nodded.

In the one concrete building in the village, the official positioned himself behind his desk, the better to assert his authority, and again went through the papers, the passports, the movement authorizations, that they carried.

'You are clearly disobeying the law,' he said. 'No foreigners are allowed in Zhongdian. I must fine you for carrying them, and fine each of them for being with you, and send you back to your town of origin.'

'Back to Jinghong?' the Abbot said, suddenly overwhelmed by a sense of failure.

But Tendzin gave his sleeve a sharp tug to silence him.

'Just a moment,' Tendzin said. 'You spoke of fines?'

The official stared at him, and after a moment, nodded.

'How large would these fines be?'

Their eyes were locked as the official tuned in to what Tendzin was suggesting, or perhaps inviting, at a level beneath his seemingly innocent question.

'The fines would be ... fifty yuan for carrying them to a forbidden area, and fifty yuan from each of them. In addition you all must write a self-critical essay.'

'That is the *official* fine?'

'That is the fine.'

'And the goat which I most inadvertently killed? I'm sure that is worth something, too.'

The official nodded, waiting.

'But writing self-critical essays can take a long time, if one is to do it with any deep and searching honesty. Perhaps we could ask that the essays be waived, and in turn perhaps the fine could be adjusted just a little higher?'

'That was a stud goat,' the official said. 'Worth at least fifty yuan.'

Tendzin gestured to say he agreed.

'And self-critical essays are not to be dropped lightly. You should be expected to contribute another fifty yuan each to the good of the country.'

'That all sounds reasonable.'

'There are four of you,' the official reminded Tendzin. 'Four times fifty for the essays. We should make it four times fifty for the original fines ...' His fingers slipped across an abacus he drew from a drawer behind the counter. '... Plus the goat. 'Eight hundred yuan!'

'Eight hundred! Where'd you learn to add ... of course, yes, eight hundred yuan sounds a reasonable sum.'

'We need fuel,' the Abbot grunted to him.

Tendzin gritted his teeth.

'To continue our journey, we will have to refuel.'

He saw the official's eyes gleam a little brighter and his fingers return to the abacus. Clearly, such a profitable day had not occurred for a long time.

Beyond Zhongdian, the road ran beside a spectacular alpine lake of clear water, almost as blue as the clothes of the Naxi women. But the Abbot didn't notice it. He sat hunched and miserable, running his beads between his fingers.

'The bribe was necessary,' Tendzin said, after watching him a while.

The Abbot looked at him guiltily.

'I encouraged that poor man's venality. I reinforced his belief that the only thing of importance in this life is the acquisition of wealth.'

'Don't talk such rot! If we didn't bribe him, we'd be heading back to Jinghong with an armed escort! What's more important — his miserable soul, or the souls of all aboard this truck?

'We have a choice. He has only ignorance.'

'It's his karma!' Tendzin said, angrily. 'He was dog shit in past lives! He's dog shit now!'

The Abbot sighed again and his mouth silently

recited his prayers as his fingers counted the beads.

In the back, Julia found herself breathing deeper and deeper, and each breath was more difficult. The cold was becoming intense, and the raw air stung her throat. She was conscious of the truck's engine beginning to falter and realized that it, too, was having trouble breathing.

She looked out ahead and gasped again as she saw the wild, white, jagged mountains towards which they had been climbing for days now suddenly and dramatically close. Then, as she stared at them glittering through wreathing clouds, all at once the air went dark, and sleety rain lanced the truck.

But the shower passed as quickly as it came. Soon the air was once more piercingly clear, and the sky ascended into unchecked blue.

The truck crested a pass with a faltering, coughing groan, and then began winding down into a wide valley, with a river at its center. Grassland stretched out on either side, and a small huddle of stone buildings showed where the road crossed the river.

'Tibet,' Tendzin said. 'We're home.'

He tried to make it sound as unceremonious as possible. But she heard the catch in his voice, and she saw the Abbot's fingers working harder on his beads. She looked across the valley. The houses, the road, a distant flock of sheep, were all dwarfed by the huge mountains that rose frowning and forbidding on either side. The mountains seemed to challenge them, to ask them just what was their purpose, and how strong was their resolve, in attempting their pilgrimage. For she realized that any journey into those mountains had to be a pilgrimage — a pilgrimage to the roof of the world. A pilgrimage into the innermost heart of your own dreams.

'Where now?' Julia asked, shivering with cold and with apprehension.

'There's a town up ahead called Markam,' Tendzin said. ' We avoid it like it had the pox. We cross our river and we pick up the road to Lhasa.'

'Our river?'

'Our river. The Mekong. It's over those hills.'

He pointed. The hills were steep, jagged peaks. She began to get a sense of geography — a sense of Asia's great rivers converging at this one point in space. Like Asia's religions, like Asia's heart, everything led into the mountains that loomed like jagged, broken glass.

'The monks told me that they have heard of a new road going all the way in to Ghenko,' the Abbot said. 'But they believe it is for military use only.'

'That'd be right,' Tendzin said.

'So how do we get in?' Julia asked.

'The way the Master and I got out,' Tendzin said. 'We walk.'

They camped for the night just off the road and in the bitter cold. There were gusting snow showers blowing against the side of the truck. They slept, exhausted, unaware of the bus that lumbered by their bivouac, en route to Lhasa with its load of pilgrims, traders, and backpackers.

In the morning they drove on through the slush,

under an increasingly brooding sky, driving into the shadows of the huge sentinels, the mountain giants who had guarded Tibet through all the centuries until the twentieth — in European reckoning — began.

CHAPTER THIRTY

The wind was cold, and full of gritty dust. The sky was sometimes clear, and sometimes suddenly overwhelmed by huge clouds that billowed up like giants, and then scattered furious showers of sleet across the barren mountainsides.

There were mountains all around them. The entire horizon was a broken porcelain bowl — rimmed with dirt in some places, gleaming white in others.

At night the travelers remained camped on the goat track on which they walked during the day — a steep mountainside lay on one side, a perilous drop on the other. They slept, huddled together for warmth, as best they could, while the wind shrieked and the clouds gusted. Sometimes a sliver of moon showed like a pulsing white knife in the sky.

They had left their truck hidden as carefully as they could in a deserted cluster of stone buildings just off the highway, after they had driven past the suspiciously upgraded track which the Abbot and Tendzin remembered as the road to Ghenko.

The road to Ghenko should have been a footpath, but now it was wide enough for a truck, and there were tire tracks in the dirt. They didn't like the feel of it and drove on.

They found a more normal pot-holed and wash-away-scoured cart track that led in to what had been the buildings of a small landowner, back in the days when the Abbot read philosophy in the quietness of the monastery's library, and the Master wandered the great halls all alone, wondering what his destiny could be to bring him such loneliness.

The chill in their hearts grew when they saw the abandoned buildings, the broken roofs, the gritty dust already smoothing and rounding the corners of exposed interior walls so that what had been abandoned no more than a decade looked as if it had always been thus.

It was as if nature was on the side of the Chinese, Tendzin thought angrily, intent on eradicating the memory of the Tibetan race forever.

The other traveler on the road to Ghenko was just a shape in the darkness. A shape with a haunted, stubbled face with blazing eyes glowering through the grit impacted into his exposed flesh — giving him the look of a mountain bandit.

He moved silent as a wraith behind them. He had waited twenty-four hours in a wind-blasted cave on the barren hillside that looked down on the highway, watching the Ghenko turnoff like a cat watching its prey. He had counted four trucks on to that track, and three out. He had watched the Polish-built buses grinding past on their way to Lhasa, and the Hungarian trucks overloaded to danger point. He had seen nomads moving their herds. He had seen one dusty, black and battered Russian limousine making heavy work of grinding up the road.

His life had shriveled down merely to sleep, and then wakefulness at the sound of a motor vehicle. The world had contracted to that turnoff, and he was impervious to his surroundings. Until he saw the old truck.

It labored up to the turnoff, and then seemed to collapse into silence. The driver's door opened and one of the old men got out and hastily kicked a rock under a back wheel.

He grinned and sat up straight, and was suddenly aware of how cold it was, how uncomfortable; aware of his hunger and his exhaustion.

Then Joe Tobias climbed out of the back and he forgot it all again.

Joe was limping. He smiled at that. Joe and the old man examined the turnoff, and looked in the dust at tire tracks.

Then they got back into the truck, grated it back into gear, and lumbered off.

For a moment he couldn't believe it.

They had to go in there! His whole plan was based upon that. They had to go and investigate the 'installation at Ghenko'. Those were the old woman's words, after he had demonstrated to her that the couple traveling with her friends were not good guys, but drug smugglers.

And now the old truck was grumbling up the road, going God knows where.

Dave Watson threw himself down the stony mountainside, slipping and stumbling in the knife-sharp scree, crashing against boulders, starting a small landslide that built up around him as he ran, until he tripped and sprawled on to the side of the road with sharp, flinty rock ringing all around him.

He got up. He was bleeding from his palms and elbow. He got up and shrugged his pack into a better position, and he ran.

The thin air made his lungs shriek. His temples pounded. Ahead he could see the truck crawling on, seeming hardly to move, yet visibly increasing the distance between them.

He ran until he collapsed. Then he got up and walked.

He saw the truck wobble off the side of the highway, and stumble down an almost invisible track. He knew then it would be all right.

'He's out there. I know he is,' Joe whispered in the night, as he and Julia clung together. 'I can feel him closing in on us.'

'He can't be,' she replied gently. 'He just can't be. It would take too much for him to get here. The odds are against him.'

'Can't you feel anything? Can't you feel it all coming together?'

She said nothing, because he was right. She could feel it, too. Whatever had brought them together in the sheltered unreality of the Beverly Center, of the artefacts shop in that far-off city of angels, was shaping their lives again.

She realized that most people went through their life without ever catching a glimpse of the pattern to it. And she also realized that perhaps that was the better way to be. Once you saw the pattern, once you realized you were not the architect of the structure that you liked to call yourself, then either fear took over, or else you became like herself and Joe ... outcasts, crazy people ... characters in a story.

She huddled even closer to him.

They woke together, with a mutual start. The sun was out, warming the hillside opposite. Something had dislodged a stone nearby and the sound of it ricocheting down the silent valley had woken them. Joe reached for his carbine, but it had gone.

He sat up.

Julia found she couldn't move. Staring up into the blue sky, with the white horizon all around her, it was as if she had shrunk almost to nothingness. They all had become such tiny, empty figures. They were insects trapped in a gigantic bowl, staring up into space that was also time, and which made every one of their gestures pitiful and absurd. Almost nauseous with the effort, she forced herself to sit up, to assert that she was real, and that effort had meaning. She looked around.

Tendzin had the gun cradled under his arm, and was watching the hillside. He looked back at them.

'Goat,' was all he said.

The Abbot was sitting up. He looked at them and said

nothing. She could see that sense of futility in his eyes, too. They got up stiffly and began walking.

Dave Watson watched them from above and behind. He saw them struggle on up a spur heading for another ridge. He slipped back behind the skyline and commenced walking. He had taken the old woman's 9 mm pistol, and had stolen a butcher's cleaver from a roadside restaurant in one of the towns where he had changed buses. The pistol was in his pocket and the cleaver wedged into his pack.

The travelers leaned into the wind, leaned up the spur, aware of the ridge ahead of them that now became their skyline, again reducing them to insignificance as it obliterated every reference-point, everything except the effort involved in pushing through the thin air.

Then they crested the ridge, saw the monastery, and immediately dropped flat on the ground.

'Oh, shit!' Joe said.

'What is it?' Tendzin asked.

The Abbot just stared, his camera forgotten.

'It's some kind of tracking station,' Julia said.

They all looked at her.

'Haven't the Chinese got satellites?' She looked up into the sky and the gathering black, white, and grey clouds. 'Isn't the Indian border over there?' She indicated the glacier beyond the next ridge.

The Abbot remembered his mission and got his

camera out and made the lens erect itself.

Squinting through the view-finder he could see two white radomes — enormous round lattices of steel covered with snow and ice — sitting atop a massive gray concrete structure. It took him a moment to orient himself. With growing anger he realized that the concrete had been poured over the top of the Master's suite, entombing it. Windows and doors had been let into the concrete. He let the view-finder track down the mountainside.

After the bombardment the Chinese had simply pushed most of the monastery into the valley below. The stream had changed its course around the rubble. The top of the rubble-heap was now a parking bay on which could be seen army trucks. The ubiquitous gray concrete block houses of Chinese architecture now replaced what the monks had labored to build over the centuries.

This was the 'installation at Ghenko.'

'Photographs, spy?' Tendzin grunted, beside him.

The Abbot nodded, and began clicking away.

Tendzin remembered the night his troops had ambushed the convoy bringing the Chinese mountain gun into the hills. He remembered the elation as they seized that big weapon, and the glee with which they proposed to turn it back on their enemy.

He remembered the blowing up of the bridge between the monastery and the village. He remembered the sharp certainty of battle.

He remembered the pit, and grunted as if he had been wounded in the stomach.

The Abbot glanced at him and knew what he was

remembering. They looked at each other.

'What have they done with the village?' the Abbot asked.

'Razed it,' Tendzin growled. 'What else? It was in their way, like we were.'

'I must photograph everything,' the Abbot said.

'Then we'll have to get closer,' Tendzin replied.

He reloaded the camera and carefully stored the exposed film in his pack.

'Over there,' Tendzin growled. 'We can hide in that cave until dark.'

He indicated a shadow in the rock face.

'Then what?' Julia asked him.

'Then we all return,' Joe said, easing himself upright.

As she got up, Julia glanced back. Something moved way back on the spur they had just traversed. She felt a chill of fear.

'What is it?' Joe asked her.

'I saw something back there.'

He stared where she pointed, but the landscape was bare; barren as the moon — with the same truncated horizon and sickeningly empty space beyond. He looked at her and nodded.

'We can handle him,' Joe said. 'He'll be acting carelessly, thinking we have no idea he's out there. That gives us an edge.'

Tendzin gave a grunt and jerked his head to indicate it was time to move out.

They began the descent towards the stream which curled around the rubble. As they dropped down the side of the ravine, they reached a point where they could see the broken remains of the bridge supports, and beyond them the remains of the village.

The radomes across from them made no sound. The whole installation was uncannily silent. No birds sang. The only sound was the eternal moaning of the wind and, as they slipped towards the cave, the rushing of the water in the stream bed below them.

At one point Tendzin stopped, staring down into the stream. Following his gaze, Julia saw the rusting remains of two trucks. The Abbot looked, too, and smiled, gently patting his old friend on the arm.

'It was a good ambush,' the Abbot said.

'But we lost, remember,' Tendzin replied.

They reached the cavern.

Dave Watson reached the ridge-top, and crawled to a point where he could look across the valley. He whistled when he saw the installation. He understood the CIA's interest, and regretted not having a camera — good photos would make a handy bargaining tool if he ever needed to rehabilitate his career. Or keep himself out of jail. But one of the old men was carrying a camera. Maybe he could get his hands on the film, after it was all over.

He had a strange feeling of regret as he scanned the landscape. Suddenly, after all these years, the Quest was almost over. His quarry had gone to ground, but that didn't worry him. They were obviously intent on getting as close as they could to the installation. Even if he missed seeing them moving, they would have to return this way. Climbing the side of the ravine they would be easy targets.

He examined the installation again. He judged it was a mile away, the distance foreshortened by the ravine. He felt relieved when he saw some tiny figures moving about on one of the many levels of the structure. They went about their business casually, keeping no lookout. And why shouldn't they? The population had been decimated, those who remained had been cowed into submission. These men were probably not even troops, but electronics technicians.

There were maybe four hours of direct daylight left before the sun dropped behind the distant, western glacier. Dave swept the slopes again with his concentrated gaze, and this time located the cavern. He studied it closely. It had to be where they were hiding.

He knew they would not be expecting him. He knew they thought he was safely locked away in the cellar. He had the advantage of surprise on his side. He could probably take them all out, right now. Get rid of the two old guys quickly, leaving the other pair to be finished off in a way which would ease the rage inside him.

A truck started up, at the installation across the ravine from him, with a grumble and a puff of blue smoke. He hesitated. He had come so far; best not to blow it through over-eagerness. Who had said, 'Revenge is a dish best sampled cold'?

It was a bitter dish. He found his eyes blinded with tears.

'What are we going to do?' Joe asked the Abbot.

They stared at each other.

'You know what needs to be done.'

'Taking photographs?'

The Abbot smiled and waved his hand dismissively.

'Taking photographs is the excuse. You know why we're here.'

Joe's eyes were dark and full of emotion. They reminded the Abbot of a boy's dark eyes, many years ago.

'There are a lot of things I have to ask you,' Joe said.

'He's here,' Tendzin said suddenly, and they all tensed.

'I heard a loose stone,' Tendzin explained.

'I should go and get rid of him,' Joe murmured.

The Abbot shook his head.

Joe looked at Tendzin and gestured at the carbine. Tendzin smiled and nodded, and Joe relaxed.

'Let me ask you this,' Joe said. 'There was a boy, right, a small boy?'

The Abbot nodded, but his expression was tense.

'He woke up to hear a battle going on. What was it?'

'The boy's servant had disobeyed the Regent Abbot's express orders to avoid violence. The servant had put together a group of nomads and some hot-headed young monks and, acting on a rumor that the Chinese were bringing in artillery to shell Lhasa, had ambushed a road convoy. That's what woke you up.'

He sighed and shook his head.

'What the servant didn't know and the Abbot did know, was that the Chinese officer in charge needed a reason to ... to enforce his will upon the people, to make an example of the monastery. The servant gave him that reason.'

Now the Abbot smiled and looked at Tendzin

who, with ears burning, refused to look back at him, maintaining his vigil at the cavern entrance.

'The officer had not reckoned with the abilities of those disobedient monks and servants. They took the mountain gun and commenced shelling the Chinese garrison. The officer, engaged as he was in making that example he needed to make...'

'He means the pit,' Tendzin growled. 'Remember the pit, Master?'

Joe stared at the old man, his face was a ghastly white.

'The officer in charge called the Chinese garrison at Chamdo for help. They sent three bombers.'

'You never had a chance,' Joe said, softly. 'Did you?'

'We could have held them off long enough for the Americans to come to our assistance,' Tendzin said. 'We could have got the rest of the world interested.'

'The rest of the world didn't give a shit,' Joe said.

The Abbot tapped his camera.

'The people who want these photographs helped us,' he said. 'They dropped food to the Dalai Lama as he escaped through the snow. But the Dalai Lama made it very clear to us that we must not meet violence with violence. And that has meant that things have taken a long time to come together, to heal. But that is how it was meant to be.'

'Meant to be?' Julia asked.

'It was foretold,' the Abbot said.

'What do you mean?'

'*When the iron bird flies and horses run on wheels, the people will be scattered like ants across the world, and the*

Dharma will arrive in the land of the Red Men,' the Abbot quoted from memory.

'What's that you're quoting?' Joe asked.

'The scripture,' the Abbot said. '*Padmasambhava.* Some commentators claim that the Red Man is the American Indian — and now anthropologists wonder if Tibetans and Indians are the same people.'

He indicated the buildings across the ravine from them, the remains of the monastery climbing up from where the bridge had stood. The installation was topped by the two round, white, domes. They could have been eggs laid by the inhabitants of this giants' kingdom.

'Perhaps we will find the scriptures untouched by our helpful Chinese friends?' he suggested.

Joe's flesh crawled.

'What do you mean?'

'A little boy once found a room containing old manuscripts. A room down in the deepest levels of the monastery, a room built when the first monks came to this valley and made their stand against ignorance. Old manuscripts and other ... other things.'

Joe shook his head.

'No,' he said.

'You've come this far,' the Abbot said. 'It would be a shame not to complete the journey.'

The Abbot walked to the mouth of the cavern and looked out. The dying sun glanced red off the glacier. Joe drew back into the shadows.

'Come on,' Tendzin growled. 'I can feel that dog up above us. Let's get over the other side.'

'You're going into the monastery?' Julia asked.

'There's a tunnel down by the stream,' Tendzin said. 'The Master and I know it well, don't we, Master?'

'No!' Joe cried. 'Not me! You've got the wrong guy!'

He looked to Julia for help, but she shook her head.

'I think we have to,' she said. 'I don't think there's any way out.'

'Come on!' Tendzin snapped. 'It's now or never!'

Joe shook his head, but he stepped forward, putting his hand in Julia's.

Dave Watson suddenly saw them almost directly below him, emerging from the cavern. He gave a start, and dragged the pistol from his pocket as he counted them. First the old man with the AK-47. Then the other old man, with the camera. Then a figure he couldn't at first identify, until he caught a glimpse of yellow hair beneath a Mao cap. She wore the bulky, padded clothes of a Chinese peasant.

And then, last of all, Joe Tobias shambling out, for some reason unwilling to follow the others. The woman glanced back at him and said something, and then tugged his hand. He followed reluctantly.

Dave's palm was sweaty. Both of them were in clear pistol range. He crouched down.

His hands were unsteady. Frowning, he saw a boulder nearby. He could steady himself on it. He took a long step towards it.

The scree beneath his foot suddenly shifted. He

swore, windmilling backwards, trying to keep everything quiet, under control. He threw himself sideways, opening out his hand to ease the fall.

The pistol slipped from his fingers.

'Run!' Tendzin yelled, glancing up at the sudden shower of stones from above.

'No!' Dave Watson yelled, lunging for the pistol. His cover was now gone. He could make as much noise as he needed. But the pistol, caught up with the moving scree, slid to the edge of the ravine, and hesitated there above the drop to the stream.

Dave cried out and gave another lunge, but fell short, and his movement pushed the sharp-edged stones away from his hand, pushed the stones up against the pistol, and in agony he watched it drop out of sight.

A few moments later there was a metallic clatter below him.

'What was that?' Julia asked, as they reached the stream.

'I'd say it was our friend dropping something,' Joe said. He grinned, and looked back up the slope, but could see nothing.

Tendzin searched among the stones and then gave a grunt of pleasure and bent down to pick up something. He showed them the pistol. Joe made his way between the boulders to him, took the pistol, and looked back up the side of the ravine. He could not see anyone, but he knew Watson could see him. He held the pistol up so Watson could see it.

In mental agony, Dave Watson saw them clambering through the rubble that half-filled the creek bed, to emerge on the other side. As he watched in the gathering dusk, he saw them climb to a large juniper bush that grew fifty yards from the edge of the rubble.

Their movements had an oddly familiar air to them. He frowned. It was as if he had seen all this before. The gathering gloom. The Master sneaking down to the stream. The Master? What fucking Master?

He rubbed his eyes angrily. When he looked up, they had all disappeared.

'Shit!' he swore. Roughly, he dropped his pack and clawed it open. He hauled out the meat-cleaver.

God! It felt like he was stepping into some weird other reality. Like he had done all this before. Everything seemed to be in some kind of super clear focus — the focus of a wide-angle lens. Every rock, every pebble, every movement of the water beneath him.

He took himself to the edge of the ravine and clambered down towards the stream.

CHAPTER THIRTY-ONE

Julia passed into the tunnel and suddenly stepped back into the other woman's reality. She gasped but made herself go on. The Abbot distributed torches, courtesy of the CIA. The circles of light showed a rough-hewn rock face, sweating with beads of moisture.

She glanced to her grim-faced husband, and he looked at her.

They stared at each other, as if staring through the centuries.

There was a low-pitched rumbling, a vibration right through the rocks. The Abbot put his hand out with curiosity, feeling the tunnel walls.

'It's a generator,' Tendzin said. 'How else would they get power for all their machinery?'

The Abbot lifted his hand and shook his head. Tendzin indicated they should continue. The torches lit the way forward.

Hand in hand now, Julia and her husband followed the old monk into the side of the mountain and into the foundations of the monastery.

As they moved forward, they began to feel the wind which blew through the tunnel. It reminded Joe of his other excursion here, as a child, and he had to force himself to keep going.

Yet his fear also puzzled him. Why was it so intense? He knew what to expect, didn't he?

Or was the fear the fact that everything to this point had been some kind of mental exercise. Now it was finally, irrevocably, real.

'Here's the hard part,' Tendzin murmured.

Both he and Joe remembered this well. The cavern became constricted with rubble at this point and the breeze gathered force, becoming a wind that tore at their clothes. Julia found herself crying.

'If they had closed off all the entrances there would be no wind,' the Abbot remarked.

'They could never find all the entrances,' Tendzin replied. 'I never could.' Pointing over his shoulder, he added, 'He never could.'

The tunnel forked on the other side of the rubble.

'Which way?' the Abbot asked Tendzin.

Tendzin moved to his left.

'No!' Julia cried out.

They turned, startled, to stare at her.

'Not in there,' she said.

She couldn't understand the terror that, like the wind, ripped at her, as if trying to tear her apart.

The Abbot looked at her, searchingly, and finally saw what he had known all along. Saw that she was, indeed, part of the pattern. He nodded.

'To the right,' he said.

A few paces later they encountered hewn steps

leading up. The throbbing of the diesel generator was all around them now. They came to another fork. Tendzin glanced to the Abbot, who gestured for them to keep climbing.

But their way was blocked with raw concrete, that had come pouring down from above, like lava, and was now set solid. The concrete vibrated with the stress of the generator above them.

'Up there's the library,' Tendzin said. 'That's where they stuck their stinking machine.'

'The generator provides them with a different form of light to the scriptures,' the Abbot said.

They retraced their steps and turned down the other fork in the tunnel.

'Where does it lead?' Julia asked, fearfully.

'I know,' Joe said, grimly.

Without a torch it was pitch black, and Dave had to grope his way forward. Occasionally the cleaver clanged against the damp walls. He went down on his hands and knees, for some reason torn with inexplicable fear, with terror. He seemed to know his way forward. Something seemed to be leading him on.

There was a mechanical rumbling all around him, which he put down to machinery, and from which he derived a small piece of reassurance. Machinery was real. The feelings he had were not. He hung on to the machinery's vibrations.

But then the wind began tugging at him, and he began to cry, like a child. The wind grew fiercer and he didn't think he could go on. He crept until he bumped against a fallen boulder and he clung to it, shivering and weeping.

He should give up the Quest, he realized. Give it up, get out and go back. He looked back over his shoulder. He seemed to sense light, as if the entrance was beckoning him back to reality.

Then something made the hair on his arms and his neck stand on end. He moaned and turned to look into the face of the wind.

She was there, lit by some strange, supernatural radiance.

She had the face of an eagle, and hideous, deformed talons. But she had a woman's body. The feathers cascaded down her back and her bright and glittering eyes were fixed on him. She lifted one taloned hand towards him, beckoning him.

'No,' he mumbled. 'No. Go away.'

But the hand beckoned again, and it was as if he was attached to it by invisible wires, for it drew him through the constriction in the tunnel, through the tearing wind, and out the other side. It walked backwards before him, with its obscenely beautiful breasts and its defiantly naked pubic mound, and its ugly bird's head. It kept on drawing him until they came to a fork in the tunnel. Without looking back, obviously knowing the way, it turned to his left.

He did not want to follow. But he had no option but to follow. The tunnel seemed to recede from him. It was as if he was in grasslands and the wind was still there, a terrifying, constant, keening wind. It was as if the light was the light of a blazing fire torn by that wind, showering sparks upwards to far distant stars.

It was as if he crouched in terror in the firelight and the eagle-headed woman was now pounding a drum, pounding it with the handle of a bronze-headed axe.

Dave Watson moaned and fainted.

There was now only one more constriction through which to squeeze to enter the final chamber. This time, though, Joe was not alone, and not a child. With the help of Tendzin and Julia, while the Abbot held the torches, Joe opened up the entrance into the most inaccessible of the chambers beneath the old monastery. But as they dragged each rock aside Joe seemed to drag more of his childhood fears into view.

It seemed that he'd lived all of his confused life avoiding those fears. It was as if he'd been running constantly through a dark maze, stumbling, fighting, killing, always trying to get away from the maze's center — when if he had just stopped in his tracks, like he was stopped now, and begun to pull aside the rocks of confusion, facing the blasts of fear that swept out of the newly revealed darkness, then he could have solved the mystery of the maze and found his way out into clear light.

Tendzin gave a grunt of final exertion and nodded his head to Joe.

'You go first, Master.'

They stared at each other a long time. Joe realized how much the old man must have loved him, to have waited so long for him to return to this place and solve this mystery for himself.

Joe nodded, accepted the torch the Abbot held out to him, and stepped into the chamber.

'So this is where it all began,' he said quietly.

The combined light of the torches showed them an ancient, black, wooden box, bigger than a man. Their footsteps shifted the dust which had sat unmoved since the Chinese poured concrete across the roof above them, sealing the entire level into forgotten history.

Joe stepped across to the box and gently eased the black lid open. Julia stared in — and jumped back in fear, as two skulls seemed to stare into her eyes, grinning their death's-knowledge grin at her. She had a glimpse of bones lying on ancient, brittle rolls of manuscript, and piles of dried-out palm-leaves — like dark, slatted venetian blinds — inscribed with some long-forgotten text.

'What is it?' she asked.

Joe knelt, like a man at prayer. He looked at her, his eyes far away, lost in some other dimension. 'It's what the boy saw, what started him running.'

She heard the Abbot let go his breath. She heard Tendzin grunt. She crept up beside Joe and knelt beside him. His eyes focused on her.

She stared at him, then she stared at the ancient bones, the empty eye-sockets, the gray teeth set in those mocking grins. The skeletons lay side by side. She imagined the feathers crowning the one, and the other clutching the statue. Then she felt that dreadful giddiness again, that she had felt staring into the bowl of sky above the bowl of mountains.

It felt as if she had been in this room before.

'It was in here I found her,' he said. 'Found Tara.'

'I know,' she heard her voice saying.

They stared into each other's eyes. The voice that spoke was hers, wasn't hers. It was also the voice of a Chinese girl. A warlord's bought bride. A girl from the lakes and pagodas of Yunnan province, with the snow-capped mountains as her constant background.

The Abbot walked over beside them. He knelt, too. His face expressionless, he began easing the manuscripts from beneath the skeleton. Joe started involuntarily, and glanced at the Abbot. They stared at each other for a moment, and then Joe gently took the bones and held them while the Abbot glanced back to Tendzin and called him over. Tendzin joined them, falling to his knees, to take the manuscripts from the Abbot. To Julia it seemed as if they were at Mass, each receiving the Eucharist in their own way.

Dust hung heavy in the air, choking them, making them cough.

'Is this what we came for?' Joe asked, standing up.

'This is it,' the Abbot said. 'You led me here many years ago, and what I found here I wanted to keep buried. Perhaps if I had brought it into the light of day, none of this would have happened.'

The Abbot shook his head, now ready to leave.

'We always say we seek the truth. But what if the truth meant the destruction of everything you believed in? Would you then have the strength to accept it?'

Julia stared at him. His question was her question. If she accepted what the box seemed to suggest to her, she was no longer herself. Or else her self was something far greater than she had ever imagined. With the baby growing in her belly she could feel herself as a pipeline connecting the generations.

'Come on,' Tendzin said at last. 'I don't like it down here. And, who knows, maybe the Chinese didn't completely seal it off.'

It was then they heard someone cough.

Panic gripped Julia so hard she felt her womb convulse. Terrified, she grabbed her belly. Joe doused his light and the others followed suit. Pure blackness enveloped them. They strained to listen, but could hear nothing but the rumble of the generator.

Then they heard a clunk; metal hitting stone. Julia felt another wave of panic. She felt a hand touch her. Joe leaned close to her ear and whispered.

'I'm going after him. Stay here.'

She tried to clutch his hand, but it was gone. She reached out, and connected with the Abbot. He squeezed her fingers in his.

Dave Watson opened his eyes and remembered what he had seen. He gasped, swiveling about in the pitch blackness, but saw nothing. He gripped the cleaver tightly. The generator kept the rocks shivering.

Then he saw the light again. He stopped himself crying out. The light flickered and flared in the distance, slowly growing brighter.

Moaning, he pushed himself upright and slid along the wall of the chamber to which he had been led. The light grew yellow. The light accompanying the apparition had been blue. This was torch-light.

He raised the cleaver.

The yellow light grew brighter, glittering off the sweaty rock about him.

A hand, holding a torch, appeared. Then the barrel of a weapon, a sub-machine-gun. Dave swung the cleaver sideways, aiming for the throat.

The Chinese soldier stepped into the cleaver's path, without seeing it coming. The blade caught his glottis, slicing through his throat, severing tendons and veins, and then bursting the artery. Bright red blood burst from the wound, bubbling with air, as the soldier splayed backwards, clattering the gun against the rock, the torch shattering on the ground.

Dave wrenched the cleaver free, blood pouring across his wrist and down his arm. The body was thumping at his feet, air gurgling in the severed windpipe. He knelt and groped for the sub-machine-gun and picked it up, but it would not come free.

'Shit!' he whispered to himself, conscious now that the others would have heard the noise; wondering if the guard had been alone.

He gritted his teeth and tugged. The weapon was jammed. He groped and found the sling caught under the dead man's shoulder.

Joe's left hand had been delicately tracing the cold rock contours when he heard the sounds of the guard being killed. He froze a moment, every nerve tingling, trying to track the noise through the labyrinth within which he was caught. He heard nothing more. He transferred the pistol to his left hand for a moment and shook out his right fingers. They had tensed so tight he was afraid they would lock. He took the pistol anew, trying to hold it lightly, and groped his way onward.

When Tendzin heard the sound, he knew immediately what it was. He touched the Abbot on the elbow and whispered to him, 'I'm going.'

Before the Abbot could prevent him, Tendzin had placed the manuscripts at his feet, and had slipped away after his Master.

Dave got his arm under the man's shoulders, and heaved. But he slipped in the warm, wet blood. He tried again, jamming himself against the rock, levering the dead man's awkward weight up, then sliding his fingers under the sling.

The gun came easily.

He stood, wet with sweat and blood. He thrust the cleaver into his belt. He groped the weapon, trying to familiarize himself with it.

Joe heard something else; a muted thump. He hesitated a moment, then pushed on into the darkness, trying to get himself back into the feel of the tunnels, into memories that came from somewhere over which he had no conscious control.

~

Dave found the trigger and then felt behind it. There was the usual lever for selecting rate of fire. He pushed it up to fully automatic with his thumb. He found the magazine in front of the trigger, a banana-like curve slotting in under the barrel. It wobbled, but it was jammed as tight as it would go in its socket. It was pitted with rust.

With his right fingers beside the trigger-guard, he stepped over the dead man, into the middle of the tunnel. He stepped into the blackness, some instinct guiding his feet.

Joe felt the wall beside him suddenly veer off to the left. He hesitated and felt to the right. His hand encountered nothingness. He took a step straight ahead and suddenly bumped into rock. He gasped and stumbled backwards.

Dave heard the sound and he shot at it. His finger came down solidly on the trigger and he squeezed a quick burst down the tunnel. There was a sudden, sharp shout from the gun, as the firing pin hurled one round on its way. The spent cartridge was ejected to clatter into the blackness. Then there was only a muted click. The gun was jammed on old ammunition.

The first shot had sent Joe scuttling back into the tunnel for safety. Hearing the click of a misfire, he had time to catch his breath.

Dave hissed a curse to himself and grabbed the stubby bolt of the weapon and dragged it back, trying to clear the breech. But the round would not eject.

Joe heard it all, and knew what it meant. He smiled and raised his pistol.

'Fuck it!' Dave yelled. 'Fuck you lazy bastard! Keep your fucking ammunition clean!'

Behind them, Tendzin heard the angry shout. He smiled and hefted his AK-47, ready to shoot, but aware that the Master was between him and the target.

Joe thought of the old scholar's clean, oiled pistol in his hand. Her ammunition wasn't split. Her magazine would not be rusted. He held his right wrist with his left hand, steadying himself, aiming for where the sub-machine-gun had flashed once.

He could feel the two of them coming back together again, back along the great river, through the solid rock of the monastery's foundations, to this moment in time — as if they had always lived in tunnels, blindly groping their way towards each other, towards what they always did at this moment. He felt the great stone wheel of karma lurching around its axis, grinding on through human misery.

He lowered the pistol and bent his head. He could see the sampans, heavy with rice, on the river. He could see those dark-eyed women, pregnant with grief, clutching the babies they were willing to trade for food, so that more babies could be born. He could see himself, thinking he was acting against his karma as he offered them the trade. But he was only acting within it. He was only setting himself to keep coming back to this point, again and again.

Joe could hear his partner in this great dance grunting as he tried to extricate the jammed round. Joe quietly laid the pistol on the ground. Then, to make clear what he was doing, he scuttered it across the rock, into the blackness, beyond hope of retrieval.

'It's me, Joe Tobias,' he called. 'Don't you think it's time to end all this?'

Dave had the magazine out, hoping to eject the jammed round downwards. When he heard the sound of gun metal scudding over rock, he froze. Then he heard the voice, and smiled, tracking it with his ears. He quietly laid the useless weapon on the ground and pulled out the cleaver.

'Can't you feel it all around us?' Joe went on. 'Don't you realize we've met here before, down these tunnels, and we'll go on meeting until it's all put behind us?'

Keep talking! Dave thought to himself. *Blabber on, you bastard!* He estimated the distance between them, and took another step, half-raising the cleaver.

Joe listened. There was only the generator's rumbling. He realized that Watson was now stalking him, that his adversary had no intention of renouncing his Quest, and that Joe Tobias must now decide how it was to be ended.

The sounds reverberated down the forking tunnels, echoing to Julia as she held the Abbot's fingers in hers. It was like memories coming back to her, confused and uncertain, but real, very real. She moaned and let go the Abbot's hand and, switching off her torch, stepped into blackness. Like her husband she was guided by those shivering, confused memories.

Now she knew, positively, that she had been in these tunnels before. And she knew she had been with the two men who faced each other somewhere ahead of her; now in pitch darkness, but once, long ago, lit by the light of a reed torch. She knew that her knees had ached as she knelt on the stone floor, unable to rise, as these two men fought their personal duel over her.

And she began to sense how that duel went back further. That perhaps her death there, unable to move, humiliated in chains, was in some way earned, brought about by something she had done at some other time.

She groped her way forward, until she touched a man's back.

She stifled the reflex scream. A hand grabbed her throat, instinctively, about to choke the life from her, and then relaxed.

'It's you?' Tendzin whispered.

She took the hand from her throat and placed it against her breast. It seemed the only way to show him who had come up from behind.

Tendzin let his hand stay there longer than was necessary, only withdrawing it when they heard the Master's voice again.

'I have put down my weapon, Brother. I kneel before you. We can end it now.'

She felt the old man's hand tense on his weapon.

'Have you got a light?' he whispered to her.

She tapped his wrist for yes.

'When I say so, switch it on. The Master is kneeling. I may be able to shoot high.'

'I prostrate myself before you, Brother. For we are both emanations of the Buddha. You and I and her. We are all One. We ...'

His voice cut off with a grunt.

'Now!' Tendzin screamed.

The cleaver tore away Joe's ear on the first stroke, and smashed his shoulder. His assailant swung again, this time connecting with the side of his skull, smashing the bone in on the brain. And as the second stroke sent bone splinters into Joe Tobias's brain, the torch lit up the cavern, freezing the scene in front of Julia, so that again she saw the tableau of the two men, caught there suspended in time in the tunnels beneath the monastery, as beside her Tendzin grunted and fired his gun.

Then the tableau was broken as Dave Watson floundered backwards to slam against the wall.

And Joe Tobias found that there was no fear after all. But there was understanding. For there was only one moment in time, ever, and all past lives were only petals on an ever-opening rose, all bursting from the same eternal bud. And the moment of the cleaver was the same moment as the moment of the axe which this same man, in different clothes and different flesh, brought down upon this same head, in the robes of a monk of high degree, in this same tunnel.

The woman, too, was there. And she, too, was an eternal woman, eternally re-enacting this moment. The axe ended her life, too. Yet there was another petal of this rose, another shimmering, illusory life, so that once it had been she who held the axe, and brought it down upon another head.

So much was revealed to Joe as he lay dying, and yet there was still so much more to know. And there was still enough life in him to hear the woman calling in anguish, 'Joe! Joe! Don't die! Please!'

Enough consciousness to see her flinging herself towards that shattered body as the reverberations of the old man's shots still thundered up and down the tunnels of time all around them.

Dave Watson, too, saw her coming. His hand still held the cleaver, and the nerves still worked enough to almost check its descent to the floor, almost make it swing towards her, as he had swung it before.

But the movement ended. Dave Watson hit the stone wall and the cleaver clattered at his feet. He died.

He died staring at her as she threw herself upon the Master's body, so they lay together, as they had once before. Dave Watson died, unable to tell if what he saw was real, or a figment of his flickering, extinguishing imagination. For as she clung, weeping, to that body, she, too, seemed to dissolve, to become more people, a telescoping tunnel of women repeating the same recurring pattern of death.

One moment she was a bright, blonde woman in a Chinese peasant costume. Then suddenly, inexplicably, she was a beautiful Chinese girl with exquisite nails and high black hair, in a silk robe which spoke of her rank.

And then she was that eagle-headed creature which Dave Watson had first glimpsed in a shop storeroom.

~

'Joe,' she whispered. 'John. Please ...'

Her voice broke off in a sob.

He looked up at her and smiled weakly. His blood was warm and sticky on her hands, in her lap. He tried to focus on her, but his head was full of pressure, full of needle points, and he seemed to be moving away from her all the time, moving into some other space. But he knew it was important for her that he say something, and so he focused all that was left of Joe Tobias on her.

'He got me at last,' he managed to say. It seemed pointless. He tried one more time. 'The wheel ... no more.'

'No!' she cried.

His eyes were fading, but for another moment they focused on her. She felt his hand move against hers.

'Thank you for bringing me back,' he whispered.

'Why?' she cried out. 'Why must you die?'

'I deserved it,' he mumbled. His eyes closed, then half-opened, clouded, confused. 'I'm sorry,' he said. 'I'm so sorry. Where's my Abbot?'

The old man knelt beside them.

'I'm sorry, Rinpoche,' Joe said. 'I failed.'

The old man took his hands.

'No,' the Abbot said. 'It was not you who failed. It was me. I could have prevented all this ... if I had been more honest.'

Joe's eyes had closed. There was a look of gentle peace on his face.

'He's going,' Tendzin said.

Julia sobbed, trying to clutch him tighter, trying to will life back into him. But the Abbot eased her away.

The Abbot glanced up to Tendzin and indicated for the old man to hold her.

The Abbot laid Joe out on the floor of the chamber, and began to recite.

O nobly born, you we have called Joe Tobias, and yet were also our Master, the time hath now come for thee to seek the Path into reality. Thy breathing is about to cease. Thy Abbot hath set thee face to face before with the Clear Light; and now thou art about to experience it in its Reality in the Bardo state, wherein all things are like the void and cloudless sky, and the naked, spotless intellect is like unto a transparent vacuum without circumference or center. At this moment, know thou thyself; and abide in that state.

She wondered if Joe could actually hear it. She wondered if he could still see them. She wondered if, this time, he had freed himself from the wheel. She felt a burning in her belly, and suddenly remembered what grew there. All of a sudden it seemed to writhe, sending warmth right through her.

The Abbot glanced curiously at her, then at her hand as it clutched her belly, then back at her face, and she realized he knew she was pregnant. Without changing his chanting, he blinked, searching his mind for a moment, and then continued. But this time he spoke in Tibetan, his voice sonorous, lilting, evoking all the centuries around them in the hand-hewn rock. He chanted:

Hear thy teacher. Ah! take birth as a Universal Emperor; or as a Brahmin; or as the son of an adept in siddhic powers; or in a spotless hierarchical line; or in the caste of a man who is filled with great religious faith; and, being born so, be endowed with great merit so as to be able to serve all sentient beings.

Thinking thus, direct thy wish, and enter the womb. At the same time, emit thy feelings of grace and goodwill upon the womb which thou art entering, transforming it thereby into a celestial mansion. And believing that the Conquerors and their Sons of the Ten Directions, and the tutelary deities, especially the Great Compassionate One, are conferring power thereon, pray unto Them, and enter the womb.

She wondered at the meaning behind the music of the words. They seemed to strike her physically, taking the strength out of her legs. She clung to Tendzin as the Abbot stared at her. His chanting had finished.

'What now?' Tendzin asked softly.

'We leave,' the Abbot said.

'And the Master?'

The Abbot stared down at Joe's drained face.

'He has achieved that which he came for,' he said, shaking his head in awe at what he was discovering about the world.

'It was he who led us back here, it was he who knew what had to be done.'

CHAPTER THIRTY-TWO

She had been out shopping for groceries when some strange seizure grabbed her belly and bent her double.

'Oh, Christ!' she said, and the woman who had just taken her cash looked at her in alarm.

'You all right, honey?'

'My belly ...' she managed to gasp.

Although the woman looked concerned, her face had also gone quite soft.

'Has it started?' she asked, gently.

Other women, pushing grocery trolleys, gathered around her.

'She's going into labor,' a young Chinese woman said. 'Quick. Call an ambulance.'

The spasm passed. Julia looked at them; looked at the mini-mart in which she liked to shop.

'No,' she said. 'No. It's only just started. I want to get home.'

'She should get straight to hospital.'

She didn't say that the birth would be at home. She didn't want to upset anyone.

'Is it the first, honey?'

She nodded, trying to push past the crowding women.

'Hey, Tony! Come and take this lady's groceries to her car!'

'Hey! I'm busy, all right! Let her take her own goddamn ...'

'Tony! Get out here this minute!'

'Jesus Christ, if it's not one fucking thing ...'

'Shut up and help this lady to her car.'

'Hey! Is she, you know ...?'

'Just shut up and carry her bags, you dumb ox.'

Tony took the bags and glanced curiously at her. If she took more care of herself she'd be a real looker. She didn't wear no make-up, and her clothes were all baggy. Lovely blonde hair which had just been sort of hacked off. He guessed it was because she was having the kid. Actually, the more he looked at her, as he carried the bags out on to the sidewalk, the more he thought he recognized her. Like, she might have once been a celebrity. Maybe checked into the Betty Ford Clinic, and got forgotten. She had the dreamy look of a boozer. But her face wasn't puffy. In fact, her face was really alive, and her skin was clear, and her dreamy eyes could focus real sharp when she chose.

When he saw the gold Mercedes he knew she must have been a celebrity.

'Nice wheels,' he said, and she smiled at him and suddenly he realized just how beautiful she was.

'You should take care of yourself,' he said, as she let him open the door for her.

'I am,' she said. 'I'm taking real good care.'

She smiled at him and closed the door and pulled into the traffic, and he stood there, watching her pull away, not even realizing she hadn't tipped him. Her smile was enough.

She was scared, and she was excited. She knew what to expect, and she didn't know a thing. Her belly had settled down, and maybe it was all just a false alarm. Maybe she'd get home and call up her midwife and the doctor, and tell the Abbot, and it would just be gas.

She got on to Santa Monica, heading for home. She was light-headed, a little dizzy. The air had that raw, purplish, Los Angeles haze to it. She had the top up and the air-conditioning on. The Mercedes sang in her ears.

It was a great car, and she was always sorry she'd not told John how good it really was.

She frowned. John? Joe? Whoever he was. Monster and, in the end, man.

She smiled, thinking of him. She smiled, thinking of Tendzin.

She and the Abbot, and an old woman who was a friend of the Abbot's, had mourned Tendzin in the grounds of the temple in the forest. It was after they got back from Ghenko. Tendzin had driven them along the well-frequented roads; driven them until he was exhausted. All the time he sorrowed for his Master, lying unburied back in the catacombs of Ghenko. Even the Abbot's recitation of all the prayers could not allay the dismay in his old heart.

They got back to the temple in the late afternoon and, next morning, Tendzin had not risen. He had died three days later — quietly, peacefully, only showing fear right at the last, as he held the Abbot's hands and looked into the Abbot's eyes and, once again, the Abbot recited the verses of the *Bardo Thodol*.

They had not buried him in the grounds. They had put his body on a stretcher and carried it over the steeply pitched tracks, down the slippery mountainside, to the great river, and there they had slipped it clear of the stretcher, clear of its bondage to earth, and let it slide out into the stream.

She had stood there, crying, watching him circle out from them; watching the current take him and point him downstream, back down to where she had commenced her journey into the mountains.

She and the Abbot had returned to the river themselves a week later. The old lady didn't want to leave. She had found them a little sampan and fitted it out with food and water, and made it comfortable for her — for the young mother.

The old lady had given them a flag to fly, and insisted that it be always visible, particularly when they got into the gorges of the border country. The old lady stressed how important it was to fly that flag.

And she told them that they would be met before they reached the Burmese checkpoint where they had previously encountered the searchlight and the soldiers in the fiberglass cruiser.

The old lady proved to be a strange storehouse of secret knowledge, of ancient wisdom, of cunning, guile, and strategy. Just above the border post they had been stopped by a group of villainous-looking bandits in an old and battered boat. Leading the bandits was an

American — a middle-aged man with faded blue eyes and a wild and lost look to him. She and the Abbot knew that look. It was the Dave Watson look. He wanted the Abbot's film.

But Julia wouldn't let him have it. She realized that the film had brought them so far. Without it they would go no further. The American had tried to bully her. She had stood her ground. When he pushed too far, she opened the top pocket of her jacket, and showed him the grenade she carried there. He had looked into her eyes, hesitated, then let them pass, petulantly warning them he was in radio contact with Thailand, and they could not expect to outwit his people.

They didn't want to outwit anyone. Julia just wanted to get home, to find a comfortable place to have her baby, whoever's baby it was. She told that — except the bit about 'whoever's baby it was' — to the man from the embassy who was waiting at Chiang Saen and, after she saw the air tickets he got for them, she let the Abbot hand over the film.

They never saw the prints. They never heard if they were useful to anyone. But someone must have been pleased with them, for there was no trouble in getting the Abbot refugee status and starting the slow process of having him eventually accepted as an American citizen.

She wheeled the Mercedes up to the gates, reached out with the gate-pass, and her belly suddenly did that weird, frightening, constriction again, made her gasp with shock more than pain. Then with pain.

She tried to sit back in the car. She tried to do the

short, sharp breathing they'd taught her. It didn't help a bit. It hurt like all bloody hell!

Then it passed, and she made it around the drive and into the garage. The only other vehicle in the garage was the Abbot's bicycle — a red and orange alloy mountain-bike. The drip tray that used to be there beside the Mercedes was gone. The Mercedes didn't drip oil.

She hurried inside and called out. The maid came running, and when she saw what was happening, called for her husband in sharp, shrill Spanish. So shrill she disturbed the Abbot and he came out of the study, his mind still obviously focused on the things he had been reading in his old, old texts.

The Abbot phoned the midwife and the doctor, just as she'd rehearsed him, and she went upstairs to prepare.

'This is it,' she thought. 'This is the one thing I have to show for everything that happened. Without this, it all might have been a dream.'

She got out of her clothes and slipped on a floral cotton nightdress. She tied her hair back. She made herself busy, until the next contraction doubled her up. She cried out, kneeling on the floor as it overwhelmed her with a rush of pure pain.

She felt a sudden terror. It was not going to be like they had told her! The midwife! The books! The magazines! They'd all lied! The pain was brutal, overwhelming. She bent double.

She saw his sandaled feet, and looked up. For a moment she thought it was her husband. His eyes were concerned. He held out his hand to her and she took it and he helped her up.

'Rinpoche' she said, 'I'm scared.'

He nodded, helping her past the great white-on-white bed to the hard, single bed in the corner of the big room.

'What if I don't make it through? What if I die?'

'You won't die,' he said.

He made her comfortable, but her mind began racing. *What if the midwife gets here late? What if the cord strangles the baby? What if … what if …?*

She grabbed his hand.

'Talk to me, Rinpoche. Tell me something.'

'What shall I tell you?'

'What were you reading when I came in? Tell me what you have found out about Ghenko.'

He was silent a moment, his fingers stroking the back of her hand. He frowned, thinking of the ancient texts, written in a script older than any he was familiar with. A script which recorded a story he had known in his heart, but refused to allow into his mind all these years. And if he had? If he had acknowledged it, then the Order would have been destroyed. Or would it? He would never know, for he had not looked at the story, and the order was still destroyed.

Now, all he could do was tell the story.

'Ghenko was founded by a young nomad,' he said, after a while. 'A youth who had no reading or writing. He came from somewhere out on the great plains. He was running away from something.'

'Running away from what? Come on, Rinpoche, you can do better than this!'

'His story was not written down until the eighth century, when he had been dead I don't know how long. Maybe two hundred years. It was written down on palm leaves, I don't know by whom, brought overland to Ghenko by Indian scholars. It was placed down there in that box with those ... those remains. It was hidden. It was forgotten. It ran contrary to everything the monastery believed about itself.

'This is what was written on the palm leaves.

'The young man's people worshipped the Great Mother, from whom all life originated, and into whom all death passed. The Great Mother was represented on earth by the shaman of her tribe.'

'Her tribe?'

'The shaman was always a woman. The people's leaders were women. They were people much feared, and legends about them spread a long way from the steppes and the grasslands.'

'Like the Naxi, Rinpoche?'

'What? The who?'

'The women in blue on the edge of Tibet. Remember them?'

'Oh, yes. Like them. The Naxi are the last of the Mother-worshippers. But these women were not just farmers. These women were hunters. And hunters are also warriors. From killing animals to killing humans is only a small step.

'They hunted on horseback. They hunted with the bow. They captured men and used them as slaves, after castrating them.

'Their supremacy in battle made them arrogant. Made them deny the humanity of all people, and the one-ness of all sentient beings.'

'And their own men? How did they treat them?'

'Their own men were little better than slaves — they did all the menial tasks. Women ruled. And of the women, the shaman was supreme. She had the power to decide over life and death.'

'It's coming again, Rinpoche. Keep talking. Make me listen.'

'The young man had acquired a place of secret power within the tribe, because he had become the shaman's lover.'

'Here it comes.'

'Breathe shallow and fast. That's it.'

'Her lover? Was that allowed?'

'No. It was not. The shaman had to be pure, unsullied by contact with creatures as debased as men. But she discovered a dreadful yearning within her to have him. She could not get him out of her mind. She was deluded. She hid their relationship from the people.

'But a slave found out. Another young man who had been taken in a raid on a settlement of farmers. Who had been castrated and was now used as a beast of burden.'

'It hurts! It hurts!'

'Shallower! Faster! It will pass!'

'It's going! That's it, it's passed. Keep telling the story, Rinpoche.'

'The young slave thought he could use his knowledge of their relationship to buy his freedom.

'He was wrong. He bought only his torture and death.'

'I think I know this part of the story,' she said.

He glanced down at her pale, sweating face, but did

not reply to her statement. Instead, he screwed up his eyes and looked again into the distance.

'Her lover, until then, had never questioned what happened among the people. He accepted that life was brutal; that they all gave homage to the Great Mother, sacrificing children when required by the shaman; that the women used the captured men for entertainment. He helped her kill the slave. But at the moment of killing, the two young men looked into each other's eyes, and he suddenly saw how there was no difference between them. He had a strange feeling that, in some distant past, he had been the sacrifice and this dying slave had been the killer. And he saw them again, in some far distant future, when this man would track him down again, and take his life.

'He broke free of the crowd of people gathered there, around the blazing fire on the grasslands, and grabbed a horse and rode away.

'He rode and he rode, with this strange pain in his breast, this awful realization that the things we do are the things which bind us to lives of misery.

'He rode until his horse died of exhaustion, and he found himself in cold lands. Then he walked.

'He came one day upon a man dying beside the track. A man who had been abused by bandits, robbed, stripped of everything, and left to die.

'Remembering what he had discovered — that we all depend upon each other — the young man took the other to a nearby cave, and nursed him back to health. They learnt to talk to each other. The other man was a monk, one sent out from India to spread Buddha's message.

'With awe, the young man heard this stranger describe a philosophy which agreed with what he had himself discovered.

'He had a sudden vision of all the lives he had led previously, and saw how they balanced each other out. He saw the eternal wheel of suffering, and he let go of the wheel and stepped into pure Bliss.'

'It's coming! It's coming!'

'Focus on emptiness. Focus on nothing but your mind, and realize that your mind does not exist in any form except the impressions it creates.'

'I've got to think about the breathing!'

'Focus on the emptiness of your mind and the breathing will look after itself.'

'Yes!' And then, more quietly. 'Yes. Oh, yes.' And then, silence.

'That's what he saw. The bliss of emptiness. A world of no form, of no thought. A world waiting to be born.'

'I can feel it beginning to move. It's time to be born! It's time to enter the world!'

'He stepped into Bliss for the merest part of a second, but it seemed like he lived there eternally. He stepped back, and the old monk, watching him, knew he had experienced Bliss, and that the old monk's purpose in this life had been accomplished. The old monk died.'

'It's passed. That one went by without hurting.'

'He took the old monk's body across the stream to a deep cave that led into the heart of the mountainside, and he built a tomb for him. And then he built a room for himself.'

'And that was the beginning of Ghenko?'

'That was the beginning of Ghenko.'

'Then what brought about its end?'

'The thing which brings the end to anything. Emotion. Fear. Old patterns of behavior.

'Men in search of freedom from the pain of existence heard of this hermit and his cave and hut on the hillside. They heard that he had magical powers.'

'Had he?'

'Most probably. After all, his lover probably had magical powers.'

'I'm sure she did,' Julia said, remembering the drum, the carvings on it, the woman rowing into the sky of night and death; remembering the feathered head-dress and the eagle's face.

'These men came and listened to his teachings, and built themselves rooms beside his, and slowly the monastery began to take shape.

'One day, a distressed woman came, wanting to hear the teachings.

'He turned her away.'

The Abbot took a deep breath and let out a long sigh. 'To him she was an unnecessary distraction, a reminder of what he had fled. There were too many emotions for him to deal with. He sent her on her way.

'But what he had done ate deep into him and, eventually, it came back to the surface. When he was an old man, much venerated, and the lower levels of the monastery had been well-established ...'

'The levels we entered?'

'Those levels, yes. When he was an old man, he

began to dream about that woman he had turned away, and he began to worry about what was her fate.

'He left the monastery in the charge of his Abbot and he set off on a pilgrimage.'

'And he found her?'

'No one knows. Many years later, a party of traders came by the monastery, which had grown bigger, had attracted a settlement of people near its base. Ordinary men and women now lived there, serving the needs of the monks, letting them spend all their time in contemplation, in meditation, in reading, analyzing, writing, teaching.

'The traders had a pair of skeletons with them. They claimed they were relics taken in a raid on the last group of Mother-worshipping nomads out on the steppes. There had been a big battle and the women had all been killed. The wheel had come full turn.

'The Abbot examined the skeletons. One was male, and one female. They were wrapped in a strange feathered head-dress, accompanied by other ritual objects — a drum, an axe.'

'It's coming! It's coming!'

'Empty the mind. Make it as flat as the grasslands.'

'Was it them, Rinpoche? Was it the shaman and her lover?'

'The Abbot thought it was. Why would these women venerate a male skeleton? The Abbot thought the old man had found his way back to his people, and somehow been reunited with the shaman. That's what the Abbot thought, but he had no evidence to support his thoughts. Nevertheless, he bought the skeletons and the objects.'

'Here it is!'

'Empty. Flat. The sea of grass. The black sky.'

'Yes, I can see them. I can feel her coming. She's coming into the world!'

Her mind was blank, was black, but then something shimmered out of it, and she was looking, in the raging red light of a fire, at a cowed, terrified young man crouched, bound, before her. She moved and the head-dress shimmered. She turned and her lover knelt there, too, his frightened eyes on her.

She felt such power! It poured up into her from the earth, from the Mother. It poured up into her and she released it to her people, all around. She held out her hands and her lover held out the axe to her.

'How far apart are the contractions?'

'About ten minutes.'

'Sorry we're late. You know what the traffic's like.'

She opened her eyes. Familiar figures moved around the bed. The midwife smiled at her and touched her forehead with a sponge.

'You're doing fine, Julia,' she said. 'Real fine. The baby's going to be fine.'

'It's a girl,' Julia said, 'isn't it?'

'We'll find out in good time.'

'The ultra-sound never showed, but I know it's a girl.'

'She was modest. She kept her legs crossed all the time.'

'I should have done the same.'

The midwife smiled at her joke. Julia looked for the Abbot. He had withdrawn to the side of the room. She held out her hand to him and he came and took it.

'It's a big story,' she said. 'But we don't know any of it for sure, do we?'

He shook his head, smiling.

'Worry about the baby,' he said, 'Not about the other things.'

'The baby will make up for it,' she said. 'The baby will bring it all together.'

'Shhh,' he said. 'Avoid exciting the mind. Keep it empty. Keep it full of Bliss.'

'That's easy for you to say. You're an Abbot.'

'You will soon be an Abbess.'

And now she could feel it coming, and she could feel that she was no longer on a journey. Instead, someone else had begun their journey, beginning it inside her. Beginning it in the mansion of her body, and now forging their way through the rivers of her being. A person bringing with her whatever it was she had known before, but bringing it fresh into the world.

She felt herself enlarging. New pain, different to the contractions. She was no longer Julia Carr, she was just a vessel, a road, a way.

She got up on to her knees, spreading her legs wide, and felt all the fluid pouring out of her. She moaned, and then screamed.

'It's crowning! Push, Julia, push!'

She roared. Sweat poured off her face. She roared and screamed and panted like a dying animal. She was not open enough. She had to open up more or it would tear her apart. She screamed again, and the midwife was at her side, whispering, trying to calm her.

The Abbot began to shout, afraid for her life. He had never seen this before. He had never seen how we come into the world.

She screamed, gripping her ankles with her hands, and he suddenly saw the top of the head beginning to show, ringed with a crown of her blood. The Abbot stopped shouting, stopped breathing.

She heaved one more time, groaning, as if on the point of death, and then there was a little face, screwed up tight, covered with slime. A little, puckered mouth, tiny, slit eyes. And then the woman gave another heave, and ejected the shoulders, and he saw the grasping little fingers all curled together, and the midwife was pulling it free. It was coming easy now, all covered with fluid, with rainbow-hued slime, accompanied by a thick, almost translucent cord, all ribbed and notched.

The midwife pulled it free and reached over the woman, turning her on her back, with the thick, slimy cord coming out of her, and the midwife pressed the tiny creature into the mother's hands, and let her grasp it to her breasts.

As the Abbot watched, he saw its mouth begin to move. The blue color began to fade, and he saw how air was entering the creature.

'Was I right?' the mother asked, feebly. 'Is it a girl?'

'You were right,' the midwife said.

Their journey had reached its end.

And every end is a beginning.

ABOUT THE AUTHOR

John Emery was born in Cairns, Queensland in 1947. His early childhood was spent on his parents' coconut plantation on the north coast of Papua New Guinea in the company of planters, prospectors and Melanesians. His parents moved to South Australia in the 1950s where John continues to live with his wife and two children.

He is the author of *Summer Ends Now*, a collection of short stories, and two novels, *Freedom* and *The Sky People*. He has won a number of awards for his writing including the National Short Story of the Year Award in 1976. He has also written screenplays for film and television. *Freedom* was made into a feature film in 1982.